THE TROJAN TRAIN

He and Zarra ran for the mail car and peered inside. The vault drew his eyes. "Slocum, it ain't locked," Zarra said, trying the bright brass handle. He pulled open the door. All Slocum saw was a small mound of greenbacks on the safe's floor. For an instant, he wondered what was wrong. Then it hit him.

"Get the money and let's clear out," Slocum ordered. "This whole damned train is a trap!"

He jumped to the ground—and almost lost his life. Hot lead sang from the direction of the caboose. As Slocum vaulted into the saddle, he saw a cloud of dust rise along the tracks from the posse's approach. More than a dozen additional men, he estimated, as a new flight of leaden death winged through the air. Slocum looked over his shoulder and saw a red blossom growing on the front of his partner's shirt . . .

DON'T MISS THESE AUTHENTIC WESTERN SERIES FROM THE BERKLEY PUBLISHING GROUP

THE GUNSMITH by J.R. Roberts

Clint Adams was a legend among lawmen, outlaws, and ladies. They called him . . . the Gunsmith.

LONGARM by Tabor Evans

The popular long-running series about U.S. Deputy Marshal Long—his life, his loves, his fight for justice.

LONE STAR by Wesley Ellis

The blazing adventures of Jessica Starbuck and the martial arts master, Ki. Over eight million copies in print.

SLOCUM by Jake Logan

Today's longest-running action western. John Slocum rides a deadly trail of hot blood and cold steel.

JAKE LOGAN

SLOCUM AT OUTLAWS' HAVEN

BERKLEY BOOKS, NEW YORK

SLOCUM AT OUTLAWS' HAVEN

A Berkley Book / published by arrangement with the author

PRINTING HISTORY
Berkley edition / October 1993

For information address: The Berkley Publishing Group, 200 Madison Avenue, New York, New York 10016.

ISBN: 0-425-13951-4

A BERKLEY BOOK ® TM 757,375
Berkley Books are published by The Berkley Publishing Group, 200 Madison Avenue, New York, New York 10016.
The name "BERKLEY" and the "B" logo are trademarks belonging to Berkley Publishing Corporation.

PRINTED IN THE UNITED STATES OF AMERICA

10 9 8 7 6 5 4 3 2 1

1

Central Wyoming was peaceful in the spring. But John Slocum didn't see any of the rugged beauty of the mountains rising to the north or the green valley with its blue ribbon of river gently rippling down to the mighty Platte. All he saw were the twin rails of iron meandering through that valley.

When the Union Pacific train came through in an hour, there wouldn't be any peace to be found. Slocum glanced over at his two partners lounging back and trying not to show any sign of concern. Clay Zarra chewed on a piece of grass, sucking at the bitter juices as if they were good. Not even Zarra's horse was enjoying the sparse feed on this rocky stretch of mountain. And Harley Benson nervously puffed at his cigarette, burning it down almost to his fingers before immediately rolling another. He got no enjoyment from the tobacco. He was too hepped up for that.

"How long?" Benson demanded of Slocum. "It's been hours. They must be held up."

"Maybe," Slocum answered, not bothering to check the time. Benson had made a similar complaint only a few minutes earlier. Benson was nervous—and so was Slocum.

The Pinkertons had been working this area lately, too hard for Slocum's peace of mind. Allan Pinkerton had bragged that he could put a stop to any train robbery for an entire month and had staked more than his reputation on it.

Slocum had heard tell of a ten-thousand-dollar bet with the Union Pacific's owners that not a single one of their trains would be robbed successfully during the month of May. This normally wouldn't have bothered Slocum unduly, but it was getting on to the end of the month and no one had successfully robbed even one of the railroad's shipments. The closer it got to June and the more it looked as if Pinkerton would win his wager, the more agents he would put onto the job of keeping the trains running unrobbed.

"We could wait till next week," he said.

"Why bother?" snapped Zarra. "You aren't getting spooked, are you?"

"No," Slocum said, his keen green eyes scanning the distance for any hint of smoke from a locomotive's smokestack. "I was just thinking out loud." He looked at Benson. The man had rolled himself another cigarette and worked to light it against the small breeze blowing down from the colder mountain heights.

"We go," Benson said unexpectedly, too loud for either Zarra or Slocum to ignore. "We've been planning this for weeks. We're not backing out." He laughed and took a long puff from his cigarette. "We want to get rich. At least, *I* do. What about you gents?"

"We'll go," Zarra said.

The other two had come to their own decision, but Slocum wasn't so sure this robbery was a good idea. The Union Pacific train had to slow when it reached the bend in the valley. Rather than taking the time to build a bridge and trestle across the river, the track crews had gone several miles out of their way with a sudden curve that forced the engineer to slow to a crawl. It was in this stretch that they'd rob the train.

If only Slocum didn't have a bad feeling about it. The Pinkertons were a concern, but not that much. Slocum had escaped from more diligent lawmen in his day. And Zarra and Benson were reliable enough. He had ridden with them for almost two months, pulling off smaller jobs, and he felt comfortable with them. Benson had nervous habits that might get him killed someday, but when the shooting started, he was as steady as any man Slocum had ever ridden with. And Zarra was cool, before, during, and after a robbery.

Slocum appreciated this as much as anything else. Zarra wouldn't shoot his mouth off while on a drunk—or if the law caught him.

But he still had bad feelings about the robbery. Slocum had done most of the planning, with Benson and Zarra agreeing. He had chosen the location and the shipment of gold going from Fort Laramie over to Salt Lake City, and the day and most everything else. He wasn't being double-crossed. But he didn't want to ride down into the valley when he sighted the train, and he couldn't say why.

"There, there it is!" cried Benson. The man shot to his feet and pointed, his cigarette dangling between his tobacco-stained fingers. "We're gonna be rich, we're gonna do it today!"

Slocum checked his Winchester and then rolled the cylinder on his Colt Navy to be sure all six chambers carried loads. He was as well armed as he'd ever been.

"Help me, Benson," called Zarra, putting his back to the lever they'd shoved under a large rock. The pair strained until Slocum threw his strength to the task. The boulder made an almost human groaning sound and then started its slow roll downhill. Slocum watched as it built up speed and took more rock with it. By the time the boulder crashed into the tracks, the steel rails were completely hidden under the avalanche, maybe mangled.

If the engineer didn't stop in time, his train would be derailed. Either way was fine with Slocum. They'd end up with the gold in the mail car and be on their way, getting at least a day's head start before the crime could be reported.

"Let's get into position," Slocum said, swinging into his saddle. His bay reared; it was a feisty animal but strong and reliable. He guided it to the thread of a trail leading down to the tracks. Benson and Zarra followed. By the time they had hidden their horses and gotten into position, the train rounded the bend.

The engineer saw the rockfall immediately and hit the brakes. Huge sparks flew as the wheels locked on the steel rails and still the train came on. Sparks shot from the wheels and the screeching caused the horses to buck and rear. Slocum had heard it took well nigh a mile for a fully loaded train running at full steam to come to a complete stop.

He had to hand it to the engineer's quick reaction and good sense. The cowcatcher crushed against the largest of the boulders on the tracks, but other than this the train suffered no damage.

Nose twitching from the hot iron smell in the air, Slocum lifted his bandanna into position and headed for the mail car. He wasn't as interested in the heavy canvas sacks as he was the small vault in the car. He had spent almost fifty dollars in greenbacks finding out about the twenty pounds of gold inside. Fifty in worthless paper for six thousand in gold. A good trade.

"Are they going to open up or do we blow it?" Slocum shouted. The threat was usually enough to make even the boldest of mail clerks fling open the door. They had a couple sticks of dynamite with them, but Slocum was hesitant to use them. He had seen too much damage done to the car's contents in other robberies.

Chasing down greenbacks fluttering on the wind because the entire mail car had been blown to splinters was ridiculous. Having to hunt through the wreckage to pry open a safe to get out the gold was even worse.

And Slocum had the uneasy feeling that time worked against them.

"It's all right. I'm coming out. Don't blow me up!" The man inside the mail car began fumbling at the inner lock—too slow for Slocum's liking.

He spun around and saw the engineer working hard in the cab to build up the lost head of steam and get the train into reverse. Slocum snapped off a quick shot, driving the engineer down.

"They're trying to back up the train," Slocum warned. "Don't let them waste any more time." He started for the engine cab to get the engineer into sight where he could cover him when he heard the mail car door scraping open. Slocum glanced over his shoulder and saw the glint of sunlight off a rifle's blued steel barrel.

"Down!" he shouted in warning. His words were drowned out by the rifle's report.

Both Benson and Zarra returned fire. Slocum wasn't able to see how effective their bullets were. Splinters exploded on the door, but it hardly seemed enough to have come from two men's six-shooters. He got off another shot in the direction of the engineer, just enough to keep the man guessing, then raced back to the mail car to aid Benson and Zarra.

The good point of having only three men involved in the robbery was the split. Each got a bigger share than if a dozen men wanted their due for risking their lives. But Slocum saw the problems with his plan. He wouldn't have minded a half dozen or more men firing into the mail car and turning it into wormwood. The mail clerk had to be the stupidest man alive if he was willing to trade his life for the contents of the safe, no matter what threats his bosses at the Union Pacific's head office might have made.

"Got him!" shouted Zarra, his six-gun hammer coming down on an empty chamber. Zarra rolled to cover and reloaded, letting Benson and Slocum take up the firing.

Slocum sent all his rounds through the door. He heard them ricocheting around inside the mail car. If this didn't convince the clerk to give up, nothing would.

"He's surrendering!" shouted Benson. "He's coming out!"

Slocum tensed when he saw the door open a bit farther. He wasn't sure surrender was what the clerk had in mind. And it wasn't. The man jumped out, firing his rifle as fast as he could lever a new round into the chamber. But the fusillade wasn't what startled Slocum. Behind the man came another and another.

They were evenly matched, any chance at surprise on the side of the defenders.

"Where'd they all come from?" demanded Zarra, swinging around and getting to one knee. He fired fast and he fired accurately. One of the three doubled over and sank to the ground.

The other two didn't seem to notice. They continued to fill the air with lead.

"The one you shot," Slocum said, "has got a star pinned on his chest. We walked into a trap. Let's get out of here."

"Not until we see what's in that vault." Zarra pointed. The black-and-gold iron face of the safe beckoned. Twenty pounds of gold. And all they had to do to get it was waltz past the two guards.

Slocum emptied his rifle at one of the guards, winging the man. The guard flopped around and then wiggled away into underbrush on the far side of the tracks. Slocum didn't bother following. Although the man wasn't dead, he was winged bad enough to keep him from returning to the fight anytime soon. He concentrated on the remaining guard. Between him and Zarra, they drove the man into hiding.

"Where's Benson?" asked Zarra. "He disappeared."

Slocum jerked his Colt Navy upward when motion on top of the car caught his eye. Benson was there, his six-shooter ready for action. If Slocum and Zarra hadn't finished off the guards, Benson would have been able to backshoot them from above. It had taken him longer than Slocum would have guessed to get to the top of the car, but it had been a smart move.

"That all of them?" called Benson.

"Watch close," Slocum said. "One's wounded and the other's turned tail. Don't let either of them come back and surprise us."

He and Zarra ran for the car and peered inside. A mountain of canvas bags showed how much mail this run carried over to the Mormons in Salt Lake City. A goodly portion of it might even go on out to California. Slocum knew if he had the time, he could go through the mail and get out hundreds of dollars in greenbacks. People sending money to friends and relatives was fairly common.

But what really drew him was the vault. Six thousand dollars in gold had to be the reason the railroad had assigned three guards instead of the usual one to this mail car.

"Slocum, it ain't locked," Zarra said, trying the bright brass handle. He pulled open the door.

"Where's the gold?" demanded Slocum. All he saw was a small mound on the safe's floor.

"Paper money. That's all there is in the safe. Maybe a thousand dollars' worth, no more than that."

"Take it," Slocum said in disgust. He eyed the U.S. Mail sacks and considered setting them on fire. He felt cheated. He and his partners had risked their lives and for what? Greenbacks? No barkeep worth his salt would take the paper money without demanding a premium for his products. What five dollars in hard gold coin could buy went for ten in scrip.

Still, a thousand dollars split three ways was better than just riding off.

"Get me a sack," Zarra said. Slocum ripped open a mailbag and dumped the contents onto the floor, then tossed the canvas sack to Zarra. For an instant, he wondered what was wrong. Then it hit him.

He knelt and pawed through the letters. There wasn't anything in the bag but cut newspapers.

"Get the money and let's clear out. This whole damned train is a trap!" Slocum jumped to the ground—and almost lost his life. Hot lead sang from the direction of the train's caboose.

"Cover me!" Slocum yelled up at Benson, but the man was nowhere to be seen. Slocum returned fire and drove back the three men firing at him.

Zarra jumped down beside him. "What's going on? Where's Benson?"

"Here, here I am!" shouted their partner. He had fetched their horses and brought them up. "I didn't see them until I got to the horses. It's a whole damned posse!"

As Slocum vaulted into the saddle, he saw that Benson was right. A cloud of dust rose from along the train tracks from the posse's approach. He wasn't much at estimating on the run like this, but Slocum guessed at more than a dozen men riding down on them. Added to the three in the car and the other three that had snuck up on them from the rear of the train meant this was one humongous ambush.

"Is it the federal marshal's men or the Pinkertons?" asked Zarra as he climbed into the saddle.

"What's the difference?" Slocum shot back. "Dead's dead either way. The Pinkertons don't have a good reputation for bringing their captives back alive."

As if to emphasize his sentiment, a new flight of leaden death winged through the air. Slocum's head jerked to one side. He wasn't hurt but a new hole appeared in the brim of his dark Stetson. Wheeling his horse, he started downhill, away from the tracks and toward the river where they stood the best chance of evading the posse. Crossing the river two or three times would throw off all but the most diligent tracker, Slocum knew. And their horses were rested. The posse riding down on them were coming at a dead gallop.

They'd be able to escape. With the thousand in greenbacks.

"That way, down that way," Benson said needlessly, pointing wildly toward the river.

"Why not just stay behind and tell them where we're heading, you dolt?" snapped Zarra. "You—" In the middle of the sentence, Clay Zarra stopped speaking and started groaning. Slocum looked over his shoulder and saw a red blossom growing on the front of Zarra's shirt.

The bullet that had hit him from behind had passed through his body. That Zarra still moaned in pain was nothing less than a miracle. Slocum had made shots like this and exploded his victim's heart.

Slocum let Zarra's horse come up beside before he turned and grabbed. Zarra sagged weakly, needing Slocum's support to stay in the saddle.

"Go on. They got me. I can hold 'em off, for a while at least."

"Shut up and save your strength," Slocum said. Benson had stopped and looked back at them. The man's expression was a curious blend of annoyance and fear. Then he resolved whatever dilemma he had and started firing at the train, driving the three gunmen at the rear back to cover. Only then did Benson ride back.

"What are you going to do, Slocum?" Benson asked.

"Get him belly-down over his saddle. That's the only way he's going to make it."

"That'll kill him!"

"Maybe. He's a goner if we leave him for them." Slocum jerked his thumb back in the direction of the train. "I make out the three from the mail car to be deputy marshals, but the others don't sport badges. That means they must be Pinkertons."

"Maybe deputies riding for the Pinkertons," Benson said. Slocum wasn't going to argue. That was a posse and they were hunting down three men who had just robbed a Union Pacific train.

Slocum dismounted and heaved Zarra over his saddle, tying the man down with lengths from his own lariat. Benson shot sporadically in the direction of the train. Slocum wasn't sure the bullets weren't wasted, but he didn't complain. He climbed back into his own saddle and put his heels to the bay's flanks. The powerful horse leapt forward as if shot from a cannon.

Hanging on to the reins of Zarra's horse, they raced for the river. Benson followed more slowly, firing faster now. When he caught up, Slocum was halfway across the rapidly flowing river.

"There's a full score of them, Slocum," whined Benson. "They're gonna catch us for sure. We got to get away. We got to go to earth and hide."

Slocum didn't answer. He was too involved getting Zarra and his horse across the river. When they got to the far side, he headed for a stand of trees, using it to shield the direction he rode. Slocum didn't much care if Benson kept up or not. He was too disgusted with the way the robbery had gone to want to palaver about how many men chased them.

It might be one or a hundred. They could be federal lawmen or county sheriffs or even Pinkertons. It just didn't matter. Whoever caught them would string them up from the nearest cottonwood.

But how had the posse just happened to be near when they'd begun the robbery? That was another question Slocum knew he'd have to think hard on later, after they got away.

2

"We can't keep them off our trail, Slocum," complained Harley Benson. The man rode with his head turned around so he could see where they had already been—and where the posse was.

Slocum had different ideas. He wanted to put as much distance between him and the pursuing lawmen as possible. To do that he had to concentrate on the land coming up. And as much as he hated to admit it, Benson might be right about their slow progress. With Clay Zarra slung over his saddle and unable to travel very fast, they were becoming sitting ducks for the eager lawmen.

"We keep riding," Slocum said. He wasn't going to abandon Zarra unless it became necessary.

"We ought to leave him," Benson said, pointing at Zarra. As if responding to his name, Zarra moaned and thrashed about weakly, straining against the ropes Slocum had used to tie him down. "He's not going to make it if we keep running like this."

"If we leave him," Slocum pointed out, "he's not going to make it longer than it takes them to put a bullet through his head."

"That might be more merciful. I wouldn't put a horse through what he's enduring," Benson said.

Again Harley Benson made sense, and for some reason that irritated Slocum. He had been called bullheaded by more than one person in his day, but he had never been called stupid. Trying to stay ahead of the Pinkertons—and Slocum was convinced that's who had fastened onto their trail like a bulldog on a thief's leg—required more speed and cleverness than they were likely to summon up if they had to care for Clay Zarra along the way.

"He's strong, and he wouldn't want to just up and quit," Slocum said, knowing the man well enough to realize the truth. Zarra would always prefer a shallow grave where the coyotes might get to him over a noose. Slocum didn't know how he knew it but the men on his trail had to be Pinkertons. They wouldn't quit, and they wouldn't take home any living prisoners.

"All right," Benson said, surprising Slocum with his easy agreement. Slocum had expected a long argument over divvying up the money and going separate ways. Slocum had even expected some treachery on Benson's part. A thousand dollars split one way was twice as good as cutting it down the middle. And no matter what Slocum might say aloud, deep down he knew Zarra wasn't going to put up a fuss over his cut from the train robbery.

Dead men don't need whiskey money.

"We ride through that pass," Slocum said, tipping his head toward the pass to their right. One led south, but he didn't want to take it. The Union Pacific tracks led down there, and the Pinkertons would be thicker than fleas on a hound dog. Their best chance for freedom lay to the north, maybe all the way up in Canada, if it came to that. U.S. money spent almost as good north of the border as it did to the south, and a thousand dollars could buy them a comfortable summer, fall, and winter. Come next spring, the danger would be past and they could consider what to do then.

"I can hear them behind us, Slocum," said Benson. "We can't keep running. Our horses are tiring quick."

"I know. We can find a place to hole up," Slocum said. "You and Zarra can rest, and I'll lay a false trail." Slocum knew his own skills and saw this as their only chance of getting away clean. The posse had to be decoyed away or they were sure to swing before sundown.

"We're in this together. You don't have to—"

"You and Zarra keep all the money," Slocum said. Benson's eyes widened in surprise.

"I didn't mean that you'd cheat us, Slocum. I want to do my part. We're partners."

Benson's sincerity startled Slocum. He thought the man had been angling for some way to get off with the money, and here Benson showed him wrong. Slocum was good at reading men, and he always managed to get the false impression of Harley Benson.

"You keep the money. I need to ride light and fast. Find a cave up yonder." Slocum indicated a rocky outcrop in the hills. "No fire, stay low, do what you can for Zarra. I'll be back just after sunset."

"And if you're not? How long do I wait?"

"Sunrise," Slocum said, knowing he'd be long dead if he didn't get back before midnight. For what he had in mind, all it'd take was a few minutes.

"All right. I still want to do what I can but you are a better trailsman than I'll ever hope to be."

Slocum wasn't used to men fessing up to their own failings. Benson was a more complicated cuss than he had thought, and he'd ridden with him for enough weeks to have seen just about every side.

Slocum watched as Benson and Zarra took off at an angle from the trail. He cut back, found some brush, and covered their tracks before starting to lay a false trail hinting that they had followed a curving path and had headed back toward the Union Pacific tracks along the other route.

Waiting in a stand of trees, Slocum saw the posse come up to the branch in the trail. The leader pointed toward Slocum, causing him to reach for his Colt Navy. He relaxed a mite when the man turned and pointed along the false trail. The men milled around, their horses confusing any track that might have been left. Slocum studied the leader, wondering if he had ever seen the man before.

Tall, straight as a ramrod in the saddle, he had a commanding air to him that was almost military. A thinning thatch of sandy hair peeked out from under his broad-brimmed hat and a sharp, straight nose looked as if someone had tried to split his face open and left the hatchet imbedded. For all the discussion going on, Slocum saw that there was no confusion.

This wasn't any ordinary posse, and the tall man leading it wasn't a hick-town sheriff.

"That way," came the faint words drifting against the wind. "A mile or so, then return."

"Yes, sir," came the immediate reply. Slocum almost expected a salute in return but it never came. A half-dozen men started along the path that would take them to Benson and Zarra, but Slocum wasn't worried. He had hidden their tracks for more than a mile. And when a scout found the minute spoor in the other direction, the tall, dour man called his men back.

They spent several minutes examining the trail Slocum had laid so carefully, discussed its truth, and then rode off, just as Slocum had planned. He waited another ten minutes and the posse didn't return. Silently walking his horse for a quarter mile before mounting, Slocum rode back toward the pass where Benson had found sanctuary. He made sure the bay kept to rocky patches and only walked across softer grass and dirt while dragging a freshly cut shrub.

An hour later the sun began dipping behind the high peaks. And a half hour beyond that, Slocum found where Benson and Zarra had made camp. He stopped and spied on Benson for a few minutes before revealing himself. Benson spent the time caring for Zarra, making sure he had a few drops of water sprinkled on his lips and a blanket under his head for support.

The canvas sack holding their booty was still slung over Zarra's saddlebags. As far as Slocum could tell, Benson hadn't even bothered taking it down to count the money.

"Slocum!" called Benson, jumping when the other man rode into the hidden campsite. "I was beginning to worry about you."

"How's Clay doing?"

Benson shook his bead. "Not good. That bullet's still inside him."

"What? Look at his shirt. Blood everywhere. The bullet went clean through him."

"He took a second one. The first one was bad enough. That must be the one that bloodied up his shirtfront. The second caught him under the rib. From all I can tell, it bounced around inside a lot." Benson shuddered at the notion of the bullet ricocheting around and not coming out.

"I got the posse turned. It'll be dawn or after before they figure out they're on a wild goose chase," Slocum said, hunkering down. He cut open a can of beans and started spooning them out. He wished he could have heated them. With coffee, even trail coffee, it would have been a decent meal, but any hint of smoke would bring the Pinkertons running back. He'd save a few of the greenbacks they'd stolen for a decent meal at the first town they passed through.

"That gives us another few hours," Benson said. He stared at Zarra and let out a gusty sigh. "He's not going to make it without a doctor."

"We can try to cut the bullet out ourselves," Slocum said.

"We'd kill him outright. This'll take a skilled hand."

Slocum snorted in contempt. The few doctors he had seen worth their fees weren't likely to patch up an outlaw without turning him in to the nearest sheriff.

"We've got to get Zarra to a doctor, and we've got to go to ground," Benson said. He stared hard at Slocum and said, "We can make Haven. It's around here somewhere."

"Outlaws' Haven?" Slocum shook his head. He had heard about it but hadn't given any of the talk much credence. There were always stories—tall tales—about entire towns given over to protecting outlaws from bounty hunters and marshals. He had never come across one himself, nor had he known anyone who had.

"It's not some yarn to spin around the campfire," Benson insisted. "I know it's around here somewhere. A friend of mine holed up there for several months and told me about it."

"Why trust anyone we don't know?" asked Slocum. He didn't like the notion of putting his life and liberty in the hands of someone likely to turn him in for a reward.

Slocum had enough wanted posters following him around, but the worst of the lot was for killing a carpetbagger judge. Slocum had been gut-shot by Bloody Bill Anderson and William Quantrill for protesting the massacre of innocent women and children. It was bad enough what they had done to soldiers and men able to defend themselves, but the senseless slaughter had galled Slocum.

It had taken Slocum almost six months to recover from his wounds and when he got back to the Slocum farm in Calhoun, Georgia, he found his parents dead and a Northern judge coveting the property. Unpaid taxes the judge had said. Pay up or get off the land he had said. Slocum had heard the rumors and knew the judge wanted the land for a stud farm. Although the judge and his hired gun had ridden in, only Slocum had ridden out.

The two fresh graves had brought about a rain of wanted posters, a modest reward for his capture, and a life of always looking over his shoulder to see who was catching up with him.

"We're going to be rotting in some prison if we don't get someone to help us out," countered Benson.

"H-he's right," grated out Clay Zarra. The man turned on his blanket and peered up at Slocum with feverish eyes. "Don't trust anyone. We can make it on our own."

"He's running a fever," Benson said, startled that Zarra had come out of his coma long enough to side with Slocum.

"There's nothing we can do for you, Clay," said Slocum. "We've got to find a town."

"And Haven," added Benson. "I don't want to spend the rest of my life in jail."

Slocum held his canteen for Zarra to drink. The wounded man slipped back into unconsciousness, but Slocum was thinking hard. They had money, and that was what it would take to get into a place like Outlaws' Haven, if it really existed. He dredged up memories of all he had heard about it. Benson was right in that rumor held it out to be nearby.

"One Ear Jenkins," Slocum said suddenly.

"Who?" Benson looked confused at the turn the conversation was taking. "Who's that?"

"Just a name I remembered," Slocum said. "Down in Denver a guy mentioned One Ear Jenkins as knowing about Haven. He said that if I ever needed a place to hole up for a while, that Jenkins was the man who could help me."

"So we'll find this Jenkins?" asked Benson.

Slocum thought awhile more on it. The best they could hope for was sending the Pinkertons on a false trail for a few hours. When they saw nothing of their quarry, they'd be back at the branch and headed north—right after Slocum, Benson, and Zarra.

"What towns are ahead of us on this trail?" Slocum asked. He didn't know this part of Wyoming that well. Due north in about three hundred miles lay Montana and to the west was Utah. If he could circle and head south, Denver beckoned. The gambling dens along Front Street seemed more and more attractive by the minute.

"Grant's Pass is a day's ride north. Once into the town, there are a couple ways we might be able to get a line on this Jenkins fellow," Benson said. He sketched a crude map in the dirt, showing Slocum where he thought they had camped and the location of the town they had to find. Finished, Benson rubbed all trace away. Slocum appreciated his caution since it wouldn't do having the posse find a map conveniently left behind showing their destination.

He almost laughed. It hardly mattered if Benson left the map in the dirt or not. They were in a canyon and had few prospects for getting out of it short of the town of Grant's Pass.

"We rest for a while, then head on," Slocum said, coming to a decision. "We make as much time as we can."

"Think the posse will camp for the night?"

"I'm hoping they will," said Slocum. If Lady Luck rode with him, the Pinkertons would give up the chase entirely, but he didn't believe that for an instant. His eyes drifted to the canvas bag with the thousand dollars in greenbacks riding easy in it. Allan Pinkerton had promised the Union Pacific that they would go an entire month without a holdup. As long as they had the loot from the train robbery, the railroad agents would never rest.

Pinkerton had once boasted he would spend a thousand dollars to recover one hundred. Slocum hated men of principle, especially when they were breathing hot and heavy down his neck.

Slocum considered their chances of making Grant's Pass with Zarra still alive if they left immediately. Then he worried that none of them might get away alive if they didn't. Zarra was a goner, one way or the other, and from what he'd said, he would prefer to die trying to reach freedom than to be turned over to the not so tender mercy of the railroad agents.

"You ready to ride?" Slocum asked.

Harley Benson nodded. They got Clay Zarra onto his horse and rode slowly through the night, picking their way slowly to keep from a nasty fall. Slocum wished for a bright full moon until he heard distant sounds echoing after him.

He looked at Benson, who shook his head. They knew that luck had run out. The Pinkerton posse was already on the right trail. No matter how bad Zarra was, they had to keep riding now.

"That won't stop them," Benson said tiredly.

"Maybe not," Slocum agreed, "but it might slow them a spell. Right now, that's all we can hope for."

They had ridden slowly all night, wary of Zarra's condition. The man moaned so loud Slocum had considered putting a gag in his mouth to muffle the noise. Zarra had fallen into a deeper coma about three in the morning. That had been good on one count and bad on another.

Slocum had been able to hear the click of horses' hooves hot in pursuit. It might have been a trick of the wind or the way the canyon walls carried sound. It didn't matter. The Pinkertons were getting closer every minute.

He had tried laying a false trail up a narrow, winding path leading to the rim of the canyon. Slocum had no hope the pursuing railroad agents would be fooled; they could see there wasn't anyone on the trail higher up. Still, Slocum had to try. He wasn't going to roll over and play dead.

"There!" cried Benson. "Look, Slocum, that's got to be the road down into Grant's Pass."

Slocum had seen the double-rutted track a few minutes earlier. It led to Grant's Pass. It also was a wide-open invitation to get caught. Benson was right about the posse not being duped by the false trails he had been leaving. But if they started down this road, the posse's greater number would work against them. Slocum didn't see how they could travel much faster than they already were, what with Zarra's condition worsening by the minute.

"Wait," Slocum said. "We can't get down into the town before they'd overtake us." He jerked his thumb backward toward the posse. "And what do we do if we get into Grant's Pass before them? There's nobody we know there likely to hide us from a Pinkerton agent."

"What do you want to do, Slocum?" asked Benson.

Slocum heard the pounding of hooves on the trail behind them. He didn't know what it would take to get away, but they'd have to figure it out quick or be prisoners within minutes.

3

"They'll cut us down like a row of wheat," Slocum said. He didn't see any way for them to get away from the posse. He looked around, wondering if they could make a fight of it. Leaving Clay Zarra never entered his mind. The man was their partner and deserved as much of a chance for escape as they were likely to have.

"You've been doing the hard work, Slocum," Benson said. "Let me have a hand at this."

"What do you have in mind?" Harley Benson continued to surprise him. Slocum would never have expected the man to have such grit.

"You head on up into the rocks yonder," Benson said, pointing out a tumble of boulders just off the road. "I'll decoy the posse away. If it works, you mosey on into Grant's Pass and get Zarra patched up. I'll be along when I can."

"How do you figure to get away? There must be well nigh twenty of them in that posse. You can't outride them on a tired horse, and you sure as hell can't outgun them."

"They may be Pinkerton agents and they may outnumber us, but they're human. All I need is one small mistake, and I'm away scot-free." Benson sounded confident, but Slocum knew it wouldn't work that way. And he had his doubts about the Pinkertons being human.

"You said I was a better trailsman. Let me—" The thunder of hooves as horses broke into a gallop silenced Slocum. The posse was closer than he had thought. Although they had maintained a steady pace throughout the night, the Pinkertons had traveled just a tad faster.

"Go on, do it!" cried Benson. He wheeled his horse around and took off down the canyon leading away from Grant's Pass. Slocum wasn't real sure where that road led, but it didn't have the look of being used much. From the signs along the way, some rotted and others badly in need of new paint, this entire area had once been a hotbed of prospecting activity. The dearth of working mines proved that neither gold nor silver was to be had.

Slocum grabbed the reins of Zarra's horse and led the tired animal toward the rocks Benson had indicated. He had barely dismounted and helped Zarra down when the Pinkerton agents rode up. Slocum worried that one of the horses might let out a neigh of fear.

He fingered his Colt Navy and waited for the inevitable.

The tall, slender man leading the railroad agents dismounted and studied the ground. Another pointed toward Grant's Pass but the leader shook his head, turning in the direction taken by Harley Benson. Slocum couldn't bear what was being said but the argument raged until the leader bent and picked up a bandanna.

Slocum wondered if Benson had dropped it on purpose. It made the trail obvious, even to a blind man. Still, he worried that the Pinkerton agent would see this as a trick.

He let out a lungful of air he hadn't even known he had sucked in when all twenty of the riders turned and raced after Benson. It wasn't too smart on their part, but Slocum wasn't going to criticize them. A few ought to have stayed behind to guard the junction in the road, but their leader obviously didn't want to split his forces, in spite of their numerical strength.

Waiting five minutes until he was sure they had swallowed the bait Benson was trailing behind him, Slocum finally ventured out. He had no idea how Benson was going to get away. For all he knew this was a box canyon filled with played-out mines and that Benson had ridden into a trap.

Slocum wasn't going to dwell on that. Zarra moaned constantly now. If the man was to be saved, he had to have a sawbones working on him quick.

The road down into Grant's Pass was deserted, but the town itself bustled with activity. Slocum couldn't see at first what kept the village alive. There didn't seem to be mining in the nearby mountains, and there certainly wasn't any farming going on. As he rode through the town, he was aware of eyes watching him.

Even worse, he heard rifles being cocked and six-shooters being slipped from holsters. The unwanted attention made him increasingly uneasy as he looked around for the town's sheriff. If the citizens were this suspicious of strangers, the law would be more than a little nosy when it came to wanting to know how Zarra had been shot.

Slocum spotted a doctor's shingle swinging in the wind. He started to dismount and take Zarra inside when he saw something strange. Not three doors down the street was another doctor. Slocum looked around, wondering why such a small hamlet had two doctors and most larger towns were lucky to have one.

Leaving Zarra hanging over his saddle, Slocum glanced into the first doctor's office. Two men sat on straight-backed chairs, waiting to be seen. He walked down past the general store and a bakery and looked into the other surgery. A man he took to be the doctor had his feet hiked up on a desk and was swilling whiskey from a silver flask.

Slocum didn't want to wait on the other doctor to be finished with his patients. He spun to go back to his horse and ran smack dab into a woman. She dropped her packages and took a step away, flustered.

"I'm sorry, ma'am," Slocum said, stooping to pick up her packages. "I'm not usually this clumsy, but I'm in a terrible hurry to get in to the doctor."

"If you are in need of a doctor, your apology is accepted," she said. The woman had hair darker than midnight and green eyes that matched his own. The tanned face gave the look of a woman who definitely was no hothouse flower, but seldom had Slocum seen a woman so lovely. Grant's Pass continued to surprise him.

"It's not for me," he said, handing her packages back.

"But there is blood on your shirt. Quite a bit, actually," she said, eyeing him closely. On impulse she reached out and pulled open his shirt. Her long fingers stroked across his chest, then darted around, probing. With a slight smile, she stepped back.

"It's not me that's been wounded," Slocum said. "It's a friend of mine. Hunting accident."

"Hunting?" She didn't sound as if she believed him. Her eyes locked on his. Slocum was a good poker player and kept his face impassive, but he felt she was looking deep into his soul.

"Yes, a hunting accident a few miles outside town. Please, I've got to get him in." He motioned to indicate the doctor still sitting behind his desk swilling his rotgut.

"You don't want that fake," she said. "Doc Mallard loses more than he saves. Rumor has it that he never graduated from any medical school and only pretends."

"The other doctor is—"

"That's Dr. Grandville. Top-notch, especially for gunshot wounds. Allow me to help you."

"I couldn't—" Slocum began. The dark-haired woman cut him off with a wave of her hand.

"Don't be silly. My name is Suzanne Crawford." She paused until Slocum introduced himself. Even as he did, Slocum cursed himself for being so stupid. He should have used a summer name rather than his real one. The Pinkertons on his trail might not know his name, but then again they might from a wanted poster.

"Pleased to meet you, Mr. Slocum," Suzanne said. She guided him back to where Clay Zarra lay across his saddle, moaning in pain.

"He must have a will of steel to have come very far like that."

"I decided it was better to bring him in rather than leave him alone and fetch a doctor."

"Reasonable," she said, and again he had the feeling she was laughing at his lie.

Slocum struggled to get Zarra over his shoulder. He was more tired than he had reckoned, having ridden all night with only a can of beans to eat. Wobbling a little, he got the wounded man into Dr. Grandville's office. To his surprise, the men who had been waiting were gone.

Grandville came from an inner room, wiping his hands clean. He looked from Slocum to Zarra and then to Suzanne.

"Well, my dear, you seem bound and determined to bring me business. What is it this time? A gunshot wound?"

Slocum didn't understand what the doctor meant, but that wasn't important. Clay Zarra needed immediate attention. He dropped him across the doctor's desk.

Grandville looked past Slocum and Suzanne Crawford to the street outside. He frowned and motioned Suzanne into his inner office.

"Bring him inside. We need more room to work on such serious wounds," the doctor said. As Slocum got Zarra through the door, he hazarded a quick look outside. The sheriff and two deputies were patrolling the street, shotguns resting in the crooks of their arms. Grandville had correctly guessed that Slocum didn't want the law sniffing around.

"No, not there," Grandville said. "Through the curtains, into the back room."

Slocum wrestled the limp Zarra past the dingy curtains and found another, smaller examining room. He put the man down on the narrow table and stepped away. Grandville looked from Zarra to Slocum, an appraising expression on his face.

"Services come high out on the frontier," he said obliquely.

"Patch him up," Slocum said coldly. "We got the money to pay."

"Of course you do, of course you do," Grandville said, smiling broadly. They understood each other well. He hesitated and then asked, "Are you injured? If so, it would take only a few minutes to patch you up."

"Just him," Slocum said coldly.

"Very well. Might I suggest that you and Miss Crawford wait outside?"

"In back?" Suzanne asked.

"Where else?" Grandville turned and began cutting away the cloth matted to Zarra's chest. As the doctor worked, he clucked his tongue like a hen looking for grain. Slocum had seen worse injuries during the war, but he didn't want to inflict such a sight on Suzanne. Again she surprised him.

She stood on tiptoe and looked over his shoulder. "I don't think he's a goner. Dr. Grandville's fixed worse than this."

Slocum smiled in appreciation. She wasn't squeamish about blood. Taking him by the arm, she guided him out the back door and into the alley at the rear of Grandville's offices.

"I'll bring your horses around. Sheriff Peña can be a mite nosy when he sees newcomers coming into town." Suzanne hurried away, leaving Slocum standing alone and wondering what he had fallen into. The beautiful woman and the doctor seemed to understand what his problem was—and they both accepted it easily.

Slocum understood Dr. Grandville. The man had told him the doctoring would be expensive, and with the hefty fee would come silence. Slocum accepted that as being fair. He had come across more than one doctor willing to fix bullet holes and never mention it to the local authorities. Such money tended to be better than setting some sodbuster's broken arm or trying to do something about the town drunk's case of consumption.

His hand flashed for his cross-draw holster when he heard sounds behind him. He swung around, his Colt Navy almost from the holster. He relaxed when he saw Suzanne leading his and Zarra's horses.

"My, you are a fast one with that hogleg, now aren't you, Mr. Slocum?" she taunted.

"You startled me coming up from behind. You left out from that end of the alley." Slocum knew how lame that sounded. There was no reason Suzanne had to return the way she'd gone. If anything, going around the block of buildings looked to be good sense if the sheriff was still prowling with his deputies.

"Are you waiting for another friend to join you?" she asked unexpectedly.

"Might be."

"So cautious. You'd think you rode into Grant's Pass with a posse on your heels," she teased. Or did she know? Slocum couldn't tell with Suzanne Crawford.

"Did you see a stranger riding into town?" he asked her.

"I did. Would you like me to deliver a message?"

"Please. Tell him I'm waiting out here and that the doc is stitching up Clay."

"I'll be back soon," Suzanne promised. She left the alley again, this time taking her packages with her. She seemed to delight in tormenting him more than a little with the way her hindquarters twitched and swayed when she walked. Slocum was almost glad when the woman was out of sight. She made him think thoughts that would only lead to big trouble.

In less than ten minutes, Suzanne came walking back down the alley, her parcels gone. Behind her rode Harley Benson, looking apprehensive. When he saw Slocum, he relaxed and dismounted.

"Slocum, you made it," he said.

Slocum motioned for the man to hold his tongue in front of Suzanne. She had been helpful but there was no need to trust her with more information than she needed. It could be dangerous not only for them but for the woman, also.

"I'll see how your friend is doing," she said, seeing Slocum's expression. She pushed between the men, her breasts lightly gliding across Slocum's chest. Suzanne smiled cheerfully and went inside, the door ajar.

"You got yourself a hot one, Slocum," Benson said in admiration. "Not in town twenty minutes and—"

"Never mind that," Slocum snapped. "How'd you get away from the railroad agents?"

Benson laughed in pure delight. "I'd be rich if I had luck like that at the poker table. I found an old mine and holed up there, waiting to shoot it out. Something went wrong with their tracking. They rode right on by, and I snuck back behind them. I don't know if that's a box canyon or if it goes to the end of the world, but they're still checking it out."

Slocum was astounded at such luck. Everything looked to be going their way—if Grandville could fix Zarra's considerable wounds.

"We can get on to Outlaws' Haven and—" Benson bit off his words as Suzanne returned. Dr. Grandville followed her.

"I've done what I can for your friend," Grandville said, looking somber. Slocum wondered if the doctor doubled as the town's undertaker. "He's still alive, but he cannot be moved."

"For how long?" Slocum asked.

"I can't rightly say. He's lost a considerable amount of blood. Rest and his own vitality are his only allies."

"What of the second bullet in him?" asked Benson.

"I found it lodged under his rib. Removal was easy enough, but the bleeding." Grandville shook his head sadly and looked even more grave. "He must rest if you expect him to ever recover. Even then, it will be a difficult fight for him."

"What do we owe you so far?" Slocum asked.

He wasn't surprised to see Grandville glance in Suzanne's direction before naming a figure.

"Fifty dollars will take care of my work this morning, but there might be additional expenses—"

"Another fifty?" suggested Slocum.

"That will be adequate reimbursement, I should think," Grandville said. He silently accepted the greenbacks as Slocum peeled five twenties from the wad he had stuffed into his shirt pocket before riding into Grant's Pass. He hadn't wanted to be seen digging in a canvas pouch for money and was glad now he'd had the foresight to take some money from their stash.

Benson looked apprehensive.

"It'll come out of Zarra's portion," Slocum said quietly. He waited until Grandville went back inside. But Suzanne didn't budge. Slocum had a great deal to talk over with Benson and wished she'd go on her way so he could get on with it.

"Outlaws' Haven?" she asked boldly. "Are you looking to get in there?"

"Why do you say that?" Slocum asked, knowing she had overheard Benson.

"You need connections to get in there safely," she said.

"Slocum here knows One Ear Jenkins," Benson blurted out.

"Indeed?" Suzanne cocked her head to one side and eyed him with frank approval. "I would never have guessed."

"He's speaking out of turn," Slocum said. "That's just a name I heard. We might be looking for this Jenkins."

Suzanne Crawford looked squarely into Slocum's unflinching green eyes again as she weighed his reply. She smiled slowly, and Slocum wasn't sure if it was lovely or diabolical.

"I can help," she said. "For a price."

"We can pay," Benson cut in.

"Good. Why don't you go see to your friend?" Suzanne suggested. "Dr. Grandville can always use someone hovering over a patient."

"What about me?" asked Slocum.

"You and I will discuss payment."

"Look, I—" Slocum waved Benson to silence. "All right, I'll go look after Zarra." Benson went inside.

"This way, Mr. Slocum," she said. She turned and walked off, not waiting to see if he would follow. The way Slocum saw it, he had little choice but to trust her. Suzanne had helped him several times already, and could have alerted Sheriff Peña to his plight—and she hadn't.

"Where are we going?"

"You'll see," she said mysteriously.

"Will I meet Jenkins?"

"Do you always ask so many questions when all you need do is wait and see?" She was laughing at him again, and this time Slocum wasn't sure he liked it. He kept a sharp eye out for any indication of betrayal and didn't see it. No one trailed them, and he didn't see how she could be leading him into an ambush because of the careful route she chose. Suzanne always made sure the alleys were empty before entering. She led him down alleys and up little used streets to a large boardinghouse with a NO VACANCY sign nailed to the gate.

"Around back," she said, walking faster now. Slocum followed her up to the rear porch and up a flight of stairs to a second-story room. Just inside the door, he stopped and stared.

"This isn't Jenkins's room," he said.

"Of course it isn't, John. It's mine." And Slocum found his arms filled with a willing, passionate woman intent on kissing him. He resisted for a moment, then succumbed.

There wasn't any reason to fight her. Suzanne Crawford was a lovely woman, and she knew her own mind. Slocum felt himself beginning to respond more and more when her agile tongue danced in and out of his mouth, teasing the tip of his tongue and luring him forth.

He fell into her trap. She bit down on his tongue, making him yelp. Or was it the way she tightened her grip on his crotch? He had grown painfully erect.

If she had tormented him up to this point, she eagerly gave him release now. Her fingers continued to stroke over the bulge at his crotch, but those same fingers worked to unfasten his gunbelt and let it fall and to get the buttons on his fly open. His lust-hard length popped out—and into the woman's awaiting mouth.

Her lips circled him, and Slocum thought his knees would give way. She reached up and grabbed his buttocks, moving in around so he could sit on the edge of the bed. Suzanne continued to move her mouth up and down his length until he was ready to pop.

"Wait, stop, can't go on," he pleaded. It had been a spell since he'd had a woman—and even longer since he'd had one as pretty as Suzanne.

"We'll see about that," she said wickedly. Suzanne spun around, sending her long skirts flying. As she turned, she reached underneath and worked free of frilly undergarments. Slocum tried to see more of what was going on, but the failed attempt was almost as exciting as if he could see everything clearly.

Suzanne stopped her whirling and stood in front of him, hands on flaring hips. She smiled even more broadly and advanced.

"I'm ready now," she said. "And I see you are, too." She reached over and gripped him hard, tugging slightly. Slocum positioned himself on the bed, then found himself buried under a sudden flow of lovely woman and her garments.

Suzanne straddled his waist and got her skirt positioned. She lowered herself unerringly. Slocum gasped when he felt himself slide easily into a hot, tight channel. A heavy sigh passed through Suzanne as she rocked back, eyes closed, and simply enjoyed the sensation Slocum was giving her by the abrupt entry.

Slocum's length twitched and jerked and he knew he wasn't going to be able to simply lie beneath the woman any longer. He arched his back slightly, lifting Suzanne up off the bed.

Her green eyes flashed with pleasure. Reaching down, Suzanne began stroking over his chest, fingers tangling in the thick mat of hair.

"You don't have to stay there," she said softly. "It was just a good place to get started."

Slocum reached behind her and cupped her firm buttocks. Lifting slightly and turning as he did so, he reversed positions. He felt her heavy breasts crushing under him. He started to free them so he could see and sample, but Suzanne stopped him.

"You've got other business to tend to right now, John," she told him.

Slocum grunted as she tensed inner muscles to tell him exactly what she wanted done. He drew back slightly, fighting her the entire way. Just before he popped free, Suzanne relaxed and gave him the signal to race back. He buried himself balls deep and with enough force to cause Suzanne to lift her knees on either side of his body.

He began moving slowly, then built the speed of his stroking as his passion mounted. He held back as long as he could, but Suzanne's sudden thrashing about robbed him of what control he had left. She moaned and sobbed and clawed at him—and he drove faster and harder into her. Every stroke pushed their mutual passion higher until Slocum was sure he couldn't endure another instant.

Somehow, Suzanne knew tricks with her inner muscles that no other woman had ever used. When he was certain he couldn't endure another minute, he found himself soaring even higher.

The white-hot tide of his passion spilled forth and inundated the woman. She shivered again and held him tightly as he rocked to and fro until his desires were spent. Only then did he lay forward across the woman, faces just an inch apart.

She was smiling with joy. Her face changed expression, then she let out a soft breath and said, "That's the first part of the payment to get into Outlaws' Haven. Now you have to pony up five hundred dollars for you and your partner."

The brusque change in her attitude took Slocum by surprise. Suzanne Crawford seemed eternally able to astonish him.

4

"That's a heap of money," Slocum said, swinging around and sitting up on the edge of the bed. His mind raced. Was it worth half their take to get away from the Pinkerton agents so hot after them? He had already paid out a hundred dollars to Dr. Grandville for Zarra's care. More than half the remainder would be spent getting into Outlaws' Haven, if it even existed.

"How do I know you aren't trying to con me out of the money?" Slocum asked suddenly.

Suzanne Crawford laughed deliciously, the sound of silver bells ringing in a summer breeze. She swung her long, bare legs up and over his head, giving him a tantalizing view of where he had just been. She came up to a sitting position beside him and took his hand in hers.

"John, there are a whale of a lot of ways of getting money, especially in Grant's Pass."

"The sheriff is on the take?"

Again Suzanne laughed. "No, poor Sheriff Peña is as honest as the day is long. He is also as poor as a church mouse."

"You're in cahoots with Grandville, that much I've figured out," Slocum said.

"And we do a good business patching up men like your friend, Clay Zarra," she said. "I did a little looking in the sheriff's office, and Mr. Zarra is a wanted man. A hundred dollars for room and board isn't too much to pay to keep him from spending some time in Sheriff Peña's accommodations."

"Reckon not," Slocum allowed, "but five hundred is a considerable sum, when Benson and I don't even need doctoring."

"Consider it an insurance policy. A policy against a necktie party." Suzanne's bright green eyes stared boldly into Slocum's. "There's nothing Doc can do about putting a stretched neck right again." Her smile broadened and the devil danced in her eyes as she stroked over Slocum's bare crotch. "Of course, there's quite a bit I can do to stretch other parts of your anatomy."

"I don't have that kind of money."

Suzanne turned away and shrugged, as if saying that it was too bad he didn't trust her more.

"I'd need to talk to Benson."

"He's over at Dr. Grandville's," the dark-haired woman said, standing. "Why don't the two of you discuss your future? It might not look too bright unless you decide to take a tour up in Haven."

Suzanne blew him a quick kiss, then whirled through the door. He heard her footsteps as she retreated down the back stairs. Slocum struggled into his trail-worn jeans and settled his gunbelt snugly around his waist. The way things were going, he might need his Colt Navy before much longer.

He was no fool, and he hadn't missed the veiled threat Suzanne had dangled before him. The sheriff might not get told about Zarra, Benson, and him if they didn't come up with the five hundred dollars, but he wasn't sure he could run the risk. Just because he and Suzanne had shared some time together didn't bind her to him.

Slocum snorted in disgust at himself. If anything, Suzanne had gone to bed with him to tie him down to her. Had it worked? Slocum wasn't sure he could come up with an easy answer to that. One thing he had to give the people running Outlaws' Haven, they knew how to recruit.

He went down the back stairs carefully, watching for any sign of a trap. The town was coming more alive as the sun sank behind the tall peaks surrounding it, but he saw no hint that Suzanne had set him up for an ambush. In a way, he almost wished she had betrayed him. That would have given him a reason for moving on.

But did he trust her or not? She was wily and clever enough to survive in a dangerous game. Slocum doubted he was the first she had recruited for Haven, and he doubted he would be the last.

Returning to the doctor's surgery, Slocum pressed his ear against the rear door. He listened hard but heard nothing unusual. He tried the doorknob and turned it slowly. In a quick move, he slid into the room, startling Harley Benson who sat at the far side, dozing off.

"Slocum!" Benson relaxed, his hand going away from the six-shooter he had lying on a table beside him. "You scared the bejesus out of me."

"Sorry," Slocum said insincerely. "How's Zarra?"

"No change. The doctor says he's in a critical stage right now and can't be moved. If we try getting him out of here, Clay's a goner for sure."

Slocum looked at the man's pale face, saw the beads of sweat and how hard it was for him to even breathe. Zarra might be a dead man, even if he wasn't moved.

"I took a turn around town," Benson said. "I asked all around about One Ear Jenkins but nobody'll fess up to knowing him. Did you have any luck with that woman? Can she get us into Haven?"

"Who all did you ask about Haven?" Slocum wasn't as interested in Benson's afternoon as he was in giving himself a few more minutes to think through Suzanne's offer.

"I was real careful, Slocum," insisted Benson. "I made sure there wasn't any law around, and then I only asked those who had the look of being on the trail for a spell."

"See anyone who might have been with the posse?"

"No!" Benson was shocked at the notion. "Do you think they're onto us already?"

Slocum grunted and shook his head. The posse had been lured away temporarily. Not even Benson could think his little ploy would keep them occupied more than a few hours. That trail might lead through the mountains. Hell, it could go all the way to South Pass and put the Pinkertons on the Oregon Trail, but that didn't mean they'd be gone for long. The tall man leading them was a good tracker, and Slocum knew he'd backtrack when he didn't find any fresh spoor.

"They have to know Zarra was hit. They'll be looking for blood, for signs we'd been through that canyon. When they don't find squat, they'll be here in Grant's Pass asking after us."

Slocum spun, his hand pulling out his six-gun when the doctor pushed through the curtain leading into the other operating room. Grandville paid Slocum no attention as he let the heavy curtain fall back into place behind him.

"We have a small problem, gentlemen," the doctor said. "It seems that Sheriff Peña is upset."

"So he gets the catarrh, and we've got trouble?" Benson asked sarcastically.

"What's wrong?" Slocum didn't have the doctor pegged as the kind of man who panicked. He hadn't batted an eye having the six-shooter leveled at him, and he had to know Slocum was the kind who could—and would—use it.

"He has been sequestered for some time with a man whose identity is unknown to me." Grandville coughed and looked apologetic. "That, in and of itself, is unusual. I have threads going throughout the fabric of Grant's Pass. A single twitch and I am aware of it in this town."

"Get to the point," said Benson, standing and beginning to pace. He was getting nervous again, just as he had been before the train robbery. Slocum couldn't ignore him. He just hoped he didn't get an itchy trigger finger and do something stupid, like plugging Grandville.

"The man who has put the bug in our dear sheriff's ear appears to be the leader of a posse hot on the trail of three robbers who held up a Union Pacific train sometime yesterday."

"Do tell," Slocum said.

"Mr. Zarra is safe here, but I'd advise you gentlemen to find other quarters. Him I can explain." Grandville jerked his thumb in Zarra's direction.

"We don't have any place to go!" wailed Benson.

"Wait a minute," Slocum said. He grabbed Benson's arm and took him aside in the small room. He knew Grandville could hear, no matter how softly he spoke, but he didn't have a wide range of choices.

"What is it, Slocum? Did the woman tell you something about Haven?"

"It'll cost us dearly," Slocum told his partner. "She wants five hundred dollars."

"That much?" Benson looked stunned.

"I don't know if I trust her, but she and the doc have played square with us so far."

"That'd only leave four hundred for the two of us," Benson said. He squared his shoulders and said, "All of it comes out of Zarra's share. He ain't got nothing coming to him."

"Hold your horses," Slocum said. "We might be able to get out of here without paying."

"We can't find Haven on our own. I spent the afternoon asking and there's nobody who'll even talk to me."

"Forget Outlaws' Haven," Slocum said. "We can just ride on. We've done what we can for Clay. We take what's left of his share, get free of the posse, then come on back later and divvy up the take."

"But we *have* to get into Haven!"

Slocum started to ask Benson why he was so hepped up about finding Outlaws' Haven, then held back. Grandville motioned them to silence when a bell in the outer office jangled twice, warning that someone had entered.

"Let's get out of here," Slocum said. "The doctor was right about us being found under his roof. He can always claim he doesn't know who Zarra is. Us, he'd have a fine time explaining away."

They slipped into the alley. Slocum pointed to the far end and started. He flattened himself against the wall of a building when two men rode slowly across the mouth of the alley. He recognized them as having been with the posse. Beside him Benson was cursing under his breath.

"We can't shoot our way out of this, Slocum. We'd be dead in a flash."

"No need. They didn't see us," Slocum said. He peered around the corner of the building but didn't like what he saw. All the posse had come to Grant's Pass, and they were patrolling the streets in pairs. They might be able to kill one or even both in a brace of Pinkertons, but the others would hear the commotion and come running.

"Where are our horses?" Benson demanded. "We can't get out of town without them."

Slocum didn't know what Suzanne had done with them. She had left them tethered in the alley, but he hadn't noticed they were missing until this moment. He considered his chances for getting across the street to the saloon, then saw big trouble.

The tall, thin Pinkerton agent leading the posse stood in the middle of the street, a rifle in the crook of his arm. His hawklike eyes weren't missing anything, and Slocum saw he didn't have a snowball's chance in hell of reaching the saloon. Slocum turned and ducked back into the alley, wondering what he was going to do. Escape down the town's main street was cut off. From the commotion all around, the posse was conducting a street-by-street search.

"We can shoot it out," Benson said, but there wasn't any conviction in his voice. "Maybe we can decoy them again, like before."

"Maybe we can turn into geese and fly south for the winter." Slocum didn't want to take refuge in Grandville's surgery but saw no other course for them. There weren't any other unlocked doors leading into the alley and getting to a roof was out of the question. They'd be spotted and filled with holes before they made it halfway.

"John?" The soft voice carried like a shout even though Suzanne spoke low. Slocum whirled around and faced the woman. She had opened a door in the building next to Dr. Grandville's offices and leaned indolently against the frame, her hand on a cocked hip.

"Are you ready to get out to Haven now?"

"Slocum?" Benson looked accusingly at him. "Did you make a deal with her?"

"The price is too high," Slocum said.

"Five hundred dollars for the pair of you," Suzanne said, coaxing him to agree. "Isn't that better than getting caught? Those Pinkerton agents are all deputized, but they have more than money or duty riding on capturing you. They have their pride."

"Pay her the money," urged Benson. "We've *got* to get to Haven."

"All right," Slocum said. He didn't see any way out of Grant's Pass, but he had to trust Suzanne. "The money's in the canvas sack hanging over—" He stopped speaking when Suzanne moved to one side and pointed. The canvas bag was at her feet.

"I'm an honest thief, John," she told him. "I stay bought—and I've taken the liberty of removing my due and not one dollar more." Suzanne tossed him the sack, paused, then sent a broken poker chip spinning through the air.

He caught the blue chip and looked at it. A zigzag pattern had been cut in it.

"What's this?"

"Your ticket to Outlaws' Haven," she said. "Now quit jawing and get moving. Through here." Suzanne stepped to one side and pointed to a trapdoor in the floor. Benson never hesitated. He dived down like a prairie dog going home. Slocum moved more deliberately, stopping beside Suzanne.

"I would hate to see you swinging from a gallows, John." Suzanne grinned and said, "I'd like more payment from you, and I don't mean money."

"Where does this go?"

"To your horses. When you come out of the tunnel, ride north along the draw for a few miles until you see a bleached steer's skull with an X cut between its horns. Turn left and try not to leave a trail behind."

"How will I know when I reach Haven?"

Suzanne laughed at this and pushed him down the hole. "You'll know. Believe me, you will know."

He heard Benson scurrying along ahead of him, and Suzanne moving on the trapdoor she'd dropped the instant he had descended into the blackness. Slocum felt trapped and wanted to run, but there was nowhere to go. Retreat was out of the question. That left only one direction. He followed Benson through the pitch-black tunnel until he saw a silver dollar of light ahead.

Slocum almost ran to get out of the tunnel and into the twilight. To his relief he saw Benson had already mounted his horse and held the reins on the bay.

"Hurry up. I think I hear 'em coming," said Benson.

"They're persistent cusses," said Slocum, climbing into the saddle. He stood in the stirrups and shook his head. It was worse than he'd thought. A half dozen of the posse was heading for them. Somebody must have spotted the horses and sent a few of the Pinkerton agents to investigate.

They had a race on their hands.

Slocum wheeled his horse and dug his heels in hard. The bay responded with a loud snort. Benson followed closely. Slocum kept bent over looking for the steer skull. He worried that there wouldn't be one. Then he worried he would miss the right one. The entire trail was littered with the bleached bones of dead animals. And some had the ominous look of humans about them.

"There, there it is," Slocum called to Benson. "Up that canyon."

"We got to hurry, Slocum," the other man called. "They're gaining on us. Can we make it?"

Slocum had no idea how close they were, but he felt the ground quiver under his horse as the posse broke into a gallop, intent on overtaking them before total darkness hid them from sight.

Slocum rode as never before, pushing his horse to dangerous limits. Somehow, Benson kept up and the posse fell back. But they couldn't keep up this pace for long without a horse breaking a leg in the darkness.

"I think they've given up the chase," Benson said, reining back. "And not an instant too soon. My horse is all tuckered out."

"My bay's not able to go on, either," Slocum agreed. "But we got other problems."

From the rocks he heard the clicking of rifles being cocked. Then a dozen men rose, each with Slocum or Benson square in his sights. They had ridden smack dab into a trap.

5

"Don't shoot!" cried Harley Benson. He threw up his hands and reared back, causing his horse to crowfoot under him. He had to grab the reins to keep from being thrown off.

Slocum was in a better position to see what was going on. The men in the rocks had the rifles, but few of them looked ready to use them. They all turned in the direction of the narrow draw for guidance. Slocum tried to figure out which of the men standing on the canyon floor was the leader.

One man was dressed in black and had a white ruffled shirt. The slicked-back hair and the quick movements told Slocum this was a professional gambler. The man to his left was more likely to be the leader of the outlaw band. He was tall, thin, had a bandanna pulled up over his nose as if he were ready to rob a stagecoach. The third man spat a gob of chaw from between broken teeth and scratched himself, as if the lice were working overtime on his filthy hide.

"We're looking to get into Haven," Slocum said loud enough for the tall man to hear. Slocum fixed his gaze on the man, who shifted uneasily, then backed off a few paces.

This startled Slocum. He looked to the gambler, then to the men in the rocks. They were intent on one of the three. Slocum doubted the gambler ruled this roost. The man wearing the bandanna was afraid of his own shadow.

"Reckon you spoke a good piece there, mister. What makes you think any of us knows about this here Haven?" It was the potbellied derelict who spoke, taking time out to spit another brown gob onto the ground. He hit a weed, which immediately began to wither under the onslaught of the nicotine.

"We've got a posse on our heels," Slocum said. "You folks don't have the look of lawmen to me."

"Now then, what *do* we have the look of?" asked the old man. He shifted a double-barreled shotgun from one hand to another.

"Might be you're One Ear Jenkins," Slocum said. "If so, you're the one I'm hunting for."

The gambler laughed harshly. "Seems he's found you, One Ear."

"Shut your tater trap, Murch." The words were cold and caused the gambler to blanch whiter than a linen sheet. Slocum knew then who was driving the buckboard and who was only along for the ride.

"We got sight of 'em," came the call from above. "What you want done?"

"Do I got to tell you everything, Nate?" complained Jenkins. "Get 'em the hell out of here."

Slocum saw the man high on the mountain wave his arm. The hillside came alive with rifle fire. The long tongues of flame leaping from more rifles than he'd thought there blinded him in the twilight. Slocum had guessed no more than five men were on the mountain. Better than two dozen opened fire on the posse agents trailing him.

"We got the firepower to keep the whole goddamn U.S. Cavalry out, if we choose," Jenkins said. He scratched himself some more and moseyed over to get a better look at Slocum. As he looked up, Slocum caught sight of a face that had seen better days.

One Ear Jenkins's face had been sliced until it looked as if he had walked through a cobweb. The tiny tracings of pink and white scars showed the results of a dozen fights won—or maybe just not lost. And his hat canted heavily to one side because of the missing ear. The entire side of his head had been stoved in, maybe from a mule's hoof or possibly from something more deliberate.

No matter how he had come by the injuries, they hadn't killed him. That made him one tough hombre.

"That's enough, dammit, Nate!" shouted Jenkins. "Don't go wastin' any more ammo than you have to."

"We run all them bastards off," the man on the mountainside called down. "I'll send out a scout or two and make sure."

Jenkins shook his head. "Nate Fogger ain't got the sense God gave a goose, but he has his uses." He turned his head to one side and studied Slocum. "Can the same be said of you? You got any purpose other than to feed the buzzards?"

"We paid for the information to get here," Slocum said. He was hesitant to mention the railroad robbery, yet it might be necessary. Then he remembered the poker chip she had tossed him. He reached for it slowly, aware that a half-dozen muzzles followed his movement. Slocum pulled it out and flipped it to Jenkins.

The man moved with the speed of a striking rattler. Slocum was astounded to see such a quick reaction in the outsize, decrepit old hulk. He told himself he shouldn't underestimate Jenkins again. It might mean his life.

"So what do I do with this cut-up chip?" Jenkins asked.

"You tell me," Slocum said.

"We paid good money for that," babbled Benson. "It was supposed to be our ticket into Haven."

"May be just that," Jenkins said. He tossed it over his shoulder. The gambler caught it and held it aloft for everyone to see. Then he fished out another chip from his vest pocket and pieced it together. Slocum let out a small sigh of relief when he saw the two halves fit like a jigsaw puzzle.

"See, we belong in Haven," Benson went on.

"He's with you?" asked Jenkins. "Keep him on a tight leash. If he goes around Haven shootin' off his mouth like that, he's gonna end up stone dead." Jenkins turned and walked back to the small knot of men on the canyon floor.

"So?" asked Slocum. "Where do we go?"

"You can go to hell for all I care," Jenkins said. "Or you can ride with us and find a place to stay in Haven."

"We did it," Benson said, wiping sweat from his forehead. Slocum wondered at the man. He got nervous at the strangest times. Jenkins wasn't about to have them cut down, even if they'd been the law. He was more curious than that—and he had a sharp mind that always moved one jump ahead. Men just didn't ride up, and for such a welcoming committee to be gathered meant Suzanne had somehow relayed the information that visitors were coming.

"I don't know what we've got ourselves into," Slocum said, "but stay alert. We might just have to shoot our way out of this."

"Why? This is *Haven.* We paid to get in!"

Slocum snorted and shook his head. Benson could be like a babe in the woods at times. If he lived to be a hundred, he wasn't sure he'd ever understand him. Slocum picked up the pace and forced Benson to ride faster. The few minutes it took his partner to catch up gave Slocum a chance to look around.

The outlaws had ridden on ahead, getting their horses from a rock corral to the side of the canyon. From the horse dung there, it was regularly used. Everything about this narrow canyon showed careful planning and some reworking of nature. Small fortresses along the walls had been built. Lookouts stationed there had a view of the entire canyon. A half dozen could keep out an entire cavalry company—maybe more. It would take a field cannon to dislodge some of the positions.

And ahead Slocum saw why Jenkins felt so secure in this canyon. Hours of backbreaking labor had gone into building the rock wall across the mouth of the canyon. The narrow gate allowed only two men riding abreast to enter at a time—about the width of a supply wagon, Slocum guessed. Along the top of the wall paced men with rifles. He didn't see what signal, if any, passed from Jenkins to the guards. They might have recognized him, or this show of force might be for the benefit of newcomers.

If it was, Slocum was duly impressed.

"Hold on there, mister," Jenkins said, turning his horse around and riding back. Slocum glanced over his shoulder and saw a tight knot of riders approaching. He didn't recognize any as being in the posse. That meant he and Benson were caught between the rock wall into Haven and the men who had been posted on the mountainside and who had driven back the posse agents. Whatever Jenkins wanted would be forthcoming or two bodies would be left to rot here on the doorstep to Haven.

"What is it?" Slocum asked. He had slipped the thong off the hammer of his Colt Navy. He didn't have any hope of shooting his way out, but if bullets started flying, One Ear Jenkins would catch the first one.

"You gave me the poker chip. That means our agent back in Grant's Pass thought enough of you to let you get this far." Jenkins scratched his stubbled chin. "Now you got to pony up the wherewithal to get into Haven."

"But we already paid—"

Slocum cut off Benson's protest.

"How much more?" Slocum asked.

Jenkins smiled and showed his broken, yellowed teeth in a ferocious smile. "How you came about the chip ain't none of my business. Maybe you paid good money for it. Maybe you stole it. Maybe you used some other form of payment." He eyed Slocum and grinned even more broadly. "But that don't butter no biscuits out here." The smile melted. "Half of all you got."

"Half! That's highway robbery!" protested Benson.

"Yep, you're gettin' the idea, boy. We ain't much on manners, but we are all real good at robbin'." Jenkins laughed harshly.

Slocum turned when Nate Fogger reached over and grabbed the saddlebags. He started to protest, then knew it wouldn't do any good. Jenkins was a cagey old bastard, but the expression on Fogger's face was one Slocum had seen too many times. Fogger slaughtered for the pleasure of it. Jenkins might enjoy the money; Fogger would get a sick thrill out of the killing.

"Slocum," complained Benson. "We can't let them do this to us. We don't have that much left."

"They got maybe four hundred in greenbacks. That's all, boss." Fogger held up the money.

"Two hundred dollars for gettin' in to Haven?" Jenkins shook his head. "Times must be gettin' hard outside, Nate. I expected these two owlhoots to bring me a passel more than that."

"We could take it all," Fogger suggested, looking wolfish.

"Half. Them's the rules. And you two gents are now members in good standing of our fine community. Welcome to Haven." Jenkins turned and rode off, letting Fogger return the two hundred dollars to Slocum. He didn't seem to much care what happened to his half of the money.

Slocum looked to the canyon cliffs to be sure that the gunmen up there had gotten the message from their unlikely leader. He didn't see any hint that rifle barrels were being turned his way. But Slocum couldn't miss the sour look Nate Fogger gave him. The man's hand twitched as he stroked the handle of his six-shooter. This one was a killer and didn't mind how or who he killed. Slocum vowed to watch his back—and to warn Benson to do the same.

"We did it, Slocum, we got in!" Benson was almost cackling with glee. Slocum looked at his partner and wondered what was going on inside the man's head. Getting into Haven wasn't anything to brag on. They had lost all but two hundred dollars from the railroad robbery, and the posse was still prowling around outside.

Slocum wondered if that might not be worse than just riding past Haven. The posse knew where they were holed up. Their leader had the aspect of a man used to waiting patiently, if he decided he couldn't smoke them out from Haven. And Slocum had to admit he wasn't sure being on this side of Haven's stone wall was any kind of accomplishment. Fogger wasn't the kind of trail mate he wanted at his back, and the others were a motley crew.

"They have an entire city up and running," Benson said, almost in awe. "Look at that! A saloon!" He hitched up his gunbelt and said, "I'm so thirsty I could spit a cotton boll."

The small town didn't impress Slocum as much as it obviously did Harley Benson. The clapboard buildings might blow over if a strong wind blew down the canyon. A fire would reduce everything to ashes in seconds. There wasn't a single stone or brick building in the small community, most of them being nothing more than tents. Slocum figured all that work had gone into the battlements protecting the valley. But one thing he saw straight out was the lack of hotels or boardinghouses. They either pitched a tent with a dozen others some distance away or unrolled their blankets and slept under the stars.

Somehow, not having anything to protect his back bothered Slocum more than it ought to.

"Come on, Slocum. Let's not keep 'em waiting." Benson urged his horse forward and jumped off in front of the saloon. Jenkins and Fogger had already gone inside. Slocum waited a few seconds, considering what he ought to do. Benson was inside the saloon; this decided him to follow. His partner was the only one in Haven he could depend on, and he didn't want to see him filled with holes.

Inside was what Slocum had expected to find. The men quieted a mite when he came in. Several looked to Jenkins and seeing no reaction on his part went back to serious drinking or poker playing. The slick-haired gambler Murch was already dealing faro, two men standing behind to count the hock and soda piles. Other games went on that looked to be more honest, whatever than meant in a place like Haven.

"A dollar!" shouted Benson. "You gotta be out of your mind!"

"That's the price. Ever'body pays it. You think yer any different?" The barkeep held the bottle back from the shot glass on the bar.

"He's trying to charge me a goddamn dollar for a single drink!" complained Benson. Slocum shrugged. This wasn't unexpected. If One Ear Jenkins controlled entry to the town, he also controlled supplies. That meant he could charge whatever he wanted. Suddenly the two hundred dollars they'd been left didn't look to be so big.

"How thirsty might you be?" asked Jenkins, lounging against the bar. He sloshed whiskey around in a water tumbler. That much booze would have cost five dollars—if he hadn't been the one doing the selling.

"Mighty," Benson allowed. He grumbled but he pushed across the greenbacks needed to buy. The barkeep poured a half shot. Benson started to go for his six-shooter, but Slocum held him back.

The barkeep smiled wickedly. "Paper money is discounted by half. Gimme gold and you get a full glass."

"You thieving son of a bitch!" Benson reached for the barkeep's throat, but Nate Fogger moved faster. He slammed the barrel of his six-gun down on Benson's wrist.

Slocum considered plugging Fogger then and there while the gunman's six-shooter was otherwise occupied. He glanced around and saw too many others just waiting for such a move. In spite of what Jenkins said, they were on probation. The residents of Haven would love nothing more than some excitement, and if that included killing two newcomers, so be it.

"Don't push it," he warned Benson. "We can get a few dollars back." Slocum's keen eyes scanned the room and he saw three or four poker games where the men were too drunk to pay much attention to odds. "Drink up." Slocum locked eyes with Fogger, who backed down.

"This isn't right, Slocum. They can't—" Benson shut up when he realized how wrong he was. They could do anything they wanted. Jenkins owned the town lock, stock, and barrel.

"Watch my back," Slocum said in a low voice. He sat down at an empty chair. The four others had been drinking but weren't so drunk they might complain if they lost. And they would. Slocum was a good player. Given enough of a stake and the time, he'd come away a winner in this crowd.

He was aware of Fogger's eyes on him as he played. Slocum saw the others cheating but said nothing. He folded those hands and took small losses. But he began winning now and again when he saw the others at the table weren't in cahoots. They were cheating each other as much as they were him, and that suited him. He managed to take small pots, but the stack of chips in front of him grew hour by hour.

Players came and went at the table, but Slocum kept winning until he was almost two hundred dollars to the good. He was just starting to feel well disposed about coming to Haven when he heard Fogger's harsh voice behind him.

"There ain't no way in hell any man can win that much money so fast without cheatin'," Fogger said, loud enough to catch the attention of players at other tables. Logic wouldn't do any good and Slocum knew it. He hadn't won fast and he hadn't won that much from any single player, considering almost a dozen men had sat at the table and been dealt cards.

"He didn't cheat," Benson said, moving to put himself between Slocum and Fogger.

Slocum pushed his partner out of the way and squared off against Nate Fogger.

"Are you saying I was cheating?" Slocum asked in a cold voice.

"No man wins like you did without stickin' a card or two up his sleeve." Fogger widened his stance. His hand twitched just over the butt of his six-shooter as he prepared to draw down on Slocum.

6

"You're a no-account, low-down cheat, and I'm callin' you out for it." Nate Fogger's expression wasn't one of outrage as much as it was blood lust. Slocum had seen the look before and knew what it would take to cure it.

Someone was likely to die.

Slocum pushed back from the table, his green eyes flinty and cold. He watched Fogger's hand twitch slightly, but the man didn't go for his six-shooter. He wanted this to be a fair fight—or as fair as it was ever possible to be.

From the corner of his eye, Slocum caught a hint of movement and knew what had to be done.

"Go on, draw," Fogger called.

Slocum took a step forward. This caused Fogger's eyes to widen in surprise.

"I won a considerable amount of money," Slocum said. "It'd be a shame to kill you and not offer everyone a drink first. Drinks are on me."

The wild rush to the bar was everything Slocum could have hoped for. Two men brushed past Fogger. The instant the killer's attention shifted, Slocum acted. He whipped out his Colt Navy and swung it hard. The blued barrel landed with a dull crunch on the side of Fogger's head. The man's eyes rolled up in his head and his knees buckled. He sank to the sawdust-covered floor without uttering a single sound.

No one noticed that Slocum was the one who stepped back—no one except One Ear Jenkins whom Slocum had seen enter a few seconds earlier. The grizzled old man was standing just inside the open door, a shotgun resting in the crook of his arm. To the other side of the door were two other men, both ready to shoot if Slocum had tried gunning down Nate Fogger.

Slocum glanced in their direction, and they looked to Jenkins for orders. The old man shook his head slightly. A smile curled at the edges of his mouth, then he turned and left. He ruled Haven with an iron fist. Slocum wasn't sure what might have happened if he had cut down Fogger, but he doubted he would have enjoyed it.

"What's going on, Slocum?" demanded Harley Benson, pushing his way through the throng.

"Free drinks. On me." Slocum watched as most of the money he had won in the poker game evaporated. The barkeep spirited it away and left only a few dollars more than Slocum had started with as a poke. But for Haven this was a gain.

And he was still alive.

"Did you—?" Benson stared at the unconscious Nate Fogger on the floor. Outlaws stepped over the fallen man on their way to the bar for more free whiskey.

"I should have," Slocum said. Then he thought on it and decided he had done the right thing. "I'm going to have to watch my back real close. You, too."

"Sure thing, Slocum," Benson said, staring at Fogger. "But why'd you tangle with him?"

Slocum considered the attack and decided Fogger had

been put up to it. "He was just taking my measure," Slocum decided.

"He paid dearly for it. Look at that cut on the side of his head," Benson said. "He's bleeding like a stuck pig. You done buffaloed him good and proper."

Slocum looked out through the doors where Jenkins spoke with his two henchmen. Someone had been taking his measure, but it hadn't been Fogger. The man was a pawn and nothing more. One Ear Jenkins called all the shots in these parts.

"Hey, no more drinkin'!" shouted the barkeep. "His money's all used up!"

Slocum slipped from the saloon, not wanting to take part in the fight that was sure to follow the announcement of no more free liquor. He stepped into the sunlight and studied Jenkins. The man didn't look as if he had a lick of sense, but Slocum knew different. Jenkins smiled and showed his broken, yellowed teeth, sardonically touched the brim of his dusty Stetson pulled low on the side of his head, and sauntered off as if nothing had happened.

Slocum's fingers tapped on the handle of his Colt. One quick shot might solve a lot of problems—and he wasn't thinking about Nate Fogger.

"Slocum, our money's almost used up, but we can get more. I saw the way those mangy cayuses gambled. If we work together, we can take them for a bundle." Benson rattled on and on, but Slocum wasn't listening.

He looked up at the tall, sheer red rock cliffs on either side of the canyon. There didn't look to be any way up to the rim. And he knew better than to scout the fortified entrance to Outlaws' Haven. Just riding over to it would get him filled with lead.

The walls closed in around him as surely as any prison cell.

"Yeah, we can make a few bucks," Slocum said, turning back into the saloon. Benson followed, still going on about his scheme to fleece other prisoners in Haven.

Slocum awoke about two in the morning. His mouth was like the inside of a cotton bale and his head was pounding from the bad liquor he had been swilling all evening. But there was something else wrong besides the start of a hangover. He sat up, hand resting on his six-shooter. Listening hard, he knew what it was. Somebody was making off with their horses.

"Benson," he hissed. Slocum didn't get an answer. He poked Benson's bedroll but didn't get any response. He came to his knees and pulled back the blanket.

Slocum frowned. Benson had put rocks under the blanket to make it look as if he were peacefully sleeping. Shooting to his feet, Slocum raced for the spot where he had tethered their horses. He wasn't too surprised to find his bay gently cropping the sparse grass—and Benson's horse gone.

Quickly saddling his horse, Slocum started out on the fresh trail. He followed Benson for almost twenty minutes before he spotted the man ahead. The dark shape moved slowly along the southernmost canyon wall. Now and then Slocum saw the sudden flare of a lucifer, as if Benson lit one cigarette after another. But there was never a burning coal to give the man away after the glare died.

The only explanation Slocum could come up with was that Benson used the match to study the walls. Harley Benson was looking for something and hadn't wanted to let Slocum in on it. More curious than pissed, Slocum edged closer for a better look.

Benson repeated his ritual, pulling out another lucifer from its tin container and striking it. He held up the light over his head and cast flickering shadows along the canyon as he studied the rocky walls. Slocum blinked and almost missed what happened next.

Harley Benson vanished.

Dismounting and going forward on foot, Slocum looked hard at the ground before he saw the narrow opening in the rock. Benson had ridden into the small gap, obviously having looked for some mark on the canyon wall and having found it. Try as he might, Slocum couldn't see anything distinguishing this section of wall from any other.

Slocum started in on foot behind Benson when he heard a horse protesting mightily. Slocum backed out and dashed for the secluded spot where he had left his own bay. In less than a minute Benson came out, leading his horse. The frightened animal pawed at the ground and kept trying to rear. Benson held the horse with a firm grip and soon quieted it.

He continued his search along the wall, Slocum following at a greater distance to keep from being overheard. The silence was enough to give a man the jitters, but it didn't bother Benson as much as it did Slocum. What was his partner searching for so diligently in the middle of the night?

Slocum started thinking—and he began having some doubts about Benson. Leaving Clay Zarra back in Grant's Pass was the only thing they could have done. Zarra wasn't up to riding. Fact was, he wasn't up to more than dying from all Slocum could tell. But Benson had insisted on getting into Haven.

"Almost from the start, he wanted in here," Slocum said softly. His eyes narrowed as he saw Benson disappear again. He tied his horse to a greasewood and hurried to the spot where Benson had gone into still another crevice in the canyon wall.

Slocum trailed his partner carefully down the fissure. This one was twice the size of the first and afforded Slocum some small chance to dodge down other cracks in the rock should Benson backtrack suddenly. But Benson was intent on moving forward and not turning back. Slocum almost walked into Benson when the man stopped abruptly.

Slocum pressed bard against a wall and breathed easier when Benson ignored his horse's warning of someone behind. Benson was too intent on studying the ground in a small, circular dirt-floored break in the passage. Someone had camped in here, but from what Slocum could see, it wasn't recently. He tried to look past Benson and see if there was another way out of the cul-de-sac.

If there was, he knew what Benson was hunting for so diligently. Harley Benson wanted an escape route from Haven. But why was he doing it like a thief in the night? He had to know Slocum's misgivings about even coming into the valley. And Benson had to know Slocum would have gladly helped him hunt for a back door since it might mean both of them staying alive if Jenkins took an impulsive dislike to them.

Benson stood, cursed in disgust, and began circling the small rocky box. Seeing there wasn't any more likely a way through the bulk of the mountains here than at any other point along the walls, Slocum backed away. It took Benson another few minutes to come to the same conclusion. The man mounted and rode along the wall, making his solitary inspection, using his lucifers now and then, and giving no clue as to what he really sought.

Slocum yawned and retrieved his own horse. He rode slowly back to where they had pitched their camp, lost in his own thoughts. Benson was up to something, and Slocum had no idea what it might be.

"Damnation, no man's that dumb," he said when details began dropping into place. Slocum snorted in contempt for Benson if the man actually considered robbing Outlaws'

Haven and trying to get away with the money. The rock wall kept out the law as effectively as it bottled up everyone in the valley.

One Ear Jenkins might have a prince's ransom hidden away from what he charged to enter Haven, and he certainly had more than any ten men were likely to see if he owned all the businesses in the valley. He had a sweet scheme going. He not only charged high passage into Haven, he extorted what money was left after his victims willingly threw themselves into his spider's web.

"Money, lots of money, and it's around here somewhere," Slocum said. Jenkins had Fogger and the others at his side constantly for a reason. They protected Haven's boss. They also acted as guards for wherever the treasure trove was hidden.

Jenkins might not tell them, but when he did a dozen rifles might be aimed at anyone foolish enough to try robbing the outlaw king. Another way out of Haven would be good, but it might not be enough. Slocum hoped Benson didn't try anything without letting him know.

Sighing heavily, Slocum dismounted and pulled his saddle from his bay. He slung the saddle over his shoulder and started back for their camp when he heard a man curse.

"Dammit, I twisted my fool ankle!" someone said, off and to Slocum's left. The voice came from within a few yards of his camp. He dropped the saddle and pulled out his Winchester, quietly chambering a round.

"I'll twist your damned neck if you don't keep quiet," came the immediate reply from farther off.

"Didn't mean nothing by it, Nate."

Slocum let out his breath and took another deep one. He knew who was stalking him now, and it didn't come as any surprise. Nate Fogger was out to ambush Slocum for the cold-cocking at the saloon.

Circling, Slocum got behind the man who had turned his ankle. The man sat on the ground, boot off and rubbing his ankle furiously.

"I can't go on, Nate. My ankle's all swole up like a rattler-bit dog."

"You stupid son of a bitch." Fogger grumbled but came to see his sidekick. A dark shape dropped down beside the injured man. Slocum considered two quick shots. The first would take out Fogger. The second would be even easier since the man with the sprained ankle wasn't able to get up and run.

He put the rifle to his shoulder, then froze when he heard a third man call out, "What's going on? We gonna kill the danged sidewinder or not?"

"You sit here till we come back for you," Fogger said. "I wouldn't want to have to shoot you to put you out of your misery."

"Yeah, sure, Nate. Whatever you say." The man's head bobbed up and down as if it were a child's jack-in-the-box popping out.

Slocum moved away, wondering how many he had to kill. The count was up to three. Had Jenkins ordered Fogger out or was the killer doing this on his own? If he had chosen to tangle with Slocum and hadn't been told to do it by Haven's boss, Slocum knew it would be easy to just bury Fogger and his confederates and deny ever having seen him.

That wouldn't cut it if Jenkins wanted him dead, though. Fogger would only be the first to come creeping in the night.

Slocum decided to cross that bridge when he got to it. He had Nate Fogger and one other moving through the night, intent on backshooting him. After he dealt with them, he could figure out what to do next.

He crept forward, rifle ready for action. He paused when he heard movement in the brush to his right. Slocum turned and strained to see who it was. He couldn't tell. He spun around when a shot came from his camp.

The shot was followed immediately by the whine of a bullet ricocheting off into the night.

"What happened, you damned fool?"

Slocum turned and waited. Fogger was the one crouching in the brush to his right.

"Nate, you ain't gonna believe it. I shot into the one's bedroll and there ain't nothin' but rock under the blanket!"

"Slocum! What about him?"

"Gone! They're both gone!"

Fogger cursed and rose, crashing through the undergrowth like a bull elephant gone rogue. Slocum lifted his rifle and squeezed the trigger. A foot-long tongue of flame momentarily blinded him. Fogger let out a shriek of pure terror and rocketed into the woods like a band of Sioux warriors was hot on his trail.

"He shot at me. The son of a bitch is out here tryin' to ambush us!" Fogger shrieked. Slocum got off a second shot that also missed. He cursed his bad luck. Fogger had moved at the wrong instant. Otherwise, he would have weighed more by a bullet's worth of lead.

Slocum twisted around and studied movement in the brush. He saw twigs shaking and waited. He could have fired wildly but there wasn't any reason. He had spooked Fogger already. It wasn't likely the man could get any more frightened into making mistakes than he already was.

The dark form rose and craned a neck to see what was happening. Slocum showed the man. The first shot took the man's hat off and sent it flying into the night like some dark, crippled bat. The second shot went lower. The would-be killer doubled over and fell facedown into a brambles.

Slocum went forward, hoping he had shot Fogger. He rolled the man over and saw one of those who had been with Jenkins earlier. Slocum cursed his bad luck in missing Fogger.

"Gotcha," came the cheerful voice from behind. Slocum heard a six-shooter cocking and knew there was nowhere to run. He got ready to take a bullet in the back and die.

7

Slocum's rifle didn't have a round in its chamber, and getting to his Colt, turning, and firing accurately in the dark was out of the question. But he had to do it if he wanted to stay alive.

Moving like lightning, Slocum crouched, dropped his Winchester, and pulled out his six-shooter just as the report from a pistol filled his ears. He saw flame stab out in the darkness—but there wasn't any bullet ripping life from him.

"You're good, Slocum. I knew you were fast, but my God!"

Walking out of the darkness came Harley Benson, his six-gun still smoking.

"Who was that owlhoot?" He gestured in the direction of the man he had gunned down.

"One of Fogger's friends," Slocum said. He looked around and saw no sign of Nate Fogger. He went to the man Benson had shot and saw he wore only one boot. Slocum shook his head at being so stupid. He ought to have slit the man's throat, then taken on Fogger and his sidekick. There wouldn't have been much noise as the man drowned in his own blood, and he would have been safer.

"You could at least thank me," Benson said. "And tell me what the hell's going on."

"Fogger came for me. I don't know where he got off to."

"Still runnin', 'less I miss my guess," Benson said, looking almost cheerful about it.

"This one's not going anywhere, though," Slocum said, returning to the man he had drilled. Two holes in the man showed Slocum's expertise with the rifle. The first bullet might have killed him. A deep groove along the top of his head was enough to shake his brains loose. But the bullet in his chest had done the worst damage.

"How many more of 'em you got to show me?" asked Benson. "I'm getting mighty tired."

"This is all," Slocum said. "Let's bury them and pretend we never saw them."

Benson paused, then laughed. "You think that'll work? If Fogger was with them, he'll know and—"

"It'll work," Slocum said. If One Ear Jenkins had sent the men, he'd be intrigued that only Fogger survived, and if Nate Fogger was solely responsible for the attack, he wouldn't dare tell his boss. Either way, he and Benson had some breathing room. Not much, but maybe enough for Slocum to find his own way out of Haven.

"Whatever you say," Benson allowed.

Slocum started to ask his partner what he had been hunting for, then decided against it. If Benson wanted to tell him, he would, but the man didn't seem inclined to mention his long search. Slocum had a suspicion that Benson was looking for a way out of Haven, too, but why had he been so eager to get inside?

After a half hour of hard work, they had the two bodies covered with mounds of dirt and enough rocks to keep the coyotes from digging up the corpses. Slocum wiped dirt and sweat from his forehead and stepped back. In the dark he was hard-pressed to see where the two would-be killers' graves were.

"I hope you know what you're doing," Benson said. The man had worked silently, and this was the first time he had opened his mouth since they had started grave digging.

"Yeah, I hope I do, too," Slocum said, thinking more about Harley Benson's nighttime hunt than the two gunmen they had just planted in the ground.

"Time for some sleep," Benson said, craning his neck and looking at the sky. It was less than two hours until dawn.

Slocum followed Benson back to their camp and sank down to the spot he had vacated hours and hours earlier. He waited for Benson to snore softly before closing his own eyes. Something was going on and he had the cold feeling it might kill him if he didn't find out soon.

Benson had saved him—but for what?

"My backbone's rubbing something fierce against my belly," complained Harley Benson. The man stretched like a cat waking from a nap, then jumped to his feet. He looked happier than he had anytime since they'd ridden into Haven, and Slocum couldn't figure out what made the man so happy.

"We can get something to eat in Jenkins's tent town," Slocum said. "I remember seeing a place that might have been a café." He stowed his gear and trailed Benson to their horses. As he passed the slight mounds of dirt on the fresh graves, he wondered if he might be pushing up daisies soon. The blow-off might come when they rode through the town and had rifles aimed at them from both sides of the street.

"We got enough money to last out a week or two. By then, the posse will have moved on," Benson said with uncharacteristic optimism. "And we might be able to rob this place and get on out with some real money."

Slocum didn't reply. His eyes roved from one side of the potholed street searching for any sign of trouble. The few men who stirred were rubbing sleep from their eyes and didn't look to be hunting for trouble—or John Slocum.

"There's the café," Benson said. He swung out of the saddle and walked to the tattered tent set up as a restaurant. He fastened his reins to a stake in the ground. Slocum had the feeling of someone watching. He moved slow and sure, taking time to look around as furtively as possible. Seeing no one did little to relieve him.

Jenkins wasn't the kind of man to do his spying from behind cover. He'd walk right on up and stare down whoever he wanted. Slocum didn't have any quarrel with anyone else in Haven other than Nate Fogger.

"What's wrong?" asked Benson, hesitating at the tent flap.

"Maybe nothing," Slocum said. He made sure his six-shooter rested free and easy in his cross-draw holster, then went into the dim, smoky interior. To his surprise he saw Fogger wolfing down food at a table at the rear of the tent. Jenkins's henchman looked up, a combination of fear and anger racing over his face. Then Fogger turned back to his meal, pretending that nothing bothered him.

Slocum sat where he could keep an eye on Fogger, but the uneasy feeling still made the hair on the back of his neck rise. Somebody was watching him. If it wasn't Fogger and wasn't likely to be Jenkins, who could it be?

Benson rattled on throughout the simple breakfast of flapjacks and bacon. Slocum paid him no heed, lost in his own thoughts. He watched Fogger leave, but the feeling of being scrutinized didn't go away.

Slocum jerked around when Benson cried, "How much for this miserable meal?" Along with the protest came the sound of hammers being pulled back. Six men had cocked their six-guns and had them pointed at Benson and Slocum.

"Twenty bucks," announced a waiter in a greasy apron. "Each."

"I ought to get a steak two inches thick for that!" Benson didn't appear too inclined to do more than grumble. He turned to Slocum and said, "We're being robbed blind. Twenty damned dollars." He peeled off a pair of greenbacks and shoved them across the table. Slocum added a twenty of his own to the pile, which vanished quickly under the waiter's once-white apron.

"That's the price for being safe," Slocum said sarcastically. It was lost on Benson. The man looked around, his head bobbing as if it were on a spring.

"Want to scout this place. See you later, Slocum." With that, Benson went off. From his attitude, Slocum expected him to pull out a piece of paper and a pencil and start making notes of everything he saw.

Slocum spun and sighted someone vanishing around the clapboard saloon across the street. He had finally caught his unseen watcher in a mistake. Rather than go straight across the street, Slocum circled. He went to the end of the street and cut back in time to see a slender figure get on a horse and ride away.

Slocum ran back and grabbed his bay's reins and swung into the saddle. He put his heels to the strong animal's flanks and slowly narrowed the gap between the fleeing figure. Slocum's eyes narrowed when the rider pulled to a halt and waved at him.

As he got closer, Slocum saw the rider had a bandanna pulled up across the nose in a vain effort to hide the face.

There was no mistaking who waved again at him.

"Suzanne, what are you doing here?" he called.

"Hush, not so loud, John." The dark-haired beauty pulled down her bandanna, took off her hat, and let her long hair whip out in the hot wind like a raven's wing banner. Her green eyes sparkled.

He reined in beside her. "This isn't the kind of place I'd expect to find you," he said.

"Who got you inside Haven?" she teased, the corners of her mouth turning up in a smile. Her eyes twinkled with devilment. "I've got friends in high places—and low."

"How do you come to know One Ear Jenkins?" asked Slocum.

Suzanne Crawford turned solemn. "There's not much time for palaver," she said. "I came for you. Clay Zarra's sinking fast and wants to see you."

"Just me or Benson, too?"

The question took Suzanne by surprise. She shrugged. "He only mentioned you. He's so weak he might not have been able to name you both." Suzanne smiled again and added, "Then again, why want to see anyone but you? I wouldn't."

"I'd go but getting out of Haven is a mite harder than getting in."

"Don't worry about that," Suzanne said mysteriously.

Slocum started to question her when she turned in the saddle and bit her lower lip. She put her finger to her lips to caution him, then pointed toward a small stand of trees. Slocum strained and heard the soft nickering of horses.

"This way," Suzanne said. She walked her horse for a few hundred yards, then picked up the pace. Suzanne led them toward the far side of the canyon. Slocum tried to determine if this was anywhere near where Benson had been prowling the night before and decided it wasn't. And

Suzanne wasn't looking for a way through the mountains as much as she was picking her way along the rocky wall as she headed for the mouth of the walled pass.

"Where are we going?" he called ahead to the woman. She looked over her shoulder. For a moment the light caught the planes and valleys of her face in such a way as to turn her into something angelic.

"Back to Grant's Pass," she answered simply.

"How do you know a way in and out of Haven? You're not thinking of just riding through the main gate, are you?"

Suzanne laughed and the sound echoed like dance-hall music in Slocum's ears. She seemed genuinely amused that he had asked such a question.

"I've lived in these parts all my life. There's not an inch of mountain or valley I haven't personally ridden over, through, or between."

"You waltzed on into Haven just to tell me Zarra wanted to talk? And you think we can just ride on out past the guards on that stone wall Jenkins built?" Slocum found this more than extraordinary. It amounted to foolhardiness surpassing anything he could believe of Suzanne Crawford.

"Why not, John?" She turned and batted her long eyelashes at him. "I'd do anything for you because you're . . . special."

And he believed she meant it.

What astounded him just as much was the way she kept riding toward the mouth of the canyon. He saw men walking along the ramparts, rifles in hand. What saved them from being seen was the way they looked out and down the narrow gap leading to the stone wall.

Or was it? Slocum considered the angles and decided this path might be in a blind spot for those guarding the entrance to Haven. The sun would work against the guards, and the canyon wall jutted out just enough to afford cover.

"Have you come and gone this way before?" Slocum asked.

"Don't ask needless questions, John," she chided. "It'll be better if you don't say anything until we're well out of here." Suzanne turned and studied the sun, as if judging where the right elevation was. Slocum couldn't believe they would be able to ride out in the middle of the day, sun in the guards' eyes or not.

And yet they did.

Suzanne walked her horse to the gateway, slipped through the open doors, and worked her way back, staying as close to the wall as she could. Slocum took his cue from her and tried to keep up. Suzanne picked up the pace, reaching a canyon wall in less than ten minutes.

"We have to wait for a few minutes," she said, again eyeing the sky. "The sun's got to be at the right spot so the guards can't see us."

Slocum studied the lay of the land and saw how deep shadows formed. Without warning, Suzanne started off, keeping to these dark areas. And again Slocum was amazed to see how the overthrust of rock hid them from above. He might not be able to get back into Haven this way, but getting out was easier than he'd ever believed possible.

When they were well down the canyon and out of sight of any patrolling guard, Slocum asked, "How'd you stumble on that way out of the valley? It's not something you just happened to find."

"Why not?" she shot back.

Slocum didn't have a good answer for that. How else would Suzanne have found the way?

The town of Grant's Pass hadn't changed one iota since he and Benson had ridden out. Slocum kept an eye peeled for any sign of the posse but saw nothing to indicate the

Pinkertons were still in the area. The people walking along the sidewalks were as edgy as before, but because he rode with Suzanne he got the notion that everyone was more curious than trigger-happy.

"I'm ruining your reputation," he told her.

She laughed and shook her head. Hair streamed out and was caught on the dry wind whipping down the street.

"Don't worry your head about it, John," she said. "People hereabouts keep their opinions to themselves. It doesn't much matter what they think of me."

"You've got to live with them." For some reason Suzanne found this argument funny, also. She waved him into Dr. Grandville's front door. Slocum entered the surgery, happy to be out of the hot sun and away from the prying eyes. Grant's Pass was a small enough town for the gossip to have started.

It wouldn't take much for the townspeople to decide he was an outlaw on the run. Putting Suzanne in his camp only endangered her life, no matter how much she denied the possibility. It would take only a mention to the Pinkertons to turn Grant's Pass into a shooting gallery.

"He's been asking for you," Dr. Grandville said, looking up from a magazine he had been reading. "Go on back. You know where he is."

Slocum pushed through the curtain separating the outer office from the first examining room, then hurried to the rear. Groans of pain greeted him as he went to Clay Zarra's side.

Bloodshot eyes flickered open. For a moment Slocum wasn't sure Zarra recognized him. Slocum reached out and touched the man's forehead. The parchmentlike skin was hot and dry. Zarra was running a fever, but the skin's texture was more what he would expect of a lizard than a man.

"It's me," Slocum said. "You're going to be all right, Clay."

"No, not, no," Zarra muttered. His eyes closed, then sprang open wide, as if he had experienced something so frightening he would die from it. "Gotta tell you. Heard. Heard it all. Gotta tell you, Slocum."

"What?" Slocum wasn't sure Zarra would be able to say anything more. His tongue was swollen and yellow and he looked panicky. Slocum poured a little water into a glass and gave Zarra a sip. This lubricated the man's mouth enough for him to lick his lips and try speaking again.

"Trap. It's a trap!"

"What is, Clay? What is a trap? Who are you talking about?" Slocum stared at the deathly pale man as he sank back to the hard bed, too weak to go on. Zarra shuddered and coughed deep in his chest, then sank into a coma.

Slocum wondered if Zarra was trying to tell him something important or if this was only the raving of a man closer to death than life. Slocum couldn't tell, and that worried him more than anything else.

8

"A trap," Slocum muttered to himself. He shook his head and figured that Zarra must have been lost in a fever dream. There couldn't be much of a trap if he was able to move around freely inside Haven—and had been able to sneak out with Suzanne's help. He looked up and down the main street of Grant's Pass and saw nothing out of the ordinary.

The citizens were jumpy, but they had been when he, Benson, and Zarra had ridden in. Being this close to Outlaws' Haven and knowing it was filled with desperate men on the run had to make law-abiding citizens high-strung and trigger-happy. He stayed out of the sun and did nothing but watch the ebb and flow of people around the town. Grant's Pass wasn't big enough to hide much, and Slocum saw everything he needed in a few minutes.

There wasn't any trap here. Maybe in Haven, thanks to Nate Fogger and One Ear Jenkins, but that was an easily avoided problem. Slocum didn't owe Harley Benson spit. They had pulled off the robbery together and that was about it. Benson wasn't quite a friend, but he surely wasn't an enemy.

Slocum came to a quick decision. Benson had wanted to hide out in Haven, so let him. Slocum felt easier away from Jenkins and his henchmen. He started for his horse when he heard movement behind him.

"John, are you going back to Haven?"

He turned to face Suzanne Crawford. His heart almost stopped. Damn, but she was a beautiful filly. Leaving her behind was about the hardest thing he had done in a spell.

"Got business," he said noncommittally. Slocum planned on just riding on, now that the Pinkertons had gone.

"I see," she said, a note of sadness in her voice. Suzanne understood what he was really saying. "If you need anything, come on back. I can help."

"Much obliged for all you've done. See that Clay rests easy." Slocum didn't like leaving the burying duties to anyone else since Zarra was his partner, but there wasn't much he could do hanging around and waiting like a vulture for Zarra to die. The man wouldn't much care who put him in the ground, and he might even like the notion that Slocum had heeded his vague warning about a trap and had ridden on.

"Take care, John," Suzanne said. She started to say something more, bit her lip, spun, and hurried off. The dry wind combed her hair back and gave Slocum a final look at her face as she turned the corner.

He mounted, wondering if he could spend a day or two longer in Grant's Pass. Riding around the doctor's office, he looked for Suzanne. If he had seen her, Slocum knew he might have decided to stay. But she was long gone.

He took that as a sign he should be, too. He put his heels to the bay's flanks and trotted from town. Slocum slowed to a walk when he got a mile down the road. There was no need pushing too hard. He wasn't running from anyone, and he sure as hell wasn't running to anywhere.

Slocum rode for another twenty minutes before an uneasy feeling of being near somebody began to make the back of his neck itch. Once, he swung around and studied his trail. Nobody was in sight. He guided his horse from the ragged path and went down into a dusty ravine, following it back along his own track for almost a mile.

Whether it was Zarra's warning or just his natural caution at work, Slocum decided to dismount and watch the countryside for a while. He and his horse were rested and this was a waste of time, but he felt better about it. Slocum found himself a spot to tether his horse, then hiked up a low rise and sat just under the crest on the far side so as not to outline himself against the sky.

Just when he thought he was being foolish, Slocum heard horses neighing. Not one or two, but many. He lay back on the sandy hillside to blend in with the brush. Less than a minute later, a half-dozen men rode along the road at the bottom of the hill.

Slocum sucked in his breath and held it, as if they might hear the air going in and out of his lungs. He recognized two of the men as riding with the posse. Even if he hadn't, the badges pinned on their chests told the story.

"Got no business doing this," complained one deputy. The rest of his gripe was lost on the wind blowing the words away, but Slocum caught the drift of the answer.

"You know what Mr. Kellerman told us. We keep that nothing town bottled up tight. You find the trail yet?"

Slocum sat up to get a better look, although it was a dangerous move. He had been right about being followed. Two of the posse were on hands and knees studying the ground for his tracks. Nobody looked up the hill in his direction.

"He's still goin' right on down the road," answered one. He laughed heartily as he stood, brushing off his hands. "Mr. Kellerman will snare him good and proper. Might have done it already, seeing as how this galoot is a good hour ahead of us."

Slocum didn't think much of the tracker's skill, but he was glad to learn he had been riding into the jaws of a trap. Zarra had been right. The Pinkertons weren't giving up. He considered what he ought to do. There wasn't any way in hell he could shoot it out with these six. He was good, but killing each Pinkerton with a single bullet was stretching luck to the breaking point.

"That way. Let's see if we can't scoop him up first. I haven't heard any gunfire, so I don't reckon Mr. Kellerman has him yet." The portly leader of the half-dozen deputies made a grand gesture, as if he led a cavalry column into battle.

Slocum almost laughed at such melodrama. The riders worked their way along the hill, and Slocum was quick to move when they were out of sight. They thought they were an hour behind but from his calculations they'd stumble across his pony in less than ten minutes, even working slowly along the dry road.

He made it back to his horse and got as much speed out of the bay as he could, going up and back over the hill. The horse slid down to where the posse had found his spoor. Behind them now, Slocum wondered if he might be able to get away. He discarded the notion. He had been lucky in avoiding capture. With six behind and more of the posse in front of him along the road, he wouldn't have stood a snowball's chance in hell of running or fighting.

With only a few minutes head start, Slocum knew he had to make the most of it. He studied the sky and saw the sun beginning to dip behind the mountains. It would be pitch-dark in another couple of hours. That might be all he needed to sneak past the Pinkertons. Or maybe not. The agent in charge—Slocum figured this was the Kellerman the posse mentioned—was no one's fool.

Slocum rode back into Grant's Pass. Haven looked better and better to him all the time.

A wry smile curled his lips. And seeing Suzanne again wasn't such a bad idea.

Slocum dismounted behind Dr. Grandville's office. He peered in and saw Clay Zarra thrashing about weakly. Sweat beaded the man's pale face and Slocum wondered how his partner hung on. He had seen corpses that looked healthier.

"Who's there?" demanded Dr. Grandville. The doctor shoved the barrel of a sawed-off shotgun through the curtains and pointed it at Slocum.

"Hold on," Slocum said, backing off involuntarily. He didn't want to be the doctor's next patient. "I was looking for Miss Crawford."

Grandville squinted at him, then lowered the shotgun. He belched, fumbled out a flask, and took a deep swig. Slocum guessed the doctor had been pulling hard at the rotgut in it from the way he spoke. "You know where to find her. Down the road, maybe a mile or two. A small whitewashed house." The doctor checked Zarra, then vanished back to the front of his offices when a tiny bell tinkled, signaling a new patient had entered.

Slocum paused for a moment, eavesdropping on the doctor. He caught his breath when he heard the town's sheriff ask Grandville, "You seen any strangers lately?"

"There's always strangers in Grant's Pass, Sheriff Peña. That's one of the problems in these parts."

"The Pinkertons are looking for a trio of men what robbed a Union Pacific train. If you see them—"

"If I see them, I'll turn them in for the reward myself," snapped Dr. Grandville. Slocum guessed there wasn't any love lost between the men. In a way, that made him feel a mite safer. Grandville wasn't as likely to turn him and Zarra over to the posse, but what was the doctor's price?

Slocum slipped from the surgery and mounted. He felt the hot breath of the law down his neck. What the doctor said puzzled him. Suzanne's room was only a short distance away, but the doctor had told him her house was down the road.

Riding slowly, Slocum went by the boardinghouse and saw no light in Suzanne's window. On impulse, Slocum turned down the road. He hadn't asked Grandville which direction Suzanne's house lay. Slocum tried to remember what he had seen riding into town and figured on the other direction. He rode hard and caught sight of Sheriff Peña emerging from the doctor's office. Slocum didn't think he had been spotted as he rode past.

He slowed when he came to a knot of houses bunched together tightly like mushrooms at the town's outskirts. None looked like the kind of place he thought would belong to Suzanne Crawford. But why did she have a house and a room at a boardinghouse? It didn't make sense.

Then he saw a simple whitewashed clapboard house standing apart from the others, a hundred yards farther down the road. Rather than approach directly, Slocum circled and came onto the house from the rear. The sun was behind the tall mountain peaks now and cast obscuring shadows.

His foot had just touched the ground when he heard a six-shooter cock.

"Hello, Suzanne," Slocum said, not turning. If he was wrong a bullet would rip his spine in half. He wasn't wrong.

"John!"

He half turned and found himself with an armful of woman. She kissed him hard on the lips and then backed off.

"Why'd you come back?" she asked. "Not that I'm complaining, mind you. You seemed bound and determined to leave Grant's Pass."

"I couldn't go off without seeing you again," he said.

"Liar."

"What are you doing out here?" he asked.

Suzanne didn't answer. Instead, she smiled and pulled him into the house. It was much as he had thought. Neat, tidy, simply furnished, it was a reflection of her elegance and beauty. This looked like the kind of place where she would live rather than just sleep. She pushed him toward a love seat and sank down beside him.

"Now what's the real reason you came back? I've seen that look you had earlier in other men's eyes. It means they're out chasing a new star."

"The posse has the town fenced off good and proper," Slocum said. "There's no way I could get out unless I had an army with me."

"So?" Suzanne's eyes danced devilishly.

"So I reckon I'm safer in Haven than I am out. I need to know how to get back inside without Jenkins seeing me."

Suzanne laughed. Then the mirth died and she stared into Slocum's green eyes. The woman moved closer. She reached out and touched his cheek, then moved still closer and kissed him again. This time it was slow and long, but it held as much passion as the first kiss outside.

"We can't get back into Haven for a couple hours. What would you like to do to pass the time?" she asked.

Slocum reached out and stroked her cheek. His hand moved to her slender throat. Suzanne caught her breath and closed her eyes. Slocum's hand moved lower and cupped the firm breast under her heaving blouse. She arched her back and pressed more firmly into his grip.

It was Slocum's turn to moan softly when he felt the woman's fingers lightly moving over his leg and moving upward. When she squeezed down at his crotch, he let out a gasp.

"The bed's over there," Suzanne said, turning toward a door off the front room. "I don't want it to go to waste."

"That'd be a shame," Slocum agreed. He kept moving his palms over the front of Suzanne's blouse and she rubbed like a cat against him, her fingers probing and making him increasingly uncomfortable in the tight jeans. Somehow, by the time they reached Suzanne's bedroom, they had both shed their clothes.

A single coal-oil lamp burned in the front room and cast dancing shadows over Suzanne's naked body. Slocum stepped away from her for a moment and appreciated the sight. Soft valleys and bold out-thrusts of flesh were revealed and hidden and revealed as Suzanne turned slowly for his appreciation.

"Just looking at you makes me want to—" Slocum didn't get a chance to finish. Suzanne rushed forward and hugged him tight.

"Me, too, John, me, too! Do it now!"

The lovely woman gave a little hop and wrapped her legs around his waist. Her arms circled his neck and supported her as her hips weaved and wobbled around until they were in just the right position. Then she sank down slowly. Slocum's hard length vanished into her.

Slocum's knees turned weak. He moved back and propped himself up against the foot of Suzanne's brass bed. He would have walked around with her so passionately joined to him but Suzanne began moving up and down. The friction was small at first but it built. She hungrily kissed his mouth and neck, burying her face in his shoulder.

"So good, John, so damned good. Don't move. Let me do it all!"

Slocum's hands slid down her sleek body and cupped her rounded buttocks. This way he was able to bounce her up and down in a motion that pushed them both to the breaking point. He felt Suzanne's breasts crushing against his chest, then moving as their flesh slickened with sweat.

"Harder, John, harder." Suzanne panted with need now.

"Can't hold out much longer," Slocum gulped. He was engulfed by her, hidden, turned every which way but loose. Together their ardor mounted until Slocum was no longer able to hold back. Just as his loins exploded, he felt Suzanne tense all over. She shrieked and threw her head backward.

He strained to hold her, to keep her from falling to the floor. The angle of her body to his heightened the sensations ripping through him. Spent, he sank slowly to the floor and let Suzanne stretch out in front of him. She grinned like a contented feline with a saucer of cream.

"We never did get to your bed," Slocum said.

"Are you complaining?" she teased.

"When do we have to start for Haven?" he asked. Slocum got the answer he wanted.

"Not too soon," Suzanne replied.

Suzanne's bed squeaked but neither of them noticed much.

Slocum had to admit Suzanne Crawford knew the mountains as good as any man could—as good as any Indian guide ever could. She led him up dry arroyos and through crevices, avoiding the main road leading to the cross canyon where Outlaws' Haven was hidden away. Slocum wasn't sure such caution was required, but tangling with the Pinkerton posse meant capture or death.

"This leads straight into Haven," Suzanne said. "We've got to be even more careful now. Guards on either side of the pass might see us if we stray away from the canyon wall."

She and Slocum were pressed against the southernmost wall, the one Suzanne had used to get out of Haven earlier. The protecting overhang kept anyone above from seeing them, and darkness cloaked their movement from any guard on the far wall.

"And stay quiet. Sounds echo to a fare-thee-well here." She stopped and let Slocum catch up with her. On impulse, she stood on tiptoe and kissed him. The loud smack rang up and down the canyon like a gunshot. She smiled wickedly and said softly, "See?"

"That sounded like a rifle report. I wonder what other sounds might turn into?" he asked.

"Let's not find out. Besides, we haven't worn out the bed yet," she said. She hurried on, a wiggle in her get-along keeping Slocum more interested in her than the guards above.

"How do we get through the wall?" he asked. "Jenkins will have the gate sealed up tight."

"You worry too much. I told you I was born and raised in these hills. I watched them build that wall. There are always a couple ways past any gate."

Slocum wasn't so sure. He had gotten a good look at the heavy portal and even sturdier stone battlements when Jenkins had first let them in, and Slocum had studied the fortifications as he and Suzanne sneaked out. It would take an army to break through.

"Can we—"

"Hush. Listen. What do you hear?" Suzanne's voice was tinged with fear now.

For a moment Slocum didn't hear anything at all. Then distant clicks and shouts and whinnies reached his sharp ears.

"Horses," he said. "Lots of them and coming fast behind us."

"The posse!" cried Suzanne. "We're caught between Haven's guards and the Pinkertons!"

9

"We're caught!" Suzanne cried. Her horse reared and almost threw her. She fought to keep the frightened animal under control. But Slocum saw that the momentary bucking and loud neighing didn't draw attention to them.

The posse galloped pell-mell up the canyon, rifles blazing away in the darkness. Slocum had seldom seen anything as foolish in his life. They couldn't see too well in the narrow confines of the canyon and several of the posse's horses slipped and stumbled. Even worse, they had lost any element of surprise they might have had.

From both walls came a withering fire that ripped through the rocky crevice. One bullet sang past Slocum's head and put a nick in the brim of his Stetson. He dismounted and held his bay firmly, trying to keep the strong animal from rearing.

"What are we going to do?" asked Suzanne. "We're going to be killed!"

Slocum didn't see any solution to their problem. The posse raced on, going past them in the darkness. He reached out and pushed Suzanne's six-shooter away as she tried to fire.

"Just wait. For a few minutes," he urged. The posse hadn't seen them yet. If they opened fire, on either posse or guards, they were sure to be spotted cowering against the sheer canyon wall. They were safe from being fired on from directly above, but anyone on the canyon floor or the guards along the far wall could cut them down instantly.

"Sorry, John, I don't usually panic. I . . . I wasn't expecting an attack."

"It's about the dumbest thing I've ever seen," said Slocum. "How can the Pinkertons hope to get through the fortifications?"

"They can't," Suzanne said. "And we may not be able to, either."

A pitched battle went on, bullets ricocheting off rocks and crawling into the night like deadly fireflies. The posse had pulled up short of the wall and concentrated their fire against the guards on the stone wall. The others, now a little behind and above the posse, kept up a devastating attack.

"They haven't seen us," Suzanne whispered, although no one could have heard her over the din of gunfire. "Let's get out of here."

Slocum paused. Things didn't add up right. Was this the trap Zarra had tried to warn him about? Or did the injured man simply mean the Pinkertons had sealed up Grant's Pass? And how could Zarra have come upon such information lying shot-up in Grandville's back room?

"How were you going to get through the gate and into Haven?" he asked.

"Not now, John. They'll have the entire valley sealed up tighter than a drum!"

He ignored her warning. Returning to Haven seemed more important now. Questions that needed answering could only be asked beyond the stone wall and the thick wooden gate.

"You can go on back to Grant's Pass. It'll be dangerous until you get free of this canyon, then there won't be any trouble." Slocum didn't think the posse would have split up and left guards at the canyon mouth. Even if they had, Suzanne's knowledge of the craggy terrain would see her past even the most vigilant lookout.

"No, John, I won't leave. You can't—" Suzanne stopped arguing when she saw the determination on Slocum's face. She heaved a deep sigh and said, "Very well. I'll go home."

"Tell me how you intended to get into Haven."

"You won't make it," she said, resigned to his intractable determination. "What I was going to do was get close to the gate, then slip to the north end of the stone wall."

"And?" Slocum pressed. Something about the way Suzanne spoke told him there was a big chink in the armor protecting Outlaws' Haven.

"There's a tiny crevice covered with brush. Get inside and it widens enough so you can walk your horse through. The rift opens a few yards past the wall inside Haven. It's dangerous, though. The guards can see you and—"

"Thanks," he said. Slocum kissed Suzanne quickly, then started for the wall. The posse was being driven back. It wouldn't be long before they gave up and retreated fully.

Suzanne started to say something more and then got on her horse and walked it off into the night. Within seconds the darkness swallowed her. He knew she would beat the Pinkertons back to the mouth of this canyon. A bigger question was if any of the posse would escape alive. The wall protected Haven, but the bigger secret of this canyon's location meant even better security. One Ear Jenkins wasn't likely to want any lawman getting away to tell others where to find some of the most wanted men in the West.

Slocum ducked involuntarily as a stray bullet sang past his ear. He knew he had to get out. Going after Suzanne might be the smartest thing he could do. He turned his horse toward the stone wall protecting Haven's valley hideout.

The closer he got to the wall, the heavier the gunfire. He had been through battles during the war that had less lead flying. The only saving grace for the posse, as far as Slocum could tell, lay in the darkness cloaking the canyon floor. That robbed the outlaws of good, clean targets.

"Cut 'em all down," came the loud command from atop the stone wall. Slocum peered up and saw One Ear Jenkins's silhouette. The grizzled old man had come to take personal command of the defenses. From all Slocum could tell, he was doing a bang-up job of it.

From the posse came wild cries of pain and rage—and utter confusion. Slocum wondered what they'd thought they were doing when they rode hellbent for leather down the canyon toward the stone wall.

He reacted instinctively when one of the posse blundered toward his position. Slocum drew and fired his Colt Navy in one smooth movement. The bullet took the Pinkerton high in the shoulder and spun him around in the saddle. The man let out a cry of pain as he fell, his foot tangled in his stirrup. As the horse raced past Slocum, the man slipped free of the stirrup cup and lay flat on his face in the dirt.

Going to him, Slocum rolled the man over. A star was pinned to the man's chest. He might not have been a Pinkerton agent at all, but only some drifter who'd been offered a few dollars to be deputized and ride along, lending the use of his six-shooter.

A piece of paper stuck in the man's vest pocket caught Slocum's attention. He pulled it out and peered at it in the darkness. It looked like a crudely drawn map of the canyon—but without any indication of a wall barring entry into Outlaws' Haven. A few Xs had been scratched around, maybe showing where the posse was supposed to form for the attack into Haven.

Slocum tossed the map away and grabbed the reins of his horse. He was too close to the wall to stand around wondering at the stupidity of the Pinkertons.

Slocum pressed hard against the wall, worrying now that the posse might see him and open fire. From the confusion still reigning in its ranks, the posse wasn't going to be much of a problem. Contradictory commands were barked out but the men got the idea of retreating, mostly on their own.

Working along the wall, Slocum found a small crevasse covered with dried brush. He shoved it aside and led his crow-hopping horse inside the dark passage. The bay tried to buck and rear, but Slocum kept a strong hand on the reins and spoke soothingly to the frightened animal. He felt his way through the fissure, taking a quick, hard right-angled turn that led him out on the far side of the wall.

Slocum had to work quick because more and more outlaws were pouring up from the valley, waving their six-shooters in the air and looking like they were going to hurrah a town. He swung into the saddle, then turned his bay's face toward the wall. He joined the crowd and stopped when Jenkins let out a roar of triumph from the top of the barrier.

"We done it, men! We run off those sonsabitches!" Jenkins fired his shotgun into the air. Three-foot-long tongues of flame leapt from the barrels.

A cheer went up from the outlaws on the battlement, then spread to those milling around on the inside of the gate.

The rider next to Slocum called, "Let's go celebrate!" This met with instant and universal approval. The charge that had brought so many of the mounted desperadoes to the barrier now reversed direction. Slocum found himself caught up in it, and not much caring.

He had developed a powerful thirst. And more than a few questions begging for answers.

At the saloon men swapped lies about their bravery in battle and how they, each and every one, had single-handedly driven back the lawmen. Slocum drank the potent whiskey but didn't join in the bragging. He stood to one side and hunted for Benson. After finishing a second overpriced drink, Slocum started to leave, only to bump into his partner on the way into the saloon.

"Slocum, there you are," said Benson. "What's the big fuss?"

"You don't know?"

"Naw, I was sleeping. Been real tired of late. Must be peace of mind that's getting to me," Benson said. Slocum thought he detected a hint of sarcasm in the man's tone but let it slide.

"The Pinkertons tried to bust through and into Haven."

Benson's eyes widened and he turned pale. His mouth opened and then snapped shut like a beached trout.

"They didn't seem to know anything about the stone wall Jenkins put across the mouth of the canyon. They smashed up against it, and the guards along the canyon walls shot them like fish in a barrel." Slocum saw Benson struggling to regain his composure. Just for the hell of it, he added, "It was a slaughter. Bloodiest I've seen since the second battle of Manassas."

Slocum wasn't sure why he was goading Benson. Wherever the man had been, he wasn't putting in time under his blanket. Slocum almost told Benson about the way around the wall to get his reaction, then stopped. To do so might endanger Suzanne's life. If One Ear Jenkins got wind of how she came and went, he'd track her down and shoot her. What Jenkins sold was a sense of safety for the outlaws entering Haven. A young woman who could get inside without anyone knowing would ruin that reputation in a flash.

"They shouldn't have done that," Benson said, getting his voice back.

"Killed most of them from the look of it," Slocum said.

"We're safe, though. They can't get past that wall. It's too thick for that."

Slocum started to press Benson on what he had been doing during the attack but he was shoved aside when One Ear Jenkins and Nate Fogger blew into the saloon. The crowd around them was enough to fill the tiny room to overflowing. Added to the crowd already there, everyone stood shoulder to shoulder.

"Men," bellowed Jenkins, "you all done good in driving them worthless bastards away." The man scratched his scraggly chin and added, "Well, some of you didn't do so good."

The cheer that had greeted Jenkins's first words now died. Silence hung over the saloon like a death shroud.

"Some of you lazy, lily-livered snakes were shuckin' off your duty to protect Haven." Jenkins found a small circle widening around him the longer he spoke. His cold eyes darted from face to face. Beside him Nate Fogger widened his stance, getting ready to kill.

Slocum looked to the door and saw he could never get outside before lead started flying. He cursed himself for not reloading the single round he had fired during the fight outside the barricade. He might need all six rounds before much longer.

"Some of you were downright cowardly," Jenkins went on, his gaze flitting from man to man. Some met him squarely. Others flinched. Jenkins seemed to home in on those. "Like him. You, Hills. What did you do beside stick your head in a hole and wait for your betters to die?"

"I fought!" the diminutive outlaw protested. "I *did!*"

"You say so, but I say different. You ran and hid. You let others do your fighting for you," Jenkins said, his fingers tapping the barrel of his shotgun.

Hills reached and fumbled, which was a fatal mistake. Jenkins's shotgun roared and cut Hills into bloody shreds. On either side of the dead man, others winced as hot buckshot tore through them. One sagged to the floor, moaning from the pellets he'd taken in the gut.

Rather than showing any remorse for the others he had shot, Jenkins roared, "And them. The ones with Hills. They're cowards, too. And we all know how we treat cowards in Haven!"

Slocum didn't want to find out, but he wasn't in any position to leave. Beside him Benson muttered constantly, his hand resting on the butt of his six-gun. Slocum hoped his partner didn't start anything. As long as Jenkins trained his wrath on others, they were safe enough.

"Get 'em outside," bellowed Fogger. He used his pistol on the side of one man's head, staggering him. The others in the saloon kicked and struck, forcing their victim into the street. Two others were sent reeling after them.

Slocum was glad for the breathing room when most of the men went outside to watch the show. Jenkins stood on a rain barrel, his shotgun resting in the crook of his arm. Beside him on the ground Nate Fogger shifted from one foot to the other, nervously waiting for his turn.

"We don't cotton much to men who don't pull their weight in Haven," Jenkins called for the crowd's benefit. They were turning nasty. Slocum had seen enough lynch mobs to know what was going to come—or so he thought.

"These three didn't do enough to defend Haven. They're traitors. And how do we treat those who betray us?"

"Hunt!" went up the chant. "Hunt, hunt, hunt!"

"Get to runnin', you miserable coyotes," Jenkins shouted. He lifted his shotgun and loosed another shattering blast at the three in the street. The buckshot tore through one man's arm, spinning him around and driving him facedown into the street. The other two grabbed for their six-shooters.

Fogger drew and fired. He was a split second ahead of a dozen others. The men who had tried to fight back were cut down where they stood.

"Ain't no fun," Fogger complained. "They didn't try to get away."

"They weren't the only pusillanimous, gutless skunks behind the wall," Jenkins said. "Them three. They didn't do their part, either."

He aimed his shotgun at a trio standing near the entrance to the saloon. Fear washed over their faces. Unlike the first three, these men turned and ran. A huge cheer went up from the crowd.

Like a swarm of bees, the outlaws went after the three who had run. Slocum and Benson hung back, able to see everything that went on.

"They should have stood their ground," Benson said uncomfortably. The trio had run less than a block before the crowd caught them and tore them limb from limb.

"Saw something like this," Slocum said. "At a Navajo sing. They call it a chicken-pull. They half bury a chicken and then ride by and try to rip it apart from horseback."

Benson shuddered. He wiped his sweaty palm on the front of his shirt as the crowd flowed back to stand before Jenkins, waiting for the next victim to be named.

"They didn't fight hard enough," Jenkins roared. "They let the rest of us down. We don't like that, do we?"

The crowd roared approval for his stand. They roared and turned more bloodthirsty by the second. Slocum felt the hate and craving for more death and suffering mount.

"We risked our lives and don't want those who didn't pull their weight next to us in Haven, do we?" Jenkins was whipping them into a frenzy of hatred. All he had to do was point out the next target and step back.

Slocum wasn't much surprised when both Jenkins and Fogger turned in their direction.

"Those two. What'd they do during the fight? Slocum was there, but was he fighting? And what of Benson? Where the hell was he?"

The crowd surged forward, and Slocum saw nothing but tombstones in their eyes.

10

Benson tried to move closer to Slocum. Three burly men shoved between them, keeping them apart and unable to protect each other's back. Slocum heard Benson mutter something about "having found it" and then he was slammed hard against the saloon wall.

"That one's a gutless son of a bitch," declared Nate Fogger, squaring off to face Benson. Light seeping from several nearby tents and buildings gave him a demonic look. His fingers tapped lightly against the butt of his six-shooter, ready to draw down at Benson's first twitch.

The men pressing Slocum against the wall turned to see what was happening. They relished a good fight, especially one where Fogger was going to put holes in a newcomer who didn't count as one of their own.

"Not man enough to have it out with me, Fogger?" called Slocum. A silence fell over the crowd, then a loud whisper started. Slocum caught enough of the murmuring undertone to know the others feared Fogger as much as they hated him. They would as soon see his blood spilled as anyone else's.

"What right you got saying that, Slocum?" Fogger swung

around but there was uncertainty in his eyes. He had faced Slocum before and come out second best. He saw no weakness to exploit.

"I'll take him, Nate," came the loud cry from the crowd. A towering man pushed through, looking like a redwood in a forest of scrub oaks. His arms were thicker than most men's thighs, and he moved with a ponderous step. In the darkness he might have been a huge boulder come to life. "I ain't killed nobody all day since I missed all the fun of potshotting those lawmen."

Fogger's attention wavered. He saw a way out and backed down, his eyes flickering nervously from the mountain of a man to Slocum and then to Harley Benson.

Slocum squared off, thinking the giant was speaking to him. To his surprise the huge man planted himself a few yards away from Benson.

"You and me got business," the mammoth man said. "I think you been cheatin' at cards. Never saw anyone so lucky."

"Let's see how your luck runs now, Treetop," Benson said, obviously recognizing the man. Slocum wondered if it would ever have been possible to sit across a card table from this behemoth and not remember him. Benson had been spending more time in the saloon than Slocum had thought.

"Better 'n yours," the man said, pushing his duster back. He wore two six-shooters stuck into his belt cross-draw fashion. Slocum tried to guess if he was left-or right-handed and couldn't. He hoped Benson was faster than he thought—and braver by half.

Benson's hand flashed to his pistol and got it out. The explosion as it went off startled everyone, including Slocum. For a split second he was blinded and thought Benson's six-gun had blown up in his hand because of shrapnel sailing past him to embed in the saloon wall. Then he saw where the first bullet had fairly ripped. The giant's hand was mostly gone in a grisly ruin of blood and sundered bone. Benson's bullet had hit the cylinder in Treetop's .44. It was *his* six-shooter that had exploded and sent metal flying in all directions.

The man dropped to his knees, clutching his destroyed right hand. He was bleeding to death and only vaguely noticed it. Seconds passed and the dumbfounded look on his dull face was replaced by the realization he was going to die. Rather than be buried alone, Treetop wanted to take Benson with him.

He fumbled for the pistol thrust into the right side of his belt. Benson's second shot stopped him dead, the bullet going through the man's head. Treetop crashed like a toppled tree and lay twitching in the dusty street.

Slocum waited for all hell to break loose. Benson had just killed someone who commanded a certain respect in Haven. To his astonishment, a cheer went up and men rushed forward to clap Benson on the back, congratulating him. Slocum was pushed back against the saloon again, forgotten in the rush to get next to Haven's newest hero. He sidled along the wall until he caught sight of Nate Fogger.

The gunman blinked at the dead man in the street. And jumping down from his rain barrel and going to Fogger's side was Haven's undisputed ruler. One Ear Jenkins said something to Fogger, who shook his head. Jenkins then cuffed Fogger and sent him reeling away. Fogger looked to be going for his six-gun until he saw Jenkins's shotgun coming up to cover him.

Even then, Slocum considered a quick shot, in spite of distance and darkness. The crowd might not notice. Too many of them shot their own side arms in the air to celebrate victory. Fogger could be dead before Jenkins figured out who had done it, not that he might care one whit. From his angry expression, he wasn't too pleased with Fogger at the moment.

Slocum's chance evaporated as more men crowded in front of him and Fogger vanished from sight. Slocum knew he'd have to get another chance—or catch a bullet in his spine when he was least expecting it. Nate Fogger was like a stepped-on sidewinder. He was too dangerous to be ignored now that he was riled up. If Jenkins was thinking of a new henchman for the number two spot in Haven, that made Fogger all the more deadly.

Going into the saloon, Slocum found the place even more crowded than before. Bottles were passed from the bar and made the rounds, each taking a deep swig before passing it along. Those closest to the source of whiskey were already tottering from too much red-eye and got pushed to one side to make room for others with just as big a thirst.

"Someday, eh, Slocum?" asked a short man pressed hard into Slocum's left side. Slocum had never seen the man before, or if he had he sure as hell didn't remember him. Such was the price of being Nate Fogger's enemy in Haven.

"Can't remember one like it," Slocum said. He took a bottle making its way through the crowd and sampled it. The harsh liquor burned his lips and throat before sliding down more smoothly than he would have thought possible.

"Them lawmen won't try gettin' into Haven again anytime soon," the short man declared, taking the bottle from Slocum and finishing it with a long loud belch of contentment.

"Did we get all of them?"

"Reckon so, though Jenkins thinks a few made it away. Dumbest stunt I ever seen, makin' a straight-ahead run at us like that. And doin' it after dark. I was up on the wall doin' my turn at sentry. I swear, I kilt three of them before they knowed what hit 'em!"

Slocum let the flow of the crowd take him away. He listened hard for more information about the Pinkertons' attack, but nobody seemed to know anything he didn't already. Most of the gossip came from men claiming to be Benson's good buddy and how much they had hated Treetop.

The towering redwood in this forest had just been felled. That left a few of the weeds like Nate Fogger and One Ear Jenkins, except Slocum didn't deceive himself that they might be harder to get rid of than an elephantine gunman who moved too slow when it counted most.

"More booze, more for everybody!" came a voice Slocum recognized. He stood on tiptoe and saw Benson pressed hard against the bar. The man was taking the whiskey bottles and passing them out into the crowd, not partaking of any as they passed through his hands. The others were getting stony-eyed drunk, but Benson looked fresher than a daisy.

Slocum tried to catch Benson's eye but failed. The din was too loud and too many men tried to get next to Haven's momentary hero. Slocum saw his chance when Benson slipped along the bar and ducked out the rear door.

It took several minutes for Slocum to work his way to the front and get out the door into Haven's dusty main street. Treetop lay where he had been killed, the flies coming in to examine a potential feast. Slocum looked up and saw a couple of vultures circling low, risking a nocturnal hunt, aware of food but not hungry enough to risk getting shot.

Slocum knew it wouldn't be long before their appetite overcame their good sense. Not only was Treetop a delectable meal, the three "cowards" who had been cut down weren't ten yards away and somewhere just beyond lay three others. Seven men dead in less than an hour.

And that didn't take into account those dying on the wall—or attacking it.

"Some haven," Slocum mumbled. These men had found death—and maybe without the shallow graves in some distant potter's field that often went with it.

He hurried around to the rear of the saloon searching for Harley Benson. The man was nowhere to be seen. Night cloaked the entire valley with a vengeance, and it wouldn't be dawn for another few hours. Slocum made his way back to their simple camp and found Benson's horse gone. From the fresh tracks, the man had hightailed it out into the canyon. Slocum wasted no time in going after him. Now that Benson had killed one of the rowdier residents of Haven and Jenkins had it in for them, they'd have to leave.

To Slocum's surprise, he had a difficult time catching up with his partner. Benson had ridden like the wind, and Slocum didn't think it was to escape further gunplay in the small town. Benson was heading straight for some spot he had already found. In the darkness, Slocum wasn't likely to be able to trail Benson quick enough to find him before first light.

"He said he'd already found it," Slocum said, thinking aloud. "What was he talking about?" He rode along, trying to put it all together. Benson might have been hunting for a way out of the canyon, a back door to escape if the need arose.

Would he have left Slocum behind and would he have gone now? Slocum took Benson to be the kind of man who'd think he had it made in Outlaws' Haven, at least for the time being. Benson had been gambling more than Slocum, and maybe winning. That would explain Treetop's desire to ventilate him.

"A passel of money pours through that canyon mouth," Slocum said, glancing over his shoulder in the direction of

Haven's entrance. He stopped and looked around, hoping to spot Benson. There wasn't any sign of him, not that he had expected there to be. Slocum chewed on his lower lip and exhaled hard. He got his fixings out and rolled a cigarette, taking the time to light it and inhale deeply. The smoke filled his lungs and took some of the edge off the sense of urgency he was beginning to feel.

"Benson wasn't in town when the Pinkertons attacked," he said to his bay. "What do you make of that?" The horse neighed softly and shook its head hard.

"You might be right," Slocum said, puffing on his cigarette. He blew a smoke ring and watched as the gentle breeze blowing from his back caught it and sent it higher into the air. The light from the cigarette's tip might betray him, but Slocum doubted anybody but he and Benson were this deep in the canyon.

"Benson might be thinking he can get really rich by finding where Jenkins stashes his take." Slocum knew there wasn't any bank in Haven that would hold Jenkins's money, and he couldn't see the outlaw riding into Grant's Pass to deposit it in a bank. Jenkins had his money hidden away someplace he thought was safe, and Benson was hunting for it.

Slocum considered his partner to be a first-class fool if that was what he sought in the canyon, but the only way to find out was to flat out ask Harley Benson. He had acted strange since they had stuck up the U.P. train and been chased by the posse.

Slocum stubbed out his cigarette and rode slowly to the canyon wall. Benson had studied the markings, as if this would give him a clue to whatever he sought. Slocum found the narrow crevice Benson had ridden down before to the sandy cul-de-sac. This time he heard no sound echoing back from the dead end. He pushed on, looking as carefully at the rocky terrain as he could for signs of Benson's passage.

An hour passed, and Slocum had to admit he wasn't likely to find his partner this way. Any track that Benson might have left would be too slight to see in the dark. And from the way Benson had run like a scalded dog from the saloon, he was hot to get back to some spot. He might have already searched this area for whatever he sought, Jenkins's money or an escape route, and ridden hard to wherever he had given up his hunt just before the Pinkertons' attack.

Slocum turned his horse's face away from the rocky canyon wall and headed back toward the center of the canyon. He wasn't even sure Benson had come down this wall. The man was moving fast inside Haven. He might have circled to the far side of the canyon in the time Slocum had spent in Grant's Pass with Suzanne.

"Suzanne," Slocum said softly, turning the name over and over on his tongue like a fine whiskey. Without realizing it, he rode faster back toward his camp. He couldn't shake the feeling she was in some kind of danger after sneaking him out of Haven to see Clay Zarra.

And the way she came and went from Haven spelled more trouble. If word got back to Jenkins from anyone in Grant's Pass who might have seen Slocum, he'd have to fight his way out. He didn't want to reveal Suzanne's secret passage past the stone wall protecting Haven from the law.

Slocum had many decisions to make. Should he abandon Benson to his own devices and get out of Haven while he could? What did he really owe the man, anyway? They'd been partners on the train robbery, but Slocum knew Clay Zarra better. And Zarra wasn't long for this world.

Fact was, he was probably dead already. And Slocum would join him if he remained in Haven much longer.

Something caused Slocum to rein back and look around.

He hadn't heard anything. He hadn't smelled anything blowing into his nostrils other than the stench from Haven.

Then he saw it. A flash of light from high atop the canyon rim. Slocum turned in the saddle and watched for a minute or more as the light winked on and off in a definite signal. Someone was sending a message down into Haven.

But who? Why? Slocum knew he might never find out for certain, but he was beginning to work out answers to some vexing questions. And the result wasn't much to his liking.

11

Slocum waited a few minutes to see if there was any more signaling. It had looked as if someone on the rim had a lantern and dropped a blanket over it to give the short and long flashes. It might have been Morse code, but Slocum didn't know it, and from the quickness of the message this might have been nothing more than a signal to alert someone inside Haven.

But who was doing the alerting and who was watching? And what information were they exchanging? Slocum shook his head, unable to figure it out. The man on the rim might be one of Jenkins's lookouts sending intelligence on the posse's condition. Or maybe not. He just couldn't say.

Slocum turned back for his camp, more determined than ever to get out of Haven. With any luck, he could backtrack through the passage Suzanne had told him about and get to Grant's Pass just after sunrise. And then he would have to play it by ear.

Clay Zarra wasn't a concern. Dead or close to it, the man wasn't going to join Slocum on the trail. Suzanne Crawford was another consideration. Slocum had taken quite a shine to her, but he doubted she would pull up stakes and come with a drifter, especially one she knew to be on the run from the law. As he rode, he thought more about the lovely woman.

Where did she fit into the puzzle that was Outlaws' Haven? She was the Grant's Pass conduit for getting men inside. She had certainly taken a high enough fee to give Slocum and Benson the information needed to find Haven. Slocum had a hard time putting her in cahoots with One Ear Jenkins, though.

Finding out what drove her wasn't possible as long as he stayed behind the stone wall across the canyon's mouth. Slocum turned his pony's face for the distant barricade. From all the hooting and hollering that was going on, he doubted if anyone was too intent on guarding the way into Haven.

He rode at a good clip for the wall, then dismounted when he came within a few hundred yards. Sentries on the mountainsides might see or hear him if he was too bold. He regretted not finding out what Harley Benson was up to, but if it came to satisfying his curiosity bump or saving his hide, Slocum knew which he'd choose. Crouching, he waited when he heard loud voices above him.

"You hear anything, Mack?" someone shouted. The words echoed back and forth across the canyon mouth. Slocum wondered if Jenkins had ever warned his pickets about giving away their positions.

"Thought it was a horse. You see anything?"

"Not down the canyon. One of them lawmen's still moaning and kicking out there. Think I ought to go cut his throat?"

Laughter greeted this.

"Come on, let's go do it. He might have a bundle riding in his pockets," urged the first man.

"Why's that?" asked Mack.

"Rewards. They musta been given a whale of a lot of money to make them so stupid. Who in their right mind would ever ride square into our guns like they done?"

Slocum held his ground, waiting for the men to argue it out about going forth and robbing the dead and wounded unable to crawl away. Jenkins must have given them specific orders not to open the huge wooden gate because neither guard stirred from his position.

That suited Slocum just fine. Having them open the gate gave him an easier way out of Haven, but it also complicated matters. He'd have to kill both of them before riding on into Grant's Pass. This way he had some idea where they hunkered down on the cliffs and could work to avoid them.

"You got a bottle?" asked Mack.

"Done finished it," came the reluctant answer. There was a long pause and then, "Why don't you go on in and get one from the saloon? It's not right we got to sit out here in the cold while everyone else is whooping it up."

"Jenkins would skin us alive."

"To hell with Jenkins. He don't own us. We pay him for the privilege of stayin' in Haven," replied the first. "Besides, I can watch just as good as the pair of us, leastwise for a spell."

"We split the bottle—and the price," demanded Mack.

"A deal."

Slocum worked his way closer to the cliff face and hoped his bay wouldn't get too edgy as Mack came down from the wall and started hiking for the saloon. Estimating distances and how fast the man walked told Slocum he had at least twenty minutes before he'd again face two sentries. And the chance was great that Mack would indulge in a drink or two on his own before returning.

Slocum waited until five minutes had passed. The remaining guard would be lulled into complacency, not expecting his partner back for a good fifteen minutes. And Mack would be far enough away so as not to hear anything from the wall.

Slocum made for the hidden crevice leading past the stone wall. He edged in past the brush he had stuffed back into the crack, his horse protesting entry into such a dark passage. He soothed the bay, patting its head and talking in a low voice.

"Won't be long. Only a few minutes, then we can ride free under the stars again," he said. He mumbled inanities but the horse settled down. Slocum started through the tight route, his shoulders scraping on the walls in places. Twice he had to untangle his stirrups from rocky spires. His horse noisily protested these brief falterings, then he burst free on the far side.

Slocum heaved a sigh, then looked up at the sky. It was only about an hour until dawn. He wanted to be far away from Haven before anyone noticed he was gone.

Hurrying, he followed the path Suzanne had taken earlier, keeping close to the side of the canyon.

"Please, oh, please," came a pitiful cry that froze Slocum in his tracks. "Help me. I . . . I can't walk. My legs. Under my horse. Crushed, oh!"

Slocum almost answered the plea. Leaving anyone to die like that was a violation of everything he believed in. If nothing else, the man deserved a quick death, a bullet through the head.

But if he went out into the floor of the canyon, he'd expose himself to the sentry still on the hillside. Slocum wasn't sure how long it had taken him to get through the tight passage, but the other guard might have returned. And there wasn't enough time for the pair to have drunk themselves into oblivion, if Mack had returned.

Slocum steeled himself and kept walking. Ignoring the pitiful cries was hard, but they faded the farther he got down the canyon. Then the walls made a quick twist to the north, Slocum patted his horse and mounted.

"Time to ride, old fella," he said.

The rifle bullet almost tore his head off. Slocum flung his arms up into the air as he fell to his left. Catching himself against the rock wall kept him in the saddle—barely. The bay reared and this did unseat him. He fell heavily to the stony ground, his head ringing.

Through the haze of pain, he got to his feet and chased down his horse. The bay stopped and pawed at the ground, giving Slocum enough time to grab the reins and pull the horse's head down, controlling it.

Slocum touched the side of his head. The bullet had dug a bloody, if shallow, channel from front to back. The damage looked and felt worse than it really was, Slocum realized. Head wounds always bled like a son of a bitch. He hung on to his horse for support until a bout of dizziness passed.

Then he heard horses moving toward him.

"I got him, I tell you," someone called out. "It was a clean shot. The owlhoot was trying to sneak out."

"Mr. Kellerman's not going to like it if you didn't hit something," came the warning.

"I wasn't shootin' any shadow. I *saw* somebody. He was in his saddle and lookin' to get away."

Slocum tried to clear his head but the ringing wouldn't leave. His vision was blurry but returning to normal quickly now. He took off his bandanna and pressed it hard against his temple. The blood was already beginning to clot. Working clumsily, Slocum tied it around his head, then settled his Stetson once more.

"I don't see nobody. You were shootin' at ghosts, Slim."

"Like hell!"

Slocum saw two riders come even with him in the canyon. They were looking back toward the wall protecting Haven and missed him. He put his hand on his horse's nose to keep the bay from whinnying. If they kept riding, he was going to make it out of the canyon just fine.

Just as he thought his chances looked good for escape, he saw three more riders coming up the canyon. He wasn't sure but he thought he saw two of the men sporting lawmen's badges.

"What are you two fools doing?" snapped the lead rider. "Get back to your posts."

"We thought we saw somebody tryin' to get away," the one named Slim shouted.

"Not so damned loud. Get your butts over here right now."

The two men joined the other three, pinning Slocum where he stood. He might have eluded two men but five was out of the question. They milled around, turning in every direction as they waited for their leader to chew out the other two.

"We saw somebody. Honest, Mr. Larrabee."

"Yeah, sure. Just like you thought you heard somebody bawling for help back up there." Larrabee pointed toward Haven.

"Could have been somebody down there," Slim complained. "We hightailed it so fast when we crashed against that blockade, somebody could have got left."

"Mr. Kellerman would never allow injured to be left behind."

Slocum almost laughed at that. This Kellerman had done just that when his attack had failed.

"Shouldn't have been a wall there. Nobody mentioned it. We was supposed to rush on in and hoorah them. Shootin' fish in a barrel, Kellerman said."

"Silence!" Larrabee fought to control his anger.

As the men argued over the abortive attack and its aftermath, Slocum edged back toward Haven. He wasn't sure but he thought the five men were drawing others from farther down the canyon. If so, that meant Kellerman had the outlaws sealed up tight. He might have been regrouping, waiting for more men or just figuring to starve them out of Haven. Whatever the Pinkerton agent's plan, it kept Slocum bottled up just as he needed to get away most.

Slocum got to the base of the wall and looked up. Two dark silhouettes walked back and forth along the wall. He saw a bottle being passed.

"Sure as hell took you long enough to get back, Mack," complained the guard who had done a double duty.

"It's a full bottle," Mack protested. "I coulda drunk some of it on the way back. I saved some for you."

"You—"

Slocum moved fast, pulling his bay behind him and once more going through the tight crevice bypassing the thick stone barrier and getting him back into Haven. He wished Suzanne had told him of some other entrance to the box canyon. If she had, Slocum knew he'd be taking it and riding wherever it led, even if it was away from Grant's Pass and Suzanne Crawford.

He heard sounds of heavy drinking and the pair on the wall getting drunker by the minute. He mounted and rode quickly, his head still swimming from the bullet crease. The cold night air cleared his head and he felt almost normal by the time he returned to his simple camp. It didn't surprise him that Benson still hadn't returned. Whatever the man was up to, it took a powerful lot of his time. Slocum considered asking outright what Benson was up to, but he knew his partner wouldn't tell him. If he'd wanted to share the information, he would have done it by now.

Slocum preferred silence to a lie.

Gunfire from the area around the tents and saloon caught Slocum's attention. He considered just pulling his gear off his horse, curling up in his blanket, and not bothering to find out what new devilment was brewing. Left to Jenkins and Nate Fogger, there would be a devil's caldron set to boil all the time.

He wasn't given the chance. He had just tossed his saddlebags to the ground when he heard drunken bellows and more gunshots. Slocum turned and saw a crowd making its way down Haven's only street—and it headed straight for him.

Before he could swing back into the saddle and hightail it, Jenkins's shotgun roared. Slocum felt the gust of air as the heavy buckshot ripped through above his head. He ducked and then checked his Stetson for telltale holes. All the double-aught shot had missed him, and he wasn't sure it was from any good shooting on Jenkins's part.

He had come too close to having his head shot off to want to risk it another time. He turned to face the crowd.

"Slocum, you goin' somewhere?" shouted Nate Fogger. The man's words were muddled with too much booze and he staggered slightly. "I'm callin' you out. You done slipped off before. Not now!"

Fogger looked to the others in the crowd for support. Slocum saw that it didn't matter to them who Fogger took on. They were eager to see more blood spilled. The dogs had been loosed and nothing would get them back into the kennel until they had their fill of suffering and death.

Slocum turned and widened his stance. He saw that he'd have no trouble cutting down Fogger, if he could hit a moving target. The man was too drunk to stand still. Fogger wobbled and weaved and looked as if he might fall over. But Slocum saw something more.

There wasn't a hint of alcoholic fog in One Ear Jenkins's eyes. The man's fingers rested on the double triggers of his shotgun. He was sizing Slocum up and had come to a decision.

Slocum was going to die. If he concentrated on Fogger, Jenkins would cut him down and probably be rid of his unreliable henchman at the same time. But if Slocum went for Jenkins, Fogger would be able to drag out his six-shooter and start spraying lead around.

As quick as he saw the problem, he came to a decision. He let his gunbelt drop to the ground.

Silence fell on the crowd as Slocum shouted, "Come on, Fogger. Just you and me. Bare knuckles—if you're man enough."

This caught the crowd's fancy. They'd rather see blood spurting from broken noses than seeping from holes in someone's belly. Slocum goaded Fogger on and pumped the crowd for their support. He kept one eye on Jenkins, wondering if this would matter to the man. Slocum was relieved to see that it did matter.

Jenkins ruled by guile and the fear men like Fogger instilled. Just looking at the old man wasn't going to put fear in many hearts among this tough bunch. If Jenkins tried to rob them of their sport, the crowd would likely turn on him.

And One Ear Jenkins knew it.

Slocum saw the broken-toothed, filthy man settle back, the shotgun resting in the crook of his arm.

Then Slocum had his hands full. Somebody had stripped off Fogger's six-shooter and pushed him forward. Fogger swung wildly, a blow powerful enough to take off Slocum's head if it had landed. Ducking under it, Slocum punched hard to Fogger's gut, landing three jabs before dancing back.

But even this brief flurry had taken its toll on Slocum's stamina. He hadn't thought the head wound would drain him, but it had. His arms were turning to lead, and his feet didn't move as quick as they should.

He took a hard punch to his chin and stumbled back. The crowd went wild. Each of the fighters had taken as good as he'd given. Now it was time to get down to serious fighting.

"Come on, you lily-livered son of a bitch," Fogger said, slurring his words. He motioned for Slocum to come get him.

Out of the corner of his eye, Slocum saw that the crowd had formed a ring around them. He wasn't going to be able to back up without someone shoving him back into the fray.

"You want to fight or talk?" Slocum asked, taking the time to study Fogger. Maybe the man wasn't as drunk as he looked. Or maybe this was some clever plan of Jenkins's to set him up for the fall.

Slocum pushed all subtlety from his mind as Fogger waded in, arms swinging like a windmill's. He took two punches on the side of his head that threatened to spill his brains. He saw red and then creeping black as Fogger continued to hit him.

Slocum got his arms up and blocked more of Fogger's punches. When he saw Fogger wind up for another haymaker, Slocum moved in. Again he drove hard to the man's belly, hammering unmercifully. Slocum knew the man had been drinking heavily. There wasn't any way in hell he could take such punishment to his middle.

And Slocum was right. The third punch stopped Fogger's windup for another blow. The fourth drove him to his knees. The crowd was going wild. A fifth blow, a right, to Fogger's face sent a shock all the way up to Slocum's shoulder.

"Go on, Slocum, finish 'im!" someone shouted. Others joined in, scenting blood.

Slocum could hardly lift his arms. He rocked back and swung but missed Fogger. He staggered into the man and knocked him to the ground. In a regular fight this would have been the end of the round. Then both fighters would have gotten up and hammered away again until one of them fell again.

Slocum couldn't go on. His head throbbed and his knuckles were bleeding from the punch he had impetuously landed on Fogger's face.

"Don't stop. What's wrong? Kill 'im!"

Slocum got his feet under him and judged the distance. Fogger was getting to hands and knees. Slocum reared back and kicked. The toe of his boot connected squarely with Fogger's chin. The man's head snapped back and Fogger fell backwards into the dirt.

Stumbling back, Slocum was caught by the men behind him. They began cheering and hoisted him to their shoulders.

"You gotta buy, Slocum! You're the winner and you got to buy us all a round!" called one man holding up Slocum. This met with unanimous and noisy approval, and Slocum felt himself being carried off toward the saloon. There was no way he could free himself from this tidal wave of humanity bearing him away.

As they carried him from his camp, he saw Harley Benson riding in, slowly looking around.

Across the man's saddle was slung a lantern.

12

Slocum tried to pace himself when it came to the whiskey drinking, but the men pushing at him from all sides made this impossible. Each drink he knocked back made him a little more giddy and turned his head into fiery, liquid pain. After a while, though, he started feeling numb and almost good.

"I whupped Fogger," he heard someone shout. This was met with great merriment. Then Slocum realized he was the one doing the bragging. His head was separated from his body, his vision was doubled, and his gut churned like the Snake River from too much booze. But worst of all was One Ear Jenkins.

Slocum saw the man sitting in the far corner of the saloon, the shotgun lying across the table in front of him. Slocum never saw the man take a drink. Jenkins was stone sober and ready for action when he could separate Slocum from the herd.

This set Slocum off on another round of drink buying. He was running out of money and knew when he pulled up broke, the party would be over. Slocum tried to moderate his drinking and to be ready for the confrontation with

Jenkins when it came, and found the best way was to spill the liquor. He made sure he turned abruptly and had his elbow jostled, but this worked only a few times. Too many tricks like this would get him embroiled in a fight he didn't want—and couldn't survive. His best tactic was simply appearing to drink heavily, and then spill most on his shirt.

Even so, he was getting drunker than a lord and this might spell his death.

"Tell us more, Slocum," a nameless voice in the crowd demanded. "Tell us how you come to be in Haven." This met with universal approval. The throng wanted to be entertained.

Slocum didn't see who spoke but knew he couldn't get involved in spinning wild tales. There wasn't a one of these men, each and every mother's son of them on the run from the law, who wouldn't turn him in for the reward on his head.

Fighting down his drunken desire to keep the outlaws diverted with the truth, Slocum started a meandering story and then ended it abruptly when he "noticed" the bottle in front of him was empty. He grabbed it and tossed it through the door. It clinked once against a rock in the street and broke with a loud crash.

"Who's gonna buy *me* a drink?" he yelled. "I deserve it!"

A dozen drinks plunked down in front of him. Slocum licked his lips and started in on the swamp of liquor. He swallowed three of the shots before a burly man to his left elbowed closer and took one of the drinks, as if daring him to protest. Slocum slapped him on the back and told him, "Drink up!"

This was greeted with another cheer and the unwanted drinks Slocum had in front of him vanished as if by magic.

He let the crowd bounce him around a little. On unsteady feet he edged away from the bar and let the men get down to real boozing. He had given them a reason. Now they were going to drink themselves blind.

Slocum kept a sharp eye on Jenkins. The man shifted his weight a little in his chair, moving the muzzle of his shotgun around. He wasn't above taking a couple men with Slocum, but if he did that he'd be a dead man. This was all that kept Slocum alive. Jenkins's grimy finger kept stroking the double triggers as if he wanted to kill but knew the response of the others in the room if he tried anything. Slocum tensed when he saw Jenkins stiffen in his chair.

Turning, Slocum saw what had caused Jenkins's reaction. Nate Fogger had stumbled into the saloon. Only a few men noticed, most too busy enjoying themselves. Two did see him and went over to his table, men Slocum had pegged as Fogger's henchmen. They sat at a table on the far side of the saloon, away from Jenkins. Slocum hoped this meant Fogger and Jenkins were on opposite sides now, but he wasn't going to bet the ranch on it. His life hung in the balance.

Almost as quick as he had recognized his danger, the slighter of Fogger's two cronies spoke loudly. "There he is, acting all regal like he was some sort of royalty. Thinks he's better than the likes of us, now don't he?"

Slocum saw Nate Fogger smile wickedly through a split lip. The man's face looked like a butchered side of beef. Slocum hadn't gunned him down before due to Jenkins. Now Slocum wondered how far and how hard he could push Fogger before Jenkins reacted. Fogger had failed and that reflected badly on his boss.

"Sure is white of him buyin' drinks," the man with Fogger kept on, trying to goad Slocum into action. "Or is he? Is he takin' *your* money for *his* booze?" The other man at Fogger's table guffawed loudly and added his own two cents' worth.

"Might be a good thing if he gets pickled. Heard tell that's about the only cure for a yellow streak up your back."

A hush fell when the second man started his taunting. Fogger tried to get ready to draw but was too unsteady. He fell back against the saloon wall and reached out to prop himself up, balancing precariously in his chair. Fogger said something to the first man, who laughed.

"Yeah, that's right, Nate. You can see the yellow better 'cuz he's just crawled out from under a rock. He—"

Slocum considered what he might do. Fogger wasn't the kind of man to leave alive at his back. But he had to deal with Jenkins, too. Maybe only with Jenkins. Slocum was all too aware of the man and his shotgun across the room.

"You got a quarrel with me, Fogger, then you say it. Don't use these two owlhoots as your mouthpiece." Slocum went and stood at the table, towering over them. He ignored the men with Fogger and focused the best he could only on Nate Fogger.

"He's makin' fun of you guys." Fogger struggled to get his chair righted. Slocum didn't give him the chance. He kicked out and caught the front leg with his toe. The kick took the chair out from under Fogger, sending him crashing into a pile on the floor.

Slocum spun on the two gunmen with Fogger. A back-hand blow sent the first one tumbling. The second started for his pistol, then froze when he saw the look of grim determination on Slocum's face. They were drunk enough to do anything anyone pushed them to, but they weren't stupid. Both backed off—for the moment.

But Slocum knew that if he didn't act fast, Fogger would incite others to come after him.

Keeping several of the crowd between him and Jenkins, Slocum kicked hard and caught Fogger just above the knee, sending him sprawling as he tried to stand. The man smashed into the wall.

"If you have a quarrel with me, spit it out," Slocum said. "Didn't I hit you hard enough before? Want to do it again?"

"Higgs, Boone, he's—" Fogger struggled to get to his feet but didn't get any further with his call for aid from his two companions. Slocum hauled off and hit Fogger with a haymaker, knocking him to the floor. Eyes brimming with hate, Fogger started for his pistol and saw this was what Slocum wanted. He would be dead before he could pull his six-shooter out of the holster pinned under him.

"Go on, try it," Slocum said in a menacing voice. He wanted Fogger to give a reason to kill him. To hell with the two with Fogger. To hell with One Ear Jenkins. To hell with everything in Haven. "Let's go outside and finish it."

A cry went up from those in the saloon. They smelled blood in the air again.

"No, I . . . Slocum, it's not that way. Jenkins!" cried Fogger. Seeing he wasn't going to get any help from his boss, he turned to the men who had been with him. "Higgs, for chrissakes, do something! Don't let him—"

Slocum stepped away and let others push between him and One Ear Jenkins. Higgs bumped into another stalwart drinker, who protested loudly. Slocum used the opportunity to judiciously shove Higgs back into the aggrieved man. Fists began flying and the entire saloon exploded in a wild donnybrook. This gave Slocum the chance he had been working for since he got into the saloon. Under the cover of the rapidly growing scuffle, Slocum ducked out and Jenkins wasn't able to do a damned thing about it.

Cold wind blew down the canyon and cooled him as he stepped out into Haven's dusty main street. Glass from the broken whiskey bottle grated under his boots, but the fresh air cleared some of the alcoholic fog in his brain and gave a chance to see that Nate Fogger wasn't going to come after him right now. The man acted like a whipped dog and wouldn't come back for more. Hair raised along Slocum's neck, though. A warning.

He had to get out of Haven and in a hurry. He had burned too many bridges tonight to hope to stay here much longer.

The roar from the saloon drowned out all other sounds, but Slocum's sharp eye caught sight of movement at the far end of town. Someone was riding out, and he knew who it had to be since most everybody had gathered inside the saloon for the celebration.

Slocum returned to his camp and saw all of Benson's belongings gone. Whatever Harley Benson was up to, he had decided to hightail it. And that suited Slocum just fine. He had reached the point of either going or staying—in a shallow grave.

Slocum mounted his horse and skirted the huddle of tents and buildings that was Haven. Men had spilled from the saloon into the street now. The fight still raged but a few stood to one side. The shadow cast by a long shotgun convinced Slocum he had spotted One Ear Jenkins. The man had four others beside him and engaged them in lively conversation. Slocum didn't much care what Jenkins was saying, but he could make a good guess.

He put his heels into the bay's sides and shot back toward the stone wall across the mouth of the canyon. Benson was several minutes ahead of him, and he wanted to catch up. He wasn't sure he trusted Benson a whole lot right now, not after seeing the lantern slung over the man's saddle, but he didn't want him riding into the posse's trap farther down the canyon on the far side of Haven's barricade. Benson was his partner and he felt he owed him something, even if Benson wasn't much on sharing with him.

Slocum caught sight of a rider ahead several times but couldn't seem to close the gap. He wanted to shout to Benson but held back. This close to the wall, he'd draw unwanted attention.

And what was Benson up to?

Gunfire caused Slocum to rein back and stare at the tall stone wall not a quarter mile distant. He saw the muzzle flash from a six-shooter and heard the furor it caused among the guards. Slocum thought Benson might have been discovered but changed his mind. There was too much confusion from the sentries atop the wall. Benson might be decoying the men from their posts with a few well-placed rounds meant only to get them stirred up.

Slocum picked up the pace and got closer to the canyon walls. He was beginning to feel at home riding along Suzanne's secret route. If he used it too many more times, his horse's hooves would cut a path in the vegetation and make the way obvious to anyone looking.

More gunfire caused Slocum to turn cautious. He couldn't tell where the shots came from. About all he knew for certain was that none was aimed at him.

"Get 'im!" came the warning from the wall.

"I did. He slithered away like some kinda lizard. Who the hell is it?"

Slocum figured both guards must be half past drunk by now. He had left them with a full bottle between them, and that had been close to two hours earlier.

"Must be one of them in the posse what got on the wrong side of the gate," answered the first guard. For all the hooting and hollering, Slocum knew they hadn't hit Benson.

A shadowy figure stood at the bar across the gate. Wood grated against wood and the locking bar slid free. The gate opened on squeaking hinges.

"Under us!"

"The son of a bitch is going through the gate? How'd he do that? Jenkins will skin us alive if we let anybody get through."

More gunfire punctuated this observation, but Slocum saw that Benson had snookered the drunk guards and had ridden through the gate. The two lookouts were firing on the wrong side of the wall. Their bullets ought to have been directed in the direction of the posse and not back toward Haven.

Slocum held back, wondering what he was going to do. Jenkins wasn't going to let him back into Haven, and he could end up with a bad case of lead poisoning if he tried following Harley Benson.

"What are you up to, you mangy cayuse?" Slocum wondered aloud. He hadn't gotten a good look at the man he'd been trailing, but it had to be his partner. Benson had taken everything he owned and left camp, and who else in Haven would be out riding instead of getting drunk?

"Close the damned gate," came an aggrieved voice. "Jenkins don't need to know anybody got past us."

"Do it quick," the other warned. "I think I see a passel of riders comin' from town."

Slocum swung in the saddle and tried to penetrate the darkness. He saw nothing, being twenty feet lower than the watchman on the wall. But he heard the thunder of horses' hooves. They were coming in a hurry for the wall—and Slocum knew it had to be One Ear Jenkins and his bunch of killers.

Slocum was trapped between the wall and the outlaws riding under Jenkins's command.

13

Slocum hesitated, not sure what to do. If he tried to sneak back into Haven, he knew what awaited him. If Nate Fogger and his cronies didn't backshoot him, Jenkins would do the deed. The man who ran Outlaws' Haven had taken a dislike to Slocum, for whatever reason. But Slocum didn't think he could get past the men riding down on him from the direction of the clapboard and tent town.

And beyond the wall lay the Pinkertons and their posse. Slocum hadn't been able to sneak past them before. He didn't see any reason he could if he tried a second time.

"Damn you, Benson," Slocum said. Thoughts of his partner finally decided him. Benson was riding blindly straight into the posse's guns. No matter what, they were partners. He couldn't let Benson do anything that dumb. Slocum heaved a sigh and smiled slightly. There was something more than just keeping Benson's neck out of a noose.

Slocum wanted to know what his partner had been up to in Haven. The man had been eager to get into the canyon and once here, he had spent too much time wandering around. The sight of the lantern dangling over Benson's saddle bothered Slocum, too. Something big was going on, and he didn't know what it was.

"Let's find out, old boy." Slocum patted his tired bay's neck and urged the horse forward. There wasn't time to make the hidden cutoff Suzanne had shown him. Slocum shuddered at the thought of getting caught in that tight passageway.

With Jenkins and his men so close and the guards on the wall especially alert, he might find himself in a stone coffin. Unable to go back, he could only follow Benson.

"Where'd he go?" Slocum shouted. "Did he get away?"

"Who's that?" One guard leaned over and tried to figure out who was calling up at him. "What are you talking about?"

Slocum had heard the discussion between the two drunken guards and knew what his words would stir up.

"The owlhoot that rode through the gate a few minutes ago, dammit!" Slocum flared. "We got to stop him!"

"Well, I don't know." There was just a hint of hesitation in the man's voice. Slocum looked over his shoulder and still couldn't see Jenkins and his men, but he heard their horses getting closer by the second. If he didn't get through the gate fast, he'd be trapped. Pinned against the stone wall, he might as well blindfold himself and wait for a firing squad to shoot.

"Open up, you fool," shouted Slocum. "I don't want Jenkins to know what went on, either. That owlhoot got away from me. I was guarding him and got to go fetch him before One Ear finds out!" The lie came from desperation. The horses were close enough for Slocum to see dust clouds rising. It was just a tad before dawn. If he didn't get away now and find some dark hidey-hole, he was going to end up dead before the sun poked over the mountains.

"Well, I reckon it's okay," the other drawled. "Just don't

go lettin' on we let him get away."

"It's on my head," Slocum assured the man.

The first guard grumbled and said, "Who *was* it what rode on out, anyway?"

"You don't want to know," Slocum said. He reached down and tugged open the gate. "Just don't go telling Jenkins."

"We won't. You get him on back here in a hurry." The guard grumbled some more but didn't shove his rifle barrel over the battlements to threaten Slocum's back.

Guiding his horse through the gate, Slocum called up, "Close the gate. Jenkins will never know!" He didn't wait to see if either of the guards obeyed. Slocum hoped Jenkins would be held up long enough to miss out on any chance of catching him.

The gate creaked closed, but Slocum didn't hear the locking bar slide into place. He bent over, fought a quick spell of dizziness, and urged his horse to as much speed as possible.

He put enough distance between him and the wall to make the first shot seeking his back fall short. Slocum kept riding, dodging from side to side, forcing the bay to an unnatural gait. When more bullets began digging up the dirt around him and he heard more than one piece of hot lead sing past his head, Slocum abandoned his evasive techniques. Putting distance between him and the outlaws was more important than trying to throw off their aim.

"Get him, damn your eyes!" he heard Jenkins shriek.

Slocum rode square down the middle of the canyon until he got to the sharp turn. He slowed and listened hard. This was the place where he had run into the posse earlier. His horse was breathing hard, and Slocum knew he couldn't push the animal much more or it would die under him. Dismounting, Slocum led his horse at right angles to the path he had been taking, going to the canyon wall.

He found a dark shadow and hunkered down, taking a rest himself and wondering where the Pinkertons were. Slocum was sure this was the spot they had set up their ambush.

"Benson," he whispered. "You simpleton. You ran smack dab into their hands." Slocum couldn't think of any other explanation for not being set upon already by the lawmen. But it wouldn't make the Pinkertons pull back from their position. They had the outlaws bottled up as much as the outlaws were safe behind their stone barricade.

Slocum stiffened and his hand went for his six-shooter when he heard echoes from up the canyon. Jenkins was coming after him. He cursed and tugged on his bay's reins. The horse eyed him skeptically, as if warning him not to ride for it.

"We've got to move on," Slocum said. "We're buzzard bait if we don't." Slocum saw his argument didn't convince the horse. He kept pulling but didn't get into the saddle, Slocum was still wary of the posse. It wouldn't do to run from Jenkins and find himself surrounded by Pinkertons.

Ten minutes of picking his way along the side of the canyon caused Slocum to wonder if he had ever seen the law and their ambush. The only others in the canyon he saw or heard were behind him. Slocum ducked down behind a creosote bush and put his hand to his bay's nose to keep it from nickering.

Jenkins and five others rode slowly down the center of the canyon, searching for him.

"We'll never catch him, boss," one man protested. "He's got too much of a head start."

"Yeah, he took off like a scalded pig. I never even caught sight of him."

"Shut up," Jenkins snapped. "Nobody leaves Haven without me sayin' so. Find him and kill him, whoever it is. I want to see his bullet-filled corpse before sunrise." Jenkins carried the shotgun in the crook of his left arm and looked as if he meant every word.

Slocum knew the daylight was going to betray him. He was in shadow now, but the first light of false dawn touched the eastern sky. Being deep in the narrow canyon would only postpone full light. There wasn't any hope he could hide much longer.

The rifle shot startled Slocum. He whipped out his Colt Navy and had it cocked before he realized the sniper wasn't shooting at him. The man riding to the far left of Jenkins jerked around, clutching at his thigh.

"I been hit, boss!" the man shrieked. "He done shot me!"

From the direction of the shot, Slocum knew this was no accident. He had seen men get buck fever more than once and end up shooting their comrades or themselves. But the man was on the flank and had been hit on the side opposite his side arm.

Another shot echoed down the canyon. Slocum wondered if Benson had laid this trap. Even as the thought crossed his mind, he knew it wasn't true. The report from two more shots sounded, almost as one. Slocum had been wondering where the Pinkertons were. He now knew. They had pulled back a little from where he'd seen them before, but they hadn't left.

"Take cover," urged one of the men riding with Jenkins. "We're being bushwhacked!"

"Get back to Haven," Jenkins snapped. "We can't fight a whole danged army."

"There's only one, boss," another said. "We can—"

The shot was either from a sharpshooter or had been fired by someone luckier than he had any right to be. The bullet caught Jenkins's henchman square between the eyes. Slocum saw the back of the man's head explode in a bloody fountain. For a moment the dead man sat in the saddle as if nothing had happened, then he slipped to one side and fell to the canyon floor.

"Get on back!" shouted Jenkins, taking his own advice. He thrashed around and got his swaybacked horse into a trot. Bullets sang around him but the man didn't appear to take much notice. The survivors with him broke into gallops and far outdistanced him.

Slocum watched the retreat and wished the sniper would get in just one more good shot. It didn't happen. Jenkins was quickly out of range and no doubt safe behind his stone wall.

Waiting a few minutes, Slocum knew what had to happen. And it did. The Pinkertons came out of hiding to see what they had bagged. Three men poked at the downed outlaw with the muzzles of their rifles. Two others caught the fallen man's horse and went through the saddlebags, no doubt hoping to find something worth stealing.

When two more joined them, Slocum made his move. Walking quickly, he pulled his unwilling, tired horse behind him. Slocum hoped the bay wouldn't kick up too much fuss. Anything bringing the posse down on his ears now would be deadly.

If there were more Pinkertons staked out around the canyon, Slocum didn't see them—and they didn't see him. A mile down the dogleg in the canyon without incident convinced Slocum it was time to ride again. The posse might have the outlaws bottled up, but they wouldn't put two ambuscades into place. There wasn't that many of them left after their harebrained frontal assault against Jenkins's impenetrable stone ramparts.

Less than fifteen minutes of riding brought Slocum to

a small dirt path. He reined back and stared down at it. The sun had come up and shone on the trail, letting him see details he might have missed otherwise. Dismounting, Slocum examined the spoor he'd seen.

"Benson?" he wondered. A horseman had passed this way within the last hour or two. How he had gotten past the Pinkertons was a mystery since this path led back through the middle of the canyon. They could never have missed a lone rider. "You're one lucky son of a bitch."

Slocum mounted and followed the path away from the main track he would have taken to get to Grant's Pass. He discovered this way meandered but finally came to Grant's Pass from a different direction. Benson had chosen well, entering the small town so that he wouldn't create much of a stir.

But where was Benson now? Slocum toot off his hat and wiped sweat off his forehead. The day was getting hot quickly, and he was badly in need of food and something to drink—even a sip of water would be like nectar.

And he didn't doubt that Benson had felt the same way.

Slocum headed into town and found a hostler to take care of his horse. He dismounted in front of the stable and poked his head inside.

"Help you, mister?" a young boy asked.

"Need some water and grain for my horse," Slocum said. He looked around the stalls.

"I keep the place real clean. You don't need to worry on that account," the boy said.

"Good," Slocum said, not telling the boy he had been looking for Benson's horse. "Here's two bits. You might see to currying the horse, too."

The boy grinned and took the reins. Slocum felt confident that his horse would get the care it deserved for such dependable service. He heaved a sigh when he realized the bay might need to be in top form to get him away from Grant's Pass. Things had fallen apart around him faster than he would have thought possible.

Wandering around the town, Slocum kept a sharp eye out for Benson. He didn't find the man in a half hour of hunting. Slocum wiped more sweat off his forehead and tried to keep his belly from grumbling. He had drunk too much the night before and couldn't remember the last food set in front of him.

But Benson was somewhere in town and Slocum wanted to find him. And Suzanne Crawford was close. Slocum found himself wanting to see her again, whether she was in her room at the boardinghouse or at the small house at the outskirts of town.

Slocum ducked into a bakery when he saw three men turn down the main street, riding slowly. The tall, thin, hatchet-faced man in the middle was the Pinkertons' leader. Slocum had heard his men call him Kellerman.

"Help you, mister?" the clerk asked.

The sweet smell of bread made Slocum's mouth water. He pointed out a freshly baked loaf, paying more attention to the lawmen in the street outside. Kellerman and his two deputies paused outside the bakery. Slocum wondered if he could enjoy as much as a mouthful of the bread before he had to shoot his way out. But the Pinkertons moved on slowly. Slocum broke off a chunk of bread and munched contentedly on it.

"Good, thanks," Slocum said. He went to the bakery door and watched as Kellerman and the other two turned down a side street.

Slocum knew whatever time he had once had to find Benson was gone. Jenkins's foray into the trap set up in the canyon had stirred up the Pinkertons. It was time to move on and to hell with anything else but saving his own hide.

Still, Slocum found himself moving toward Dr. Grandville's office. No one sat in the waiting room, and the doctor was nowhere to be seen. Slocum went around into the alley and waited a few minutes, devouring the bread until he was spitting cotton. He went to a watering trough and drank of the murky water, then returned to the surgery's back door.

It looked safe enough. Slocum went inside.

His eyes narrowed when he didn't see Clay Zarra on the hard bed. Slocum drew his Colt and glanced back into the alley, fearing a trap. The only people he saw were townspeople at the mouth of the alley, and all were peacefully going about their business. He turned his attention to the doorway leading into Grandville's main surgery.

Slocum whipped through the door, six-shooter leveled at the man sitting at a desk.

Grandville looked up, his eyes bloodshot. The doctor blinked and held up an empty whiskey bottle. "Wanna pull? Good stuff here. Best in the whole damn town." Grandville almost fell out of his chair.

Slocum checked the outer room. It was as empty as when he had peered in the window.

"Where's Zarra?" he demanded.

"My patient?" slurred the doctor. He tried to drink from the empty bottle and looked confused when he got nothing from it. "Smooth. About the smoothest."

"Zarra," repeated Slocum, going to the doctor. He grabbed the front of Grandville's jacket and shook him hard. Slocum thought about sticking his Colt in the man's face and hesitated. It wouldn't do any more good than shaking some sense into Grandville.

"Gone," said the doctor, hiccuping. "They took him."

"Who did?" Slocum asked, cold hands clutching at his heart. He knew who "they" were. He had seen Kellerman and knew the Pinkerton wouldn't hang around town without a good reason.

Grandville shrugged. When Slocum released his grip, the doctor crashed facedown onto his desk. Slocum stepped back, cursing to himself. He shouldn't get involved, but he couldn't ride out of town and let the posse keep Zarra to themselves.

He slipped out the back way and hurried down the alley. If Kellerman had nabbed Zarra, there was only one place the Pinkerton agent would put a prisoner. Slocum crossed the street and walked along, as if looking at merchandise. He positioned himself in the right way to see the reflection of the town jail in a plate-glass window.

Slocum saw Kellerman and his two flunkies stop there and dismount. Not wanting to appear too curious, yet needing to know what was going on, Slocum worked along the sidewalk slowly, drawing more stares than he wanted when he took too long in front of a women's dress display.

"Help you, mister?" asked a man at the business next door. "You have the look of someone screwing up his courage. It's understandable. Nobody likes to talk about their need."

Slocum recoiled when he saw the dour, black-clad man in the next storefront's doorway. He knew an undertaker when he saw one, and he counted this as an ill omen.

"Might be in need soon," he said. Slocum turned and faced the jail across the street. Kellerman and his men came out and continued their mounted patrol of the streets of Grant's Pass.

"We have many fine coffins, or if that's not your concern, we also make fine furniture. A man of your culture would surely see the quality in each and every piece."

"Furniture?" Slocum blinked. He had found an undertaker and cabinet maker. He shook his head and pointed at the jail. "I was wondering what the ruckus was over there. Never seen so many men coming and going."

The undertaker smiled and reminded Slocum of a vulture waiting for a meal. "A sorry tale, that. Sheriff Peña has found a miscreant and has imprisoned him."

"Miscreant?"

"A lawbreaker the sheriff caught, being treated at Dr. Grandville's office," the undertaker said. "He's about the most interesting thing that's happened in Grant's Pass in the past week, even counting the other prisoner." The mortician cocked his head to one side and asked, "What is your interest?"

"Nothing," Slocum said, knowing it was Zarra in the town jail and maybe Harley Benson as well. The uncertainty of the jail's occupants made him edgy. Zarra was dying and would never stand trial, much less have a noose dropped around his neck. But he had been a friend. And was Benson sitting alongside Zarra?

"May I—" the undertaker started, taking out a tape measure to gauge Slocum's height and girth.

Slocum didn't let the mortician finish. Walking away, he cut across the street and went down the alley beside the jail. Slocum was alert for a guard posted behind the hoosegow, maybe on the roof or in a nearby building, but he saw nothing. Sheriff Peña obviously trusted the sturdy walls and iron cage inside to hold his prisoners.

Slocum chanced a quick look into the small barred window and saw a pale Clay Zarra lying on the bunk. But there was no sign of Harley Benson.

Slocum wasn't sure if this was good or bad.

14

Slocum ducked down when he saw movement inside the jail. He pressed hard against the jail wall and listened to what went on inside.

"You wantin' any breakfast?" the deputy asked Zarra. There wasn't any answer. "You ain't upped and died on us, have you?"

The jail cell door rattled. Slocum pictured what was going on in his head. The guard put down a breakfast tray and pulled out a ring of keys. The clank in the lock, the unoiled cell door opening. The guard going over to Zarra didn't fit, though.

Slocum heard a squeaky noise that was all wrong. He heard a strangled cry from in the cell and had to look. He popped back up and peered in, seeing Zarra rise from the bunk and grab the guard by the throat.

Zarra might be near death but he wasn't buried. His fingers tried to snuff the life from the deputy—or at least keep him from crying out. Slocum started to lend his aid when he saw Zarra was bound to fail in his escape attempt.

The guard let out a strangled cry that brought two more deputies to his rescue.

"Goldarn it, Seth, you got to be more careful," the deputy coming to the rescue said, prying Zarra's fingers loose from the other lawman's throat. "Mr. Kellerman warned you he was a tough hombre."

"Son of a bitch. I'm gonna kick the shit out of him!"

Slocum ducked back and listened again. There was a scuffle inside, and the moan from Zarra told him he was being worked over.

"What's going on? Stop it, stop it right now!" came the harsh command. Slocum chanced another look. Sheriff Peña had entered. "You two, don't do that. We need him alive."

"But, Sheriff, he—"

"Kellerman is going to skin you alive if he dies and can't be used as bait for the others," Peña said.

"Who do you take orders from, Sheriff, the town council or this Pinkerton agent?" shot back the deputy.

"Watch your mouth, Seth, or I'll cut out your damned tongue. You boys leave the prisoner alone."

Slocum heard boots shuffling across the cell floor and then there was a loud clanging as the cell door was relocked. He sank down and thought hard. Zarra was still fighting. Dr. Grandville must have patched him up better than Slocum would have ever thought possible, but where did Slocum's responsibility end?

He walked out of the alley, looking up and down the street. The posse had ridden in, showing deputy badges and Pinkerton credentials, and had taken over Grant's Pass. He caught sight of another trio patrolling the street. Kellerman wasn't with these men. That meant several Pinkertons made the circuit.

"Where's Benson?" Slocum wondered aloud. The undertaker had mentioned two men in jail. Slocum hadn't seen Benson, but it was likely he was locked up in another cell.

He couldn't have avoided riding squarely into Kellerman's trap back in the canyon. Even Jenkins with four armed men at his back couldn't get through, had he wanted to try. The firepower—the perseverance—of the Pinkertons was as commendable as it was treacherous.

Slocum turned from the trio riding sentry in the street and came to his conclusion. He couldn't leave Zarra in that cell. The man's injuries were healing enough to make him feisty, but he wouldn't last another day if the deputies came back to work him over.

"How? How am I going to get Zarra out?" And Slocum couldn't forget Benson. He might be rotting away in the jail, too. Before he could figure that out, he needed information.

Asking the undertaker or any other citizen was risky. The only two in town Slocum even halfway trusted were Dr. Grandville and Suzanne Crawford. Grandville was too far in his cups to be a reliable source of information any longer. More to the point, Slocum wasn't sure he trusted the doctor.

He wasn't even sure he trusted Suzanne, but she had given him valuable help before when he had needed it most. It wasn't fair trying to corral her to help him spring Zarra from the town jail, but Slocum didn't have too many other routes open.

Rather than tire his horse, he left it in the stable and walked to the boardinghouse where Suzanne's room was still empty. Deciding to keep looking, Slocum hiked to the edge of Grant's Pass. Suzanne's house was some distance down the road. He used the walk to clear his head and put together a plan for getting Zarra free.

Slocum slowed as he approached Suzanne's neat, whitewashed house. Four horses were tethered out front. Hunkering down, Slocum decided to wait and see who was visiting Suzanne. An hour later still gave no clue. Slocum felt the pressure of time weighing down on him. Sheriff Peña might want to keep his prisoners in good health, but his deputies weren't inclined that way.

Clay Zarra had to be freed soon. Slocum decided it wasn't fair to Suzanne to involve her. He smiled crookedly as he thought of how much she had taken of his money for instructions on getting into Outlaws' Haven. She might want more, and he just didn't have it.

Worrying about the riders belonging to those four horses but not daring to investigate further, Slocum turned back to town. He didn't think Suzanne was in trouble from anything he had done. She looked to be a real wheeler-dealer, so she might have brought down the law from trying to get others into Haven. He felt a pang of guilt in leaving her to Kellerman and the Pinkerton agents, but not much. Suzanne could look after herself, and he might be getting antsy over nothing.

He had no proof those horses belonged to Kellerman's men or the law. She had a life he knew nothing about.

The wicked flee when no man pursues, Slocum thought. He walked back to town, torn between finding out about Suzanne's mysterious visitors and getting Zarra free. Why did she keep two residences?

As he approached the town, he stopped and squinted into the bright sun. Slocum started to call out but held back, not being sure he could trust his eyes.

Harley Benson stood half in shadow talking to someone completely hidden from sight. Slocum saw the flare of a lucifer and blue smoke rising. Whomever Benson spoke to had lighted a cheroot. Being too far away Slocum couldn't make out the words, but Benson was madder than a wet hen. He waved his arms and balled his fists.

Slocum kept walking, working closer to see who his

partner was so angry with.

"... nothing to do with this," Benson declared. "You did it all wrong."

The answer was muffled, but another puff of blue smoke rose from the deep shadow.

Slocum got closer and then waved, trying to attract Benson's attention. The man who stood with his back to Slocum puffed quietly on his cheroot. And Benson didn't see Slocum. Slocum neared the pair, just as the man smoking the cigar seemed to fade away. Slocum tried to figure out what had happened, then saw the door in the side of the building. Whomever Benson had been speaking to so angrily had simply gone inside.

"Benson!" he called, but his partner had spun and stalked off, fists still balled. Slocum broke into a run to catch up with him. If Benson wasn't in the town jail, he would be able to help spring Zarra. But by the time Slocum got to the corner of the building, Benson had mounted his horse and was galloping off.

He stopped and considered his chances of overtaking Benson. They didn't look good. By the time he reached the stable, saddled, and got on the trail, Benson could be long gone. Slocum wasn't up to doing serious tracking when Zarra was dying by inches in jail.

Slocum knelt where Benson and the other man had spoken and lifted the stubbed-out cheroot. He sniffed in appreciation. It was good quality, not something he would have expected in a jerkwater town like Grant's Pass.

Turning to the door, Slocum tried to open it and look into the building. It had been locked on the inside. More curious than ever, Slocum circled and stopped in front. Inside a telegrapher worked on his key, chewing his tongue and pressing the black button to send a message with almost grim determination.

Slocum went inside and the telegrapher looked up. "Be right with you," he said, returning to his message. In less than a minute, he heaved a sigh of relief and settled back in his chair. "What can I do for you?"

Slocum started to inquire after the man who had entered but decided to be more cautious. Too many ill-considered questions might cause the clerk to tell Sheriff Peña about a nosy stranger.

"I was looking for somebody else. I was told he worked here, but you're not him."

"I'm the only telegrapher in Grant's Pass," the man said proudly.

"Hmmm," Slocum said, mind racing. "You got a smoke? I'm fresh out." He patted his pockets as if searching for his bag of fixings.

"Don't smoke, leastwise not on duty." The man pointed to the stacks of yellow flimsies scattered in front of him. "One spark and somebody might lose his message. Can't have that."

"Reckon you go out back to smoke," Slocum pressed.

"Reckon I could, if I thought much on it," the telegrapher answered, frowning. "Is there something I can do for you?"

"Just wondering if anything had come in for me," Slocum said on impulse. "The name's Benson. Harley Benson."

The clerk pushed back his green eyeshades and shook his head. "We been gettin' a lot of traffic—that's what we call telegrams—but nothing for any Harley Benson."

"Why so much traffic?" asked Slocum.

"It's those Pinkerton fellows. An entire posse of them breezed into town, but you know that, don't you?"

"Now why would I know anything of the sort?" Slocum replied carefully.

"You're one of them, ain't you?"

"Excuse me, I see my friend now. Much obliged for your time," Slocum said, sauntering from the telegraph office, trying to keep from going too fast. He wasn't sure if he had stirred up a hornets' nest or not. Most of the business coming along the wires must originate in Pinkerton offices back East. Would his questions make the clerk hunt out Kellerman or the sheriff?

Slocum decided he had to get Zarra out of the jail fast. His time was running out.

Slocum couldn't remember having ever been jumpier. Every sound in town made him start for his six-shooter. He had crawled into the stall next to his bay and tried to sleep, but it wouldn't come. Even the young boy's comings and goings kept him on edge.

Slocum lay back, hands folded under his head as he stared up at the hayloft. He went over everything in his mind, practicing mentally what he would do and how he would get Zarra from his cell. He had no idea how many deputies he faced. Sheriff Peña had two, from the look of it. But Kellerman had brought a veritable army with him.

Even after getting blown to bloody ribbons in his assault on Haven, the Pinkerton agent had enough deputies to patrol Grant's Pass regularly. Slocum wondered if Kellerman had pulled his men from the canyon leading to Haven. Somehow, he doubted it. The man might have telegraphed his main office in Chicago authorizing more men, all duly deputized and able to run in any lawbreaker they found.

Or just kill them on the spot and save the trouble of going to trial.

"Zarra, you damned thorn in my side," Slocum muttered. He ought to have left Grant's Pass that morning but obligation held him like a sticky glue. If Zarra had died on schedule, Slocum wouldn't have the problem he now faced.

And Slocum kept thinking about two other thorns worrying in his brain and festering something fierce. Suzanne's visitors. Four riders. Who were they? More vexing was the man Benson had argued with. What was Harley Benson up to?

Slocum had no good answers. All he could do was get Zarra free and try to escape.

He sat up and peered around the edge of the stall. The sun was going down and it was starting to turn cool again, or as cool as it was ever likely to get in Grant's Pass. With any luck, he'd heat it up a mite before moving on.

Slocum saddled his bay and led it out into the street. He walked to the edge of town and tethered the horse, then went looking for a mount suitable for Clay Zarra. He smiled when he saw the horses outside the jail. This couldn't have been better if he had asked the sheriff for them. Slocum craned his neck around and saw a slow line going toward the saloon, looking more like ants than men. He couldn't help but think of the saloon inside Haven and how crowded it always was.

Still, this suited his purposes even better. Slocum walked behind the line of buildings facing Grant's Pass's main street and found a pile of debris stacked against the wall of a millinery. It took him a few tries to get a lucifer ignited. Slocum held it up and watched it flicker in the twilight, then tossed it into the rubbish.

The sudden *whoosh!* almost singed his eyebrows. He backed away, startled at how voracious the fire was and how quickly it jumped to the wooden wall of the store.

Slocum hurried to the main street and positioned himself near the jail's front door. He wanted to sound the alarm before the fire spread. He had been in terrible fires that gutted entire towns in the wink of an eye and knew the horror. But he kept his peace, waiting for the inevitable.

"Fire!" came the cry less than a minute later. "Bessie Livingston's store's on fire!" The words had hardly died down when a fire bell sounded, shattering the calm.

Sheriff Peña and his two deputies erupted from the jail. The sheriff still had a fork in his hand and some food caught in his mustache. The lawmen took off at a dead run for the fire to lend a hand.

Slocum held back for a moment, then drew his six-shooter and rushed into the tiny office. Another deputy sat at a desk, poring over a newspaper.

"Fire, the sheriff needs help," Slocum gasped out, as if he had been running.

"Can't. He just tole me to—" That was all the deputy got out. Slocum swung his pistol and caught the man alongside the head. He dropped like he had been poleaxed, falling over the newspaper spread in front of him.

Slocum grabbed the ring of keys and opened the door leading into the cell block. He fumbled as he hunted for the right key that would open the door to Zarra's cell.

"Clay, get your ass moving. I'm breaking you out of here," Slocum shouted.

Clay Zarra stirred and moaned softly, forcing himself to a sitting position in the cell. He turned a white face and dark eyes in Slocum's direction. A smile split his face, giving him the look of a death's head.

"Glad you came, John. Knew you wouldn't let those Pinkerton bastards keep me."

"Have you seen Benson?" Slocum asked, taking a shot in the dark.

"Nope." Zarra got to shaky feet and had to hang on to the iron bars to keep himself erect. He was in worse shape than Slocum had thought.

"Did the deputies beat you up after you tried to escape?" Slocum asked. Slocum looked around but Zarra was the only prisoner in the cell block.

Zarra's startled expression told the story. "How'd you know I tried to get out of here? And how'd you know they thrashed the bloody hell out of me?"

"Just a guess," Slocum said, putting his arm around Zarra's shoulders and helping him to the outer office. The three horses were just outside. Slocum planned to steal all three and then pick up his bay on the way out of town. That would give them each a horse to ride and another to rest. When the first horses tired, they could switch over and keep riding. With any luck, they could outdistance any posse Kellerman might put on their trail.

Slocum saw their luck was running thin when he stepped into the street. The fire he had started hadn't burned long enough to keep many men occupied. Sheriff Peña and his two deputies were already on their way back to the jail.

"A gun, Slocum, give me a gun!" demanded Zarra. "If we have to shoot it out, I want to do what I can. I won't rot in that jail another night."

Slocum pulled the rifle from the saddle scabbard of the sheriff's horse and tossed it to Zarra. The man almost fell over when he grabbed it. Zarra had been pale before. Now he looked as if all the blood had drained from him. Slocum didn't think the man could fire the rifle, much less ride with the skill and speed needed to get away from Grant's Pass and its lawmen.

"Jailbreak!" went up the cry. Peña went for his six-shooter a split second before his deputies.

Zarra fired his rifle and Slocum got off a round from his Colt, but the fight was only beginning. If they didn't get out of town fast, they'd be buried here.

15

Slocum felt exposed in the middle of the street. Bullets whirred past his head and he returned fire, driving both Sheriff Peña and one deputy to cover. The other deputy was either foolish or very brave. He stood his ground and took careful aim.

"Ride!" Slocum called to Zarra. They'd lose any gunfight if it went on even a minute longer. Already the shots were bringing unwanted attention from those who had worked to put out the fire. Facing an armed town meant certain death, even if the Pinkertons weren't alerted.

"Hard getting up," grunted Zarra. He fired his rifle and struggled to get into the saddle. Slocum leapt onto the skittish horse he had chosen, leaned and grabbed the reins of the third horse.

"He's stealin' your horse, Sheriff!" the deputy in the middle of the street cried, as if this were worse than burning down the town or breaking a prisoner out of jail.

"Slocum!" shouted Zarra. The injured man lunged forward, almost falling from horseback. Slocum caught the man and propped him up. Getting away was going to be harder than he'd thought. When Zarra had tried to escape earlier by strangling his guard, Slocum had mistakenly thought Zarra was in better shape than he was.

"Let's get out of here," Slocum said, heaving Zarra back into the saddle. Something was wrong but he didn't have time to stop and think on it.

Shooting over his shoulder, wildly throwing lead at anything that moved, Slocum emptied his Colt Navy. The deputy in the street didn't budge. He kept firing with a mechanical pace that, luckily, wasn't any better than bad. Slocum bent low and put his heels into the skittish horse's sides and raced the wind out of town. He slowed when he got to the edge of Grant's Pass and saw his horse standing patiently, waiting for its owner.

"They'll be coming after us pronto," Slocum called to Zarra. "We can outrun them, though. We change horses when—" He reined back a little and came up behind his partner. A giant red blossom had appeared in the middle of Zarra's back. He had taken a slug in the brief fight in front of the jail.

"Clay, can you keep on?"

"We got to, Slocum. We got to keep riding. Can't go back. Die. Will die." Zarra almost fell from the saddle. Slocum grabbed and pulled the man upright again. He saw the pain etched on Zarra's face. The man had taken a bullet for Slocum.

"We can hole up somewhere and—"

"No!" Zarra's spirit forced the answer. "They'll catch us for sure if we do that. Ride."

Slocum knew Zarra wasn't going to make it, but they had to try. He had beaten the odds by getting Zarra out of the jail when Kellerman had used him as bait for just such an attempt.

The thought of the Pinkerton agent made Slocum sit straighter and look around. The sun was long set behind the mountains and had turned the valleys around Grant's Pass into inky gloom. The posse might be lurking out there, waiting to swoop down and trap them.

"We can make it, Slocum. We got to." Zarra sounded confident but he wobbled in the saddle and had to clutch the saddle horn to keep from falling off. "Where's Benson?"

"I wanted to ask you that," Slocum said, trying to keep a sharp lookout as he rode. He had the feeling of walking into the steely jaws of a trap. "Was he ever held in the jail?"

"Haven't seen him since the robbery," Zarra said. "Thought he might have gotten ventilated. They brought in some other fellow, a gambler from the look of him. Don't know what they did with him."

Slocum said nothing about them making it into Haven—or Benson returning to Grant's Pass. What was Benson up to? The more Slocum found out, the less he understood.

"Off the road. Now!" Slocum barked. He had an uneasy feeling about the way the road wended around a tall rock before heading on up into the mountains.

"What do you see?" Zarra turned his pony's face for the ditch running alongside the road, then he fell off. He landed with a heavy crash and moaned. Slocum dismounted and knelt beside him.

"Are you all right?" He touched the man's back and was rewarded with a cry of pain. The bullet Zarra had taken rather than letting it find a berth in Slocum's chest was killing him faster than his other wounds.

"Didn't mean to bawl like that," Zarra said. "Why not go scout the road? I'll be fine. For a while."

Both men knew it was a lie. Sheriff Peña would have had enough time to raise a posse of his own by now and would be hot on their trail. And although Slocum hadn't seen anything in the road ahead, experience told him it was a good place for an ambush. A handful of men could take on an army and win because of good crossfire positions.

Slocum didn't want to leave Zarra, but he had to know if the road was clear. Skirting a trap would add hours to their flight, but if he rode ahead without checking they might not be alive long to make any escape.

"Lie low. I'll be back in a few minutes." Slocum considered riding the horse he had stolen, then decided his bay was a better choice. He mounted and the animal snorted in disgust at the weight on its back again. Slocum tried to see back down the road and failed. There had to be pursuit, but Sheriff Peña hadn't gotten this far yet.

Slocum angled across the road and came up behind the large boulder, straining to hear anything that might give away ambushers. The soft sighing of the wind covered any low noises. Slocum dismounted and walked on cat's feet around the boulder, coming up from the far side. Anyone could be between him and the road.

He blinked when he saw the size of the trap waiting for any unsuspecting rider. Three men on either side of the road sat with their rifles trained on the notch in the rocks. Six rifles firing meant a whale of a load of lead in the air, should any gunplay start. If they had kept riding, he and Zarra would have been cut to bloody ribbons without knowing what had happened.

Slocum sized up the six men and decided they belonged with Kellerman and his posse. He didn't see any badges shining in the dark, but they had to be deputies. There wasn't any profitable traffic along this path for a band of outlaws to rob.

He started to slip back when he took a bold and possibly foolish risk. Slocum whispered loudly, getting the attention of the man closest to him.

"Psst, hey, any sign of them yet?" Slocum asked.

The man never looked at Slocum. He shook his head,

rubbed a sweaty palm on his jeans, and finally said, "No talkin'. You know what Mr. Kellerman said about too much jawin'."

"Sorry," Slocum said in an even lower voice. He backed off before the man got suspicious as to who spoke. He wanted to run, to keep riding until his horse dropped and then keep on until Grant's Pass and all of Wyoming was far behind him.

Slocum had just climbed back into the saddle when he heard a commotion from the other side of the boulder.

"Who was it, then?" came the loud question. "Somebody was talkin' to me. Who the hell was it, if you galoots weren't shootin' off your mouths?"

Slocum turned his bay and galloped back to where Zarra sat on the ground, his rifle resting on his raised knees. The man's eyes burned with fever and his hands shook uncontrollably.

"I heard shouts. Is it a trap ahead?" Zarra asked.

"Yeah, six of them. All from the Pinkertons' posse," Slocum said. "When the Pinkerton Agency gets a bug in its ear, it never quits."

"They'll spend thousands to recover a hundred-dollar theft," Zarra said, laughing. "Don't make good sense. Why send so many men out for the likes of us?"

Slocum wasn't going to discuss the merits of prevention. If the Pinkertons caught them, it would discourage anyone else from trying to rob a Union Pacific train for months and months. He spun when he heard the pounding of hooves down the road.

"That'll be the sheriff," Zarra said.

"Get in the saddle. We've got to—" Slocum stopped when he saw Zarra sadly shaking his head.

"John, I can't go on. My legs don't move right, and I'm gettin' cold all over. And that bullet in my back. It burns like hellfire. You know what that means."

"It means we have to get to a doctor who can patch you up."

"It means I'm a goner. Thanks for what you tried to do." Zarra turned his pasty face in Slocum's direction and gave a feeble smile. Then he made a brushing motion, as if shooing away flies.

Slocum looked back down the road toward Sheriff Peña's men and then in the other direction toward the Pinkerton agent's ambuscade. They might play one off against the other, get them fighting and escape unnoticed. Slocum saw that the same notion had already occurred to Zarra.

"I'll help them along in thinkin' they got us," Zarra said. "Now get the hell out of here."

Slocum rummaged through the saddlebags of the stolen horses and got all the rifle ammo he could find. He dropped it and two spare rifles on the ground where Zarra could reach them. Then he mounted his bay and rode like the demons of hell were on his heels.

A minute later he heard a rifle begin firing, slowly, almost painfully as if the sniper had trouble with the lever and trigger. The return fire was more energetic and was accompanied with loud whoops of glee, of a fugitive run to ground.

Before Slocum began circling in the dark, trying to find a canyon wall to follow out of the locality, he heard a second volley of gunfire, a deeper thunder indicating that Kellerman's men had opened fire, too. Slocum hoped the Pinkertons and the deputies from Grant's Pass were blasting holes in each other, but he doubted it would happen that way long, if it had even started.

Clay Zarra had sacrificed himself so that Slocum could get away. It was only right that Slocum not waste the man's act. But Slocum didn't have any good idea where he was going. This part of the mountains was new to him, and he had the gut feeling he was getting lost, maybe turning around and riding back into the trap.

"Out for an evening's ride?" came a soft voice.

Slocum swung in the saddle, his hand going for his six-shooter. He stopped when he saw Suzanne Crawford sitting astride a horse not ten feet from him. He had ridden even with her and never noticed.

"I must be getting careless," he said.

"I know these hills," she said. "You just don't seem to believe it."

"You'd better get on out of here," Slocum said, worrying that the posse might be closer than he thought. "I'm in a bit of trouble."

"Breaking Clay Zarra out of jail will certainly do that," Suzanne said, mocking him. "And there you were, all safe and secure in Haven. Why did you leave?"

Slocum didn't want to go into the details. He wasn't any safer on the far side of One Ear Jenkins's stone wall than he was on this side. It all boiled down to whether he wanted to be shot by the law or the lawless. As far as Slocum was concerned, dead was dead. It didn't amount to a hill of beans who killed him.

"I've got two posses after me," he said. "I can get away by myself, but together, well, you wouldn't want to get caught."

"Oh?" Suzanne tossed her head back and sent a mane of midnight hair flowing on the wind. "So you can get away? Do you have any idea where you are?" She laughed her musical laugh when he didn't answer. "You're lost. Admit it, John. You don't know where you are."

"I'm right here," Slocum said resolutely. "I just don't know where the posses are, or how to get away from them."

"Men," Suzanne said, shaking her head. "Do you want some help?"

"I don't have any more money. I spent it all."

"Haven's drinks *are* expensive," she said, still taunting him.

Men shouting caught Slocum's attention. The way the canyon walls carried echoes for long distances, he wasn't sure if the posse was ahead or behind him.

"Down that way," Suzanne said, seeing his uncertainty. "You're not two miles from where they killed Zarra."

"So they cut him down?"

"You inspire people to do the damnedest things, John." Suzanne shook her head as if in wonder at this sudden thought and then said, "This way. No talking. And keep your horse from rearing. The way's going to get real tight before it gets better."

Slocum's horse had no problem with the tight crevice into which Suzanne led them, but Slocum did. He'd never thought he had any fear of being closed in like this, but the walls were so close his knees scrapped and his shoulders banged painfully. He tried looking up to see the sky but couldn't see as much as one star. And the route seemed to go on forever. He thought they would end up in the heart of a mountain or the edge of the world.

When his horse burst into open space again, it was Slocum who let out a long sigh of relief.

"That's as closed in as I ever want to get," he admitted.

Suzanne laughed. "If James Kellerman catches you, you'll be lucky to spend time in a cell any larger than that."

Slocum said nothing. Even Suzanne knew of the Pinkerton agent on his trail. There didn't seem to be much that got past her.

"Where now?" he asked.

"My house is only a mile or two in that direction,"

Suzanne said. "You can lie low there until the posse gets tired of looking for you."

"That'll be a cold day in hell," Slocum said.

"Kellerman is a persistent cuss, isn't he?" Suzanne treated this as a joke, something to laugh at. For Slocum it meant life and death. He looked behind him at the narrow crevice in the rock. She wasn't too far wrong saying he might end up in a cell that width for the rest of his life.

He vowed to go down shooting, just as Clay Zarra had.

"What's happened to Harley Benson?" Slocum asked suddenly.

"Your other partner? Can't rightly say," Suzanne said. "Last I heard, he was safe up in Haven. You know something about him that I don't?"

"No." Slocum didn't want to go into the matter. If Suzanne was telling the truth, and he saw no reason for her to lie after she'd saved his hide again, Benson's intentions lay well beyond the ordinary. Just how far and to what purpose, Slocum was at a loss to decide.

"Put your horse in the shed out back so Sheriff Peña won't spot it. Even if he does, he might not connect it to you."

Slocum almost asked Suzanne about the four horses he had seen tethered beside her house and then bit back the question. It didn't concern him. He didn't have any call getting her more involved than she was already.

"I'll find my own way out of Grant's Pass," he said.

"John, don't be ridiculous. Zarra died for you. Don't throw away his noble act." She smiled wickedly and added, "Besides, by the time noontime rolls around, Sheriff Peña's deputies will be hot, hungry, and ready to quit. That's a much better time to ride on."

"They might find me here."

"You worry so. Put your horse in the shed and then find

me." Suzanne vaulted from her horse, tethered it at the rain barrel so it could drink, then went to the back door. She stood there a moment as Slocum put his horse in the small shed.

He started for the house when she ducked inside. It took Slocum only a few seconds to get there, but Suzanne Crawford had vanished as if she'd never existed.

Slocum paused just inside, listening for any sound that might betray her. "Where are you hiding?" he called, waiting for her reply. It didn't come.

He quickly searched the small house. He was puzzled when he didn't see her. Suzanne hadn't had time to get out the front way. Even if she had, Slocum would have spotted her. A second hunt failed to reveal her hiding place. He frowned and looked carefully at the walls, thinking there might be a hidden closet where she could hide. He found nothing. The back of the wardrobe in her tiny bedroom was solid.

Slocum turned to go outside and see if she had somehow sneaked onto the roof when he heard a soft chuckle behind him. He spun and faced Suzanne. She was completely naked, except for a simple red ribbon tied around her throat.

"Worried now that the sheriff will find you?"

Slocum saw that she had came out of the wardrobe, but not through a false door in the back. The floor folded upward to reveal a ladder going down into a cellar.

"He'd think I robbed you of all your belongings," Slocum said, unable to take his eyes off her naked beauty.

"Come over here and see what I've got."

"You don't seem to be hiding anything, now," Slocum said.

Suzanne kissed him with a fervor that made his heart race. She threw her arms around his neck and pulled him down into the cellar, lit by a single coal-oil lamp. He had trouble disengaging from her long enough to go down the ladder. Pulling the trapdoor shut over his head put him in a vulnerable position for the woman's advances.

Slocum gasped when he felt Suzanne's fingers working to open the buttons at his fly. He had been getting harder by the minute, and now Suzanne discovered his hidden secret. She popped the tip of his manhood into her mouth and worked her tongue over the top.

Slocum's knees turned weak on him and he sank down, balanced precariously on the ladder. Suzanne swarmed all over him, her fingers probing, her lips kissing, her tongue dancing wetly on his exposed flesh.

"Let me down," Slocum said. In the dim light he saw that a comfortable bed stood to one side of the cellar. A table and four chairs were pushed to one side. Rows of canned foods lined the walls, making this hideout capable of concealing a man for a month or longer.

"Here, over here," Suzanne said eagerly, hungrily. As Slocum made his way to the bed, he stripped off the clothes Suzanne hadn't already removed.

She lay on the bed, legs raised slightly, her lips pursed as if ready for another kiss. Slocum found himself drinking in her beauty. Somehow, the red ribbon around her neck made her seem more naked than if she wore nothing at all.

He dropped beside her on the bed, his hand cupping her breast. He squeezed gently. She moaned and arched her back, shoving herself fully into his grip. He tensed his fingers and felt the pliant flesh flow beneath them. Suzanne moaned even louder. Her legs drifted farther apart in wanton invitation.

Slocum was hurting by now, and he wasn't going to deny her what he also wanted. He slipped on top of her and moved quickly, positioning himself so that the tip of his shaft lightly brushed her nether lips. Tingles went through his body, and he felt her responding strongly.

"John, you're such a tease," Suzanne said. "Don't do that anymore. Give it all to me. All!" She reared up and grabbed his buttocks. Pulling hard, she showed him exactly what she wanted.

Slocum sank balls deep into her heated interior. For a moment he hung there, suspended in time and lost in the sensations rippling through his loins. Then he began stroking. Slowly at first, he built up the speed until friction burned at their flesh.

"That's what I need, John. More, yes, more, more!" Suzanne arched her back to take even more of him into her. Fingers clawing at him, she urged him on.

Sweat streamed down Slocum's body and he knew he couldn't hold back much longer. He wanted to build up the greatest tension possible in the demanding woman before letting go himself. Just when he thought he'd never be able to go on, Suzanne gasped and shuddered like a leaf caught in a twister. She thrashed around and mumbled incoherently as passion possessed her totally.

As she relaxed, Slocum exploded like a stick of dynamite. He felt Suzanne's hands stroking along his back and arms and over his chest, even reaching between them to tease him more.

Sated, he sank down onto her.

"You do have a way about you, John," Suzanne said.

"So do you. It's never been this good."

"Don't lie," she said sharply.

Slocum sat up abruptly when he heard footsteps just above his head.

"The law!" he whispered.

"So? They'll never find us," Suzanne said, toying with the hair matted on Slocum's chest.

"You anywhere around, Miss Crawford?" came Sheriff Peña's voice. "We're looking for an escaped prisoner. You in here?"

At least four sets of boots marched back and forth. Slocum tried to bat Suzanne's hand away when it drifted lower and began playing with the limpness she found at his groin.

"Spoilsport," Suzanne said. "They'll never find us."

"They might."

"Want to hide?" she asked. "Or can I just hide this again?" She applied her lips to his limp organ. Slocum lay back on the bed, caught between worry over the sheriff discovering them and the stimulation Suzanne was giving him. He didn't want to respond to her, but he did.

They made love again, the sheriff's deputies still patrolling Suzanne's house.

16

"Ummm, that was nice," Suzanne Crawford said, stretching on the bed like a contented cat. She almost purred. Slocum sat up and glanced toward his six-shooter when he heard boots moving around in Suzanne's house just a few feet above his head.

"Don't worry, John," she said, sitting up and putting her arms around him. He felt the woman's warmth and softness and could almost follow her advice. Almost. The sheriff and his deputies patrolling the house worried him. Staying hidden for a few hours or even a day or two wasn't bad, especially if Suzanne stayed with him, but he couldn't postpone leaving Grant's Pass forever.

He was as much a prisoner here as he would be in Sheriff Peña's jail—or in Haven.

"How can you be so sure they won't find the way down here?" he asked, almost whispering. He could hear the lawmen talking as if they were in the same room. He assumed they could hear any noise he and Suzanne made. She seemed not to believe this. She spoke in her usual throaty voice.

"No one ever has. And people have looked," she said. "Sheriff Peña isn't a stupid man, but he lacks imagination. If something isn't as plain as the nose on his face, he'll miss it."

"His nose was mighty plain," Slocum pointed out. Suzanne laughed at this.

"You worry too much, John. Or is it that you don't trust me?" The dark-haired woman swung around on the bed. The dim light from the coal-oil lamp cast intriguing shadows across her lush body. She began dressing. Slocum hated to admit it, but this was a good idea. He didn't know when he'd have to shoot his way free.

"There's a great deal about you I don't know," he said, getting into his jeans.

"That's as it should be," Suzanne said. "A woman ought to be just a tad mysterious."

He flat out asked, "Who were the four men here earlier?"

"Earlier?" she asked, puzzled. "Oh, yesterday? You were by here then?"

"Who were they?" Slocum settled his six-gun onto his left hip and slipped off the leather thong over the Colt's hammer. He was ready for anything now.

"One Ear Jenkins and three of his henchmen," she said. Slocum's eyes widened in surprise. He hadn't expected her to be so forthcoming.

"What did they want?"

"John, I act as Jenkins's agent. You knew that. He comes by now and again for his share of the money I collect. It's only fair. I wouldn't get a red cent if it weren't for him and Haven. I keep a place in Grant's Pass to sleep and this place we use as a rendezvous."

Slocum shook his head in wonder. Jenkins collected from those entering Haven, then came and collected again from Suzanne. The man had to be swimming in money. That had to be what Benson was hunting for in his midnight searching inside Haven's protective walls.

"There's no way I can go back into Haven," Slocum said. "I crossed Fogger and—" He bit back adding Jenkins's name to the roster of those wanting to see him dead. He enjoyed the time he spent with Suzanne, but she was the one who had pointed out how little he knew of her.

Mysterious, yes, and definitely dangerous. He found it hard to believe she shared her bed with One Ear Jenkins, but stranger things had happened. That might be part of the tariff the outlaw charged for allowing Suzanne to send along men to his keeping.

If he didn't, Jenkins was a damned fool.

"Oh, Nate? He's a blowhard. He wouldn't give a man like *you* any trouble."

"Not much trouble. I took care of him once." Slocum looked at his skinned knuckles and remembered the fight and the drunken celebration after. And he remembered how Jenkins had followed him around with the shotgun ready for action. He had slipped out of Haven after Benson without creating too much of a stir, but he had been recognized.

Jenkins had to know what was going on.

"You ought to have put a slug in his head," she declared with some passion. "No, not his head. His balls. That'd hurt him even more. There's nothing in that worthless skull of his that he'd ever miss as much."

The floorboards over his head squeaked as Sheriff Peña began pacing. And he caught the faint odor of cigarette smoke as someone lit up.

"What do you think they're looking for?" Slocum asked, indicating upstairs.

"Who knows? The sheriff is all the time sniffing around here. I'm sure he's wondering where I am, and who belongs to the horse out in the shed."

Slocum had been too occupied to think of that. The lawman had found his bay. If Peña was sweet on Suzanne, he might hang around for some time, worrying that she had been kidnapped or been the victim of other foul play.

"I don't want this to drag on much longer," Slocum said. He was already making plans for shooting his way through the sheriff and his deputies when he heard Peña let out an explosive snort of disgust.

"We can check back later, men," Sheriff Peña said. "Miss Crawford's not likely to be in any trouble she can't get out of on her own."

"What about the horse?" asked a deputy.

They had found his bay.

"She's all the time horse trading. It might be a new one," Sheriff Peña said, no conviction in his voice. "Let's get to work finding the owlhoot who broke Zarra out of jail."

Slocum hesitated when he heard the men leaving. They might know he and Suzanne were hiding somewhere and were only faking a retreat. Slocum had visions of walking square into their guns when he poked his head through the bottom of Suzanne's wardrobe.

"They're going, John. All of them." Suzanne stood on a crate at the far end of the room, her eye pressed to a small hole. Slocum went and looked over her shoulder. She silently relinquished her position to give him a better view.

Peering into the hole, Slocum was startled to see a view of the house's front yard. The tiny system of mirrors reflected everything back down to whoever hid in the cellar. He looked around and saw several more of the peepholes. Suzanne could check every room in her house without leaving the safety of the cellar.

"All clear," she said. "The only spot I can't see is out back, near the shed. But I counted three men with Sheriff Peña and all four have left."

"They might have the place watched," Slocum said.

"So wait until dark before getting back to Haven."

Slocum stiffened at this. He wasn't planning to return to Haven, Nate Fogger, and One Ear Jenkins. Now that Zarra was dead and Benson had gone to heaven knows where, he was free to hightail it out of Wyoming.

"I'm not going back there," he said. "I'm riding west, over to Oregon, maybe."

"You can make South Pass in a couple days hard ride," Suzanne observed. "From there, it's not too bad following the Oregon Trail on to the Northwest." The dark-haired woman spoke matter-of-factly, as if she had considered this herself.

Slocum almost asked her to come with him but something held him back.

"Now might be a good time to sneak out," she said. "It's not long till sundown."

"Sundown!" Slocum was startled. He hadn't realized they had been in the cellar that long. Between lovemaking bouts, he had dozed. He checked his watch and saw the woman was right.

"You won't get far," Suzanne said. "You'll be back."

"Maybe," Slocum said, thinking of all the reasons he might return. Suzanne Crawford was a big one. But it would be much later, after the Pinkertons and the sheriff had forgotten about him.

"Go on, John. You want to try this crazy escape thing. Trust me. You're safer in Haven, Nate Fogger or no."

Slocum still hesitated to bring up how Jenkins might want him dead, too. He bent and kissed her quickly, then jumped onto the ladder and cautiously pushed up the trapdoor in the bottom of Suzanne's wardrobe. The tiny bedroom was hidden in shadow. Slithering like a snake, he made his way to the window and looked out.

Seeing nothing, Slocum slipped out and made his way to the shed, worrying that the sheriff might have left a guard on the horse. The bay snorted and pawed, wanting out of the tiny building. Slocum obliged, still worrying that he was in the jaws of a trap. He mounted and rode off slowly, seeing no sign of the law.

A mile down the road he began to breathe easier. Two miles off, he knew that Sheriff Peña hadn't left any lookouts. Slocum would have spotted them on his trail by now, if the lawman had. As he rode, Slocum thought hard about Suzanne Crawford. She was a mystery to him, and maybe that appealed as much as anything else about her. Pretty as four aces in a high-stakes poker game, she wasn't the kind of woman Slocum came across often. He damned himself as a fool for riding on and not asking her to come with him, then decided she would have turned him down.

Whatever kept her in a miserable hole like Grant's Pass had to be powerful. It didn't seem to be a beau, though Slocum couldn't be certain. If Sheriff Peña thought he had any chance with her, that meant there wasn't another man sniffing around. Not obviously, or the sheriff would have had it out with any suitor.

Slocum's speculations were cut short by the sight of men moving in the road ahead. He saw ghostly images of three armed men moving from the left to the right, firelight outlining them. He reined back and took a deep sniff. No fire. He was upwind.

He rode off the road and dismounted, waiting to see what was going on. Slocum had barely missed getting caught by Kellerman's men the night before. The Pinkerton agent might not have given up. Slocum cursed the man's persistence, even as he grudgingly admired it. The only major mistake Kellerman had made was the frontal assault on Outlaws' Haven.

"Be out with vittles soon," Slocum heard as the wind died down suddenly. The breeze at his back picked up again and the rest of the conversation was lost.

"Don't move. I got you covered," came a cold voice behind. Slocum stiffened, his mind racing. He had been too absorbed in what went on down the road to think about watching his back.

"Shut up, you fool!" Slocum hissed. "We got him. He's down there. In the arroyo. You want to spook him?"

"What? I thought—"

Slocum turned, drew, and swung his Colt Navy as hard as he could. He caught the man by surprise. The diversion had caused the lawman to look just long enough into the ravine Slocum had indicated. He lay moaning at Slocum's feet.

"You get him, Gus?"

"Yeah," Slocum said, growling deep in his throat to conceal his identity.

"What's wrong with you? You're not supposed to say that. What's the password?"

Slocum scooped up the fallen man's rifle and tried to find the deputy challenging him. He couldn't locate him, and his lack of quick response drew fire. The bullet nicked Slocum on the upper thigh. He sagged slightly, involuntarily reaching for the minor wound.

This saved his life. More bullets tore through the space where his body had been a split second earlier.

"Over here. Somebody's got Gus. Here!" went up the cry.

Slocum saw new tongues of flame licking out in the darkness. He started firing the captured rifle and drove the sentry to cover. But the rifle jammed and he had to draw his Colt Navy. Hobbling along, trying to get to his horse, Slocum was greeted with new gunfire. This time the bullets came from behind him. The men in the ambush along the road had come to the aid of the pair outside the camp.

He kept low, wondering how he was going to get out of the trap. Luck had turned against him at the last possible instant. Otherwise, he would have been able to bull his way through and be free. It hardly mattered who it was circling him, but Slocum guessed it was Kellerman's posse.

"There he is! Get 'im. He done up and kilt poor ole Gus!"

Slocum hadn't done any such thing. Gus lay in the dirt, groaning from the lump on his head. But Slocum wasn't in any position to argue the charges. He wasn't in a position to do much more than die.

Rolling, he came to a halt beside Gus. The man rubbed his head and looked stunned. Slocum propped him up and said, "You got to save us, Gus. They've gone crazy. They think we're outlaws."

"Wha—?"

"The password. Give them the password!" Slocum shook the man, who wailed at the pain rummaging through his head.

"Dang nab it!" Gus bellowed, wincing and holding his head again. "Stop shootin' at us. Allan, Allan Pinkerton's the password!"

"Gus, is that you?"

" 'Course it's us." Gus stopped, as if finally realizing he had gone out on patrol alone. He turned and stared at Slocum, slow realization coming into his numbed brain. "You. It's you!"

Slocum slugged him again. Gus sank to the ground, but the confusion was spreading throughout the Pinkerton ranks. Men came out from cover, arguing about firing on their own men. Slocum didn't hesitate. He stood and moved around, shouting and cursing and spreading as much dissension as he could. He made his way to where his bay nervously pawed the ground. Slocum mounted quickly, then turned for the spot where the ambush had been set up.

He wasn't going back into Grant's Pass if he could get away scot-free. A tall, thin figure walked into the road and Slocum knew he was lost. Kellerman wasn't the careless sort who would allow anyone to ride past without taking note of their face.

Wheeling his horse, Slocum backtracked, riding through the middle of the milling deputies. A fistfight had broken out between three men. Slocum would have liked to stay and see how this three-way fight turned out but knew better than to use up what luck he had coming his way.

"I say, who's that on horseback?" Kellerman called. "It's him. That's the one we want!"

Slocum bent low but was far out of range before any of the deputies got their wits about them and opened fire. He turned off the road and found a dirt path meandering along the canyon wall, then cut across country and tried to leave as complicated a trail as possible for the Pinkertons to follow.

An hour later Slocum came to the conclusion they might not be able to find him in the dark, but he'd never get past their patrols. They had sealed up Grant's Pass tighter than any drum.

Slocum rode back to Suzanne's house, worrying that Sheriff Peña might spot him. He approached the woman's house carefully, hunkering down just off the road to study the place. Her horse was gone, but Slocum knew she might have moved it around to the back. He was getting ready to ride in to find her and ask for help when rocks grated against boot soles behind him.

"Don't go getting all jumpy on me, John," came Suzanne's soft voice. "I heard what was going on, so I figured I ought to find you. Kellerman's got the whole danged town in an uproar."

Suzanne had dressed for the trail in a man's jeans and shirt, but no one could ever mistake her sleek, full figure for a man's.

"I ran into the Pinkertons out on the road."

"Every road," she said with some disgust. "The telegraph office has been doing a land office business. Seems Kellerman has called in a small army of deputies. They mean to clean out Haven once and for all."

"How do we get away?" Slocum asked, aware that he included her in his plans now.

"Nobody can get into Haven," she said scornfully. "It's too well guarded, and Jenkins is too damned smart for them."

"I can't go back there," Slocum said.

"It's more than just Fogger, isn't it?" The dark-haired woman came closer and looked up into his eyes. "You've got a feud going with Jenkins."

"Something like that. He would have cut me down with that double-barreled shotgun of his if he'd had the chance."

"He does what he wants inside Haven, more or less. He must not have meant to—"

"He means it," Slocum said firmly. "I see how he keeps control. He runs things, but he can't push too much or there'll be men willing to go against him. Nate Fogger keeps most of them in line."

"But not you," Suzanne said, chuckling. "No man can keep you in line." She kissed him quickly. Slocum knew she was right. No man could manage him, but Suzanne obviously thought a woman could. And Slocum heard the sureness in Suzanne's voice as to who that woman might be.

"I reckon we ought to lie low for a few days. Kellerman can't keep the town bottled up forever."

"No," she said firmly. "He's got the men, and he's got the authority from the territorial governor. Haven's been a sore point with the governor for years. Wasn't till Kellerman came along that they even found it. They'll keep the pressure on now that success is within their grasp."

"All the more reason for getting away," Slocum insisted.

"You might be right." Suzanne frowned as she thought. Slocum saw she was working on some powerful decisions. "We'll get the hell out of here, but we have to get into Haven first."

"No."

"John, we *have* to. There's no other way. Will you trust me on this?"

He didn't and it must have showed on his face.

"There aren't any roads out of Grant's Pass that aren't knee-deep in deputies. Grant's Pass is crawling with Sheriff Peña's men. And there's no way to ever get over those mountains. So we have to get into Haven—and out the back way."

Slocum wasn't too surprised at what she was saying. "There's a secret way out?"

"At the far end of the canyon. But we have to get inside before we can get to it. And once through the back way, we'll be twenty miles beyond James Kellerman and his damned Pinkerton men."

"You know a way to Haven that's not guarded?"

Suzanne laughed. "I told you. I was raised in these hills. I know every stone. Of course I can get us in. And don't fret none over Fogger or Jenkins. We won't be inside Haven long enough for them to bother you none."

"Which way do we head?" was all Slocum asked. Suzanne Crawford laughed in delight, gave him another kiss, and swung easily into her saddle. Then they rode like the wind for Haven.

Slocum just hoped he was doing the right thing going back into that snake pit.

17

"We can't go there without being caught," Slocum protested. Suzanne Crawford had led them through canyons and valleys and across ridges until Slocum was turned around—until they came out in the narrow canyon leading to the stone wall protecting Outlaws' Haven. Slocum saw a dozen deputies strewn around like so many leaves from a tall tree. They sat by small fires, not making any secret of their presence. For each fire, Slocum guessed there might be as many as three or four men. This meant they had eliminated Jenkins's guards in their positions higher on the mountainsides.

"The guards on the wall wouldn't open the gate and greet us with open arms, either," said Suzanne. The midnight-haired beauty laughed in delight. To her this was little more than a game. Slocum wondered how he had let her talk him into this suicidal attempt.

"How do we get close enough to use that special passage of yours? If the Pinkertons don't see us, the sentries on the wall will. Jenkins has them spooked and ready to shoot anything that moves."

"Looks like a real battle's brewing," Suzanne allowed.

"So?"

"We don't use that path. I reckon you've been in and out through it too many times. There might even be a sentry posted inside ready to cut down anybody using it."

Slocum didn't acknowledge this with anything more than a shrug. He had the feeling he had gone to the well once too often using that narrow crevice route. A deep down feeling told him if they tried it now, they'd be dead.

"Ready, John? You've got to be brave now." Again she seemed to be laughing at him, and this rankled.

"I'll do whatever it takes," Slocum said, "but—" He didn't get a chance to ask Suzanne what she intended. The woman let out a whoop and put her spurs to her horse's flanks. The horse leapt forward, snorting and neighing as it went.

Slocum thought she had lost her mind and intended to take him with her. His choices flashed through his mind. He couldn't stay now that she had drawn so much attention from the posse camped in front of the wall. Men were already stirring, wondering what was going on behind their lines. And if he followed, he was likely to get cut down.

"The hell with it," Slocum muttered. He put his bay into a hard gallop to catch up with Suzanne. She looked over her shoulder and flashed him a bright smile. Then she bent over and urged her horse to even more speed.

Slocum thought Suzanne was crazy, rushing straight for a blank wall. The woman's horse tried to shy away from running head-on into rock. Slocum blinked when it seemed that Suzanne simply vanished. Then his horse shot through the darkness and past the brush stuffed into the crevice. Ahead in the narrow crack rode Suzanne, still hellbent for leather. Behind, Slocum heard the deputies getting to the spot. A bullet sang down the crevice past his head and kept him moving.

As suddenly as he had plunged into the dark, narrow passageway, he burst into Haven. Cold air blew into his face and the stone walls expanded left and right. They had emerged from the course a hundred yards south of Jenkins's stone wall. The men standing watch there were taken by surprise when Suzanne and Slocum rode out.

"Keep riding, John," she called. "We have places to go and people to see."

He tried to overtake her. Suzanne was heading straight for the pitiful cluster of tents and buildings that constituted Haven's heart.

"Suzanne, wait! I can't go there without getting into trouble."

She didn't listen. Slocum pulled up a little and finally came to a complete halt. She didn't slow in her rush to get to Haven. Whatever pulled Suzanne, Slocum wasn't likely to be able to trail along unnoticed.

But a commotion from behind told him that James Kellerman was finally making his play. This time the Pinkerton agent had enough men to storm the bastion One Ear Jenkins had built. There was no way Slocum could return to the passage. If anything, his and Suzanne's entry to Haven might have precipitated the posse's attack.

When gunfire came from the area near the hidden entry into Haven Suzanne had used, Slocum knew what had happened. The deputies had followed them. The crack in the dam allowed the lawmen to pop the cork and flood into the outlaws' hideout.

Slocum got his powerful bay moving again, heading in the direction Suzanne had taken. She was his only chance for getting out alive. He would be crushed like a bug between the Pinkertons' heel and the rock that was One Ear Jenkins.

He saw Suzanne's horse behind the saloon, but he didn't

see the woman anywhere. What Slocum did see turned him cold.

"There you are, Slocum," came Nate Fogger's loud cry. "I want you. I'm gonna gun you down where you sit if you don't get over here." Fogger stood in front of the saloon, his stance wide and his hand hovering over the butt of his six-shooter.

Slocum wondered that Fogger hadn't simply opened up on him when he first sighted him. An ambush was more what he'd come to expect from the gunman. Then he saw Jenkins in the saloon's doorway. This was One Ear Jenkins's way of making sure he got rid of a thorn in his side.

If Fogger didn't kill him, Jenkins would.

Slocum dismounted, keeping his horse between him and Fogger. Slocum settled himself, getting ready to draw.

"You been outside the wall," Fogger said loudly, screwing up his courage. "You brought that posse in. You might even be a lawman yourself!"

Slocum went for his Colt Navy when he saw the other man's cheek twitch. Slocum cleared leather and got off the first shot. The lead took Fogger in the thigh, spinning him halfway around. Fogger continued trying to draw. His first shot went into the dirt.

Slocum's second bullet tore through Fogger's belly and doubled him over. The gunman sank to his knees, fighting to raise his own six-shooter for another shot. Slocum's third shot finished off Nate Fogger.

And then he spun, ready to empty his six-gun in One Ear Jenkins's direction. To his surprise, Haven's leader had vanished from his post in the saloon door. Others poked their heads out and then came timidly into the street to see what the results were.

"You done it, Slocum," crowed one outlaw. "You fixed his wagon good and proper." The man let out a whoop and began dancing around Fogger's fallen body like some demented Indian brave celebrating his first victory.

Slocum hurried into the saloon, hunting for Jenkins. The saloon was almost empty—and he knew why.

Killing Fogger had been a momentary diversion. The Pinkertons breaking through the wall occupied most everyone. Slocum knew there was good reason for them to fear for their lives. He didn't think Kellerman was the kind of man who appreciated long trials as much as he did quick lynchings.

"Jenkins!" Slocum bellowed. "Where are you?" He wanted to have it out with One Ear Jenkins or he wouldn't feel safe until he got out of Haven.

Slocum blasted back through the swinging doors into the street. The outlaws were saddling up and getting ready to fight for their lives. Nate Fogger lay in a pathetic pile, already gathering flies. But where was Jenkins?

Movement caught Slocum's attention. He swung around, pistol ready. He hesitated when he saw Harley Benson astride his horse. The surprise at seeing his one-time partner caused Slocum to freeze. Benson didn't see him because his attention was focused somewhere down the dark valley, away from the gunfire coming from the posse's attack.

Benson used his reins to whip his horse into motion. Slocum lifted his six-shooter and started to shoot, then lost his target. He wasn't sure what Benson was up to. What was he doing back in Haven?

"What am I doing here?" muttered Slocum. He took time to reload as he walked around looking for Suzanne. Without her knowledge of the small crevices in and out of Haven, he'd never escape James Kellerman's men.

"Suzanne!" he bellowed. He looked around. Haven was a ghost town now, the outlaws having hightailed it looking for shelter or a place to make their stand against the law.

"John, here. Back here!" came the woman's cry. He saw her behind the saloon. She hadn't been there a few seconds earlier. Hurrying around, he stopped. Suzanne was mounting.

"Where do we go?" he demanded.

"This way," she said breathlessly, indicating the direction Benson had just taken. "There's a tiny path leading out of the canyon at the far end. And there's something more there."

"What?" Slocum wasn't budging until he got some answers. Bullets began whining through the air, lofted from the fight at the stone wall. He didn't know how long Jenkins's defenders could hold out against the waves of lawmen. Not too much longer, Slocum guessed.

"There's no time, John. Please!"

"What else? We don't go until you tell me."

"Get mounted. I'll tell you as we ride. Please!" The woman's mood had changed from one of pleasure to panic. Slocum climbed into the saddle and trotted to stand beside her. Suzanne looked around anxiously.

"That way," she said, taking off with a start. When Slocum pulled alongside, she said, "There's someone I've got to see, to talk to."

"Benson?" Slocum said, taking a shot in the dark.

"What?" Suzanne shook her head, sending dark hair fluttering behind her. "Heavens, no. Why'd I want to talk with him?"

Slocum didn't have any answer to that, and that was the problem. He had more questions than solutions to them. Looking over his shoulder, he saw one tongue of flame after another leaping out along the stone wall. From the constant roar echoing down the valley, a full-scale battle now raged. It wouldn't be long before James Kellerman rode through the gate, the new ruler of Outlaws' Haven.

"The Pinkertons have busted this place wide-open," he said. "We'll never get back that way."

"We can escape just as we planned," Suzanne said, but a new note of worry tinged her words. She wasn't as sure as she had been before entering Haven. Slocum wondered how much he ought to worry over that.

Then he caught the sound of hooves from ahead, down the canyon in the direction they rode. He had been looking for Harley Benson but hadn't caught sight of the man. The pounding hooves must signal Benson making his escape.

"Does Benson know the way out?"

"Why do you keep asking about Benson?" snapped Suzanne. "I don't know anything about him. He might have found the way out of Haven, but I doubt it. The path isn't obvious."

"Is it marked?"

"What? No, John, it doesn't have a sign on it saying THIS WAY OUT. How stupid do you think we are?"

Slocum didn't reply. Benson had been scouring the canyon walls, looking for some kind of mark. He had entered the sand pit and hadn't been satisfied with that hidey-hole. That meant he wanted another way out, other than through Haven's main gate.

"Hold up, John. Wait!"

Slocum obeyed as Suzanne stopped at the far end of the canyon and frantically looked left and right. She said, "I need to find two thin spires of rock. We ride between them."

"It's too dark to see much," Slocum said. "It'll be dawn in another hour or two. We don't have time to wait." More gunfire sounded, but it was dying down. He didn't hear the cheers of triumph that would have accompanied an outlaw victory. The Pinkerton posse was slowly wiping out the pockets of resistance remaining. It would be a good day for them when the sun finally peeked over the canyon rim.

"There!" she cried. She dismounted and tugged on her horse's reins to get it to follow. Just as she stopped between a pair of rock pylons, two shots rang out.

"Wait," Slocum cautioned. "Who's up there?"

Slocum was talking to thin air. Suzanne had rushed ahead on foot. Slocum cursed, whipped out his Colt, and crashed into her. She had stumbled over a body stretched out in the sandy stretch leading into the mountains.

"No," muttered Suzanne, hands covering her mouth. "It can't be."

Slocum pushed past her and dropped to one knee. At first he didn't recognize the dead man, then saw the barrel of a shotgun poking out from under the body. Slocum turned the man's head and saw the jagged yellow teeth and stubbled chin. Even in death One Ear Jenkins was an ugly son of a bitch.

"What happened?" Suzanne said in a whisper.

"Looks like he got shot in the back," Slocum said. Jenkins's head was pointed toward Haven. He had been leaving the escape route, not entering, when he had been cut down.

Clanking from behind caused Slocum to turn slowly, his Colt leveled. He whispered to Suzanne, "Tell me about this way out. Everything, every detail."

"It . . . it goes along narrow like this for another ten yards, then widens into what was once a pool under a waterfall."

Slocum looked at the sides of the rocky corridor and saw they had been washed smooth by years of running water.

"The water dried up years back," Suzanne went on.

"So there's a wider area ahead, and we have to pass through it to get out of Haven?"

Suzanne nodded.

"Get the horses," Slocum ordered. He saw that Suzanne was still shaken by Jenkins's death. She simply stood and stared until Slocum shook her gently and pushed her in the direction of the opening. When Suzanne started for the horses, Slocum turned and walked quickly down the rocky chute toward the dried-up pond Suzanne had described.

He heard the clink and clank of heavy chains and strongbox lids. A dark figure hunched over a stack of canvas mailbags.

"Finding enough to satisfy you, Benson?" Slocum asked.

Harley Benson whirled, his six-shooter coming up in a smooth movement. He hesitated when he saw Slocum. He didn't put down his pistol and he didn't crack a smile at seeing his old partner. Slocum didn't take either as good signs.

"There's thousands here, Slocum. More. Jenkins has been robbing and stealing for years. This is his entire stash."

"So this *is* what you've been hunting for." Slocum allowed his six-shooter to sink off-target.

"It's the only reason I came into Haven," Benson said.

As he turned dim starlight glinted off a badge hung on Benson's chest.

"You're a Pinkerton agent," Slocum said, all the pieces of the puzzle coming together.

"Everything's been set up to get me inside Haven," Benson said.

"The train robbery was a fake. We were 'given' the greenbacks so we could buy our way in. But did you know Zarra would get shot?"

"It didn't matter. All that counted was Jenkins letting me into Haven. I'm sorta glad you weren't hurt. I've taken a liking to you, Slocum. But I've got to arrest you."

"Are you going to arrest me or are we going to split this loot? It's quite a haul. We'll both be rich, and Kellerman would be satisfied with a fraction of it."

"You don't know him, Slocum. He's a devil! He doesn't miss a thing. No, this all goes back to the railroads where it was stolen from. Don't try lifting that hogleg of yours. I'll kill you. I swear it!"

Slocum saw the resolve in the man's face. Benson had been impatient to get into Haven, just to break the place wide-open for the railroads and the Pinkerton Agency. He didn't look to be a man driven as much by greed as by ambition. Slocum worried about men like that.

"Why'd Kellerman launch that first attack? He must have lost half his men butting head-on into Jenkins's defenses."

"That was a mistake," Benson said. "He thought I'd signaled him to come ahead when I wanted him to hang back and wait."

"The lantern. You were signaling Kellerman up on the rim, telling him what to do."

"Nobody tells Mr. Kellerman what to do. We were exchanging times. He told me when he was going to come ahead."

"I'd wager he jumped the gun," Slocum said, remembering how the posse had come after him and Suzanne when they entered Haven. "What else did he fail to tell you?"

"This won't work, Slocum, trying to sew discord," Benson said. "Mr. Kellerman might have started the attack early, but he had a good reason. He always does. And I've done what I was sent in to do. Don't raise your six-shooter if you want to keep on living." Benson aimed his pistol square at Slocum. At this range he couldn't miss.

"What were you supposed to do, besides find the loot Jenkins had accumulated?"

"Get rid of Fogger. You did that for me. And I was to take out One Ear Jenkins. That old galoot was a mad dog killer. One of the worst what ever rode."

"And he was my father, you son of a bitch!"

Slocum jerked to one side when Benson turned to face Suzanne. She fired her rifle, the bullet taking Benson square in the face. His six-gun discharged, but the bullet went wide of Slocum's body and kicked around the rocky arena until it ran out of steam.

Suzanne cocked the rifle again and walked forward slowly. She fired a second round into Benson's chest, just for insurance.

"Thanks," Slocum said. "I never had him pegged for a Pinkerton agent. I wonder if Benson was what Zarra was trying to warn me about when he mentioned I was riding into a trap." Slocum would never know. Zarra might have been delirious, or he might have overheard something.

On impulse, Slocum asked, "Does James Kellerman smoke cheroots?"

"What? Yes, I think he does," said Suzanne.

Everything fit. When Slocum had last seen Benson in Grant's Pass, he'd been reporting to his boss. Kellerman had stayed in the shadow and Slocum hadn't gotten a good look at him. If he had, things would have gone a lot different.

Slocum poked around in the chests filled with gold coins, gold dust, and silver bars. The canvas mailbags were stuffed with more greenbacks than he thought existed. Opening one, he dug through it. Most of the scrip was worthless, being issued by local banks, but enough of it was federal paper to make lugging the bags worthwhile. But it would take a dozen mules to get all the gold and silver moved.

He looked up. Suzanne just stood, her face stricken. Tears rolled down her dusty cheeks.

"Jenkins was your father?" This was about as outrageous as anything Slocum had ever heard. Suzanne Crawford was beautiful. Jenkins had been uglier than sin.

Suzanne nodded numbly. "Haven was *ours.* I took my mother's maiden name to help Papa get suckers in here so he could fleece them. He liked the notion I was out in Grant's Pass and he was ruling the roost here. Kept me out of trouble, he always said."

"You made quite a bit off outlaws on the run, didn't you?"

"I've never seen his stash before. I can't believe this is all of it. John, we made a *lot* of money. What I took outside I used to keep us safe."

"Like building that cellar in your house."

"That," Suzanne said, animation coming back to her voice. "And there was much more. I bought most of the deputies so they'd look the other way. Sheriff Peña was always too honest." She laughed harshly, almost hysterically. "He'd never believe I had anything to do with this place. He was sweet on me."

Gunfire from the direction of the canyon reminded Slocum of how thorough James Kellerman was. He wouldn't stop until he had rounded up every outlaw in the valley. And there was a chance Benson had already given his boss the location of this secluded way out of Haven. Harley Benson had been clever enough to fool Slocum, and he must have done other work for the Pinkertons well.

"Kellerman couldn't know of this way out," Suzanne said. "Papa guarded it too well. He must have led Benson here."

"I don't think so," Slocum said. "The way I make out the spoor, Benson was already here and your pa surprised him. Jenkins turned and tried to run and Benson cut him down. That means Benson might have told the posse about your private bank." He made a sweeping gesture with his hand, encompassing the entire dried pond area.

"We don't have to go back, John," Suzanne said, taking

a deep breath. He wondered if he would ever again enjoy the sight of her breasts rising and falling as they'd just done. Too much had happened in the last few minutes.

She turned, her rifle muzzle moving in his direction. Disjointed thoughts flashed through Slocum's head. He had been Benson's partner. Did she hold that against him? Was she cutting out a possible rival for all the gold in this small mountain pocket?

"There," Suzanne said. "Behind you is the route out of here." She whistled and her horse trotted into the rocky arena. Behind it came Slocum's bay, again protesting at being penned up by the high rock bulwarks.

"What do you think we should take?" Slocum asked, trying to decide between the gold and weighing down his horse and the bags of greenbacks and speed.

"A little of each," she said. "There's a chance Kellerman won't find this place." Suzanne let out a deep sigh. "Papa worked so hard to get the money, and what good did it do him? Shot in the back like a common criminal."

Slocum said nothing. As far as he was concerned, One Ear Jenkins was a low-down, no-account common thief. Maybe worse. But he was dead and had left his rich legacy for those best able to use it. Slocum settled twenty pounds of gold coins into his saddlebags, then added a couple canvas mailbags stuffed with greenbacks.

Suzanne had similarly laden her horse. Without so much as a glance in his direction, she rode out through the crevice she had shown him. Slocum followed closely, seeing how a posse could get lost in the winding maze of cracks and passages through the mountains. An hour later he and Suzanne emerged on the far side of Haven.

"That way's Montana," Suzanne said, pointing north. The sun was just poking up behind her, sending out rays in an arc that turned her into an angel. The light caught her dark hair and gave it a radiance of its own.

"How long would it take getting there?" Slocum asked, not sure what to say.

Suzanne shrugged. "A week, maybe more. Depends on how fast you travel."

Slocum started his bay north toward Montana. A week, Suzanne had said. He could do it in less, if he put his mind to it.

He turned and saw Suzanne riding up alongside him. An almost shy smile greeted him.

Or it might take longer, Slocum decided, if two people were making the journey and neither of them was in much of a hurry to get anywhere.

JAKE LOGAN

TODAY'S HOTTEST ACTION WESTERN!

__SLOCUM'S WAR (Giant Novel)	0-425-13273-0/$3.99
__SLOCUM AND THE SHARPSHOOTER #160	0-425-13303-6/$3.50
__DEATH'S HEAD TRAIL #161	0-425-13335-4/$3.50
__SILVER TOWN SHOWDOWN #162	0-425-13359-1/$3.99
__SLOCUM AND THE BUSHWHACKERS #163	0-425-13401-6/$3.99
__SLOCUM AND THE WYOMING FRAME-UP #164	0-425-13472-5/$3.99
__SAN ANGELO SHOOTOUT #165	0-425-13508-X/$3.99
__BLOOD FEVER #166	0-425-13532-2/$3.99
__HELLTOWN TRAIL #167	0-425-13579-9/$3.99
__SHERIFF SLOCUM #168	0-425-13624-8/$3.99
__VIRGINIA CITY SHOWDOWN #169	0-425-13761-9/$3.99
__SLOCUM AND THE FORTY THIEVES #170	0-425-13797-X/$3.99
__POWDER RIVER MASSACRE #171	0-425-13665-5/$3.99
__FINAL DRAW #172	0-425-13707-4/$3.99
__SLOCUM AND THE TIN STAR SWINDLE #173	0-425-13811-9/$3.99
__SLOCUM AND THE NIGHTRIDERS #174	0-425-13839-9/$3.99
__REVENGE AT DEVILS TOWER #175	0-425-13904-2/$3.99
__SLOCUM AT OUTLAWS' HAVEN #176	0-425-13951-4/$3.99
__AMBUSH AT APACHE ROCKS #177 (November)	0-425-13981-6/$3.99
__HELL TO MIDNIGHT #178 (December)	0-425-14010-5/$3.99

For Visa, MasterCard and American Express orders ($15 minimum) call: 1-800-631-8571

Check book(s). Fill out coupon. Send to:
BERKLEY PUBLISHING GROUP
390 Murray Hill Pkwy., Dept. B
East Rutherford, NJ 07073

NAME ____________________

ADDRESS ____________________

CITY ____________________

STATE __________ ZIP __________

PLEASE ALLOW 6 WEEKS FOR DELIVERY.
PRICES ARE SUBJECT TO CHANGE WITHOUT NOTICE.

POSTAGE AND HANDLING:
$1.75 for one book, 75¢ for each additional. Do not exceed $5.50.

BOOK TOTAL $____

POSTAGE & HANDLING $____

APPLICABLE SALES TAX $____
(CA, NJ, NY, PA)

TOTAL AMOUNT DUE $____

PAYABLE IN US FUNDS.
(No cash orders accepted.)

202d

AF538562

पानदान

युवान बुक्स - अनबाउंड स्क्रिप्ट का उपक्रम

पानदान : मुज्तबा ख़ान

प्रथम संस्करण : नवम्बर, 2025

ISBN : 978-93-48497-67-3

प्रकाशक : अनबाउंड स्क्रिप्ट
2/41, अंसारी रोड,
दरियागंज, दिल्ली - 110002

वेबसाइट : www.unboundscript.com
ई-मेल : books@unboundscript.com
फोन : 011- 35807601

PAANDAAN
by Mujtaba Khan

मुद्रक : यश प्रिंटोग्राफ़िक्स, नोएडा, उत्तर प्रदेश

मूल्य : ₹ 199/-

मुज्तबा ख़ान

पानदान

“बेटे मैं भी एक माँ हूँ और बहुत सारे काम करती हूँ जो मेरा दिल नहीं करता और सिर्फ़ इसलिए करती हूँ क्यूँकि उसमें मेरे बच्चों की ख़ुशी होती है।” अम्मी ने अपना पानदान उठाते हुए कहा।

मुमताज़ बेगम दालान के बीच-ओ-बीच पड़े अपने जहेज़ में आए हुए नमाज़ के तख़्त पर बैठी दुआ माँग रही थीं। इतनी देर में उनकी मुलाज़िमा फ़रीदन दौड़ती हुई आई और कहने लगी, "बी, नसीम आपा का ख़त आया है।"

मुमताज़ बेगम ने इशारों-इशारों में उसको हज़ारों गालियाँ दीं, जिसको देख फ़रीदन तेज़ी से ख़त छोड़ वापस दौड़ गई। फ़रीदन दालान के दर के पीछे छुपी उनकी आवाज़ का इंतज़ार करने लगी। पंद्रह-बीस मिनट लम्बी दुआ माँगकर मुमताज़ बेगम ने ख़त की तरफ़ निगाह डाली। ख़त उनकी बेटी नसीम का था। मुमताज़ बेगम अपनी ऐनक ढूँढने लगीं, जब नहीं मिली तो ज़ोर से आवाज़ दी, "अरे नेकबख़्त! अरे ख़ुशनसीब कहाँ गई, घोड़े पे सवार आई और ग़ायब हो गई?"

फ़रीदन दर के पीछे से बोली, "बी, क्या हुआ? मैं तो बावर्चीख़ाने तक गई थी, आपका खाना लगाने का इंतज़ाम करने।"

"बस-बस बातें कम बनाओ और ज़रा जल्दी से मेरी ऐनक ढूँढ दो। नसीम की लिखाई पढ़ना भी एक जंग है। उस्ताद थक गए थे लेकिन ढीठ इतनी थी कि लिखाई पर कभी काम नहीं किया। कहना मानना तो फ़ितरत में ही नहीं था इसके। बिलकुल बाप पर गई है इस मामले में।" बी बड़बड़ाती रहीं।

फ़रीदन ने हँसते हुए कहा, "बी, ये लीजिए, अपनी ऐनक और मेरा ग़ुस्सा नसीम आपा की लिखावट पर मत उतारिए।"

बा-एहतेराम ऐनक लगाकर, मुमताज़ बेगम ख़त पढ़ने लगीं-

अम्मी अस सलामुआलैकम,

उम्मीद करती हूँ आप बा-सेहत होंगी और घर में भी सब ख़ैरियत होगी। माज़रत चाहूँगी मैं आपके पिछले दो ख़तों का जवाब नहीं दे पाई। दरअसल मैं उन्हें पढ़ ही नहीं पाई थी। हम लोग कहीं घूमने-घामने चले गए थे उस चक्कर में इधर-उधर हो गए थे वो ख़त।

बशारत और सकीना कैसे हैं? उनसे कहना जल्दी से ख़ुशी की ख़बर सुनाएँ, कान तरस गए।

अम्मी पिछले तीन चार महीने से आपका नवासा मेहराज मेरी जान खा रहा है कि नानी के घर जाना है। बाप को भी मना लिया इसने। पर मेरी समझ में नहीं आ रहा है कि क्या करूँ? अगर मना करती हूँ तो भी ग़लत और भेजती हूँ तो आपकी जान आफ़त में हो जाएगी। दिन-रात शैतानी करता है और ऊपर से कभी आपके घर आया तक नहीं है और अब अकेला भेजने में भी घबरा रही हूँ। बताइए क्या करूँ? आपके जवाब की मुन्तज़िर हूँ।

आपकी ढीठ बेटी
नसीम

फ़रीदन पीछे खड़ी कुनियाई आँखों से ख़त पढ़ने की कोशिश कर रही थी। इतने में मुमताज़ बेगम ने ख़त को तह करके लिफ़ाफ़े में डाल दिया। फिर उनको कुछ याद आया और बोलीं-

"फ़रीदन, तुझसे कब से कह रही हूँ लिहाफ़ों को धूप दे दे लेकिन तेरे तो कान पर जूँ तक नहीं रेंगती। तेरी माँ को बुलाकर तेरा हाथ दे दूँगी, अब मुझसे नहीं सँभल सकती तू।"

उन्नीस साल की फ़रीदन इकलौती इंसान थी, जो मुमताज़ बेगम से थोड़ा बहुत मज़ाक़ कर लेती थी। मुमताज़ बेगम और उनके इन्तेज़ामात दूर-दूर तक मशहूर थे। वो जिन लिहाफ़ों को निकलवाने की बात कर रही हैं, कोई चार-पाँच नहीं बल्कि पच्चीस-तीस लिहाफ़ हैं। जिनको हर साल सर्दियाँ जाते ही धूप देकर कमरे की मचान पर बक्सों में संभालकर रख दिया जाता है। ये सारा काम लल्लन मियाँ ही करते हैं लेकिन धूप में डालना और उठाना तो फ़रीदन और रुख़साना ही करती हैं।

लल्लन मियाँ पिछले चालीस साल से इस घर के मुलाज़िम हैं। इनके बाप दादा के ज़माने से ये लोग इस घर की ख़िदमत करते आ रहे हैं। लल्लन मियाँ दरवाज़े पर कुर्सी डाले बैठे रहते और घर में जैसे ही किसी काम की ज़रूरत होती वो अंदर आ जाते।

लल्लन मियाँ एक मर्तबा अपने घर से भागकर बी के पास आए और रोते हुए कहने लगे-

"बी, मेरे माँ बाप को समझाइए।"

बी ने घबराकर पूछा, "अरे लल्लन, हुआ क्या? पहले वो तो बताओ।"

रोते हुए लल्लन मियाँ बोले, "वो लोग मेरा निकाह करने को कह रहे हैं। मैं ज़हर खा लूँगा, शादी नहीं करूँगा।"

बी हँसते हुए बोलीं, "सही तो कह रहे हैं। तीस साल के पहलवान हो, शादी की उम्र है। वजह बताओ तभी उनसे बात करूँगी।"

बिना रुके लल्लन मियाँ बोले, "मुझे कोई ज़िम्मेदारी नहीं चाहिए। मुझसे ये नहीं हो पाएगा, बी।"

बी ने उसी दिन लल्लन मियाँ को अपने घर ये कहकर रख लिया कि "पहलवानी करो और खाओ-पियो। घर का काम-काज देख लिया करना और आराम से यहाँ रहो।" पिछले पंद्रह साल से लल्लन मियाँ यही कर रहे हैं।

बी की डाँट सुनते ही फ़रीदन दरवाज़े पर गई और बोली- "लल्लन मियाँ कब तक यहाँ बैठे ऊँघते रहोगे। बी बुला रही हैं, जल्दी अंदर चलिए।" लल्लन मियाँ अपनी कुर्सी पर दोनों पाँव रखे नींद के झोंके में जा ही रहे थे लेकिन बी का नाम सुनते ही उछल के खड़े हो गए। मुमताज़ बेगम को सब लोग बी ही कहते थे।

खड़े होते ही लल्लन मियाँ बोले, "फ़रीदन, तू कब बड़ी होगी। ऐसी चीख़ें मारी तूने कि मेरा दिल काँप गया।"

फ़रीदन हँसते हुए बोली, "हाहाहा, मुर्दा उठ जाए बी के नाम से। आप तो ख़ैर अभी ज़िंदा हैं।"

"चल मैं तेरी शिकायत करूँगा बी से।" झुंझलाकर कहते हुए अगले मिनट में लल्लन मियाँ दालान में बी के सामने हाज़िर थे।

फ़रीदन भी जाकर बी के पीछे खड़ी हो गई। लल्लन मियाँ कुछ बोलते इससे पहले बी बोलीं, "लल्लन, जल्दी से अपनी पहलवानी का हुनर दिखाओ और मचानों पे चढ़कर लिहाफ़ उतार दो।"

फ़रीदन पीछे खड़ी लल्लन मियाँ को दाँत दिखा रही थी। इतने में बी पलट के उससे बोलीं, "आँगन में पलंग कौन डालेगा?" फ़रीदन पल में वहाँ से छू हो गई।

लल्लन मियाँ ने बी की निगरानी में लिहाफ़ उतारे। उधर फ़रीदन और रुख़साना आँगन में पलंग बिछाने लगीं, जिनपर लिहाफ़ों को धूप दिलाने के लिए डाला जाना था।

फ़रीदन ने रुख़साना से कहा, "आज ज़रूर बी किसी गहरी सोच में चली गई हैं।"

रुख़साना उसको घूरते हुए बोली, "तुझे इसी सब की पड़ी रहती है। बी तो रोज़ किसी-न-किसी काम में लगती ही हैं।"

"अरे तुझे कुछ पता नहीं है। ग़ौर करियो, बी जिस दिन कुछ सोच में होंगी उसी दिन ज़्यादा कामों में लग जाएँगी।" फ़रीदन ये कहते हुए बावर्चीख़ाने में चली गई।

मुमताज़ बेगम तो नानी भी कब की बन गईं लेकिन उम्र अभी सिर्फ़ अट्ठावन साल ही है। चौदह साल की थीं, जब इनकी शादी हुई और घर में सबसे बड़े लड़के की दुल्हन बनकर आईं। तो ज़िम्मेदारी तभी से इनके सर पर पड़ना लाज़मी थी। वैसे तो इनका सबसे छोटा देवर भी इनसे पन्द्रह साल बड़ा था लेकिन बड़ी भाभी थीं तो उन लोगों

के लिए माँ की जगह आने में ज़्यादा वक़्त नहीं लगा। इनकी सास भी काफ़ी सीधी-सादी औरत थीं, बस अगर सुबह पाँच बजे से एक मिनट देर से उठती थीं तो मुमताज़ बेगम के वालिद को शिकायत करवा दिया करती थीं। इनकी सास इनसे इतनी मोहब्बत करती थीं कि शादी के कुछ वक़्त बाद उन्होंने कहा, "बेटी, मैं इस घर में आज से खाना सिर्फ़ तुम्हारे हाथ का खाऊँगी।"

वो दिन था और फिर मुलाज़िम होने के बावजूद खाना तो मुमताज़ बेगम के हाथों का ही खाया जाता था। अपनी सास की मोहब्बत को भला दरकिनार करतीं भी तो कैसे?

बी की सास इनकी शादी के पाँच साल बाद ही गुज़र गईं। इन्हें लगा शायद अब कोई इनके हाथ का खाना पसंद नहीं करेगा इसलिए इन्होंने कुछ वक़्त बाद मुलाज़िमों से खाना बनवाना शुरू कर दिया। लेकिन इनकी ख़ुशनसीबी कि इनके शौहर ने कह दिया, "अम्मी चली गईं लेकिन उनकी ख़्वाहिश यही थी कि घर का खाना घर की दुल्हन ही बनाए इसलिए कल से खाना आप ही बनाना।"

अब ये वक़्त आ गया है कि काम न करें तो बेचैनी हो जाती है। इसलिए लिहाफ़ सर्दियाँ आने से एक महीना पहले ही धूप देकर रख दिए जाते हैं। शायद आज कोई सोचने की वजह मिल गई इसलिए मुमताज़ बेगम ख़ुद को कामों में मसरूफ़ रखकर सोचेंगी।

दोपहर का खाना खाकर मुमताज़ बेगम अपना पान मुँह में दबाए कुछ देर के लिए सो जाती थीं। एक बजे दोपहर का खाना और उसके बाद तीसरे पहर तक आराम करना इनका मामूल था। चाहे दुनिया इधर से उधर हो जाए लेकिन वो अपने मामूलों की पाबंद रहती थीं। आँख खुलते ही फ़रीदन को चाय के लिए आवाज़ दे दिया करतीं और ख़ुद असर की नमाज़ पढ़तीं। नमाज़ के बाद दालान में

अपने जहेज़ में आई आरामकुर्सी पर बैठ जातीं। उसी पर बैठकर मुमताज़ बेगम ने अपना राज चलाया।

उस दिन फ़रीदन ने जैसे ही उन्हें चाय लाकर दी, उन्होंने उससे अपनी क़लम और डायरी मँगवाई। फ़रीदन ने डायरी अभी हाथ में दी भी नहीं थी कि उन्होंने उसको रुख़साना को बुलाकर लाने को कहा।

"बी, उससे क्या काम है मुझे बताइए न, मैं कर दूँगी," परेशानी में फ़रीदन बोली।

"अगर तुम्हारे बस का होता तो मैं तुमसे कब का करवा लेती। अब दफ़ा हो जाओ और रुख़साना को भेजो।" ये कहकर बी ने लिखना शुरू कर दिया।

दरअसल फ़रीदन और रुख़साना हैं तो सगी बहनें लेकिन ये दोनों एक-दूसरे को एक आँख नहीं भाती हैं। दोनों ही मुमताज़ बेगम के साथ रहती हैं। इनकी माँ मुमताज़ बेगम की ख़ादिमा थी, जो उनके साथ शादी के बाद यहाँ ससुराल भी आ गई थी। वो बी से दस साल बड़ी थी लेकिन उसकी शादी काफ़ी वक़्त बाद हुई और वो भी बी ने ही करवाई थी। बी इन बच्चियों को पढ़ा-लिखा रही हैं और ये बच्चियाँ घर का ऊपर का काम-काज भी करती रहती हैं। मुमताज़ बेगम को लड़कियाँ बेहद पसंद हैं और उसी वजह से वो अपनी बेटी की ज़िद के आगे झुकती रहीं।

फ़रीदन बुरा मुँह बनाए आँगन से आसमान में पतंगों की तरफ़ देखती हुई जा रही थी इतने में दरवाज़े से लल्लन मियाँ ने अंदर आकर बताया कि "चार पाँच औरतें बी से मिलने आई हैं"। फ़रीदन दालान की तरफ़ इशारा करके बोली- "ख़ुद पैरों का इस्तेमाल

करने की ज़हमत करें और बता दें बी को।" हँसते हुए भाग कर बावर्चीख़ाने में घुस गई।

लल्लन मियाँ उन औरतों को अंदर बी के पास दालान में ले गए। उनमें से एक औरत बुर्क़ा नहीं उतार रही थी तो मुमताज़ बेगम ने पूछा, "क्या हुआ?"

दूसरी औरत जो कि बी के पास आती रहती थी, उसने बताया कि "ये अख़्तरी है, मेरी छोटी बहन है। ये कह रही है कि क्या पता कोई मर्द आ जाए तो बेपर्दगी होगी।"

बी ने अख़्तरी को अपने क़रीब बिठाया। फिर उससे पूछा- "तुम्हारी शादी हो गई?"

अख़्तरी ने रोते हुए कहा, "मेरा मर्द घर में बीमार पड़ा है।"

उसके आगे बोल नहीं पाई तो बी ने उसके सर को हाथ से सहलाया। इतने में उसकी बड़ी बहन बोली, "बी, इसका मर्द रंगरेज़ है। किसी के घर की दीवार काफ़ी ऊँची थी। बाँस की दो सीढ़ियाँ जोड़कर चूना कर रहा था और वो टूट गई। उस हादसे में उसके दोनों पैरों की हड्डी टूट गई।"

"हाय अफ़सोस! तो इलाज-विलाज नहीं कराया?" बी ने घबराकर पूछा।

अख़्तरी रोती हुई बोली, "उसी के ऑपरेशन के लिए मदद को आई हूँ।"

बी ने उसके कंधे पर हाथ रखकर कहा कि, "तुम बुर्क़ा उतार लो इस दालान की तरफ़ कोई मर्द मेरी इजाज़त के बिना निगाह नहीं उठा सकता।"

उसने झट से अपना बुर्क़ा उतार दिया।

फ़रीदन इतनी देर में उनके लिए नाश्ता ले आई, क्यूँकि बी को बिना ख़ातिर किए किसी को वापस भेजना बिलकुल पसंद नहीं। जाते-जाते अख़्तरी ने बी से कहा, "बी, आप अगर चाहें तो मेरे घर किसी को भेज कर दिखवा लें। मेरा मर्द पलंग पर पड़ा है, मैं झूठ नहीं बोल रही हूँ।"

"इंसान को अगर एक निगाह में नहीं पहचाने तो ज़िन्दगी के तजुर्बों का क्या फ़ायदा। तुम इत्मीनान से जाओ, तुम्हारा काम ज़रूर हो जाएगा।" बी ने उसके सर पर हाथ रखकर कहा। अख़्तरी के चेहरे पर बी को कुछ इत्मीनान दिखा।

"लल्लन मियाँ को घर का पता देती जाना", कहते हुए बी ने उनको रुख़सत कर दिया।

इतने में रुख़साना भी फ़ारिग होकर बी के पास आ गई। बी ने उसको बोला, "मुल्लानी के पास जाकर ग़रारों की ख़बर लाओ और साफ़ बोल देना, अगले इतवार तक अगर ग़रारे नहीं सिले तो वो उनके लिहाफ़ बनाकर ख़ुद ओढ़ लें।"

दरअसल ये ग़रारे दस लड़कियों के लिए बनाए जा रहे थे, जिनके निकाह बी करा रही थीं। अगले पीर को इन सबका निकाह बी के घर ही होना था।

बी साल में एक बार ऐसी लड़कियों की शादियाँ कराती हैं। रिश्ते भी ख़ुद ही कराती हैं और फिर निकाह और खाने-पीने का इंतज़ाम भी। साथ में थोड़ा-बहोत लकड़हट (फर्नीचर) वगैरह भी देती हैं। जिसमें एक दीवान, दो मसहरियाँ, एक सिंगारमेज़ और एक अलमारी होती है। ये सारा सामान बी घर में अपने पुश्तैनी बढ़ई से बनवाती हैं। बी

के आँगन में से ही एक छोटा-सा दरवाज़ा है, जो बराबर वाले छोटे घर में जाता है, जिसमें ये तमाम काम होते हैं।

शाम होते ही ये मज़दूर बी के पास अपनी मज़दूरी लेने आ गए। बी इनको देखते ही बोलीं, "मग़रिब की अज़ान हो गई?" एक ने सर हिलाकर 'हाँ' कहा। "पूरे शहर की सबसे पहली आज़ान की आवाज़ तुम लोगों को आ जाती है।" बी अपने पानदान में से पैसे निकालते हुए बोलीं। "अरे नहीं बी, ऐसा नहीं है, बहुत वक़्त हो गया अज़ान हुए तो।" उनमें से एक बोला।

रोज़ के रोज़ बी उनका मेहनताना देती हैं और पूरे दिन के काम का ब्यौरा भी ले लेती हैं।

हर बरस ऐसा लगता था जैसे इस घर में किसी की शादी हो रही है। मोहल्ले के लोग और अक्सर औरतें, साल के इस हफ़्ते का इंतज़ार करती थीं। बी के सामने पूरा मोहल्ला काँपता था इसलिए औरतें बी के पास अपनी शिकायतें लेकर आती थीं; किसी की सास परेशान करे तब, किसी का मियाँ परेशान करे तब, हर मसला सुलझाना बी का ही काम था। लेकिन सारे हल प्यार से करतीं, सिवाए जहेज़ माँगने या बहू पे उस वजह से ज़ुल्म की शिकायत के।

एक मर्तबा रात को दस बजे, एक औरत भागते हुए बी के घर आई और चीख़ते हुए कहने लगी-

"बी, मुझे मार देंगे। मुझे मार देंगे।"

बी कमरे में लेटी अपने पसंदीदा शायर दाग़ देहलवी की शायरी की किताब पढ़ रही थीं। बी निकलकर दालान में आईं तो वो औरत भाग के उनके पास कहती हुई आई- "बी, मेरे साथ घर चलिए। मेरे ऊपर बहोत हाथ उठाया है।"

बी ने कहा, "इस वक़्त तुम अपने घर जाओ, रात में ऐसे भागकर आना सही बात नहीं है।"

वो औरत रोती हुई वापस चली गई। बी ने अपना बुर्क़ा पहना और उसके पीछे-पीछे निकल गईं। वो औरत अपने घर में घुस गई और बी उसके दरवाज़े पर कान लगाकर खड़ी हो गईं। मोहल्ले के लोग भी अपनी-अपनी छतों से झाँककर उस घर में देख रहे थे। जैसे ही उस औरत के चीख़ने की आवाज़ आई बी घर में घुस गईं। उस औरत का ससुर उसको बुरा-भला कह रहा था और उसकी सास उसपर हाथ उठा रही थी। बी ने उन दोनों को बुरा-भला कहना शुरू कर दिया, इतने में उसका ससुर बोला, "बी, ये हमारे घर का मसला है। ये बाहर भागकर क्यों गई थी? आप यहाँ से चली जाएँ।" बी बिना कुछ बोले वहाँ से वापस हो गईं।

बी ने थानेदार को एक ख़त लिखा और लल्लन मियाँ को थाने फ़ौरन भेजा। रात में उन दोनों सास-ससुर को पुलिस ने उठा लिया। सुबह को थानेदार उन दोनों को बी के घर ले आया, कहने लगा, "बी, बताइए इनका क्या करना है?" बी बोलीं, "भाई, अब तो क़ानून का मामला है, मैं क्या बोलूँ।"

वो बोला, "ठीक है, फिर इनका चालान काटकर इन्हें जेल भेजता हूँ।" ये सुनते ही दोनों बी के पैरों पर गिर गए। गिड़गिड़ाने लगे, माफ़ी माँगने लगे। बी ने उनकी तरफ़ नहीं देखा और थानेदार से कहा, "इनको इनके घर छोड़ दीजिए और इनकी बहू से कह देना कि अगली बार वो सीधे आपके पास आए।"

इस मोहल्ले के ज़्यादातर लोग तो वही हैं जो कभी बी के ससुराल में अलग-अलग कामकाज करते थे। कोई बी के ससुराल की

घोड़ागाड़ी पर था, तो कोई बच्चों की देख-रेख करने को, तो कोई ज़मीनों पर जाने के लिए, तो कोई सफ़ाई के लिए। बी का ससुराल एक ज़माने में शहर के बड़े और मशहूर दौलतमंद ख़ानदानों में माना जाता था। लेकिन बी के सामने वक़्त ऐसा बदला कि सब बर्बाद हो गया।

बी के शौहर अभी सात-आठ साल पहले ही गुज़रे लेकिन उन्होंने अपने सामने-सामने सब कुछ फ़ना कर दिया था। बी के शौहर के भाई तो उनसे पहले ही मर गए थे। किसी के बच्चे नहीं हुए तो कोई शादी से पहले ही मर गया। तो सारी विरासत बी के शौहर के ही पास आई। लेकिन वो अपने बीवी और बच्चों को ज़ेहमत नहीं देना चाहते थे इसलिए उन्होंने सब कुछ अपने सामने ही ख़त्म कर दिया। घर से ज़्यादा बाहर वक़्त गुज़ारते थे और लोगों ने उन्हें बेवक़ूफ़ बनाकर ख़ूब फ़ायदा उठाया।

बी के भाई का भला हो, जो उसने जायदाद में बी का हिस्सा नहीं हड़पा और उन्हें जायदाद में से उनका वारिसाना हक़ दे दिया। बी ने उसके ज़रिये अपने ससुराल की विरासत को ही आगे बढ़ाया।

बी के कारोबारी काम-काज की देख-रेख उनके मुंशी प्रेम ने संभाली। प्रेम दरअसल बी के बचपन के दोस्त भी थे। मुंशी प्रेम के वालिद, मुंशी आनंद, बी के अब्बा के मुंशी थे। जब बी को उनके वालिद की जायदाद का हिस्सा मिला तो बी को कुछ मालूम नहीं था कि उसको कैसे संभालें। बी ने कुछ ही वक़्त बाद मुंशी प्रेम को ये ज़िम्मेदारी दी और उनके साथ मिलकर सब कुछ बख़ूबी संभाल लिया। देखते ही देखते ऐसा वक़्त आया कि मुंशी प्रेम की कारोबारी समझ को बी ने पार कर दिया। कुछ सालों में बी की जायदाद उनके भाई से ज़्यादा हो गई।

बी की दो औलादें हुईं, एक बड़ी बेटी नसीम और उससे छोटा बेटा बशारत। नसीम का तो काफ़ी कम उम्र में निकाह हो गया। बशारत सिर्फ़ चार साल छोटा था नसीम से, लेकिन उसका निकाह नसीम के निकाह से बारह साल बाद हुआ।

दरअसल एक रोज़ बशारत अपनी ग्रेजुएशन ख़त्म करके बी से कहने लगा, "मुझे कारोबार करना है।" बी ख़ुश होकर बोलीं- "शाब्बाश बेटे, दिल ख़ुश कर दिया आपने मेरा। क्या शुरू कर रहे हो?"

"सोच रहा हूँ पीतल के शोपीस बनाने का कारखाना डाल दूँ," बशारत ने ख़ुशी-ख़ुशी बताया।

"चलो इस बहाने हम भी घर सजा लेंगे।" बी ने हौसलाअफ़ज़ाई करते हुए कहा।

"अरे आपका ही होगा वो कारोबार, बी आप कैसी बात कर रही हैं।" बशारत बोला।

"भाई, हिसाब-किताब में साफ़ रहना चाहिए। बच्चे जो कमाते हैं, वह उनका ही होता है। आपका ख़ुद का कारोबार होगा। पैसा आपका, काम आपका। तो भला मेरा क्यों होगा वो?" बी बोलीं।

"अरे बी, जब पैसा आपका होगा तो आपका ही होगा ना। काम शुरू करने को मैं कहाँ से लाऊँगा इतना सारा पैसा?" बशारत थोड़ा परेशान होकर बोला।

"भाई, मैंने तो कोई ऐसा इरादा नहीं करा है कि आपको कारोबार के लिए पैसे दूँ। पहले कुछ कमाकर दिखा देते तो सोचती।" बी ने ये कहकर साफ़ मना कर दिया।

"बी, कारोबार के लिए पैसे चाहिए होते हैं और उससे ही पैसे कमाए जाते हैं।" झल्लाकर बशारत बोला।

उस दिन बी ने साफ़ कह दिया कि जब तक ख़ुद के पैसे कमाना शुरू नहीं करोगे तब तक निकाह भी नहीं करूँगी। बी ने बशारत का रिश्ता अपनी छोटी बहन की बेटी से बचपन में ही तय कर दिया था। एक रोज़ बेचैन होकर बशारत ने कह दिया कि उसका भी हक़ है जायदाद में। बी ने उसको उसी वक़्त घर से निकाल दिया। वो लड़कर दिल्ली चला गया और अपनी मंगेतर को बोल गया कि वो उसका इंतज़ार ज़रूर करे। बी ने भी अपने दिल को मज़बूत रखा और अपना इरादा नहीं बदला। उधर उनकी छोटी बहन ने भी अपनी बेटी का निकाह कहीं और नहीं किया।

दिल्ली से उसको मौक़ा मिला सउदिया जाने का। वहाँ लगातार चार साल काम करके वो घर वापस आया और शादी करके अपनी बीवी सकीना को भी साथ ले गया।

घर पर सिर्फ़ बी और उनके कामकाज करने वाले थे, जिनमें से फ़रीदन उनकी ख़ास-अम-ख़ास थी। बी को तो ख़ैर वैसे काफ़ी काम रहते थे- किसी की शादी कराना तो कभी ख़ानदान में लोगों के मसले सुलझाना। पैसों से भी लोगों की मदद करती रहती थीं। बी के पास मोहल्ले के बच्चों को सलीक़ा सीखने के लिए उनके घरवाले भेजते थे। इसलिए घर में तो हमेशा रौनक़ रहती थी। जब बी ने अपनी बेटी के ख़त का जवाब देकर अपने नवासे मेहराज को बुलाने का फ़ैसला लिया तो बी के लिए अपने दोनों बच्चों के देख-भाल के बाद घर के किसी बच्चे की देख-रेख की ज़िम्मेदारी सालों बाद आई। बेटी दूसरे शहर में ब्याह कर चली गई और बी तो ख़ैर सिर्फ़ शादी के बाद एक ही बार उसके घर गईं।

बी ने मुंशी प्रेम को बुलवाया और उनसे बात की।

बी ने उनसे कहा, “मुंशी जी, मेरी समझ में यही आया कि बेटे को अगर आने दे रहा है नसीम का शौहर तो कुछ दिल में नरनी आई ही होगी। आपके नज़दीक क्या सही रहेगा, क्या मैं उसको लेने ख़ुद जाऊँ?”

मुंशी प्रेम बड़े ऐहतराम से बोले, “आप तो ख़ुद हर बात हम सब से बेहतर जानती हैं। माफ़ कीजिएगा लेकिन मुझे लगता है आपको नहीं जाना चाहिए।”

बी ने अपने पानदान से निकालकर मुंशी जी को पान देते हुए कहा, “अरे आपकी बात बिलकुल जाइज़ है लेकिन आप ख़ुद सोचिए अगर मैं किसी मुलाज़िम को भेज दूँ और हमारा कमअक़्ल दामाद नाराज़ हो गया तो उस बच्चे को भी नहीं भेजेगा।”

मुँह में पान लेने से पहले मुंशी जी फ़ौरन बोले,“मैं आपकी बात समझ रहा हूँ। मैं तो ख़ैर आपके घर का नहीं हूँ लेकिन अगर आपको ऐतराज़ नहीं हो तो मैं जाकर मेहराज को लेकर आ सकता हूँ।”

“मुंशी जी, आपने ये बात कहकर हमारे दिल का बहुत बड़ा बोझ हटा दिया।” बी ने कहते हुए एक पान अपने मुँह में रखा।

मुंशी प्रेम का पूरा परिवार बी के लिए अपने ख़ून के रिश्ते-जैसा था। मुंशी प्रेम ने बी के दोनों बच्चों को अपनी गोद में खिलाया था। हमेशा उनसे लगाव रखा और उन लोगों के हर कामों में आगे से आगे रहे। इसीलिए उन्होंने बेझिझक मेहराज को लाने के लिए बोल दिया।

नसीम को बी का ख़त मिला और मेहराज की ख़ुशी सातवें आसमान पर हो गई। तेरह साल का मेहराज अपने घर का इकलौता बच्चा था। माँ और दादी की जान तो हलक़ में थी, क्यूँकि मेहराज पहली बार कहीं अकेला जा रहा था और वो भी एक दो हफ़्तों के लिए।

दादी ने मेहराज को समझाना शुरू कर दिया, "बेटे, बहुत तमीज़ से रहना वहाँ जाकर। शैतानी बिलकुल मत करना। वरना लोग कहेंगे कि दादी ने क्या तमीज़ सिखाई है। ऐसे रहना कि सब तारीफ़ें करें कि कितना अच्छा बच्चा है, जिसको माँ और दादी ने बहुत अच्छी परवरिश दी है।"

मेहराज ने मज़ाक़िया अंदाज़ में कहा, "दादी अम्मी, अगर तमीज़ सिखाई होगी तो लोग ऐसा ही बोलेंगे, उसमें इतना सोचने की क्या बात है। आपको मैं तमीज़ का नहीं लगता हूँ क्या?"

दादी ने दिल पर लेते हुए कहा, "नहीं, मेरे जिगर के टुकड़े, ऐसा कब कहा मैंने। आप तो सबसे तमीज़ के बच्चे हैं।"

मेहराज हँसकर बोला, "सही है, फिर मुझे कुछ पैसे दे दीजिए, ग़लत बात होगी अगर मैं बिना पैसों के जाऊँगा।"

मेहराज अपनी दादी के साथ ही हमेशा उनके कमरे में सोया करता था। मेहराज के वालिद मोईन ख़ान अफ़रीदी बचपन से ही मूडी थे। मूड में होते तो वो अपने बेटे से प्यार करते, नहीं होते तो देखते तक नहीं। लेकिन मेहराज उनके साथ बाहर जाने का कोई भी मौक़ा नहीं छोड़ता। दादी भी उसकी ज़िद पूरी करने में कभी पीछे नहीं रहीं और इस बात से नसीम को हमेशा परेशानी रही। नसीम चाहकर भी उसको डाँट नहीं पाई क्यूँकि दादी ऐसा होने नहीं देती थीं।

मोईन ख़ान अफरीदी क़तई नहीं चाहते थे कि मेहराज नानी के घर जाए। लेकिन दादी ने मनवा लिया मोईन ख़ान को। पहली बार मेहराज नानी के घर तब गया था, जब उसकी माँ छिल्ला नहाकर अपने चालीस दिन के बच्चे को लेकर अपने माईके गई थीं। तभी आख़िरी बार मोईन ख़ान भी अपनी ससुराल गए थे। उस दिन बी ने एक दावत रखी थी, जिसमें बी ने तोहफ़े भी दिए। मोईन ख़ान को जिसपर ऐतराज़ हुआ और उन्होंने कहा,"इन तोहफ़ों की कोई ज़रूरत नहीं है। अल्लाह का दिया सब कुछ है।"

अब बी जवाब न देतीं ऐसा तो हो नहीं सकता था, बी कह बैठीं- "तोहफ़ा लेना-देना रिश्ते को मज़बूत करता है।"

जिस पर मोईन ख़ान ग़ुस्से में बौखला गए और बोले, "तो आप ये तोहफ़े देकर रिश्ता ख़रीदना चाहती हैं? हम आपके लिए तोहफ़े नहीं लाए तो इसका मतलब हुआ हम रिश्ता अच्छा बनाना नहीं चाहते?"

बी थोड़ी देर ख़ामोश रहकर बोलीं, "अगर दामाद नहीं होते और मेरे अपने बेटे होते तो इसका जवाब ज़रूर देती।"

मोईन ख़ान फ़ौरन खड़े होकर बोले, "नसीम, तुम्हें अपनी माँ के जवाब सुनने हैं तो रुको, नहीं तो मेहराज को उठाओ और घर चलो मेरे साथ।"

जिसके बाद मोईन ख़ान न ख़ुद बी के यहाँ गए और न अपने बच्चे को जाने दिया।

बहुत लोगों ने बात करने की कोशिश की लेकिन बात बनी नहीं। बी भी आख़िर में थक गईं और बात संभलवाने की कोशिश करना बंद कर दी। मोईन ख़ान और बी का ही कुछ मसला है, जो कभी समझ

नहीं आया कि आख़िर हुआ क्या था। लेकिन ये दोनों एक-दूसरे को शुरू से ही बर्दाश्त नहीं कर पाए। मेहराज जब बड़ा हुआ तो अपने स्कूल, आस पड़ोस के बच्चों को नानी के घर जाते देखता था। एक वक़्त आया जब वो ज़िद पर अड़ गया नानी के घर जाने की।

एक रोज़ मोईन ख़ान को उनकी माँ ने अपने कमरे में बात करने को बुलाया और कहा, "मोईन बेटे, तुमने ये आख़िरी बची हुई ज़मीन का टुकड़ा बेचने का दिल बना लिया? अच्छे से सोच लिया है? मतलब इसके बाद कुछ बचेगा नहीं।"

मोईन ख़ान तसल्ली देते हुए बोले, "अम्मी, मैं तो सबके ख़याल का ही सोच रहा हूँ। कारोबार इस बार दिल से करूँगा वरना घर चल नहीं पाएगा। आपकी फ़िक्र जाइज़ है।"

अम्मी कुछ देर ख़ामोश रहकर बोलीं, "नहीं, अगर आपने सच्चे दिल से इरादा किया है तो मुझे तो ख़ुशी ही होगी लेकिन इस बार अगर कुछ चूक हो गई तो संभल नहीं पाएँगे हम लोग। पहले भी हमेशा आपने यही किया है और हम सब जानते हैं कि हर बार ज़मीन बेचने का नतीजा क्या हुआ है।"

मोईन ख़ान ग़ुस्से में कुर्सी से उठने लगे। उनकी अम्मी माहौल को ठंडा करते हुए बोलीं, "बेटे, मुझसे ज़्यादा कौन ख़ुश होगा अगर आपका इतना नेक इरादा हो गया है। आज तक लोगों से आपकी बुराइयाँ सुन-सुनकर मुझसे और आपकी बीवी नसीम से ज़्यादा कौन शर्माया है।"

मोईन ख़ान ग़ुस्से में बोले, "अम्मी, आप अपनी बात करिए, उसकी बात करने से कोई फ़ायदा नहीं है। अपनी माँ के जैसी एकदम तेज़ तर्रार औरत है। बच्चा है इसीलिए घर में है और आपकी ख़िदमत की

ख़ातिर। एक बार अपनी माँ या भाई को बुरा कहने के लिए तैयार नहीं होती। उन लोगों ने मेरी कभी इज़्ज़त नहीं की लेकिन इसने मेरी तरफ़दारी आज तक नहीं की।"

उनकी अम्मी समझाते हुए बोलीं, "देखो, इंसान को अपना दिल बड़ा करना चाहिए और पुरानी बातों को भूलकर आगे बढ़ना चाहिए। नसीम तो बेचारी अच्छी है, इतना सब ख़याल रखती है और तुम्हारे ही तो साथ है, कभी घर नहीं जाती क्यूँकि तुम्हारी मर्ज़ी नहीं है।"

मोईन ख़ान उनकी बात काटते हुए बोले, "अम्मी, उसको मना नहीं किया है, मैंने सिर्फ़ ख़ुद और अपने बेटे का जाना बंद किया था। लेकिन उसने ये सब ख़ुद किया है कि अगर मेरे शौहर नहीं जाएँगे तो मैं भी नहीं जाऊँगी। ये घर जाती और अपनी माँ से कहती वो मुझसे माफ़ी माँगें तो बात कब की सही हो चुकी होती।" और कमरे के दरवाज़े की तरफ़ बढ़ने लगे।

जिसपर उनकी अम्मी बोलीं, "चलो छोड़ो, बस मेरी एक बात है, अगर सच में आप अब संजीदगी से ज़िन्दगी जीना चाहते हैं, और चाहते हैं कि मैं अपने हिस्से की ये आख़िरी ज़मीन बेचकर आपका कारोबार कराऊँ, तो आप मेरी एक बात मत नकारिएगा।"

मोईन ख़ान कमरे के दरवाज़े की तरफ़ बढ़ते-बढ़ते ये सुनकर रुके और पलटकर हैरानी से अपनी माँ को देखने लगे।

उनकी अम्मी बोलीं, "मेहराज कई महीने से अपनी नानी के घर जाना चाहता है। अब बच्चा बड़ा हो रहा है, उसपर बुरा असर पढ़ेगा अगर ये सब बातें उसकी समझ में आने लगेंगी। मेरा इरादा है कि अब उसको छुट्टियों में भेज दिया जाए।"

मोईन ख़ान बोले, "अम्मी, आप क्यों मेरी बात ख़राब करवाना चाहती हैं। मेरा बेटा क्यों जाएगा, जहाँ मैं नहीं जाना चाहता?"

"बेटे, मैं भी एक माँ हूँ और बहुत सारे काम करती हूँ, जो मेरा दिल नहीं करता और सिर्फ़ इसलिए करती हूँ क्यूँकि उसमें मेरे बच्चों की ख़ुशी होती है।" उनकी अम्मी ने अपना पानदान उठाते हुए कहा।

मोईन ख़ान समझदार इंसान थे, फ़ौरन समझ गए कि उनकी माँ का इशारा कहाँ था। डर गए कि कहीं उनकी अम्मी ज़मीन बेचने का इरादा बदल न दें। कुछ ही देर में वो कह गए- "अम्मी अब आपकी मर्ज़ी के आगे मैं क्या ही बोल सकता हूँ। अगर आपको बेहतर लगे तो भिजवा दीजिए। उसकी माँ भी अगर जाना चाहे, तो वो भी जा सकती है।"

ऐसे हुआ मेहराज का अपनी नानी के घर जाने का फ़ैसला।

मेहराज को नये कपड़े सिलवाने के लिए मोईन ख़ान उसको बाज़ार लेकर गए। कई क़मीज़ें और पतलून सिलवाई गईं और कुछ कुर्ते-पजामे भी। मेहराज की तैयारी ज़ोरों पर होने लगी।

मेहराज की दादी ने उसकी माँ नसीम से भी कहा, "दुल्हन अगर तुम चाहो तो तुम भी चली जाओ। मैंने मोईन से बात कर ली है, उसको तो कोई ऐतराज़ नहीं है।"

नसीम थोड़ी देर ख़ामोश रहकर बोली, "अम्मी, मैं नहीं जाना चाहती। अब तो ज़माने में मेरा मज़ाक़ बन ही चुका है। किसी की शादी हो या कोई ख़ुशी हो, कभी गई ही नहीं। अब क्या करूँगी जाकर। मेहराज चला जाए और मेरी दुआ है उसका भी एक बार में ही अरमान पूरा हो जाए कि दोबारा जाने की बात ही न करे।"

नसीम की सास बोली, "दुल्हन, वक़्त लगता है लेकिन सब्र का फल मीठा ही मिलता है। देखना मेरा दिल कह रहा है कि जल्द ही सब ठीक होने वाला है। अल्लाह तुम्हें अब ख़ूब सुकून देने वाला है।"

नसीम अपनी आँखों में आँसू भरे बोली, "अम्मी, मैंने अब इसी को अपनी असलियत मान कर सब्र कर लिया है। कुछ हो-न-हो, ज़िन्दगी कट गई, और जितनी बची है, वो भी कट जाएगी।"

सास चाय की प्याली रखकर बोली, "बेटे, ऐसी बुझे दिल की बातें नहीं करते हैं। अभी तो तुम्हें अपनी औलादों की ख़ुशियाँ देखनी है। तुम मेरा और इस घर का बहुत ख़्याल रखती हो। मुझे तो तुम अपनी सगी बेटी से कम नहीं लगी कभी और न ही मुझे तुमसे कोई शिकायत है।"

नसीम उस पर बोली, "अम्मी, मैंने तो वैसे कोई भी ऐसा काम नहीं किया है, जिससे किसी को शिकायत हो। आपसे हमेशा बहुत ढारस मिली है, तभी मैं रह पाई हूँ इस घर में।"

यह कहकर नसीम चाय की प्याली उठाकर कमरे से चली गई।

मुमताज़ बेगम के पास बशारत का ख़त आया, जिसमें उसने अपने और सकीना के आने की इत्तिला दी थी। बी के ऊपर एक नय काम आ गया, उन्होंने फ़ौरन फ़रीदन और रुख़साना को लेकर बशारत के कमरों की सफ़ाई शुरू कर दी।

बातूनी फ़रीदन का चुप रहना मुश्किल था, उसने बी से सवाल करना शुरू कर दिए।

फ़रीदन ने पूछा, "बी, आपका इतना बड़ा मकान है फिर आपने बशारत भाई के लिए नये कमरे और दालान क्यों बनवाया?"

बी बशारत के दालान में बैठी चादरें और रज़ाइयाँ देख रही थीं। उन्होंने मुस्कुराते हुए कहा, "फ़रीदन, तुझे ख़ामोश न रहने का बहाना चाहिए होता है। नये-नये सवाल ढूँढकर लाती है।"

रुख़साना अपने दुपट्टे से मुँह ढके हुए छड़ी से कमरे के जाले साफ़ कर रही थी। वो फ़रीदन को देखकर हँसी।

फ़रीदन खिड़कियों से परदे उतारते-उतारते रुक गई और बोली, "बी, आप मेरा मज़ाक़ क्यों उड़ाती रहती हैं।"

बी हँसते हुए कहने लगी, "ख़ुशनसीब लोग होते हैं, जो दूसरों को हँसने का मौक़ा देते हैं।"

इसपर रुख़साना का ठहाका नहीं रुक पाया और बी ने उससे कहा,"रुख़साना, ज़्यादा मुँह खोलकर हँसोगी तो धूल-मिट्टी मुँह में घुस जाएगी।"

फिर बी ने फ़रीदन की बात का जवाब दिया, "अरे यहाँ पर पहले भी दो कमरे और दालान था लेकिन काफ़ी पुराना हो गया था। इसमें बशारत के चाचा रहा करते थे। उनका और उनकी बीवी का जल्दी ही इंतेक़ाल हो गया था। फिर ये कमरे हमेशा ही बंद पड़े रहे।"

फ़रीदन खिड़की से कूदकर नीचे आई और बी से पूछने लगी, "बी, फिर आपने क्यों दिया ये बशारत भाई को। मेरी दोस्त बता रही थी कि कुछ जगहें मनहूस होती हैं।"

बी चादरें एक तरफ़ रखकर बोलीं, "ऐसी बातें इंसान को कमज़ोर बनाती हैं। ये सब शिर्क की बातें हैं। अल्लाह पर भरोसा रखना चाहिए इंसान को।"

फ़रीदन थोड़ी देर सोचकर बोली, "ख़ैर आपने इसको नया करवा दिया, ये सही किया।"

बी ने बताया, "मैंने नहीं कराया, तुम्हारे बशारत भाई से साफ़ बोल दिया था कि तुम्हें अपनी शादी पर सब कुछ ख़ुद ही करना होगा।"

फ़रीदन हैरान होकर बोली, "बी, क्या आप मेरी शादी भी तब ही करेंगी, जब मैं ख़ुद पैसे कमाने लगूँगी?"

बी अपनी हँसी को रोक नहीं पाईं और फिर कुछ देर बाद बोलीं, "नहीं, ऐसा नहीं करूँगी लेकिन जब तक तुम और रुख़साना बी. ए. पास नहीं करोगी, तब तक नहीं करूँगी।

लल्लन मियाँ अंदर दौड़े-दौड़े बताने आए कि, "बी, आपसे मिलने मुंशी जी आए हैं।" बी ने मुंशी प्रेम को अंदर बुलाया। मौसम चल रहा था धान उठने का और बी के खेतों के बासमती के चावल हमेशा बहुत अच्छी कमाई देते रहे थे। बी ने मुंशी प्रेम से पूछा, "मुंशी जी, फ़सल का क्या रहा। सुना है इस बार बहुत भारी फ़सल निकल रही है। क्या भाव मिला?"

मुंशी प्रेम का चेहरा नीचे ही झुका रहा।

बी ने दोबारा पूछा, "क्या हुआ मुंशी जी, सब ख़ैरियत है? कुछ बोलिए।"

मुंशी प्रेम बहुत हल्के से बोले, "बी, वो एक हादसा हो गया।"

"हाय क्या हुआ, सब ख़ैरियत से तो है?" बी ने अपने हाथ का पंखा झलते-झलते रोक दिया।

मुंशी प्रेम घबराकर बोले, "बी, वो फ़सल कल कट गई थी, आज धान निकालने थे पर ख़ुदा जाने सुबह-सुबह उसमें आग लग गई और सारी कटी हुई फ़सल जल गई।"

बी ने सुकून की साँस ली और बोलीं, "आपने मुझे डरा दिया था। माल है, आता-जाता रहता है। किसी की क्या ग़लती? हवा तेज़ चल गई होगी। एक चिंगारी भी काफ़ी होती है सूखी हुई फ़सल को जलाने के लिए।"

मुंशी प्रेम बोले, "बात वो नहीं है दरअसल मसला है नगद का और दो-तीन जगह पैसे देने के वादे हैं। ऊपर से बच्चियों की अगले हफ़्ते शादियाँ हैं, उसमें भी खर्च है। और वो बराबर वाली जो दस बीघा ज़मीन ख़रीदी थी, उसके भी बचे हुए पैसे देने हैं वरना बयाना मारा जाएगा।"

बी ने मेज़ पर से प्लेट उठाकर मुंशी जी के सामने बढ़ाई और कहा, "आप परेशान न हों। अल्लाह ज़रूर इसका हल भी दे देगा। मसला आया है तो ज़रूर इसका हल भी निकलेगा। शादियों का तो ख़ैर मैं कर लूँगी। आप उस ज़मीन वाले से बात कीजिए, अगर कुछ वक़्त की मोहलत और मिल जाए तो।" मुंशी जी ने एक सेब की फाँक उठा ली।

मुंशी प्रेम ने दबी आवाज़ में कहा, "मैं अपनी ज़िम्मेदारी अच्छे से पूरी नहीं कर पाया। मैं उसके लिए बहुत शर्मिंदा हूँ। आप जैसा कह रही हैं मैं वैसे ही बात करता हूँ। फिर देखते हैं क्या रहता है।"

चाय का घूँट लेते हुए बी बोलीं, "अब जो हो चुका उसको कोई बदल नहीं सकता। माल का नुक़्सान जान का सदक़ा होता है। ख़ैर आप मेहराज को लेने जाने को कब का सोच रहे हैं? जैसा भी हो मुझे एक दो दिन पहले बता दीजिएगा, कुछ भेज दूँगी नसीम के लिए।"

मेहराज ने नानी के घर जाने का सब दोस्तों को बताना शुरू कर दिया। मेहराज का एक दोस्त उसको बताने लगा कि तुम्हें मालूम है मेरी नानी के घर के पास एक बहुत बड़ा पेड़ है और उस पेड़ पर जिन्नों का साया है। लेकिन मेरे नाना थे ना, वो उस पेड़ के जिन्नों के बच्चों को रात में पढ़ाया करते थे।"

मेहराज हँसते हुए बोला, "कितनी झूठी बातें कर रहा है यार। कम फेंक।"

दोस्त चिढ़कर कहने लगा, "भाई सच में! घर चल अम्मी से पुछवा दूँगा।"

मेहराज थोड़ा सोचकर बोला, "अच्छा मैं भी एक बात बताता हूँ लेकिन किसी और को मत बताना। ठीक है?... वो हमारे जो नाना थे ना, वो शिकार पर बहुत जाते थे। एक बार क्या हुआ कि वो शेर के पीछे बंदूक लेकर भागे। उनके दोस्त पीछे रह गए। शेर झाड़ी में ग़ायब हो गया लेकिन थोड़ी देर बाद झाड़ी में से दो शेर निकल के उनके सामने खड़े हो गए। नाना ने बन्दूक देखी, उसमें सिर्फ़ एक गोली थी और उनकी जेब में एक चाकू पड़ा था। उन्होंने दोनों शेरों के बीच में चाकू फेंका और चाकू पर गोली मारी। गोली चाकू से दो टुकड़ों में हो गई और दोनों शेरों को एक-एक गोली का टुकड़ा लग गया। मेरे नाना ने एक गोली से दो शेरों का शिकार कर लिया।"

"ओ झूठों के सरदार मेहराज ख़ान साहब, आपका घर आ गया। अब कुछ वक़्त तुम लोगों की छुट्टियों में कानों को सुकून मिल जाएगा।" ये कहते हुए उसके स्कूल के रिक्शावाले ने उसे घर पर उतार दिया।

अगले दिन मुंशी प्रेम मेहराज को लेने पहुँच गए। मुंशी जी ने मेहराज की दादी से पूछा, "मोईन ख़ान नहीं दिख रहे हैं। कहाँ हैं?"

दादी ने बताया "वो सुबह-सुबह काम पर चला गया लेकिन आ जाएगा थोड़ी देर में।"

मुंशी जी ख़ुश होकर पूछे, "तो आजकल क्या मसरूफ़ियत है उनकी?"

दादी केतली से मुंशी जी के कप में चाय डालते हुए बोलीं-"प्रेम भाई, बेचारे के साथ पता नहीं क्या रहता है। पिछले तीन कारोबार बर्बाद हो गए। मेहनत भी करता है। पर जब काम ख़राब होने लगता है तो चिड़चिड़ाहट में ग़लत फ़ैसले कर जाता है।"

मुंशी जी एक थैला दादी के हाथ में देते हुए बोले, "ये बी ने आपको देने के लिए कहा था। चलें हमारी तो दुआ है कि मोईन ख़ान का कारोबार जम जाए। कारोबार में मिज़ाज का ताल्लुक़ बहुत बड़ा रहता है।"

दादी ने थैला लेते हुए कहा, "मुमताज़ और उसके तौर-तरीक़े कभी नहीं बदल सकते। वैसे जागीरदार लोगों के मिज़ाज तो ख़ैर मुश्किल से ही बदलते हैं। इसलिए मोईन को भी मुश्किल हो रही है।"

मुंशी जी समझदार इंसान थे फ़ौरन समझ गए कि दादी का इशारा कहाँ था। उन्होंने चाय की प्याली रखते हुए बात बदलने की कोशिश की,

"नसीम कहाँ गईं? उनको बुला दें। मेहराज तो बाहर दरवाज़े पर मिले थे, कह रहे थे एक दोस्त से मिलकर आ रहा हूँ।"

मेहराज इतने में भागता हुआ घर आया और अपनी माँ को आवाज़ देते हुए उनके पास बावर्चीख़ाने में चला गया, "अम्मी आप बहुत अच्छी हैं आपने मेरी बात मान ली। मैं अब वापस आकर आपका हर कहना मानूँगा क्यूँकि आप मुझे नानी के घर भेज रही हैं।" और उसने नसीम के कंधे पर सर रख दिया।

नसीम बिरयानी के भगोने का ढक्कन ढककर मेहराज को गले लगाकर उसके माथे पर प्यार करने लगी और कहने लगी, "तुम ही तो मेरे जीने का सहारा हो, तुम्हारी ख़ुशी से ज़्यादा क्या हो सकता है? अब तो तुम्हारा क़द भी मुझसे कुछ ही कम रह गया है। जल्दी-जल्दी जवान हो रहा है मेरा शहज़ादा।"

मेहराज अपनी माँ की आँखों को गीला देखकर बोला, "अम्मी क़द लम्बा होने की वजह से आप तो रोने लगीं।"

नसीम हँसकर बोली, "नानी के घर शैतानी मत करना। उनको परेशान मत करना और यहाँ की कोई भी बात किसी को मत बताना।"

"जी जी, ठीक है", कहता हुआ मेहराज वहाँ से चला गया।

मेहराज सवार होने से पहले दादी से मिलने उनके कमरे में गया। मुंशी प्रेम और नसीम दरवाज़े पर खड़े बात करने लगे।

मुंशी जी ने जेब में से एक लिफ़ाफ़ा निकालकर नसीम को दिया। नसीम ने लिफ़ाफ़ा खोला, जिसमें उसके बचपन की तस्वीरें थीं। नसीम ख़ुश होकर बोली, "अरे ये आपके पास कहाँ से आईं?"

मुंशी जी तस्वीर देखते हुए बोले, "मैं ही तो लाया था इस फ़ोटोग्राफर को जब आप दसवीं में पास हुई थीं। याद है? बी ने दावत रखी थी। कितनी ख़ुश थीं बी उस दिन।"

नसीम ने तस्वीरें वापस रख दीं और कहा, "हाँ, और उसके कुछ वक़्त बाद ही मैंने उनकी ख़ुशियाँ छीन लीं।" पीछे से मेहराज आया और मुंशी जी का हाथ पकड़कर कहने लगा- "चलिए अब मुंशी नाना।" नसीम ने उनको सवार करा दिया और अपने कमरे में जाकर अपनी बचपन की तस्वीरें देखकर रोती रही।

मेहराज और मुंशी जी रेलवे स्टेशन की बेंच पर बैठकर ट्रेन का इंतज़ार करने लगे। मेहराज ने घबराते हुए मुंशी जी से पूछा, "यहाँ इतनी सारी ट्रेनें आ रही हैं। लोग तो ग़लत ट्रेन में बैठ के पता नहीं कहाँ चले जाते होंगे?"

मुंशी जी हँसते हुए बोले, "आप कितनी बार ग़लत जगह पहुँचे हैं?"

मेहराज अपने बैग को अपने पैरों के बीच में दबाते हुए बोला, "बिना कभी स्टेशन आए कैसे ग़लत जगह पहुँचता। पता है एक बार मैं अब्बा के साथ बस से गया। बस में जगह ही नहीं थी तो मैं ड्राइवर के साथ बैठ के गया। क्या मज़ा आया था।"

मुंशी जी हँस कर बोले, "चलो आज ट्रेन में भी बैठ जाएँगे आप। देखते हैं सही जगह पहुँचेंगे या ग़लत।"

मेहराज बोला, "क्यों आप भी पहली बार जा रहे हैं?"

इतनी देर में वहाँ प्लेटफ़ॉर्म पर कुछ नट अपने करतब दिखाने लगे। मेहराज तो उनके बिलकुल क़रीब जाकर खड़ा हो गया और देखने लगा। मुंशी जी बैग की हिफाज़त करते रहे और मेहराज को देखते रहे। जैसे ही करतब ख़त्म हुआ मेहराज बेंच पर वापस आया। मेहराज के पीछे-पीछे एक नट बच्चा अपनी थाली लेकर आ गया, जिसमें वो लोगों से पैसे ले रहा था। मेहराज उसकी थाली को देखता रहा और वो बच्चा थाली को उसके मुँह के सामने घुमाता रहा। मुंशी जी ने जेब से निकाल कर उसकी थाली में कुछ सिक्के डाले। मेहराज फ़ौरन बोला, "अम्मी ने मना किया है कि माँगने वालों को पैसे नहीं देते हैं। आपको नहीं पता है ये बात?" और उसने अपने थैले में से केला निकाल कर उसकी थाली में रख दिया। वो बच्चा वहाँ से चला गया।

मुंशी जी बोले, "जी मैं भी नहीं देता हूँ। लेकिन वो बच्चा अपने नाटक के टिकट के पैसे लेने आया था, जिसका आपने कूद-कूदकर लुत्फ़ उठाया।"

मुंशी जी ने ख़ूब बातें कीं, जिससे मेहराज उनके साथ थोड़ा घुल -मिल गया। ट्रेन आई तो मुंशी जी उठने लगे। मेहराज भी डरते-डरते उठा। मुंशी जी ने उसका बैग उठा लिया। बोगी में घुसते वक़्त मेहराज ने अपने बराबर खड़े यात्री से पूछा, "ये ट्रेन कहाँ जा रही है।"

उसने जगह का नाम बताया और मेहराज से पूछा, "आपको कहाँ जाना है?" मुंशी जी बराबर खड़े मुस्कुराते रहे।

मेहराज बोला, "मुझे तो नानी के घर जाना है।"

ट्रेन में बैठने की देर थी कि मेहराज ने मुंशी जी की नाक में दम कर दिया कि, "मुझे खिड़की पर बैठना है।"

मुंशी जी बेहद संजीदा मिज़ाज के इंसान थे, उनकी समझ में नहीं आ रहा था कि कैसे किसी को कहें कि खिड़की वाली सीट दे दो। मेहराज के सब्र का पारा ऊपर चढ़ा और उसने ख़ुद ही जाकर खिड़की पर बैठी औरत से कह दिया, "आप ट्रेन में पहली बार बैठी हैं?"

वो चिढ़कर बोली "नहीं! पर इस बात का क्या मतलब हुआ?"

मेहराज बोला, "तब ठीक है। आप मुझे यहाँ पर बैठने दीजिए क्यूँकि मैं पहली बार ट्रेन में बैठा हूँ।" उस औरत ने मुस्कुराकर मेहराज को अपने पास बिठा लिया।

नसीम ने मेहराज को बताया था कि रास्ते में एक नदी पड़ेगी और जब पुल पर ट्रेन दौड़ती है, तो पानी देखना बहुत ख़ूबसूरत लगता है। नदी के पार एक मंदिर दिखाई देता है, जिसका नदी पर गिरता हुआ अक्स बहुत ख़ूबसूरत लगता है। अपनी माँ को वापस जाकर ये सब ख़त के ज़रिये लिखना भी था। इसलिए मेहराज के लिए खिड़की पर बैठना और ज़रूरी हो गया था। सफ़र तो ख़ैर सिर्फ़ चार घंटे का ही था। सड़क से तो सिर्फ़ डेढ़ घंटा ही लगता पर सड़क बरसात के बाद नदी में बदल जाती है। बरसात गुज़रने के अगले तीन-चार महीनों तक पानी-कीचड़ ख़त्म नहीं होता। इसलिए पैसेंजर ट्रेन से सफ़र करना पड़ता है, जो हर छोटे-बड़े स्टेशन पर रुकती हुई जाती है। जहाँ भी ड्राइवर का मूड हो, ट्रेन रुक गई। न चाहते हुए भी इंसान ख़ुद-ब-ख़ुद सोने लगता है। ट्रेन की धीमी गति लोरी का काम करती है। मेहराज को जैसे ही नींद का झोंका आया उसने अपने थैले से पानी निकालकर पिया फिर उसमें से एक स्टील का टिफ़िन निकाला, जिसमें नसीम ने अपने बेटे के पहले सफ़र के लिए पराठे और हलवा बाँधकर दिया था। मेहराज ने बराबर बैठी औरत से कहा, "मेरी अम्मी ने हलवा पराठा बनाकर दिया है। आपने मुझे सीट दी है, आप भी खाइए।"

वो औरत मना करने लगी तो उसने कहा, "हमारी अम्मी कहती हैं खाना बाँटे बिना नहीं खाना चाहिए। खाकर देखिए आपकी अम्मी भी इतना अच्छा खाना नहीं बनाती होंगी।"

सामने बैठे मुंशी जी ने उस औरत से कहा, "बेफ़िक्र रहिए शुद्ध शाकाहारी ही है।" मेहराज बोला, "नहीं-नहीं हलवा पराठा है।" उस औरत ने एक पराठा और हलवा ले लिया। मेहराज ने इधर-उधर बर्थ पर बैठे लोगों को दिया कुछ ने खाया कुछ ने मना कर दिया। किसी के मुँह में पान था तो किसी को मीठा पसंद नहीं था। उस औरत ने मुंशी जी से पूछा, "ये आपके बेटे हैं?" जितनी देर में मुंशी जी कुछ कहते मेहराज बोल पड़ा, "अरे नहीं ये तो हमारे मुंशी नाना हैं। हमारे अब्बा तो इतने गुस्सेनाक हैं कि अब तक मुझे कितना डाँट चुके होते।" मुंशी जी और उस औरत के समझ में ही नहीं आया कि क्या बोलें। मुंशी जी ने फ़ौरन बात बदलते हुए उस औरत से कहा, "आप और पराठा लीजिए।" उसने शुक्रिया कह कर नना कर दिया। थोड़ी देर बाद मुंशी जी की और उस औरत की आँख लग गई। ट्रेन, पानी के पुल से जब गुज़र चुकी और मेहराज पेड़ों को उल्टी तरफ़ दौड़ता हुआ देखकर थक गया तो वो सीट से उठ गया और ट्रेन का मुआइना करने निकल गया। उसको एक बोगी से दूसरी बोगी में जाने का रास्ता दिखा। वो फ़ौरन दूसरी बोगी की तरफ़ निकल गया लेकिन थोड़ी देर में उसको लगा कि वो ट्रेन के उल्टी दिशा में जा रहा है। उसे डर लगा कि कहीं वो वापस घर की तरफ़ न चला जाए। वो पलट कर दूसरी तरफ़ चलने लगा। दिल में सोचने लगा कि अगर अम्मी भी होतीं तो कितना मज़ा आता। क्यूँकि उसने माँ के साथ कभी सफ़र ही नहीं किया था। सोचने लगा बड़े होकर ख़ूब पैसे कमाऊँगा और अम्मी को ख़ूब घुमाऊँगा।

अगले डिब्बे में टीटी टिकट चेक कर रहा था। उसने एक आदमी को पकड़ा, "बिना टिकट अपने बाप की ट्रेन समझ के घुस जाते हो?"

वह आदमी बोला, "साहब मैं टिकट लेने खिड़की पर खड़ा था पर वहाँ भीड़ थी और ट्रेन निकल रही थी इसलिए घुस गया।" मेहराज ये सब दूर से देख रहा था।

"हाँ तुम्हारे घर पर टिकट भिजवाना चाहिए। हमारी ही ग़लती है। चालान काटके तुम्हें जेल भेजेंगे।" टीटी उस आदमी से बोला।

टीटी ने पुलिसवाले को इशारा किया। पुलिसवाले ने उस आदमी का कॉलर पकड़ लिया और आगे लेके जाने लगा। मेहराज ने किसी से पूछा- "ये क्या हो रहा है?" तो उसने बताया- "ये आदमी बिना टिकट ट्रेन में चढ़ गया इसलिए टीटी ने उसको पकड़वा दिया।" मेहराज बोला, "अब इसका क्या होगा, इसको कहाँ लेकर जाएँगे?"

"इसको अब जेल भेजा जाएगा। तुम्हारे पास टिकट है वरना तुम्हें भी जेल भेज देंगे।" वो आदमी हँसते हुए मेहराज से बोला।

फिर उसको टीटी और पुलिस से नफ़रत होने लगी क्यूँकि वो उस बिना टिकट के आदमी को छोड़ नहीं रहे थे। थोड़ी देर बाद ट्रेन रुकी और उस स्टेशन पर उस आदमी को पुलिसवाले ने स्टेशन के एक पुलिसवाले को दे दिया। फिर टीटी और पुलिसवाला आगे बढ़ गए टिकट चेक करने। मेहराज सोचने लगा कि क्या ये इसी ट्रेन में रहते हैं? तभी ये किसी को भी बिना टिकट यहाँ नहीं रहने देते। वो यही सोचता रहा और उनके पीछे-पीछे चलता रहा। पर उसे कहीं उनका घर नहीं दिखा। उसे देखना था कि इन दोनों का घर और घरवाले कहाँ हैं। मेहराज पानी की बोतल साथ में लिए हुए था, जिसे उसने लगभग ख़ाली कर लिया था। घबरा-घबराकर पानी के बड़े-बड़े

घूँट पी रहा था। काफ़ी देर वह उन दोनों के पीछे चलता रहा लेकिन उसको उनका घर नहीं दिखाई दिया। इतने में उसको टॉयलेट जाने की ज़रूरत पेश आई। वो गया तो उसने देखा कि वो बेहद गन्दा था। उसको उसकी माँ और दादी ने इतनी सफ़ाई, पाकी और-नापाकी सिखाई थी कि वह गन्दा टॉयलेट उससे बर्दाश्त नहीं हो रहा था। पान की पीक से घिरा हुआ और बेसिन में पानी भरा हुआ। लेकिन जब उसको सीट के छेद से पटरी दिखी तो वो हैरान हो गया। जैसे तैसे करके उसने पेशाब करने की कोशिश की इतने में ट्रेन ने झटका लिया और रुक गई, जिस वजह से उसकी पतलून पेशाब से गीली हो गई। उसकी समझ में नहीं आ रहा था कि वह क्या करे। वह टॉयलेट में बंद रोता रहा। वह पेशाब में सना हुआ तो कभी भी बाहर नहीं जा सकता था। ट्रेन अलग-अलग स्टेशन पर रुकती रही और मेहराज डरता रहा कि कहीं मुंशी जी उसको बिना लिए न चले जाएँ।

उधर मुंशी जी की भी आँख खुल गई और उन्होंने देखा मेहराज अपनी सीट पर नहीं है। मुंशी जी ने उस औरत से पूछा, बोली मेरी भी आँख लग गई थी। मुंशी जी ने उसको ढूँढना शुरू कर दिया- एक बोगी से दूसरी बोगी, लेकिन मेहराज का कहीं पता नहीं लगा। अलग-अलग बोगियों में लोगों से बात करते हुए पूछते रहे। कुछ लोगों ने बताया- देखा तो था एक बच्चे को। उन्हें डर था कि कहीं वो ग़लती से किसी स्टेशन पर उतर तो नहीं गया। उनसे एक ज़िम्मेदारी नहीं सम्भली, क्या कहेंगे वो जाकर बी से! हर एक टॉयलेट देख लिया पर वो कहीं नहीं दिखा।

एक टॉयलेट काफ़ी देर से बंद था, वो उसके बाहर खड़े हो गए। जब कोई नहीं निकला तो उन्होंने धबधबाया और मेहराज को आवाज़ दी। मेहराज ने रोते हुए अपना मुँह बाहर निकाला, "मैं यहाँ हूँ मुंशी नाना।"

उन दोनों की जान में जान आई।

मुंशी जी बोले, "अंदर क्या कर रहे हो, चलो स्टेशन आने वाला है।"

मेहराज रोते हुए बोला, "मैं बाहर नहीं निकलूँगा क्यूँकि मेरी पतलून पेशाब से सन गई।"

"अरे बेटे कोई बात नहीं आ जाओ ऐसे ही। घर चलकर बदल लेना अब।" मुंशी जी ने उसको समझाया।

उसने कहा, "मैं बाहर नहीं निकलूँगा, मुझे बहुत शर्म आ रही है।"

मुंशी जी बोले, "रुको मैं तुम्हारे बैग में से कपड़े लाता हूँ।" मुंशी जी ने उसको लाकर साफ़ पतलून दी।

मेहराज ने लेकिन पतलून लेने से मना करते हुआ कहा, "मैं बाहर ही नहीं निकलूँगा जब तक मुंशी नाना आप मुझसे वादा नहीं करेंगे।"

"अरे बेटे बोलो क्या वादा करूँ।" मुंशी जी बेचैन होकर बोले।

मेहराज रोता हुआ बोला, "आप किसी को ये बात कभी नहीं बताएँगे।"

मुंशी जी ने उसे भरोसा दिलाया। उसने पतलून पहनी और अपना मुँह साफ़ करके सूजी हुई आँखें लेकर बाहर निकला। जैसे ही वो अपनी सीट पर पहुँचे तब तक उनका स्टेशन आ चुका था। स्टेशन से घर दस मिनट ही दूर था।

मेहराज जब सूजी हुई आँखें लेकर अपनी नानी के घर पहुँचा तो वो परेशान हो गईं।

बी को लगा कि मेहराज रोता हुआ आया है और उसको माँ की याद आने लगी होगी।

बी बोलीं, “मेहराज बेटे, ट्रेन में मज़ा आया?”

वो मुंशी जी को देखते हुए बोला, “जी, बहुत मज़ा आया। मैं तो खिड़की पर बैठकर आया हूँ।”

बी ने अपने होठों से पान की लाली साफ़ करते हुआ कहा, “बड़ी ख़ूबसूरत नदी पड़ती है और उसके पीछे एक मंदिर है, जो बहुत चमकता हैं। देखा आपने वो?”

“हाँ अम्मी ने भी बताया था लेकिन आज वो चमक नहीं रहा था।” मेहराज मायूसी से बोला।

उसपर मुंशी जी बोले, “अरे बादल थे। अगर धूप होती तो चमकता।”

मेहराज तो वैसे ही शरमाया हुआ था क्यूँकि पहली बार अपनी नानी से मिल रहा था। ऊपर से इतना बड़ा हादसा हो गया था उसके साथ ट्रेन में। डर था उसको कि कहीं ये बात नानी को न मालूम हो जाए। शर्म में वो यहाँ रह कैसे पाएगा। इतने में नानी ने फ़रीदन से कहा कि मेहराज के नहाने का इंतज़ाम कर दे। मेहराज को लगा कि इनको कैसे मालूम हो गया? वो तो मुंशी जी और नानी के साथ ही बैठा था, फिर उनको कैसे पता लगा! मेहराज को उठकर जाना पड़ा नहाने के लिए। मुंशी जी ने बी को एक ख़त देकर कहा, “नसीम ने आपको ये ख़त भेजा है।”

फ़िर वो ये कहते हुए खड़े हुए ,“वो मैं कल जाकर ज़मीन वाले लोगों से बात करूँगा।” बी ने उनको भरोसा देते हुए कहा, “आप फ़िलहाल अपने घर जाकर आराम करें। हर काम का वक़्त होता है। ये ज़मीन का मसला भी हल हो जाएगा अपने वक़्त पर।” मुंशी जी बिना कुछ बोले चले गए।

लेकिन मेहराज पूरे वक़्त डरता रहा कि अब नानी के पास जाऊँगा तो उनको पता चल चुका होगा जो कुछ ट्रेन में हुआ।

ख़ैर मेहराज जैसे-तैसे करके वापस आया तो नानी अम्मी ने उससे कहा कि, "बेटे, कभी भी सफ़र से आओ तो सबसे पहले नहा लेना चाहिए। सफ़र में बहुत गंदगी होती है, आपके कपड़ों और बदन पर लग जाती है।"

मेहराज तो सिर्फ़ सर हिला कर हाँ-हाँ किए जा रहा था। जैसा कि उसकी अम्मी ने कहा था कि नानी का कहना मानना। लेकिन ये शुरुआत थी सिर्फ़। इसके बाद शुरू हुआ, मुमताज़ बेगम का सलीक़ा और तमीज़ सिखाने का सिलसिला। हर बात पर टोकना और हर बात पर समझाना।

मेहराज खाना खाने बैठे तो उससे पहले बी उसके हाथ-पैर धुलवातीं। मेहराज को हर वक़्त की अज़ान होते ही मस्ज़िद में नमाज़ पढ़ने भेजना। मेहराज से उसके गंदे कपड़े रोज़ के रोज़ धुलवाना। खाना खाने के बाद मेहराज से उसके इस्तेमाल किए बर्तन धुलवाना।

लेकिन बी ने उसकी आते वक़्त की सूजी आँखें देखी थीं इसलिए बहुत ज़्यादा सख़्ती भी नहीं कर रही थीं।

एक दिन फ़रीदन ने मेहराज से पूछा, "कैसा लग रहा है यहाँ? तुम्हें अपने घर से क्या अलग लगा यहाँ?"

मेहराज ने बिना सोचे जवाब दिया, "ये तो जेल है। घर कौन कहता है इसको?"

हँसकर फ़रीदन बोली, "आज से इस जेल में मज़े लेना सिखाया जाएगा आपको।"

दोपहर का खाना खाकर बी तो हमेशा सोती ही थीं। लेकिन घर में अब दो लोग हो गए थे जो सोते नहीं थे। पहली थी फ़रीदन और अब मेहराज भी। फ़रीदन और मेहराज बी के सोने के बाद निकल जाते। छतों पर दौड़ते-फिरते। दरवाज़े के बाहर उनका एक बड़ा-सा फ़ाटक था, जहाँ लल्लन मियाँ कुर्सी डाले बैठे रहते। एक दिन मेहराज ने लल्लन मियाँ से पूछा, “लल्लन मियाँ इस फ़ाटक में हमेशा से रिक्शे खड़े होते थे?”

“अरे छोटे मियाँ कैसी बात की आपने। यहाँ तो आपके नाना की मोटरगाड़ी, घोड़ागाड़ी वगैरह-वगैरह खड़ी हुआ करती थीं।” अपनी कुर्सी से उछल-उछलकर लल्लन मियाँ बोले।

“आप तब भी यहाँ कुर्सी डालकर बैठा करते थे? आप बैठे थे उन गाड़ियों में?” मेहराज ने बहुत जोश में पूछा।

लल्लन मियाँ कुर्सी से खड़े होकर बोले, “अरे तब तो मैं काफ़ी छोटा था, हाँ देखा था सब। मेरी उम्र इतनी ज़्यादा थोड़ी है। यहाँ लोगों का जमावड़ा रहता था। क्या दौर था वो, छोटे मियाँ क्या-क्या बताऊँ आपको।”

मेहराज हैरान कर बोला, “तो आप अब इन रिक्शों की निगरानी करते हैं?”

“छोटे मियाँ, ये मोहल्ले वाले मनहूस, बी के सामने रोकर रिक्शा खड़ा करने लगे।” बेहद तकलीफ़ से लल्लन मियाँ बोले। इतने में पीछे से फ़रीदन एक रिक्शा चलाते हुए बोली, “लल्लन मियाँ, इतना ग़ुस्सा मत करो। बुज़ुर्गी में दिल का दौरा पड़ने में ज़्यादा वक़्त नहीं लगता है।” ये सुनते ही मेहराज से अपनी हँसी नहीं रुकी।

“तेरी तो मैं बी से शिकायत करूँगा फ़रीदन।” लल्लन मियाँ कुर्सी पर बैठ गए और हाथ का पंखा झलने लगे। गुस्से में मुँह लाल हो चुका था उनका।

ग़रीब लोगों के पास अपना रिक्शा हिफ़ाज़त से खड़ा करने के लिए बी के फ़ाटक के अलावा कोई दूसरी जगह नहीं थी। लेकिन अब आ गए थे बी के शैतान नवासे, जो फ़ाटक को बंद करके दोपहर भर रिक्शा चलाते। फ़ाटक इतना बड़ा था कि आराम से गोल-गोल चक्कर लगाते। लेकिन कभी रिक्शा की चेन की ग्रीस से पजामा ख़राब होता तो कभी कुर्ता फट जाता। फ़रीदन इन सारे जुर्मों के सुराग़ मिटाती रहती। बी को इस सब का कभी पता नहीं लगने देती।

एक रोज़ शाम को फ़रीदन से बी ने मुल्लानी को बुलवाया। मुल्लानी से कुछ दिन बाद होने वाले निकाहों के ग़रारों का हिसाब-किताब लेना था। वैसे तो बी थोड़ा परेशान थीं क्यूँकि फ़सल भी बर्बाद हो गई थी लेकिन बी तो ख़ैर बहुत हिसाब से चलती थीं इसलिए उनको पैसों की ऐसी दिक़्क़त नहीं हुई। फ़रीदन के साथ मेहराज भी बी से पूछकर मुल्लानी के घर चला गया। मुल्लानी का घर तो बी के घर के पीछे ही था लेकिन उधर जाने के लिए रास्ता बहुत घूमकर जाता था। रास्ते में फ़रीदन को बच्चों में खेलता हुआ एक दोस्त मिल गया। वो दरअसल था तो बीस बाईस साल का पर उसका क़द मेहराज से भी काफ़ी छोटा था और दिखने में बस दस-ग्यारह साल का लगता था। फ़रीदन बच्चों को देख कर रुकी तो मेहराज ने पूछा, “क्या हम भी इन लोगों के साथ खेलेंगे?”

उसने अपने दोस्त की तरफ़ इशारा किया और आवाज़ दी- “बौने, इधर आ। कुछ काम-काज कर ले, बच्चों में ही खेलता रहेगा?”

बौना आया और कहने लगा, “फ़रीदन ये अपने साथ क्या चीज़ लेकर टहल रही है?”

“औक़ात से ऊपर मत उड़। देख कर बात करा कर। जा काम कर अपना।” फ़रीदन ये कहकर मेहराज का हाथ पकड़कर आगे बढ़ने लगी।

इतने में मेहराज बोला, “इस चीज़ का नाम मेहराज है। आपका क्या नाम है, बौने भाई?”

बौना दौड़कर फ़रीदन के आगे खड़ा हो गया, “तुझे क्यों इतना बुरा लग गया? चीज़ ने तो अपना नाम भी बता दिया।” मेहराज की तरफ़ इशारा करते हुए बोला।

“ये हैं मेहराज मियाँ। बी के नवासे।” ये सुनते ही बौना काँप गया और मेहराज से कहने लगा, “मियाँ मुझे मालूम नहीं था। माफ़ करना। बी को मत बताइएगा।”

“सब कुछ बता दूँगा अगर अपना नाम नहीं बताया तुमने तो।” मेहराज एकदम सूखे मुँह से बोला।

“फ़हीम... फ़हीम। अरे अम्मी के अलावा सब बौना ही कहते हैं, आप भी वही कह लें।” बौना कह ही रहा था कि पीछे से रिक्शा में दो औरतें गुज़रीं। एक औरत ने कहा, “बौने हवा चल रही है। घर चला जा कहीं उड़ न जाए तू।”

फ़रीदन उस औरत से बोली, “नरगिस, इसको तू ही उड़ा सकती है।”

बौना भी फ़रीदन और मेहराज के साथ मुल्लानी के घर चला गया। उसने न इधर देखा न उधर, सीधा मुल्लानी की छत पर चढ़ गया और पतंगें उठाकर ले आया।

मुल्लानी के घर से निकलकर मेहराज बोला, "फ़हीम भाई, क्या ये मुल्लानी आपकी रिश्तेदार हैं?"

बौना बोला, "क्यूँ?"

"अरे आप बिना झिझक उनकी छत पर चढ़ गए," मेहराज ने पूछा।

"झिझक की बात कहाँ से आ गई। मियाँ साहब एक ज़माना था, जब ये आधा मोहल्ला हमारा था।" हल्की आवाज़ में फ़रीदन को देखते हुए बौना बोला।

फ़रीदन और मेहराज उसके बाद घर चले गए।

मुल्लानी आईं बी से मिलने और उनको तसल्ली भी दे गईं कि बच्चियों के निकाह से एक दिन पहले वो सारे ग़रारे दे देंगी। उधर लकड़हट वालों ने भी लगभग सब कुछ बना दिया था। मेहराज दिन भर बैठकर उनको काम करते देखता और उनकी आरी से लकड़ी के टुकड़े काटता रहता। सब कुछ बन चुका था बस अब उनपर रंग होना बाक़ी था। बी के इंतज़ाम एकदम ज़ोरों पर चल रहे थे।

रोज़ दोपहर में बौने ने फ़ाटक में आना शुरू कर दिया। अब दो नहीं बल्कि तीन लोग फ़ाटक में दोपहर भर शैतानी करने लगे। मेहराज और बौने की दोस्ती भी गहरी होने लगी। बौना तो बड़े-बड़े का मज़ाक़ उड़ा लेता और हर किसी की ख़बर थी उसके पास। मेहराज था कि उसके क़िस्से कहानियों पर लोट-पोट हो जाता। मोहल्ले की कोई भी बारात हो बौना हर जगह चला जाता। बुलावा हो या न हो। बच्चों में गिनती हो जाती उसकी हर जगह। लल्लन मियाँ बौने को क़तई नापसंद करते थे। बौना भी कम नहीं, वो हमेशा लल्लन मियाँ

की जान आफ़त में रखता। उनका मज़ाक़ बनाता, जिसपर नेहराज की समझ में नहीं आता कि वो हँसे या ख़ामोश रहे।

एक दिन लल्लन मियाँ बहुत तमीज़ से मेहराज से बोले, "छोटे मियाँ, आपसे एक बात कहूँ। बुरा मत मानना।"

मेहराज बोला, "अरे आप ऐसे क्यों बोल रहे हैं। आराम से बोलिए, आप तो बड़े हैं हमारे।"

लल्लन मियाँ झिझकते हुए बोले, "वो मैं ये कह रहा हूँ आप बड़े अज़ीम ख़ानदान के वारिस हैं। आप फ़ाटक में रिक्शा चलाते हैं, ये बात बी को मालूम होगी, तो वो नाराज़ हो जाएँगी।"

मेहराज ने उनको देखा और बोला, "आप मत बताइएगा उनको। हमें बहुत डाँट पड़ेगी वरना।"

लल्लन मियाँ घबराकर बोले, "नहीं नहीं मैं क्यों बताऊँगा भला। बस मेरी राय है कि आप और फ़रीदन खेलते थे, उतना ठीक था। लेकिन ये बौना आपके मयार का नहीं है। आप उसके साथ मत खेला कीजिए, उसका असर आपके ऊपर बुरा साबित होगा।"

मेहराज थोड़ा नाराज़गी से बोला, "लल्लन मियाँ आपको उसका नाम मालूम है?"

लल्लन मियाँ घबरा से गए, "सब बौना ही कहते हैं उसको। नाम वही पड़ गया।"

मेहराज ग़ुस्से से बोला, "उसका नाम फ़हीम है और हमारे दोस्त का कोई मज़ाक़ उड़ाए, वो हमें पसंद नहीं होगा।"

लल्लन मियाँ, "अरे बेटे मैं तो बस..." मेहराज उनकी पूरी बात बिना सुने ही वहाँ से चला गया।

उस दोपहर जब बौना आया तो मेहराज ने कहा, "फ़हीम आज हम तुम्हारे घर चलते हैं वहाँ पर ही खेल लेंगे।" बौना कुछ देर हिचकिचाया, अगर-मगर करने लगा लेकिन मेहराज भी कम ज़िद्दी नहीं था। आख़िरकार उसको मनाकर उसके घर चला गया। घर ज़्यादा दूर नहीं था पर मेहराज को अपनी नानी के उठने से पहले ही वापस आना था ताकि उनको ख़बर न हो पाए वो बाहर गया था। वैसे मेहराज को इतना तो इत्मीनान था कि फ़रीदन कैसे न कैसे बातें बना लेगी और मेहराज को बचा लेगी।

अपने घर के टूटे हुए दरवाज़े से पर्दा हटाकर बौना घुस गया। उसके पीछे जैसे मेहराज घुसने ही वाला था इतने में बौने की माँ ने बौने को डाँटना शुरू कर दिया। मेहराज वहीं दरवाज़े की आड़ से लगकर खड़ा हो गया और पर्दे के छेद से अंदर झाँकने लगा। अंदर एक कमरा और उसके आगे टीन की चादरों का दालान, जिसमें लाल ईंटों का फर्श था। फर्श के ईंटों के एक-एक कोने साफ़-साफ़ चमक रहे थे। एक लड़की ज़मीन पर बैठी एक बड़े तसले में आटा गूँध रही थी। कुछ पलंग पड़े थे और एक पलंग पर बौने के बुज़ुर्ग बीमार वालिद लेटे हुए थे। मेहराज ये सब देख ही रहा था कि बौना वापस आकर कहने लगा, "कहाँ रह गए मियाँ? चलो अंदर अम्मी बुला रही हैं।"

बौने की अम्मी ख़ुशी से पागल-सी हो गईं। कहने लगीं, "पहली बार ढंग का काम करा है फ़हीम ने जो आपको हमारे घर ले आया।" एक पलंग पर चादर के ऊपर दूसरी साफ़ चादर बिछाने लगीं। मेहराज को उस पलंग पर बिठाया गया। बौने की अम्मी, वो तो मेहराज

के सामने उसकी नानी के गीत गाने लगीं, उनको दुआ देने लगीं। मेहराज से कहने लगीं, "हमारी लड़की का भी निकाह बी अगले हफ़्ते करा रही हैं।" अपनी बेटी से उन्होनें बिना देर किए बोला, "अरे शरबत बनाओ जाकर मियाँ साहब के लिए।"

मेहराज आया था खेलने और वहाँ घिर गया इन सब में।

लड़की दालान से निकलकर अपने छोटे-से बावर्चीख़ाने में चली गई, जो छत पर जाने वाले ज़ीने के नीचे बना हुआ था। आँगन मिट्टी का कच्चा-सा खुरदुरा था। ये ज़ीना और बावर्चीख़ाना मस्ज़िद की दीवार से चिपका हुआ था। बड़ी-सी मस्ज़िद की गुम्बद इनके छोटे-से घर को अपनी छाँव में ढक लेती थी। गर्मी में सुकून होता लेकिन सर्दियों में धूप मिल नहीं पाती।

बौने का सब्र ख़त्म हुआ और वो मेहराज को लेकर पतंग उड़ाने छत पर चला गया।

मेहराज ने बड़ी छत देखते ही हैरानी में पूछा, "फ़हीम ये छत आपकी है?"

"हाँ क्यूँ?" बौने ने पतंग में मंझा बाँधते हुए कहा।

"नहीं वो आपका घर नीचे तो..." बौने ने उसकी बात काटते हुए कहा, "मियाँ, आप पतंग उड़ा लेते हो?"

मेहराज ने पहली बार पतंग उड़ाई और एक दो पेंच भी काट दिए।

उधर बौने की बहन ने एक नया चमकता हुआ स्टील का गिलास निकाला। रूहअफ़ज़ा की बोतल लगभग ख़त्म ही थी बस तली में लाल रंग चमक रहा था। उसने बोतल में पानी डाल कर घुमा लिया

और जिससे कुछ लाली-सी आ गई पानी में। एक नीम्बू मिला जो कि बेहद सूखा था। वो भागती हुई छत पर गई और बराबर वाले घर में रहने वाली नरगिस को आवाज़ देने लगी। नरगिस ने अपने घर के पेड़ से एक नीम्बू तोड़ कर दिया। नरगिस के हाथों और गर्दन पर उबटन साफ़-साफ़ लगा दिख रहा था। दरअसल नरगिस का भी निकाह मेहराज की नानी करा रही थीं। बौना पतंग में सुत्तल बाँध रहा था, नरगिस को देखते ही बोला, "मेरे लिए तूने पतंगें नहीं लूट कर रखी ना? ससुराल चली जाएगी फिर तो बंद ही हो जाएगा तेरा पतंगें देना।" नरगिस शर्माकर बोली, "तुझे पतंग मैं अपनी ससुराल से भी दूँगी। देख लियो!" उसकी निगाह मेहराज पर पड़ी, जो मंझे की अटिया सुलझाने में मसरूफ़ था। नरगिस ने पूछा, "ये कौन हैं? तेरे दोस्त इतने अच्छे लोग कब से बनने लगे?" बौना बहुत रुआब से बोला, "तुम्हारा जो निकाह करा रही हैं ना उनका नवासा है।" नरगिस हैरान हो गई, "आप नसीम ख़ाला के बेटे हैं? रुकिए मैं मैं... अम्मी को बुलाती हूँ।" नरगिस ने ज़ोर-ज़ोर से आवाज़ देकर अपनी अम्मी को बुला लिया।

नरगिस की अम्मी फ़ौरन ऊपर आ गईं और मेहराज को बताने लगीं कि कैसे वो और उसकी माँ दोपहर भर खेलती थीं छतों-छतों और फ़ाटक में वो लोग रिक्शा चलाते थे। मेहराज ने फ़ौरन पूछ लिया, "तो आप लोगों को लल्लन मियाँ मना नहीं करते थे?" नरगिस की अम्मी बोली, "लल्लन मियाँ पर नसीम बाजी का ख़ौफ था। वो चूँ नहीं कर पाते थे।" फिर आँखों में आँसू लिए कहने लगीं, "अल्लाह कितना मज़ा आया करता था। पीछे एक बेरी का पेड़ था। नसीम आपा छत से लटककर बेर तोड़ती थीं और हम सब बच्चों को खिलाती थीं।" मेहराज हैरान हो गया कि उसकी माँ भी कभी ये

सब किया करती थीं! क्यूँकि उसने तो उन्हें हमेशा सिर्फ़ काम करते या ख़ामोश ही देखा था।

इतने में बौना नरगिस की तरफ़ इशारा करके बोला, "चच्ची आप जाइए नरगिस के उबटन लगाइए अब। वरना इसका दूल्हा भाग जाएगा इसको देखकर।" नरगिस भी कम नहीं, जाते-जाते कह गई- "वो भाग गया तो तुझसे कर लूँगी निकाह फिर सबसे पहले तेरा पतंग उड़ाना बंद कराऊँगी। बूढ़ा घोड़ा बच्चों में जान डाले हुए है।" हँसते हुए नीचे भाग गई और साथ में उसकी माँ भी चली गई। मेहराज ने हँसते हुए पूछा, "फ़हीम ये तुम्हारी रिश्तेदार हैं?"

बौना बोला, "नहीं पड़ोसी हैं। क्यूँ?"

"अरे आपकी छत और इन सारे घरों की छत एक ही है न इसलिए मुझे लगा।" कहते हुए मेहराज ने पतंग को हवा में ठुमकी दी।

बौना बोला, "मियाँ बड़ी लम्बी कहानी सुननी पड़ेगी।"

"अब तक मेरे बिना पूछे कितनी फालतू की कहानियाँ सुना चुके हो। जो मैं पूछ रहा हूँ, वो भी सुना दो।" हँसते हुए मेहराज बोला।

"अच्छा मियाँ साहब आपकी मान ली। बस मुझे पीछे की बातें करना पसंद नहीं है।" ये कहकर बौना थोड़ी देर ख़ामोश रहकर बोला, "तो नरगिस के दादा मेरे दादा की बग्गी गाड़ी चलाया करते थे। उनका ये घर हमेशा से पीछे ही था। हमारा ये बहोत बड़ा घर था, जो अभी सिर्फ़ कमरा और दालान ही बचा है। पूरा घर छोटे-छोटे टुकड़े करके बेचते गए और कभी कोई कारोबार कर नहीं पाए। आज नरगिस का घर हमारे घर से बड़ा है। वो घर भी मेरे दादा ने दिया था उनको।"

मेहराज ने पूछा, "तो तुम्हारे दादा भी हमारे नाना की तरह रईस आदमी थे?" बौना बोला, "नहीं-नहीं उतने रईस नहीं थे लेकिन सुना है मोहल्ले में दूसरे नंबर के रईस थे।"

इतनी देर में बौने की बहन शरबत का गिलास ले आई और मेहराज के हाथ में दे दिया। मेहराज ने बौने की तरफ़ देखा। बौना फ़ौरन बोला, "मैं शरबत पीता ही नहीं हूँ, तभी तो वो मेरे लिए नहीं लाई।" बहन भी बोली, "और क्या तभी तो नहीं लाई मैं। आप पीजिए आराम से बिलकुल साफ़ गिलास है।" गिलास मेहराज को देकर नीचे चली गई। मेहराज ने आधा गिलास पीकर बचा हुआ बौने को दे दिया और बौने ने बिना मना किए फ़ौरन एक ही बार में पूरा पी लिया।

इतने में भागती हुई फ़रीदन मेहराज को बुलाने के लिए बौने के घर आ गई। कहने लगी, "बी उठ गईं। मेहराज मियाँ इससे पहले कि वो आपको पूछें, जल्दी वापस चलिए।"

वो मेहराज को छोटे वाले घर से लेकर गई और मेहराज वहाँ पहुँचकर ऐसा दिखाने लगा कि जैसे वो लकड़ी के काम का मुआइना करने आया हो। इत्तेफ़ाक़ से उसने दो अलमारियों में कमी निकाल ली और सीधा बी को जाकर बता दिया।

बी ने मेहराज के माथे पर चूमते हुए कहा, "शाब्बाश मेरे जिगर के टुकड़े। आप एक ज़िम्मेदार इंसान हो गए।" फ़ौरन बी छोटे घर की तरफ़ चल दीं।

फ़रीदन ये सब देख रही थी, उसने आकर मेहराज से बोला, "ये सब झूठ बोलना आप पर बौने का असर है।"

मुस्कुराते हुए मेहराज ने जवाब दिया, “फ़रीदन आपा घर में भी कुछ लोग हैं, जिनसे ये सब सीखा जा सकता है।”

बी ने जाकर बढ़ई की क्लास ले ली और उन दोनों अलमारियों को तुड़वा कर दोबारा से बनाने को कहा। बी उनसे बोली, “मैंने साफ़-साफ़ कहा है कि हर एक चीज़ एक जैसी होनी चाहिए। एक कील का फ़र्क़ भी नहीं होना चाहिए।” बी अपने पास से हर लड़की को निकाह पर ज़रूरत के लायक़ सामान देतीं थीं और वो भी हर एक को बिलकुल एक जैसा।

रुख़साना ने दालान में चाय लगा दी और कुछ नमकपारे भी। मेहराज और बी बैठे चाय पी रहे थे कि लल्लन मियाँ बाहर से बड़े-बड़े बैग लाकर आँगन में रखने लगे। वो देख फ़रीदन दरवाज़े की तरफ़ दौड़ी और फ़ौरन वापस आकर बी से चीख़ कर कहने लगी, “बी, आइए जल्दी से, बशारत भाई और भाभी आ गए।”

बी और मेहराज उठे, इतनी देर में बशारत और उसकी बीवी सकीना अंदर आ गए। बशारत बी के गले लगा और हैरानी से मेहराज की तरफ़ देखते हुआ बोला, “अम्मी, ये जनाब कौन हैं?” बी ने सकीना के माथे पर चूमते हुआ कहा, “ये आपकी इकलौती बहन का इकलौता बच्चा है।”

मेहराज उन दोनों को देखकर थोड़ा परेशान-सा हुआ, शायद नये चेहरे देख कर या फिर ख़ुद पर से तवज्जो कम होने के डर से। बशारत ने उसे गले लगाया और कहा, “मेहराज ख़ान आपका आज तक नाम ही सुना था और वो भी ख़तों में। आपने तो आज हमें घर वापस आने का लाजवाब तोहफ़ा दे दिया।” सब लोगों ने साथ बैठकर चाय पी और फिर बशारत कुछ देर बाद मेहराज को लेकर बाज़ार चला गया।

ये पहली दफ़ा था जो मेहराज घर से कहीं बाहर तफ़री के लिए गया। बाज़ार में बशारत अपने दोस्तों से मिला, कुछ रिश्तेदारों से मिला। एक दोस्त ने कहा, "बशारत भाई आपके आने से ज़्यादा मेहराज से मिलकर ख़ुशी हुई।" बशारत ने मेहराज के कंधे पर हाथ रखकर कहा, "इनकी दुकान पर साइकिल मिलती हैं। चलो तुम्हें दिला देते हैं।" मेहराज गर्दन हिलाकर मना करता रहा। बशारत ने हरचंद कोशिश कर ली कि वो मेहराज को तोहफ़ा दिलवा दे लेकिन मेहराज ने रुआँसा होकर कहा, "मैं नहीं लूँगा कुछ भी मामूजान, अम्मी से पूछे बिना।" इसके आगे बशारत कुछ बोल नहीं सकता था। आख़िर में रबड़ी वाली आइसक्रीम खाने को जब बशारत ने पूछा तो उसपर मेहराज बोला, "हाँ खाने-पीने को अम्मी ने मना नहीं करा।" वो दोनों गंज की मशहूर, सौ साल पुरानी दुकान की रबड़ी आइसक्रीम खाने चले गए, जहाँ शहर के कोने-कोने से लोग आते और दुकान का सारा सामान एक घंटे में ख़तम हो जाता। जामा मस्जि़द के दरवाज़े के ठीक कोने में लाला रबड़ी वाले की दुकान थी और नमाज़ी शाम में मस्जि़द से बाहर निकलते ही रबड़ी लेते हुए ही जाते थे। बशारत को वहाँ दुकान पर उसके अब्बा के दोस्त मिल गए। आइसक्रीम लेकर जब बशारत ने देने के लिए पैसे निकाले तो उसके अब्बा के दोस्त ने मेहराज के कंधे पर हाथ रख कर कहा, "हमारी औलादें नहीं हुई तो नाना दादा बनना भी नसीब नहीं हुआ। बेटे आप हमारे सबसे अज़ीज़ दोस्त के नवासे हैं। अपने मामू से कहिए कि वो पैसे वापस रख लें। ये आइसक्रीम हमारी तरफ़ से है।" बशारत की आँखों में आँसू आ गए।

मेहराज ने आगे जाकर पूछा, "मामू, उन्होंने पैसे क्यों नहीं देने दिए?"

बशारत अपने अब्बा के दोस्त की बात सुनकर किसी गहरी सोच में पड़ गया था। उसने मेहराज का सवाल नहीं सुना तो मेहराज ने उसका हाथ पकड़ के दोबारा पूछा।

बशारत ने अपनी आँख के आँसू पोंछते हुए उसको बताया, "हम लोगों का रिवाज़ है कि अपने छोटे को पैसे नहीं देने देते हैं।"

"अगर बड़ों के पास पैसे ही न हों हैं तब?" मेहराज ने सोचते हुए पूछा।

"तब वो ऐसी जगह रुकते ही नहीं हैं," बशारत बोला।

"फिर तो जो बड़े ग़रीब होते होंगे, वो अपने छोटों से बाज़ार में मिलते ही नहीं होंगे।" परेशान होकर मेहराज बोला, "मामू आपके बच्चे मेरे छोटे होंगे। मैं भी उनको पैसे नहीं देने दूँगा।"

बशारत ने आसमान की तरफ़ देखते हुए हल्के-से कहा, "अल्लाह, मेहराज को ये मौक़ा ज़रूर देना।"

"क्या मौक़ा मामू?" मेहराज ने हैरान होकर पूछा। बशारत ने उसके सर को सहलाते हुए कहा, "तेज़ चलो आइसक्रीम पिघल ज एगी।"

उधर सकीना और बी बातें करने बैठ गए। सकीना ने बी को बताया कि उन दोनों को एकदम से आना पड़ा। दरअसल सकीना और बशारत की शादी को कई साल हो गए लेकिन उनके औलाद नहीं हुई। सऊदी के डॉक्टरों को दिखा-दिखाकर थक गए तो यहाँ इलाज कराने आना पड़ा। सकीना ने बताया कि दिल्ली में कुछ अच्छे डॉक्टर हैं, उनको दिखाएँगे। बी किसी भी बात से आसानी से घबराने वालों में से नहीं थीं। बी ने सकीना को कहा, "देखो, औलाद

देना न देना अल्लाह की मर्ज़ी है और मायूस होना कुफ्र है। क्या बशारत औलाद की वजह से दूसरी शादी की बात कर रहा है?" सकीना की आँखों में आँसू भर आए और वो कुछ कहने ही वाली थी कि इतनी देर में बशारत और मेहराज घर आ गए, सब के लिए रबड़ी आइसक्रीम लेकर।

दूसरे दिन बी ने सकीना के सभी घरवालों की दावत रख दी। तमाम घर दावत के इंतज़ाम में लग गया। लेकिन सकीना तो एकदम बेजान-सी बेदिल दालान में बैठी थी। मेहराज अपने नाना का लकड़ी का शतरंज कहीं से निकाल लाया और मोहरे लगाने लगा। सकीना ने देखा तो उसके साथ जाकर खेलने बैठ गई। मेहराज ने तो अभी तक सकीना से शर्म में बात तक नहीं की थी। सकीना का कुछ दिल बहल गया। मेहराज को भी एक इंसान मिल गया, शतरंज खेलने और बातें करने को।

मेहराज ने सकीना से पूछा, "आप हमारी दादी से मिली होंगी पिछले साल सऊदी में।"

"नहीं तो। वो कब गई थीं?" सकीना ने जवाब दिया।

"अरे मुमानी वो हज करने गयी थीं ना। आप वहाँ थीं तो कैसे नहीं मिलीं?" मेहराज ने हैरत में पूछा।

"बेटे सऊदी कोई इतना छोटा थोड़ी है। हम लोग तो दम्माम में रहते हैं।" सकीना अपना मोहरा बढ़ाते हुए बोली।

"अरे सऊदी में तो बस मक्का है दादी ने बताया था। और कोई शहर है ही नहीं। आप शायद कहीं और रहती होंगी मामू से पूछिए।" कह कर मेहराज ने घोड़ा बढ़ाया और फिर फ़ौरन वापस उठा लिया।

“हाहाहाहा! कोई बात नहीं। तुम्हारे मामू भी मुझसे हारते हैं, तो चाल बार-बार बदलते रहते हैं। ख़ैर सऊदी में कई सारे शहर हैं और उसकी राजधानी है रियाद।”

उसके बाद सकीना ने सारे शहरों के नाम बताए और मेहराज को अगली तीन चालों में हरा दिया।

सकीना को जाना था बाज़ार, वो फ़रीदन को लेके जाने लगी इतने में बी ने कहा, “फ़रीदन की ज़रूरत है घर में। आज बहुत काम हैं तुम कल चली जाना या फ़िर मेहराज को अपने साथ ले जाओ।” फ़रीदन का मुँह बन गया और सकीना अपने साथ मेहराज को लेकर चली गई।

मेहराज ने बाज़ार में सकीना को बताया कि मैं आज तक अपनी अम्मी के साथ कहीं बाहर नहीं गया। यह सुनकर सकीना हैरान थी। इस बच्चे की मासूम बातों की वजह से वह अपनी तकलीफ़ को भूल गई। सकीना ने मेहराज को अपना कॉलेज दिखाया। उसको पुराने क़िले लेकर गई। मेहराज ने अपनी अम्मी का स्कूल भी देखा। सकीना ने अपने सारे काम छोड़ मेहराज को घुमाया और शहर दिखाया। वो दोनों रिक्शा में बाज़ार से गुज़र रहे थे इतने में सकीना को ऊन की एक दुकान दिखायी दी। वो वहाँ रुक गई और मेहराज से रंग पसंद करवा-करवाकर उसने काफ़ी ऊन खरीदे। पीछे सड़क पर एक रिक्शे में लाउडस्पीकर से एलान हो रहा था, “मुल्क की सबसे अज़ीम नुमाइश आपके शहर से जा रही है। सिर्फ़ चार दिन और बचे हैं। इससे पहले कि आपसे दुनिया के नायाब सामान देखने-ख़रीदने का और एक से एक लाजवाब झूलों में बैठने का मौक़ा छूट जाए, नुमाइश में अपने-अपने परिवारों को लेकर ज़रूर

आइए। बच्चे-बूढ़े, जवान, औरत, मर्द हर एक का दिल लग जाए ऐसी जगह का लुत्फ़ आख़िर आप क्यों न उठाएँ।"

मेहराज ने कभी नुमाइश नहीं देखी थी और वो ये एलान सुनकर उतावला-सा हो गया। उसने सोचा नानी के घर तो सब लोग उसका कहना मानते ही हैं, तो लोग उसको नुमाइश भी ले जाएँगे।

वापस घर पहुँच कर मेहराज ने बी से कहा, "नानी अम्मी, आपको मालूम है नुमाइश लगी हुई है। आप हमें लेकर चलेगीं?"

जिस पर फ़रीदन बोली, "हमें तो बी हर साल लेकर जाती हैं। बी को वहाँ की सॉफ्टी आइसक्रीम बहोत पसंद है।"

मेहराज ने दोबारा पूछा, "नानी, बताइए ना चलेंगे हम?"

बी शाम की दावत के कामों में मसरूफ़ थीं, उन्होंने कह दिया "हाँ भाई चलेगें, अब तुम दोनों ज़रा बाहर जाके लल्लन मियाँ को बुला लाओ।"

मेहराज दरवाज़े से लल्लन मियाँ को बुलाने पहुँचा तो बैठक में बशारत अपने दोस्तों के साथ बैठा था। दिल्ली के एम्स के डॉक्टरों को लाया था। मेहराज बैठक का दरवाज़ा खुला देख उस तरफ़ आगे बढ़ने लगा। बशारत अपने दोस्त को कह रहा था, "कैसी बातें कर रहे हो मियाँ। मैं दूसरी शादी का सोच तक नहीं रहा हूँ। इलाज से बेहतर हो जाएगा तो ठीक, वरना यही नसीब में होगा।"

दूसरा दोस्त बोला, "बशारत भाई, बुरा न मानें तो एक बात कहूँ, कमी मर्दों में भी निकल सकती है। आप अपनी भी जाँच करवा लीजिएगा।" बाक़ी दोस्त ये सुनकर मुस्कुराए, बशारत का मुँह गुस्से में लाल-सा हो गया। इतने में दरवाज़े पर किसी की आहट हुई।

मेहराज को देखते ही बशारत ने उसको डाँटा और वहाँ से भगा दिया।

मेहराज को पहली बार यहाँ आकर डाँट सुनने को मिली। अपने घर में तो बाप से अक्सर बिना बात के डाँटना आम था।

दोपहर में दावत के कामों की वजह से कोई सोया नहीं और मेहराज का बौने से मिलना भी उस वजह से नहीं हो पाया। वो रुख़साना से साथ बावर्चीख़ाने में बैठकर बातें करने लगा। रुख़साना बहुत कम बात करने वालों में से थी। रुख़साना से मेहराज ने कॉपी और क़लम माँगी और अपनी माँ को ख़त लिखने लगा।

रुख़साना को मेहराज मायूस-सा लगा तो उसने हँसते हुए पूछ लिया, "अपनी अम्मी से क्या हमारी बुराइयाँ लिख रहे हो?"

वो हँसते हुए बोला, "नहीं तो। बस अम्मी की याद आ रही थी। मेरा पहला ट्रेन का सफ़र था ना तो अम्मी को अपने पहले सफ़र के बारे में लिखूँगा।"

वो बोली, "हमें भी बताओ न कैसा था। हम तो आज तक स्कूल के अलावा कहीं गए ही नहीं हैं।"

मेहराज ने कॉपी क़लम रखकर सब कुछ तफ़सील से बताना शुरू किया। उसने बताया खिड़की की सीट सबसे बढ़िया होती है। सब कुछ दिखाई देता है वहाँ से। रास्ते में एक नदी पड़ी जिसके पार एक मंदिर था। वो मंदिर धूप की वजह से सोने जैसा चमकता है। उसने टीटी के बारे में बताया कि कैसे वो लोगों को परेशान करते हैं और पुलिस वाले उनकी मदद करते हैं। रुख़साना उसकी बातें ग़ौर से सुन रही थी कि इतने में फ़रीदन आ गई। लकड़ी के चूल्हे पर खीर बन

रही थी और रुख़साना मगन थी मेहराज की बातों में। उसका ध्यान खीर से हट गया और खीर उफन गयी।

फ़रीदन को रुख़साना की शिकायत करने का मौक़ा मिल गया। कहने लगी "अभी जाकर तेरी शिकायत करती हूँ बी से।" उसपर मेहराज बोला "अगर आपने रुख़साना आपा की शिकायत की तो मैं भी नानी अम्मी को बता दूँगा कि आप उनका हुक़्क़ा छुप-छुपकर पीती हो।"

"मैं वैसे भी नहीं करती," कहते हुए फ़रीदन निकल गई वहाँ से।

शाम में सकीना के घरवाले आ गए। उसकी माँ वैसे तो बी की बहन भी थी। मेहराज के लिए ख़ूब सारे तोहफ़े आए। मेहराज को समझ नहीं आ रहा था कि वो ख़ुश हो या क्या करे! उसने अपनी नानी के पास पलंग पर तोहफ़ों को रख दिया। सकीना की अम्मी ने मेहराज से उसके घर के बारे पूछना शुरू कर दिया। मेहराज ने ठीक वैसे ही बताया जैसे उसकी माँ ने उसको कहकर भेजा था। बी और सकीना की अम्मी एक ही पलंग पर बैठे बातें कर रही थीं और उनके साथ ही मेहराज बैठा था। जैसे ही सकीना की माँ बोली, "हाय तुम्हारी माँ की क़िस्मत!" बी ने उनको इशारा करते हुए मना किया। बशारत सकीना के भाई से बातें कर रहा था। वह पूरे वक़्त कोफ़्त में था कि उसने मेहराज को क्यों डाँटा। आख़िरकार वो मामला सही करने के लिए बाज़ार से पान लाने के बहाने मेहराज को साथ ले गया।

सकीना की माँ और बी की बातें बिना रुके चलती ही रहीं। वो कहने लगी, "बी, दुनिया का दस्तूर देखो तुमने कितनी लड़कियों के घर बसवा दिए। पर तुम्हारी इकलौती बेटी ही अपना घर बचाने के

चक्कर में तुमसे नहीं मिल पाती है।" बी ने पान उनके हाथ में देते हुए कहा, "जब रिश्ता आया था तो मैंने नसीम से उसी वक़्त कह दिया था कि यह लड़का सही नहीं है। इसका बाप भी इसकी माँ को अच्छा नहीं रखता है। ख़ैर दुआ है कि वो ख़ुश रहे, चाहे मिल पाए या नहीं।"

"हाँ, अब किया भी क्या जा सकता है," सकीना की माँ मुँह में पान रखते हुए बोली।

"करने को बहुत हो सकता था और अभी भी हो सकता है। लेकिन अपना खूँटा ही मज़बूत नहीं है।" बी बोलीं।

"नसीम की शराफ़त है। हम लोगों की परवरिश भी तो ऐसी की जाती है ना। शादी हो गई तो निभाना ही है, चाहे कुछ हो जाए। तुमने भी तो बी... ठोकर खा के ही सीखा था ना।" सकीना की माँ ने कहा।

"वो बात तो सही है। पर मलाल मुझे भी है। एक बार नसीम तलाक़ लेने को राज़ी हो गई थी पर मैंने उससे दूसरा निकाह करने का ज़िक्र कर दिया। आज तक ख़ुद को कोसती हूँ कि आख़िर क्यूँ बोले मैंने वो अलफ़ाज़।"

"अरे बी ख़ुद को कोसने से क्या होगा। तुमने अच्छे के लिए कहा था। लेकिन नसीम का भी दिल बुझ गया होगा। उसको वक़्त लगता वो सब कुछ सोचने के लिए।" तसल्ली देते हुए सकीना की माँ बोली।

"ख़ैर अब तो बस यही दुआ है कि मेहराज अच्छा निकले और बड़ा होकर अपनी माँ को ऐश कराए।" बी ने कहा।

"क्या रिवाज़ है कि हमारी ख़ुशियाँ भी इन मर्दों के भरोसे ही रहती हैं तमाम उम्र।"

वो दोनों बातें कर ही रही थीं कि बशारत और मेहराज बाज़ार से वापस आ गए। सब लोगों के खाने के लिए दालान में दरी और चाँदनी बिछाई गई और उसपर ख़ूब लम्बा दस्तरख़्वान लगाया गया। कुछ मिनटों में सब लोग अपने-अपने ग़म भूलकर खाने के ज़ायक़े और हँसी ठट्ठों में मगन हो गए।

खाने के बाद उस दरी पर दूसरी चाँदनी बिछाई गई। पान और मिठाइयाँ छोटी-छोटी प्लेटों में रख दी गईं। शेर-ओ-शायरी का सिलसिला शुरू हो गया। सब लोगों ने अपने-अपने लिखे हुए शेर सुनाना शुरू किया। इस घर में कोई भी ऐसा नहीं था, जिसको शायरी का शौक़ न हो। यहाँ तक रुख़साना और फ़रीदन ने भी एक दो शेर सुना डाले। ये देखकर मेहराज तो कश्मकश में था कि बस आख़िर मैं ही हूँ जिसने कुछ नहीं लिखा है। इतने में सकीना बोल गई, "मेहराज मियाँ आप भी कुछ हुनर आज़माइए।"

मेहराज ने न इधर देखा न उधर और ये शेर पढ़ डाला-

मिटा दे अपनी हस्ती को अगर कुछ मर्तबा चाहे,
कि दाना ख़ाक में मिलकर गुल-ओ-गुलज़ार होता है।

सब हँसने लगे और कहने लगे कि ये तो अल्लामा इक़बाल का शेर है। मेहराज फ़ौरन बोला, "नहीं-नहीं, ये मेरी अम्मी का शेर है। जब कोई तकलीफ़ होती है, तो वो ये पढ़ती हैं।"

किसी को कुछ समझ नहीं आया कि इस बात पर क्या बोलें। इतने में फ़रीदन ने एक अपना लिखा हुआ बचकाना-सा शेर पढ़ा, जिस

पर सब ख़ूब हँसे। फ़रीदन ने ये काम सोचकर किया या नहीं, ये उसको ही मालूम होगा, लेकिन बी के लिए फ़रीदन इन्ही सब बातों की वजह से सबसे अज़ीज़ थी।

दूसरे दिन बशारत और सकीना दिल्ली चले गए। उन्होंने बहुत कोशिश की मेहराज को अपने साथ लेकर जाने की मगर बी ने सख़्ती से इंकार कर दिया। बी ने कहा मेहराज उनकी ज़िम्मेदारी है और ज़रा-सी कोई चूक हो गई तो क्या जवाब देंगी उसके माँ बाप को? बी तो ख़ैर वैसे भी अगले कुछ दिन काफ़ी मसरूफ़ रहने वाली थीं। क्यूँकि अब कुछ ही दिन ही रह गए थे निकाहों में। दस निकाह एक ही दिन कराना और सब कुछ उनके घर से ही होना था। दस दुल्हनों के ख़ानदान और दस दूल्हों के ख़ानदान कुल मिलाकर कम से कम सात-आठ सौ लोगों का इंतज़ाम करना। सबकी ख़ातिर तवाज़े बाइज़्ज़त करना और सबके दिल का भी ख़याल रखना कोई आसान बात नहीं, लेकिन बी सब बख़ूबी कर लेती थीं।

बी को जब उनके वालिद की जायदाद से हिस्सा मिला, उन्होंने तभी ये अहद कर लिया था। जैसे ही उनके कारोबार में कुछ फ़ायदा होना शुरू हुआ उन्होंने ये निकाह कराना शुरू करा दिए। शुरुआत में तो हर साल दो लड़कियों की ही शादी कराती थीं। बढ़ते-बढ़ते दस लड़कियों की शादियाँ होने लगीं बी के ज़रिए।

अगले दिन सुबह-सुबह मुंशी जी आ गए और साथ में एक पंचायत ले आए। पंचायत वही, जो उन्होंने बी के लिए ज़मीन ख़रीदी थी। जिसका बयाना दे दिया था और फ़सल के बाद बाक़ी के पैसे देने का वादा किया था। पर फ़सल जलने की वजह से नुक़्सान हो गया और उसके बाक़ी पैसे नहीं दे पाए। उस ज़मीन का मालिक बाग़वान

और उसकी बीवी मुंशी जी के साथ आ गए। वो ज़मीन उसकी बीवी के ही नाम थी।

बी ने उन सब को दालान में बिठाया और पहले तो चाय नाश्ता कराया। फिर उन्होंने पूछा उन दोनों से, "साफ़ साफ़ बताओ आप लोग क्या चाहते हो?"

बाग़वान बोला, "हमें ज़रूरत थी उसी वजह से हमने ज़मीन बेची थी। अब अगर ज़रूरत के वक़्त पैसा नहीं मिलेगा तो क्या फ़ायदा?"

बी ने उसकी बीवी के हाथ में केला छीलकर देते हुए कहा, "हमारे पास अगर इस वक़्त उतने पैसे होते तो ये सब बातें हो ही नहीं रही होतीं। इस मसले का कोई हल तो निकालना पड़ेगा ना।"

उसकी बीवी बोली, "बेगम साब, ये ज़मीन मेरी है और मैं इसको अपनी बेटी की शादी के लिए बेच रही थी। दस दिन बाद शादी है। थोड़ा बहोत सामान ख़रीद लिया है जहेज़ का, पर माँग काफ़ी ज़्यादा है।"

बी ने अपने पानदान से पान निकालकर मुँह में रखते हुए कहा, "वैसे तो जहेज़ की शर्तों की जगह पर अपनी बच्ची को देना ही नहीं चाहिए। लेकिन अगर ये मसला है, तो आप लोग उस ज़मीन को किसी और को बेच दो। हमारे पैसे लौटा देना अगर हो सके तो। नहीं तो हमारे ऊपर वक़्त निकलने का दंड मान लिया जाएगा।"

मुंशी जी फ़ौरन बोले, "अरे बी, ये इतने सीधे नहीं हैं, इन्होने ज़मीन बेचने की पूरी कोशिशें कर ली। लोग मजबूरी का फ़ायदा उठाकर कौड़ियों के दाम लगा रहे हैं। आपने तो इनसे बाज़ार के दामों से भी ज़्यादा पर सौदा किया था।"

“मुंशी जी, इंसान परेशान होता है तो कुछ भी करने को तैयार हो जाता है। औलाद के लिए तो इंसान बड़े-बड़े जुर्म कर लेता है, तो फिर ये तो छोटी-सी बात है। मसले का कोई हल तो सोचना पड़ेगा मुंशी जी।”

इतने में बढ़ई, बी को बताने आ गया कि रंग हो गया सारे लकड़ी के सामान पर, आकर देख लें। बी ने उसे इंतज़ार करने को कह दिया।

बाग़वान बोला, “हमारी समझ में कुछ नहीं आ रहा है बेगम साहब कि क्या करें। हमने तो हमेशा आपके खेतों में काम किया है। आज आपसे मदद माँगने के अलावा हमारे पास कोई सहारा नहीं।”

बी ने उसकी बीवी से पूछा, “बहन क्या तुम्हें इसी जगह अपनी बेटी की शादी करनी है?”

वो बोली “जहाँ भी करेंगे जहेज़ तो इतना ही देना पड़ेगा या हो सकता है और ज़्यादा माँग रख ले कोई। ऊपर से अगर लड़की का रिश्ता ख़त्म होता है तो हज़ार बातें बनेंगी।”

बी बोली, “देखो मैं अगर कोई भी फ़ैसला लूँगी तो तुम क्या उसको मान लोगी? तुम्हें लड़की की शादी करनी है, ये ज़रूरी नहीं कि इसी जगह हो। सही?”

बाग़वान बोला, “आप बस हमारी इज़्ज़त बचा लो। हमें आप पर यक़ीन है। पूरा गाँव आपकी क़समें खाता है। हमें भरोसा है।”

“ठीक है, तुम लोग घर जाओ, मुझे शाम तक का वक़्त दो। मुंशी जी तुम लोगों को आकर बता देंगे। मैं कोशिश ही कर सकती हूँ। संसार की लीला तो ऊपर वाले के हाथ है।” बी ने उन्हें समझाकर वापस भेज दिया।

बी ने मुंशी जी से पूछा, पूरन प्रधान के बेटे के लिए लड़की देखी जा रही थी। उसका ब्याह हो गया?

मुंशी जी ने बताया, "नहीं। उसके बेटे की तो बेवजह झूठी ख़बर उड़ा दी कि वो टी बी का मरीज़ है। प्रधान के दुश्मन बहोत हैं, उस चक्कर में बेटे का ब्याह ही नहीं हो पा रहा है।"

इन सब मसलों में बी का दिमाग़ घोड़े की रफ़्तार से भी ज़्यादा तेज़ चलता था हमेशा। बी ने पूरन प्रधान को बुलवाया और उससे बाग़वान की बेटी लक्ष्मी से बिना किसी माँग के शादी करने की बात की। प्रधान तो ख़ुशी में बी के पैरों में पड़ गया। बी ने बाग़वान के घर मुंशी जी से कहलवाया कि उस रिश्ते को ख़त्म करो, ये कह कर कि जहेज़ का लालच बढ़ता ही जा रहा है इसलिए यहाँ शादी नहीं कर सकते। शाम तक उनके घर पूरन प्रधान का परिवार आ जाएगा, लक्ष्मी का रोका करने।

बी ने दस निकाहों के साथ एक मंडप का भी इंतज़ाम करा दिया। बाग़वान की लड़की के लिए भी ज़रूरत के सामान का इंतज़ाम होना शुरू हुआ। अब दस लड़कियों के निकाह के साथ साथ एक लड़की के फेरे भी उसी दिन के लिए तय हो गए। उसके भी जहेज़ के लिए लकड़ी का सामान बनाने के लिए बोल दिया। बिलकुल ठीक वैसा ही जैसा बाक़ी की दस लड़कियों के लिए बना था।

बी इन सब इन्तज़ामों में लगी थीं, उधर मेहराज नुमाइश में जाने के लिए उनसे ज़िद करने लगा। बी के समझ में नहीं आ रहा था कि क्या करें। सीधा-सीधा मना करने के बजाय उसको टाल रही थीं। फ़रीदन भी कम नहीं, वो उसको चिढ़ाने लगी कि हमें तो बी हर साल

लेकर जाती थीं। फ़रीदन अब मेहराज से चिढ़ने लगी थी, जबसे मेहराज ने उसे हुक़्क़े वाली बात बताने की धमकी दी। मेहराज को वैसे ही बेचैनी थी जाने की, ऊपर से फ़रीदन की बातें उसका ख़ून और खौला रही थी।

दोपहर में कई दिन बाद बौना आया और मेहराज ने उसके साथ फ़ाटक में खेला। बौने के लिए मेहराज ने अपने घर की छत से ख़ूब सारी पतंगें इकट्ठा करके रखी थीं। लल्लन मियाँ के पास बुरा मानने के अलावा कुछ बस में नहीं था और बौना उनको छेड़े बिना रह जाए ऐसा भी नहीं हो सकता था। मेहराज ने उसको ताक़ीदन कह दिया कि अगर वो लल्लन मियाँ का मज़ाक़ उड़ाएगा तो वो उससे मिलना छोड़ देगा।

मेहराज ने बौने से तय किया कि कल हम लोग नुमाइश जाएँगे। पर बौने को मालूम था कि वो होना मुमकिन नहीं क्यूँकि उसके पास तो पैसे थे नहीं और मेहराज भी कहाँ से लाएगा पैसे। मेहराज ने लेकिन कह दिया था कि उसको किसी भी हालत में कल नुमाइश जाना है। क्यूँकि नुमाइश एक दिन बाद बंद होने वाली थी।

घर में शादियों के इंतज़ाम ज़ोर शोर से चल रहे थे। बी सारी लड़कियों के परिवारों को बुलाकर जो भी जहेज़ का इंतज़ाम उन्होंने किया हुआ था, दिखाती थीं और उन सब के लिए चाय नाश्ते का इंतज़ाम करती थीं। तो बी ने तमाम लोगों को अगले दिन बुलवा लिया। मेहराज और फ़रीदन एक-एक के घर जाकर बुलावा देकर आए। मेहराज ने वापस आकर बी से फिर पूछा कि, "नानी अम्मी, कल नुमाइश का आख़िरी दिन है, क्या हम जाएँगे?" बी के जवाब से मेहराज समझ गया कि उनका जाना मुश्किल है।

दूसरे दिन सुबह से जहेज़ का सामान लगना शुरू हो गया। पूरा घर जहेज़ के सामानों से भर गया। सारी लड़कियों के परिवार के कुछ लोग सुबह से आ गए। उनमें से ज़्यादातर तो मोहल्ले के ही थे। बौने की माँ और नरगिस की माँ भी थीं। क्यूँकि बी उन दोनों की लड़कियों का निकाह भी करा रही थीं।

जहेज़ में बी ने सब लड़कियों को एक सिलाई मशीन भी दी। ताकि कभी ज़रूरत पड़ने पर कपड़े सीकर अपना खर्चा तो निकाल सकें। घर के आँगन में ये सामान लगा दिया गया। फ़रीदन इन सब कामों में आगे आगे थी। इस सब के बीच भी उसने मेहराज को चिढ़ाने का मौक़ा नहीं छोड़ा। बौना बी के घर अपनी माँ से कुछ कहने आया, तभी मेहराज ने उससे कह दिया कि नुमाइश जाने के लिए ठीक दो बजे वो फ़ाटक के बाहर आ जाए।

बौने ने उसको बोला, "ऐसे जाना सही नहीं है। बी बहुत डाँटेंगी।"

उसपर मेहराज ने साफ़ कह दिया, "फ़हीम अगर तुम्हें नहीं जाना है तो मत जाना मगर मैं तो आज नुमाइश जाकर ही रहूँगा।"

बौने को समझ आ गया था कि मेहराज नहीं मानेगा और उसको अकेला भेजना और ज़्यादा ग़लत होगा।

बी को बाग़वान की लड़की लक्ष्मी के लिए साड़ियाँ ख़रीदने बाज़ार जाना था। लक्ष्मी की माँ और बहन भी आ गए थे। बी ने दोपहर का खाना खाया और उन दोनों को साथ लेकर बाज़ार निकल गईं। लक्ष्मी की माँ और बहन की ख़ुशी देखने के क़ाबिल थी। वो तीनों एक ही रिक्शे में बैठकर निकल गईं।

और बुलंद थे। मेहराज ने हामी भर दी फ़ौरन और आख़िर क्यों नहीं? अभी तक उसका एक भी निशाना नहीं चूका था। लोगों में जोश देखने लायक़ था। दाना एयरगन में डाला गया और फिर एक टंगी हुई पतली-सी कील का निशाना मारना तय हुआ।

मेहराज ने निशाना लगाया और एयरगन चलने की आवाज़ आई लेकिन कील अपनी जगह से हिली तक नहीं। हैरान मेहराज बौने का मुँह देखने लगा।

लेकिन अबकी बौना बोला- "एक बार और लगाते हैं शर्त। तुम दाना डालो।"

स्टाल वाले लड़के ने फिर से एयरगन भरने के लिए अपने दांतो के बीच दबे दाने को निकाला। उसपर बौना फ़ौरन बोला, "नहीं ये वाला दाना मत डालो।" बौने ने टेबल पर रखे दानों से भरे मग की तरफ़ इशारा करते हुए कहा उसमें से निकालो।

वो बंदा बहस करने लगा। कहने लगा, "जब निशाना चूक गया तो दाने पर शक करने लगे। भागो यहाँ से।" ज़ोर से चिल्लाया।

बाक़ी लोग भी यही कहने लगे। बौना बोला, "ठीक है यही डालो।"

मेहराज ने निशाना ताना और जैसे ही उसने ट्रिगर दबाया बौने ने अपना हाथ एयरगन की नाल के आगे कर दिया। मेहराज और वहाँ खड़े लोग एकदम चीख़ पड़े। जब बौने का हाथ देखा तो वो बिलकुल ठीक था। तब पता लगा कि दाना सिर्फ़ मसाले का था। वो स्टाल वाला बंदा धोखेबाज़ी कर रहा था। बौना उससे लड़ने लगा। बच्चा समझकर स्टाल वाला बौने को मारने चढ़ गया। बौना भी समझदार था, उसको कुछ दूर पर मोहल्ले के लड़के दिख गए और उसने उन लोगों को आवाज़ दे दी। मामला रफा-दफ़ा हो गया।

लेकिन मेहराज ने काफ़ी देर तक बौने से बात नहीं की। बौना परेशान हो गया, बार-बार कहने लगा, "कुछ तो बोलो, कुछ तो बोलो क्या हुआ"।

मेहराज एकदम ग़ुस्से में बोला, "फ़हीम अगर तुम्हारा हाथ कट जाता, तो तुम्हारा क़द और छोटा हो जाता। मेरा तो दिल बैठ गया था ये सोच के।"

बौने ने मेहराज को ग़ौर से देखा और दोनों ज़ोर-ज़ोर से हँसने लगे। मेहराज ने बौने के कंधे पर अपना हाथ रखा और दोनों नुमाइश में टहलने लगे। निशाने लगाकर मज़े में दोनों निकल गए- न एक पैसा दिया न ही मिला। मेहराज एकदम बेफ़िक्र था न उसे वापस जाने की कोई जल्दी थी और शायद बी का भी डर नहीं था।

बी और लक्ष्मी की माँ बहन बाज़ार में टहल रही थीं। उनको भी देर हो रही थी बाज़ार में। क़ुदरत भी मेहराज का साथ दे रही थी। दरअसल बी अपने मिज़ाज के ख़िलाफ़ तो कोई काम करने का सोच ही नहीं सकती थीं। उन्हें अभी तक उतनी अच्छी साड़ियाँ नहीं दिख रही थीं। और वो ऐसा नहीं करना चाहती थीं कि जल्दबाज़ी के चक्कर में लक्ष्मी का दिल छोटा हो। इसलिए वो उसे लेकर पहुँच गईं पुराने बाज़ार, उनके घर से काफ़ी दूर था।

इस बाज़ार में कभी बी के वालिद की दस दुकानें थीं, जिन्हें उनके भाई ने बेच डाली थीं। पर एक दुकान उनमें से बी के हिस्से में आई थी, जिस दुकान पर बी पिछले कई सालों से मुक़दमा लड़ रही थीं। दरअसल उस दुकान पर किरायेदार ने क़ब्ज़ा कर लिया था और उसका कहना था कि उसने बी के भाई को पैसे देकर दुकान ख़रीद

ली है। मुक़दमा तीन लोगों में चल रहा था– बी, उनके भाई और मोहनदास। इस बड़ी खिचड़ी में कौन सही है और कौन ग़लत का फ़ैसला बी ने अदालत पर छोड़ दिया था।

बाज़ार में उन दोनों के साथ बी को टहलते हुए जैसे ही उस दुकानदार मोहनदास ने देखा, उसने बी और उन दोनों को दुकान में बुला लिया। इसने बी की दुकान पर क़ब्ज़ा किया हुआ था, फिर भी बी की बेपनाह इज़्ज़त करता था। उसने उन सब के लिए लस्सी मंगाई और बी के लिए उसने ताकीद करके कम मीठा रखने को कहलवाया। कितने अजीब लोग थे- एक तरफ़ मुक़दमा, दूसरी तरफ़ एक-दूसरे की ऐसी इज़्ज़त! ये दुकान इस बन्दे के बाप के पास किराए पर थी। यह बचपन से यहीं बैठा था। बी बचपन से ही इस दुकान पर आया करती थीं। अब मुक़दमा भी हो गया लेकिन न तो इस बन्दे ने और न ही बी ने ये रिवायत तोड़ी। मोहनदास की दुकान में वैसे तो मर्दों के धोती लुंगी और बनियान हुआ करते थे। लेकिन उसने बी के लिए दूसरे साड़ी वाले दुकानदारों का सामान अपनी दुकान पर ही मँगवाकर पसंद करवाया। साड़ियाँ पसंद करना इतने कम वक़्त में आसान काम नहीं था।

मेहराज और बौना घुस गए थे, मौत के कुएँ का शो देखने। वो दोनों सबसे आगे खड़े थे और मेहराज चीख़ें मार-मार के मज़े ले रहा था। तमाशा ख़त्म हुआ और दोनों भीड़ के साथ बाहर निकलने लगे इतने में उस मौत के कुंए में काम करने वाला उन दोनों के पास पहुँचा और बौने से कहने लगा, “हमारे पास जो बौना काम करता है उस कमीने का पेट ख़राब हो गया। क्या तू सिर्फ़ अगले तमाशे के

लिए मोटरसाइकिल और जीप में ड्राइवर के साथ बैठ सकता है?" मेहराज उस बन्दे को घूरने लगा। इतने में बौना बोला, "कितने पैसे मिलेंगे?" मेहराज डर गया और बौने से मना करने लगा। इतने में वो बंदा बोला, " दो रूपए मिलेंगे और तुम दोनों को नुमाइश के हर झूले के टिकट और साथ में छोला-चाट भी।"

बौना इतने सब को कैसे मना कर सकता था आख़िर। वो मेहराज को भरोसा देकर उस बन्दे के साथ चला गया। थोड़ी ही देर में वो तमाशा दोबारा से शुरु हो गया। मेहराज फिर सबसे आगे खड़ा होकर देखने लगा। लेकिन इस बार वो सिर्फ़ घबराया हुआ था। बौना उधर चीख़ें मार रहा था। जैसे डर रहा हो। जैसे वो घबरा रहा हो। लोग बौने की उन डरी हुई चीख़ों से और मज़े ले रहे थे। उधर बौना डरे-डरे मुँह बना रहा था और उसके साथ बैठा ड्राइवर उसका मज़ाक़ उड़ाकर लोगों को इशारे कर रहा था। मेहराज ज़ोर-ज़ोर से आवाज़ देकर पूछ रहा था,"फ़हीम तुम ठीक हो? फ़हीम तुम ठीक हो?" मेहराज के दिल की रफ़्तार कुएँ में चलती हुई मोटरसाइकिल से ज़्यादा तेज़ चल रही थी। उसकी आँखों से लाचारी के आँसू निकलने लगे। उसे कुछ समझ नहीं आ रहा था कि क्या करे। वो बस तमाशा ख़त्म होने का इंतज़ार कर रहा था। जैसे ही तमाशा ख़त्म हुआ वो फ़ौरन भागता हुआ बौने के पास पहुँचा, कहने लगा, "तुमने रोकने को क्यों नहीं कहा इन लोगों से? जब तुम इतना ज़्यादा घबरा रहे थे तो।" ये कह कर उसने अपने आँसू पोंछे।

बौना शर्मिंदा हो कर बोला, "मियाँ आप मुझे माफ़ कर दीजिए मैं आपको बताना चाहता था पर वक़्त इतना कम था। मैंने वो सब उनके कहने पर किया था। उन लोगों ने मुझे झूठी चीखें निकालने के लिए बोला था।" यह कहते हुए उसने अपने हाथ में ढेर सारे टिकट दिखाए।

मेहराज ने वो टिकट उसके हाथ से छीन लिए फिर बोला, "मैं अकेले ही जाऊँगा इन सब में। तुम जाओ कुएँ में चीख़ो।" और कहते हुए वहाँ से बाहर निकल गया। बौना उसके पीछे हँसता हुआ भागा। दोनों हाथों में हाथ डालकर सबसे पहले छोले-चाट की दुकान पर पहुँचे।

बी की साड़ियों की खरीदारी हो चुकी थी। अब उनका एक ही काम बचा था और वो था सारी दुल्हनों के लिए मेवे के हार। इस हार में कई तरह के मेवों में छेद करके एक मोटे लाल डोरे में डाले जाते हैं। ये रिवाज़ था दुल्हनों और उनकी माँओं के गले में डालने का, उनके निकाह से एक दिन पहले। वो दिन आज ही था। बी ने लक्ष्मी की माँ को साड़ियाँ लेकर अपने घर वापस भेज दिया और उनकी बेटी को अपने साथ बाज़ार में रोक लिया। ख़ुद बैठ गईं हार वाले दुकानदार के पास, ताकि वो इतने सारे हारों में कहीं बेकार मेवा न डाल दे।

नुमाइश में भीड़ इतनी बढ़ गई कि मेहराज की तबीयत ख़राब होने लगी। बौना जल्दी से शिकंजी की दुकान ढूँढ़ता हुआ उसको ले गया। शिकंजी पीकर उसकी जान में कुछ जान आई। फ़िर बौने ने मुस्कुराकर कहा- "इतनी झूठी-झूठी चीख़ें मारकर मैंने हम दोनों के लिए टिकट कमाए हैं। अब चलिए ना मियाँ झूले वालों को भी कुछ परेशान करते हैं।"

हँसता हुआ मेहराज बोला, "फ़हीम तुम इतने शैतान कैसे हो भाई?"

आँख मारते हुए बौना बोला, "रोज़ सुबह उठकर इसके लिए वर्ज़िश करता हूँ।"

उन दोनों ने नुमाइश का कोई झूला नहीं छोड़ा। एक आख़िरी झूला बचा था और वो उसकी तरफ़ बढ़ रहे थे, इतने में ऐलान हुआ कि, "एक बच्चा जिसका नाम नंदन है। वो अपनी नानी को ढूँढ रहा है। उसकी नानी जहाँ कहीं भी हों वहाँ से एलान वाली जगह गेट नंबर दो के सामने आ जाएँ।"

ये सुनते ही मेहराज कि रूह काँप गई। उसने कहा, "अरे नानी मेरा बुरा हाल कर देंगी। अब बस जल्दी से घर ले चलो मुझे।"

दोनों नुमाइश आकर बेहोश हो गए थे कि उनको पीछे की दुनिया की कोई ख़बर ही नहीं रही। दोनों तेज़ी से भागे। जैसे तैसे उस भीड़ को पार करते हुए बहुत मुश्किल से नुमाइश के गेट से बाहर निकले। रिक्शा लेकर वहाँ से निकल पड़े। पन्द्रह बीस मिनट का सफ़र काटने से नहीं कट रहा था मेहराज से। बौने ने उसको बहुत भरोसा दिलाया कि वो सब कुछ अपने ऊपर ले लेगा और मेहराज पर डाँट नहीं पड़ने देगा। मेहराज किसी क़ीमत नहीं चाहता था कि नानी को ये सब कभी पता लगे। जैसे ही उन लोगों का रिक्शा उनकी गली तक पहुँचा बौना कूदकर रिक्शे से उतर गया और बोला, "मियाँ साहब बस यहीं उतर जाइए। अगर किसी को बाहर दिखेंगे तो यही लगेगा कि मोहल्ले में कहीं गए होंगे।" जल्दी से रिक्शे का किराया देकर वो लोग भागे। जाकर अपने फ़ाटक के पास खड़े होकर मेहराज बोला, "चलो तुम भी मेरे साथ आज घर के अंदर चलो। तुम्हारी अम्मी और बहन भी तो हैं।"

बौना बोला, "अरे वहाँ सिर्फ़ औरतों को बुलाया है बी ने।"

"हाँ और बच्चों को भी। तुम भी चलो।" मेहराज बोला।

“मेहराज मियाँ, मैं बाईस का हूँ। आप हो बच्चे। अच्छा सुनिए वो पान....” बौने के ऊपर चीख़ते हुए इतनी देर में बौने की माँ बी के घर से निकल कर आ गई।

“फ़हीम, तुझे होश है तेरे बाप अकेले घर पर पड़े हैं। जल्दी चला जा घर।” मेहराज की तरफ़ देखते हुए बोलीं, “मेहराज मियाँ को भी बिगाड़ देगा तू।” और मेहराज को अपने साथ लेकर घर में चली गई। बौना अपनी बात अधूरी छोड़कर घर की तरफ़ बढ़ा, इतने में दो उसकी उम्र के लड़के उसका मज़ाक़ उड़ाकर भाग गए। बौने ने एक पत्थर उठाया वैसे ही पीछे से बी का रिक्शा आ गया। उन्हें देखकर वो तेज़ी से अपने घर की तरफ़ भागा। उधर लल्लन मियाँ दरवाज़े पर पड़ी अपनी कुर्सी पर ऊँघ रहे थे फ़ाटक में रिक्शे को घुसते देख वो अपनी कुर्सी छोड़ कर भागे।

बी घर में गईं। पूरा आँगन सामान से भरा हुआ था। लल्लन मियाँ उनके पीछे-पीछे मेवे वाले हारों का बोरा उठाए हुए थे, जिसे उन्होंने दालान में पड़ी बी की आराम कुर्सी के पास रख दिया। लक्ष्मी की माँ ने भी साड़ियाँ और बाक़ी सामान सजा दिया था।

बी किसी से भी बात किए बग़ैर सीधे गईं अपने कमरे में और नमाज़ के लिए वुज़ू करके दालान में नमाज़ पढ़ने बैठ गईं। फ़रीदन रोज़ाना के मामूल के हिसाब से बी के लिए चाय बनाने दौड़ गई। मेहराज भी जाकर नमाज़ पढ़के बी के पास दालान में पलंग पर बैठ गया, इतना मासूम बनकर जैसे वो सुबह से बस घर में ख़ाली बैठा हो। बी ने नमाज़ पढ़कर जैसे ही उसको देखा, कहने लगीं, “बेटे आपको नुमाइश नहीं लेकर जाने पर हम बहुत शर्मिंदा हैं। लेकिन आप बेफ़िक्र रहिए हम अगले साल ज़रूर चलेंगे।”

मेहराज बोला, "जी, लेकिन मैं अगले साल यहाँ होऊँगा या नहीं क्या मालूम।"

"देखना हम बुला लेंगे आपको।" बी अपनी आराम कुर्सी पर बैठते हुए बोलीं। उन दोनों ने चाय पी फिर बी बोलीं, "आप जाकर इन लोगों का हाथ बटाओ काम में। सामान रखवाओ। दुआएँ मिलती हैं लोगों का काम करने में।" यह कहते हुए बी ने चाँदी की प्लेट से पान उठा कर मुँह में रखा। बी के लिए फ़रीदन ने सुबह में ही एक चाँदी की प्लेट में कई पान लगाकर रख दिए थे। बी इतने भीड़ भाड़ के मौक़ों पर पानदान अपने कमरे में छुपाकर रखती थीं। क्यूँकि बी का पानदान बा-सलीक़ा रहता था। लोग अक्सर आते थे और चूने का चम्मच कत्थे में डाल देते और कत्थे का चूने में। इसलिए उन्होंने भीड़ भाड़ के दिनों में, ख़ून जलाने से बेहतर पानदान ही छुपाना बेहतर समझा।

मेहराज जाकर सामान लगाने में लोगों की मदद करने लगा। अँधेरा होने से पहले सब लोगों के नाश्ते का इंतज़ाम करा दिया गया। आँगन में कई मेज़ों पर बड़ी ताम्बे की परातों में इमरतियाँ, कटे हुए सेब, केले, मसाले वाली दालमोठ, समोसे, पकोड़ियाँ और बड़ी बाल्टी में रूहअफज़ा का शरबत। इतना इफ़रात में सारा सामान होता था कि लोगों का जैसे खाना ही हो जाए। मेहराज ने तो दोपहर का खाना भी नहीं खाया था, वो सबसे पहले भूखों की तरह लिपट गया नाश्ते पर। बी ने ये देख कर उसको गुस्से से बुलाकर कहा- "बेटे पहले मेहमानों को खाने दो। कितनी बत्तमीज़ी की बात है कि मेज़बान ही सबसे पहले खाने लगे।"

"लेकिन नानी अम्मी भूख लग रही है हमें।" मेहराज बोला।

"क्यों आपने दोपहर ठीक से खाना नहीं खाया था क्या?" ये सुनते ही मेहराज बात काटकर निकल गया वहाँ से। उसको तो दोपहर में हुई हर बात को ग़ायब करना था, जैसे इस दिन की दोपहर कभी हुई ही नहीं थी।

सब लोगों ने नाश्ता कर लिया और फिर बी ने सारी दुल्हनों और उनकी माँओं के मेवे वाले हार डालना शुरू किए। सब के डाल दिये बस लक्ष्मी नहीं आ पाई थी इसलिए उसका हार उसकी माँ को ही दे दिया।

इस सब के बाद सारी औरतों ने बैठकर ढोल बजाया और गाने गाए। बी ने भी गानों में शिरकत की। पूरा घर औरतों की आवाज़ों से गूँज रहा था खिलखिला रहा था। किसी के मुँह में पान की लाली चमक रही थी तो किसी के हाथों पर से मेहँदी अपना रंग दे कर छूट कर गिर रही थी। मेहराज और बाक़ी बच्चे भी उन गानों का मज़ा ले रहे थे। मेहराज ने तो ये सब पहले कभी देखा ही नहीं था। मेहराज भी ज़ोर-ज़ोर से गा रहा था। "सज रही बन्नो मेरी सुनहरे गोटे में" झूम-झूमकर रुख़साना के साथ ज़ोरों से तालियाँ बजाकर गा रहा था।

बी मेहराज को इतना ख़ुश देखकर उसकी माँ नसीम को याद करने लगीं। उनकी ज़बान पर इन गानों के बोल लेकिन आँखों में आँसू थे। फ़रीदन उनको देखकर ही समझ गई कि उन्हें अपनी बेटी की याद आ गई। फ़रीदन फ़ौरन ही बी का पानी का कटोरा लेकर बी के पास चली गई।

गानों का सिलसिला चलता रहा और जैसे-जैसे रात होती गई लोग अपने-अपने घरों को जाते रहे। ज़्यादातर का तो घर क़रीब में ही था बस लक्ष्मी का परिवार दूर रहता था। इसलिए बी ने पहले ही

उन्हें रुकने के लिए बोल दिया था। रात होते होते गाने वालों में बस रुख़साना, फ़रीदन, लक्ष्मी की बहन और उनके साथ मेहराज ही बचा था। बाक़ी सब अपने-अपने घर वापस चले गए थे। बी भी अब अपने कमरे में लेटने जाने लगीं। फ़रीदन को उन्होंने आवाज़ देकर उनके कमरे में पानी का जग लेकर आने को कहा। ये सब लोग गाने में मशगूल थे बी की आवाज़ फ़रीदन सुन नहीं पाई।

थोड़ी देर बाद बी ने चीख़कर फ़रीदन को आवाज़ दी। गाना रोक दिया उन लोगों ने। "बी, बस अभी पानी लाई।" कहते हुए फरीदन उठने लगी।

बी की आवाज़ आई, "नहीं! मेरा पानदान यहाँ कमरे से ग़ायब है।" फ़रीदन भागते हुए कमरे में गई। पानदान ढूँढने लगी। जब काफ़ी देर कमरे में ढूँढने पर पानदान नहीं मिला तो बाकी लोग भी ढूँढने में लग गए। घर का कोना-कोना ढूँढ लिया पर पानदान कहीं नहीं मिला। आँगन में फैले हुए जहेज़ के सामानों को भी उठा-उठाकर देख लिया। छोटे घर में जाकर सब लोगों ने रात में ही ढूँढा लेकिन पानदान का तो कोई सुराग़ नहीं मिला।

बी ने थककर कहा, "अब सब लोग लेट जाओ। कल लम्बा दिन है। सुबह को देखा जाएगा।"

सब लोग लेटने चले गए। फ़रीदन बेचैन थी, पूरा घर दोबारा दोबारा देख रही थी। आख़िर में उसको भी थककर सोना ही पड़ा। मेहराज को बी ने पहले ही सोने के लिए भेज दिया था। पूरा घर लगा था पानदान ढूँढने में पर नानी के कहने की वजह से उसको लेटना पड़ा। सुबह में सब जल्दी ही उठ गए। उस दिन वैसे भी ग्यारह शादियाँ होनी थीं। लेकिन बी के लिए तो पानदान का नया मुक़दमा आ गया था।

आख़िर घर से पानदान ग़ायब कैसे हो सकता था। बी का कोई सामान ऐसे ग़ायब हो गया और किसी को कोई ख़बर नहीं! बी ने सोचा की अगर नाक के नीचे से चीज़ ग़ायब हो जाएगी तब तो मेरी पकड़, और चीज़ों पर भी कमज़ोर लगने लगेगी।

उन्होंने फ़रीदन को अपने कमरे में बुलाया और कहा, "जितने भी परिवार आए थे उनके घरों पर जाकर पूछकर आओ। शायद किसी बच्चे ने शरारत की हो।"

फ़रीदन जैसे ही जाने उठी तो बी बोलीं, "और सुनो, कल जितने भी लोग घर में काम-काज कर रहे थे, उन सब से कहो, मुझसे आकर मिलें।" बी ने चाँदी की प्लेट में से कल का सूखा हुआ पान उठाकर मुँह में रखा। फ़रीदन भागकर गई सारे लोगों को बी का पैग़ाम देने।

एक-एककर सारे लोग आने लगे। इन लोगों में थे- लल्लन मियाँ, रुख़साना, एक बावर्ची और दो औरतें, जो बी की मदद के लिए हर साल शादियों के वक़्त रहती थीं।

ये तमाम लोग एक-एककर बी के कमरे में जाने लगे। बी का सवाल-जवाब का सिलसिला चलता रहा। इतने में फ़रीदन आ गई और उसने बी को बताया कि वो हर एक घर में हो आई पर किसी को कुछ नहीं मालूम। बी ख़ामोश रहीं, उस वक़्त कमरे में बी और लल्लन मियाँ थे। फ़रीदन वापस चली गई। बी ने लल्लन मियाँ से कहा, "लल्लन, तुम पूरा दिन कुर्सी पर ऊँघते ही रहोगे ज़िन्दगी भर। किसी मर्ज़ की तो दवा बन जाओ लल्लन।" लल्लन ख़ामोश, शर्मिंदगी में वहाँ से उठकर वापस चले गए। फिर आई रुख़साना, तब तक बी का पारा बहुत गरम हो चुका था। कोई बी की आँखों में धूल कैसे झोंक सकता है, यही बात उन्हें सता रही थी। बी बोलीं,

“रुख़साना, अगर कुछ मालूम हो तो बता दो वरना तुम सब के सब बहुत बुरा खामियाज़ा भुगतोगे।” रुख़साना वैसे ही काँप रही थी और ये सुनकर तो उसकी ज़बान ही जैसे बंद हो गई।

“कुछ बोलोगी। मुँह में फफूंदी जमाकर क्यों खड़ी हो?” बी ने ग़ुस्से में कहा।

वो डरते-डरते बोली, “छोटे मियाँ को बाहर... लेकर जाते देखा था।”

बी की आँखें खुली की खुली रह गईं। रुख़साना छोटे मियाँ कहा करती थी मेहराज को।

सुबह के आठ बज चुके थे और मेहराज अब तक सो रहा था। बी ने उसको फ़ौरन अपने कमरे में बुलाया।

मेहराज को पहले तो रुख़साना ने उठाया। चाय नाश्ता कराया। फिर जब वो अपने होश-ओ-हवास में आ गया तब रुख़साना ने कहा कि, “छोटे मियाँ, मुझे माफ़ करियेगा। लेकिन मैंने...” इतने में पीछे से फ़रीदन कहते हुए आई कि मेहराज मियाँ आपको बी बुला रही हैं।

मेहराज जैसे ही कमरे में घुसा बी ने उसको इशारे से कुर्सी पर बैठने को कहा। बी ख़ुद तो इतने ग़ुस्से में थीं कि उसे क़ाबू करने के लिए टहलने लगीं।

मेहराज के बैठते ही बी बोलीं, “हमें मालूम है हमारा पानदान आप ही लेकर गए थे। अब आप ख़ुद बताइए सब कुछ सच -सच।”

मेहराज बोला, “हमें नुमाइश जाना था। आपके पानदान में पैसे नहीं मिले। हम ग़ुस्से में उसे उठाकर बाहर ले गए और हमने पानदान ही बेच दिया।”

बी ये सुनते ही आग बबूला हो गईं, “हाय, अफ़सोस आपने हमारी नाक कटवा दी। कहाँ बेचा, किसको बेचा?” मेहराज की माँ ने सिखाया था कि कुछ हो जाए झूठ नहीं बोलना कभी। अब सच तो बोल दिया मेहराज ने। बोलते-बोलते ही ख़ुद को एहसास हुआ कि शायद कुछ ज़्यादा ही ग़लत कर दिया उसने।

“बताइए जल्दी अब।” बी बोलीं।

“वो सब हमें नहीं मालूम। हम तो पानदान को लोहा टीन ख़रीदने वाले कबाड़ी को बेच रहे थे।” बी इत्मिनाम से कुर्सी पर बैठ गईं। मुँह पर हाथ रख के मेहराज को देखती रहीं और सर हिलाती रहीं। मेहराज भी उस वजह से बिना डरे बोलता गया, “लेकिन मोहल्ले में हमारा एक दोस्त बना है। उसने कहीं ज़्यादा पैसों का बेच दिया। जितने पैसे नुमाइश में खर्च हुए वो हो गए, बाक़ी सब हमने आपके सरहाने लाकर रख दिए थे।”

बी ने ज़ोर से चीख़ मारी, “लल्लन लल्लन...”

लल्लन मियाँ भाग कर कमरे में आए। जैसे ही आए, बी बोलीं, “दरवाज़े से ये पानदान लेकर चले गए। तुम कहाँ थे?” लल्लन मियाँ इससे पहले कि कुछ कहते बी उठकर अपने पलंग के सरहाने गईं। उन्होंने अपना तकिया उठाया तो उसके नीचे एक रूपए के तीन नोट निकले। उन्होंने पलटकर मेहराज को देखा और कहा, “हमारी दादी का सौ साल पुराना असली चांदी का पानदान कौड़ियों के दाम में बेच दिया। वाह बेटे! वाह!” मेहराज लल्लन मियाँ को देख रहा था। लल्लन मियाँ मेहराज की तरफ़ से निगाह हटा रहे थे क्यूँकि इस वक़्त आसमान भी अगर गिर जाए लेकिन वो बी के अलावा किसी की नहीं सुन सकते। बी ने लल्लन मियाँ से कहा, “इनके दोस्त को

जानते हो? उसको लेकर जाओ और जहाँ भी वो पानदान बेचा है, वहाँ से लेकर आओ। अगर पानदान नहीं ला पाओ तो ख़ुद भी घर लौटकर नहीं आना।" लल्लन मियाँ जाने लगे, बी बोलीं, "पैसे देकर आना। नहीं हों तुम्हारे पास तो पहले पूछ कर आओ फिर पैसे लेकर जाना। अब अपनी सूरत यहाँ से दफ़ा करो जल्दी।" लल्लन अपना सर झुकाकर वहाँ से निकल गए।

फिर बी ने कमरा अंदर से बंद कर लिया और मेहराज के ठीक सामने कुर्सी डालकर बैठ गईं। उन्हें समझ नहीं आ रहा था कि उनके घर का बच्चा ऐसी हरकत कर कैसे सकता है। पहली बार आया था तो बी उसको डाँट भी नहीं सकती थीं ज़्यादा। बी ने लम्बी साँस ली अपना गुस्सा क़ाबू किया फिर बोलीं- "बेटे, आपको मालूम नहीं है चोरी करना गुनाह होता है?"

"चोरी? घर का सामान बेचना तो चोरी नहीं होती।" मेहराज ने इत्मिनान के साथ जवाब दिया।

"हाँ, लेकिन बिना पूछे बेचना चोरी हुई ना।"

"नानी अम्मी, ऐसे तो हमारे अब्बा भी घर का सामान बिना पूछे बेच देते हैं।"

"हाँ, तो वो अपना सामान क्यों किसी से पूछकर बेचेगें।"

"नहीं, वो दादी और अम्मी का सामान उनसे बिना पूछे बेच देते हैं।"

बी हैरानी में बोलीं, "अच्छा तो आपकी अम्मी और दादी फिर मना करती होंगी उन्हें।"

"हाँ, हर बार वो दोनों कहती हैं, लेकिन फिर भी वो बेचते ही रहते हैं। कई बार मैं भी उनके साथ गया हूँ।"

बी के लिए नई परत खुल रही थी अपनी बेटी नसीम की ज़िन्दगी की। बी बोलीं, "तो आपकी अम्मी से लड़ते भी हैं क्या?"

"अम्मी उनसे जब भी कोई बात करती हैं। वो उनपर ग़ुस्सा करने लगते हैं।"

"क्या आपकी अम्मी को अब्बा मारते भी हैं?"

मेहराज ने ख़ामोश होकर गर्दन झुका ली। बी बोलीं, "बेटे, मैं आपसे कुछ पूछ रही हूँ। आप डरिए नहीं, मैं आपकी अम्मी को नहीं बोलूँगी कुछ।"

वो हलके से बोला, "मुझे नहीं मालूम लेकिन अम्मी अक्सर रोती रहती हैं। जब कभी रात को अब्बा घर आते हैं तो बहुत शोर करते हैं।"

बी खड़ी होकर मेहराज का सर सहलाने लगीं। बी समझ गई थीं कि बच्चा किस माहौल से अपने घर में गुज़र रहा है। बी मेहराज से बोलीं, "अच्छा तो आपके अब्बा आपको तो बहुत प्यार करते होंगे ना?"

"मैंने मना कर दिया था काफ़ी पहले ही, उनके मुँह से बहुत गन्दी बदबू आती है। पहले करते थे अब तो हमेशा देखते ही डाँटते हैं।" मेहराज आँखों में आँसू लिए बोला।

बी ने उसकी तरफ़ देखा और कहा, "देखो आपने जो हरकत की है उसका सबक़ तो आपको सिखाना पड़ेगा।"

मेहराज रोते हुए बोला, "नानी अम्मी अब कभी नहीं करूँगा।"

"हाँ, मेरे बच्चे हम हर चंद कोशिश करेंगे कि आप ऐसी कोई हरकत ज़िन्दगी में कभी न करें।" मेहराज को ये सुनते ही थोड़ा सुकून आया।

फिर बी ने अपनी कड़क आवाज़ में आहिस्ता-आहिस्ता बोलना शुरू किया, "आपकी सज़ा है कि आप रोज़ाना पूरे घर की मच्छरदानियाँ लपेट कर रखेंगे। बाहर जाकर लल्लन मियाँ की भी। फिर आप दिन में बावर्चीख़ाने में मुलाज़िमों की मदद करेंगें। कल शाम से आपको पढ़ाने उस्ताद आया करेंगें और अब आपका दरवाज़े से बाहर क़दम निकालना बंद, जब तक हम नहीं कहेंगे।" मेहराज अपने आँसू पोंछते हुए उनको देखने लगा।

बी बोलीं, "अब जाइए, अभी से मुलाज़िमों के साथ कामों में लग जाइए, आज वैसे भी बहुत काम हैं शादियों के।"

मेहराज फ़ौरन वहाँ से उठकर भाग गया। बी ने अपनी ऐनक हटाकर अपनी गीली आँखों को पोंछा।

उधर लल्लन मियाँ बौने के दरवाज़े पर बैठे इंतज़ार कर रहे थे। जैसे ही बौना कहीं बाहर से लौटकर अपने घर आया लल्लन मियाँ ने उसका गिरेबान पकड़कर बोले, "चोट्टे, तूने बच्चे को बेवक़ूफ़ बनाकर बी का पानदान बेच दिया।" लल्लन मियाँ की आँख को बौना कभी नहीं भाया और आज तो उनको मौक़ा मिल गया। ऊपर से बी ने भी उनकी ग़लतियों के लिए उन्हें ख़ूब ज़िल्लत दी थी।

बौना बोला, "लल्लन मियाँ अपना हाथ मेरे गिरेबान से हटाओ।"

"चल चोर तुझे तो थाने लेके जाऊँगा, अगर पानदान तूने वापस नहीं लौटाया।"

बौना गुस्से में बोला "तमीज़ में बात कर सकते हो?"

"बताता है या तेरे बाप से अंदर जाके बात करूँ। जो औरत तेरे घर की इतनी मदद करती है उसी को लूट लिया।"

बौने ने झटककर लल्लन मियाँ को ख़ुद से दूर किया और बोला, "ये मत भूलो के आपके दादा इसी फ़ाटक पर मेरे बाप दादा के दरबान थे। हमारे हालात ख़राब हो गए लेकिन ज़मीर ख़राब नहीं हुआ है।" लल्लन मियाँ ये सुनकर थोड़ा पीछे हटे।

बौना उनको घूरते हुए बोला, "बी का नवासा उनके पानदान को तीन रूपए में कबाड़ी को बेच रहा थ। मैंने बचा लिया और जाके सलीम बीड़ी वाले के पास अमानत के तौर पर रख के 5 रूपए ले लिए थे। मेहराज को नुमाइश जाना था, इसलिए किया ये सब। होंगे वो बड़े लोग और तुम बड़े घर के नौकर।"

लल्लन मियाँ थोड़ा शर्मिंदा होते हुए बोले, "अरे बेटे, मुझे मालूम थोड़ी था ये सब।"

"तो तमीज़ से पूछते ना आकर।"

लल्लन मियाँ गर्दन डालकर वापस जाने लगे। बौने ने उनसे पूछा, "कहाँ जा रहे हो अब?"

"सलीम से जाकर पानदान ले लेता हूँ। बी बहोत गुस्से में बैठी हैं।"

"मैंने और अम्मी ने पैसों का इंतज़ाम करके पानदान सलीम से ले लिया। मैं अभी फ़रीदन को पानदान देकर ही आया हूँ।" ये कहता हुआ बौना अपने घर में घुसने लगा।

लल्लन मियाँ बोले, "फ़हीम, बड़ा समझकर माफ़ कर देना।"

“आज के बाद मुझसे तमीज़ से बात करना या फिर कभी बात मत करना।” ये कहता हुआ बौना अपने घर में चला गया।

उधर फ़रीदन ने बी को पानदान दिया और कहा, “ये जहेज़ के सामान के नीचे मिला, शायद किसी बच्चे ने छुपा दिया होगा।”

बी को तब तक सब मालूम हो चुका था। झूठ बोलने पर उन्होंने फ़रीदन को ख़ूब बुरा-भला सुनाया।

लल्लन मियाँ जब तक बी के पास पहुँचे तब तक पानदान बी को मिल चुका था। लल्लन मियाँ ने फ़हीम की सारी बात तफ़सील से बताई कि क्या हुआ और कैसे हुआ। बी ने लल्लन मियाँ को मेहराज पर हर वक़्त निगाह रखने का काम दे दिया।

दोपहर तक घर लोगों से भर गया। सारी दुल्हनें आने लगीं और बी के घर पर ही तैयार होने लगीं। मेहराज को बी ने सारे मेहमानों को पानी पिलाने पर लगा दिया। मेहराज पानी का जग और गिलास लिए पूरे घर में फिरता रहा।

शाम को छह बजे मस्ज़िद में एक साथ दस जोड़ों के निकाह होने थे और रात को दस बजे घर पर एक जोड़े के फेरे। लक्ष्मी का परिवार भी अपने कुछ रिश्तेदारों के साथ बी के घर आ गया। बी अपने दालान में पड़ी आराम कुर्सी पर बैठे-बैठे सारे कामों को देख रहीं थीं। वैसे अंदर से तो बी काफ़ी मायूस और परेशान ही थीं। उनका दिमाग़ अपनी बेटी के बारे में ही सोचता रहा। उन्हें अंदर की जो बातें आज मेहराज के ज़रिये मालूम हुईं, उस सब का उन्हें कभी इल्म तक नहीं था।

सारे दूल्हे अपने रिश्तेदारों के साथ निकाह के मुक़र्रर वक़्त से पहले पहुँच गए। सबके साथ कुछ औरतें भी आईं, दुल्हन को रुख़्सत कराकर साथ ले जाने के लिए, क्यूँकि ज़नाने में मर्द नहीं आ सकते थे। मर्दों को छोटे घर में बिठाया गया और सब लोगों को नाश्ता कराया गया।

सब का वक़्त पर निकाह हो गया और वक़्त से रुख़्सती भी हो गई, सिवा एक दुल्हन के। वो दुल्हन थी बौने की पड़ोसन नरगिस। दरअसल नरगिस का दूल्हा और उसके रिश्तेदार निकाह के वक़्त से काफ़ी देर बाद आए। इस बात पर बी ने शर्त रख दी कि अब निकाह दूसरे दिन सहर में फ़ज्र की नमाज़ के बाद होगा। नरगिस की माँ और बाप भी बी के सामने कुछ कह नहीं सकते थे। उनको बी ने बोला, "अगर ये दूल्हा निकाह के दिन ही देर से आया है तो फिर ख़ुद सोच लो बच्ची की क्या ही क़दर करेगा। इसीलिए ये सज़ा इनके लिए ज़रूरी है।"

नरगिस के सामने ही बी ने बोला ये सब। वो तीनों बी की बात से सहमत हो गए। उधर बौना अपनी बहन की रुख़्सती के बाद माँ के साथ बैठा हुआ रो रहा था। नरगिस उसकी बहन की और उसकी बहुत अच्छी दोस्त थी। बौना और उसकी माँ नरगिस के निकाह का इंतज़ार कर रहे थे और उसकी बारात का ख़याल रख रहे थे। मेहराज का काम अभी तक वही था, सबको पानी पिलाना।

नौ लड़कियाँ इज़्ज़त से रुख़्सत हो गईं और बी ने हर बारात को नाश्ता कराया और साथ में हर बारात को दो-दो बिरयानी के पतीले दिए, बहोड़े के तौर। ये खाना बारात को देने का रिवाज़ था, जिसे बहोड़ा कहा जाता था। वो लोग उसको अपने साथ ले गए, रात के

खाने के लिए। नरगिस की बारात को नाश्ता कराया और छोटे घर में बिठा दिया।

इस सब के बाद आई लक्ष्मी की बारात, जिसके फेरों का इंतज़ाम बी ने अपने ही आँगन में किया था। मुंशी जी के ऊपर पंडित और सारे रीती रिवाजों को करने की पूरी ज़िम्मेदारी थी। मोहनदास दुकानदार भी आया था, बी ने उसको भी बुलावा दिया था आने के लिए। मुक़दमा अपनी जगह, ताल्लुक़ अपनी जगह। दूल्हे के अलावा सारे मर्दों को छोटे घर में ही बिठाया गया, जहाँ पहले से नरगिस की बारात बैठी थी।

एक दो घंटे में लक्ष्मी का भी ब्याह हो गया। उसकी भी रुख़्सती हो गई।

अब तक नरगिस के दूल्हे और उसके रिश्तेदार नाराज़ हो चुके थे कि हमें अभी निकाह करना है या फिर हम शादी ही नहीं करेंगे। बी ने ये सुनकर नरगिस के माँ बाप को बुलाया और पूछा, “देखो भाई, तुम्हारी बेटी है अगर तुम लोग चाहो तो कर दो अभी निकाह। मेरी वजह से मत करना किसी मजबूरी में।” वो दोनों बोले, “नहीं, हमें आपकी बात समझ आ गई। आप जो फ़ैसला लेंगी वो ही हम मानेगें।”

“देख लो, सोच लो ठीक से। कही हुई बात वापस नहीं होती है।” बी ने कुछ देर सोचकर कहा।

“आप जो कहेंगी, उस पर हम चूँ नहीं करेंगें,” वो दोनों बोले।

बी ने मुंशी जी को बुलाया और नरगिस की बारात को वापस भेजने के लिए बोला। नरगिस की बारात वापस चली गई। ज़्यादातर लोग

घर से जा चुके थे। अब बी के घर में बौना और उसकी माँ, लक्ष्मी का परिवार और नरगिस का परिवार था। सब लोग घर के अलग-अलग कोनों में बैठे बात करने लगे। मेहराज अभी भी पानी का जग और गिलास लिए टहल रहा था। उसने रोती हुई नरगिस को पानी पिलाया और उसके माँ बाप को भी।

मुंशी जी सब काम होने पर घर जाने लगे तो बी ने उनको रोक लिया। बी ख़ुद वुज़ू करके नमाज़ पढ़ने चली गईं। दस पंद्रह मिनट बाद बी अपने कमरे से नमाज़ पढ़के निकलीं और इतनी देर में उन्होंने नरगिस के मसले का हल भी सोच लिया। उन्होंने अपने कमरे में मुंशी जी को और बौने के साथ उसकी माँ को बुलाया। कुछ देर बाद वो तीनों बाहर निकले। बौना और उसकी माँ अपने घर चले गए। मुंशी जी ने मेहराज को बुलाया और खाना खाने के लिए कहा। फ़रीदन ने मुंशी जी और मेहराज को खाना खिलाया। मेहराज ने पानी पिला-पिलाकर आज ख़ूब सवाब कमा लिया था, जैसा उसकी नानी ने कहा था।

बी ने फिर नरगिस और उसके माँ बाप से बात की। बी ने कहा, "देखो, मर्ज़ी तुम लोगों की होगी पर मेरी राय ये है कि नरगिस का निकाह फ़हीम से कर दो।"

नरगिस की माँ घबरा कर बोली, "अरे बी, वो बौना तो एक नंबर का आवारा है।"

"उसका नाम फ़हीम है और शक्ल सूरत का अच्छा ख़ासा है, सिर्फ़ क़द कम है। दूसरी बात हमने उसको मुंशी जी के साथ काम पर लगवा दिया है। वो हमारे काम काज में उनकी मदद करेगा।" बी उन लोगों को समझाने के अंदाज़ में बोलीं।

"फ़हीम किस ख़ानदान का बच्चा है ये आप दोनों ख़ूब अच्छी तरह जानते हैं।"

नरगिस के बाप हलके से बोले, "बी अब तो मतलूब ख़ान साहब के घर का सिर्फ़ एक ही कमरा बचा है। रखेंगे कहाँ वो हमारी बेटी को।"

बी ने नरगिस की तरफ़ देख कर कहा, "मैं एक महीने में उसका एक कमरा बनवा दूँगी और उसके बाद ही रुख़्सती करना। लेकिन मैं नरगिस से अकेले में बात करना चाहूँगी पहले।"

नरगिस और बी कमरे में अकेले रह गए फिर बी ने कहा, "बेटी, तुम्हारी मर्ज़ी ज़रूरी है। मैं आज तक अपनी बेटी का घर सही नहीं कर पाई। मैं तुम्हारी कोई नहीं हूँ जो इतना बड़ा फ़ैसला ले लूँ। अल्लाह के घर मुँह दिखाना है, मुझे जो बेहतर लगा मैंने वो रख दिया, तुम लोगों के सामने।"

"अरे बी, आप ऐसी बातें मत करिए, आप हमारे लिए बहुत कुछ हैं। पूरा बचपन आपके घर गुज़रा है।" नरगिस रोते हुए बोली।

"नरगिस, मैं अपने तजुर्बे से कह सकती हूँ कि तुझे फ़हीम बहोत अच्छा रखेगा। बहोत समझदार लड़का है। मुझसे मना कर रहा था कि नरगिस मेरी दोस्त है, मैं नहीं करूँगा उससे निकाह।"

नरगिस ये सुनकर मुस्कुराने लगी। थे तो वो दोनों बचपन के अज़ीज़ दोस्त ही।

"बेटी, मर्द का क़द, शकल, पैसा सब बुरा लगने लगता है अगर वो अच्छा नहीं हो तो। देख लो अपनी नसीम ख़ाला का हाल। घर तक नहीं आई है पिछले पाँच साल से।"

नरगिस बी की बात ग़ौर से सुनते हुए बोली, "आपको जैसा बेहतर लगे मुझे वो मंज़ूर है।"

बी ने फ़ौरन उसके माँ बाप को बुलाकर कहा, "फ़हीम के घर जाओ और मतलूब ख़ान से बात करके आओ। अभी एक घंटे में नरगिस और फ़हीम का निकाह होगा।"

वो दोनों अपनी बेटी को ख़ुश देखकर कुछ बोले बिना फ़हीम के घर चले गए।

ग्यारह बजे के क़रीब फ़हीम अपना सबसे नया कुर्ता पजामा पहनकर बी के पास सर पर हाथ रखवाने आया। मस्जिद के मौलाना को बुलाकर नरगिस और फ़हीम का निकाह कराया गया। बी ने इनकी रुख़्सती एक महीने बाद की तय कर दी। ये सब होने के बाद एक ही दस्तरख़्वान पर बैठकर बी के साथ फ़हीम और नरगिस ने खाना खाया और दोनों अपने अपने माँ बाप के साथ अपने घर चले गए।

जिस दिन सुबह में लल्लन मियाँ ने फ़हीम को चोर कहकर उसका गिरेबान पकड़ा था उसी रात को वो उसके बाप के लिए खाना लेकर गए। निकाह के बाद फ़हीम को सबसे पहले मुबारकबाद देने और गले लगने वाले भी लल्लन मियाँ ही थे। फ़हीम ने भी उनसे कान में माफ़ी माँग ली, क्यूँकि वो भी हमेशा से लल्लन मियाँ को छेड़-छेड़कर भागता था।

सब उस रात सुकून से सो गए, सिवाए बी के। उनको तो पूरा दिन अपनी बेटी नसीम का ख़याल सताता रहा। पूरी रात वो वही सोचती रहीं जो सूरत-ए-हाल मेहराज ने उनको बताया था। पूरी रात करवटें

बदलती रहीं लेकिन जो एक पल को भी नींद आई हो। सुबह होने से पहले बी ने अपना पलंग छोड़ दिया और उठकर साफ़-सफ़ाई के काम-काज में लग गईं।

रुख़साना की जैसे ही आँख खुली वो बी के पास भागती हुई जाकर कहने लगी, "बी, आपने मुझे क्यों नहीं उठाया। आप मत करिए मैं कर दूँगी। आप बैठ जाइए, मैं आपके लिए चाय लाती हूँ।"

बी आँगन में पेड़ों को बाल्टी से पानी दे रही थीं। उन्होंने बाल्टी रखकर कहा, "तुम सबसे पहले मेहराज को उठाओ और उसको कहो जो मैंने कल बोला था वो करे।"

बी पानी देती रहीं।

रुख़साना ने मेहराज को उठाकर कहा, "मियाँ, उठिये और सबकी मछरदानियाँ लपेटकर रख दीजिए। बी बहोत ग़ुस्सा हैं।"

वो उठा और सबकी मछरदानियाँ लपेटकर दोबारा अपने पलंग पर जाकर सो गया।

बी अपने बराबर वाले घर में थीं। फ़रीदन उनके लिए चाय लेकर गई। आँगन में कुर्सी पर बैठे बी ने कहा, "कम्बख़्त ये लकड़ी के सामान पर रंग करने के चक्कर में मेरी दीवारें भी ख़राब कर गए। मुझे पहले नहीं दिखा वरना इनके पैसे रोकती।"

फ़रीदन बोली, "हाँ बी, और ये देखिये बारातियों ने पान की पीकें उस दीवार पर कितनी मारी हैं।"

बी ग़ुस्से में बोलीं, "बहोत ही कम मर्द होते हैं जिन्हें इस सब का लिहाज़ होता है। फ़हीम आएगा दस बजे उससे कहकर रंग करने वालों को बुलवा लेना।"

बी चाय का घूँट लेने लगीं पर जैसे ही फ़रीदन दूसरे घर में वापस जा रही थी बी ने उससे पूछा, "मेहराज ने मच्छरदानियाँ लपेट दीं?"

"हाँ बी कब का।" इससे आगे और कुछ बोले बिना फ़रीदन भाग गई दूसरी तरफ़।

फ़रीदन ने मेहराज को उठाकर बोला, "मियाँ, बी आज बहोत गुस्से में लग रही हैं। बेहतर होगा आप उठ जाइए। आपके बारे में बार-बार पूछ रही हैं।" मेहराज कसमसाकर उठा और सीधा बाहर जाकर लल्लन मियाँ की मछरदानी लपेटने लगा। इतने में बशारत और सकीना का रिक्शा आकर रुका। वो लोग दिल्ली से डॉक्टर को दिखाकर वापस आ रहे थे। मेहराज को सकीना ने गले से लगाकर प्यार किया। वो तीनों एक साथ अंदर बी के पास चले गए।

थोड़ी देर बाद वे लोग नाश्ता करने बैठ गए। सकीना ने मेहराज के गिलास में दूध निकाला। फिर वो बशारत के गिलास में दूध डालने लगी, जिसपर बशारत ने बहोत बत्तमीज़ी से मना कर दिया। यह देखते ही बी बोलीं, "जुआरियों की तरह बौखलाकर अपनी बीवी पर क्यों मुँह मार रहे हो। तुम कौन सा जुआ हार आए।" बशारत ये सुनते ही अपना आपा खोकर बोला, "आपको क्या मतलब। दूसरों के घर बसाइए। आपके अपने बच्चे मरें या जियें। क्या फ़र्क़ पड़ता है।"

ये माहौल देखते ही सकीना ने बशारत को चुप कराने की कोशिश की मगर वो नहीं रुका और गुस्से में बी से बोला, "अपनी सारी दौलत लुटा दिए दूसरों पर। हम पागल हैं जो परदेस में जाकर ख़ुद को तबाह करें।"

सकीना माहौल की नज़ाकत को देखते हुए मेहराज को वहाँ से अपने साथ ले गई। बी और बशारत अकेले रह गए। बी बोली, "मेरी

दौलत है, मुझे उसपर किसी से कोई राय नहीं चाहिए। जिसको रहना है रहे, नहीं रहना है न रहे।"

"हाँ, आपने तो निकाल ही दिया था न मुझे। कारोबार कराने को कहा था आपसे, लेकिन आपको अपने बच्चों की फ़िक्र हो तब ना।"

"क्या कारोबार करते तुम। मेरी ज़मीन बेचकर सब पैसे बर्बाद कर देते। मुझे एक रुपया कमाकर दिखाते तब मैं पैसे लगाने का सोचती भी।" बी चाय का घूँट लेते हुए बोलीं। बशारत ग़ुस्से में बड़बड़ करता ही रहा।

"इसलिए हमने तुम्हें पाल-पोसकर बड़ा किया ताकि तुम हमसे ऐसी बत्तमीज़ी करो। बहोत ख़ुशी है मुझे जो मैंने तुम्हारे ऊपर अपनी ज़मीन का पैसा बर्बाद नहीं किया।" बी ने ग़ुस्से में कहा।

"नसीम आपा के लिए कुछ कर लेतीं। दुनिया की बेटियों की फ़िक्र है, उनके बारे में ही कुछ सोच लेतीं।" बशारत ने कमज़ोर बात पकड़ने की कोशिश करते हुए कहा।

"तुमसे पूछकर करूँगी? मैं अपनी मर्ज़ी की मालिक हूँ। अपने हिसाब से करूँगी।" आग बबूला होकर बी ने कहा।

"आपको सिर्फ़ अपने नाम और शान की फ़िक्र रहती है। उसी के लिए करती हैं सब कुछ। सब मालूम है। वो तो ये घर मेरे बाप का था वरना आप तो घर में भी नहीं रहने देतीं।" बशारत झुँझलाकर बोला।

"तुम्हारे मसले जो भी हैं, जाकर पहले उन्हें सही करो। उसके बाद मुझसे बात करना। अपने बाप की कमी पूरी कर रहे हो आज तुम। बड़े हो ही गए आख़िर।" ये कहते हुए बी अपने कमरे में चली गईं।

फ़हीम को बी ने अपने साथ काम पर लगा लिया था। वो ठीक दस बजे आकर लल्लन मियाँ के पास बैठ गया। मेहराज ख़ुशी से उसके पास गया और खेलने को कहने लगा। फ़हीम ने उसको समझाया, “अब मैं आपकी नानी का मुलाज़िम हूँ तो मैं काम के वक़्त आपके साथ नहीं खेल सकता।” इतने में लल्लन मियाँ ने मेहराज को घर में जाने को बोल दिया। न चाहते हुए भी उसे उठना पड़ा, क्यूँकि बी का हुक्म था।

बी पहले से ही इतना परेशान थीं ऊपर से सुबह-सुबह बशारत की बत्तमीज़ी ने उनको और हिला दिया। सकीना कुछ देर बाद बी के कमरे में गई। उसने बशारत की तरफ़ से बी से माफ़ी माँगी। बी ने उसको अपने पास बिठा लिया। सकीना ने बी का हाथ पकड़ा और उसको सहलाने लगी। उसने बी को बशारत के इतने बुरे निज़ाज के पीछे की वजह बताई। दरअसल डॉक्टर ने सकीना को तो बिलकुल ठीक बता दिया था। उसमें कोई भी कमी नहीं निकली, जिसकी वजह से उसको औलाद होने में परेशानी हो। डॉक्टरों ने उल्टा बशारत को अपनी जाँचें कराने को बोल दिया। बशारत ने उसके बाद सकीना को चार-पाँच और डॉक्टरों को दिखाया और हर एक ने वही बात बोली जो पहले डॉक्टर ने कही थी। उसने बताया इसी सब की वजह से बशारत के होश जगह पर नहीं हैं। बी ने सकीना को गले से लगा लिया।

बी ने पूरा दिन कमरे में अकेले ही गुज़ारा। बस मेहराज को अपने पास बिठाकर क़ुरान पढ़वाया बाक़ी उन्होंने किसी से भी कोई बात ही नहीं की। सकीना भी अपने मायके चली गई कुछ दिनों के लिए। घर का माहौल मायूस-सा ही रहा।

रात में बशारत ने बी से उनके कमरे में जाकर माफ़ी माँगी, अपने रवइये के लिए। बी ने उसको बस इतना ही बोला, "मैंने आपसे सुबह भी कहा था और अभी दोबारा कह रही हूँ। आपके जो भी मसले हैं, उनको ठीक करिए। हक़ीक़त को मान लेना ही इंसान की सबसे बड़ी कामियाबी होती है।" बशारत आँखों में आँसू लिए अपनी गर्दन डालकर सब सुनता रहा और बी के पैर दबाता रहा।

दूसरे दिन सुबह-सुबह बी ने मुंशी जी से बात की और उसके बाद बी ने अपनी बेटी नसीम को ख़त लिखा। जिसमें लिखा था-

"उम्मीद है आप ख़ैरीयत से होंगी। उम्मीद तो कर ही सकती हूँ कम-से-कम। हमने आप दोनों के नाम अपनी कुछ जायदाद करने का फ़ैसला लिया है। हम अपनी ग़लतियों की माफ़ी चाहते हैं। मोईन ख़ान को ये बात ज़रूर बता दीजिएगा। उनसे कहिएगा हम अब सब कुछ ठीक करने की कोशिश करेंगे। ख़ैर कागज़ात बनाने को तहसीलदार साहब ने बुध का दिन दिया है। आप लोग उससे पहले आ जाएँ। बाक़ी बातें मिलकर करेंगे।

अल्लाह हाफ़िज़।"

नसीम ख़त पढ़कर हैरान हो गई।

आख़िरकार नसीम और मोईन ख़ान बुध की सुबह-सुबह पहुँच ही गए। मोईन ख़ान को लल्लन मियाँ ने बैठक में बिठा दिया। नसीम बीमार और कमज़ोर हाल में कई साल बाद अपने घर आई थी। जैसे ही नसीम दरवाज़े से घुसी मेहराज भागता हुआ उनसे चिपट गया। अपनी माँ को लेकर बी के पास उनके कमरे में पहुँच गया। बी ने

मेहराज को बोला, "आप अपने वालिद के पास जाकर बैठिए।" वो वहाँ से बिना कुछ बोले पलटकर चला गया।

नसीम अपना बुर्क़ा उतारने लगी इतने में बी बोलीं "बुर्क़ा मत उतारिए हमें बस निकलना ही है।" नसीम वैसे ही बी के पलंग पर बैठ गई।

बी ने कहा, "हमने अपनी जायदाद आपके और सकीना के नाम करने का फ़ैसला लिया है।" नसीम फ़ौरन बोली, "अम्मी, क्यों कर रही हैं आप ये सब। बशारत और सकीना को दे दें सब कुछ।"

बी इस पर बोलीं, "हमारी बात मुकम्मल नहीं हुई है अभी। आपका तलाक़नामा तैयार किए हुए वकील साहब हमारा इंतज़ार कर रहे हैं।"

ये सुनते ही नसीम खड़ी हुई और बोली, "अम्मी... आधी से ज़्यादा ज़िन्दगी गुज़र गई। अब इस सब का क्या मतलब है। मुझसे पूछे बिना ये फ़ैसला..."

बी उसकी बात काटते हुए बोलीं "आपको मालूम है ना कि नोईन ख़ान बिलकुल अपने बाप की तरह हैं? अगर ये फ़ैसला आपने अभी नहीं लिया तो मेहराज को मोईन ख़ान की तरह निकलने से कोई नहीं रोक सकता।"

इसके आगे नसीम के पास कोई जवाब नहीं बचा, वो अपनी माँ के गले लग कर फूट-फूट के रोने लगी।